Alan Savage is t
established au
storyteller, with a
history and milit
bestsellers as Al
Moghul and

Also by Alan Savage:

OTTOMAN
MOGHUL
THE EIGHT BANNERS

ALAN SAVAGE

Queen of Night

WARNER BOOKS

A *Warner* Book

First published in Great Britain in 1993
by Little, Brown and Company

This edition published by Warner Books in 1993

A CIP catalogue record for this book
is available from the British Library.

ISBN 0 7515 0037 2

Typeset in Century Schoolbook by Leaper & Gard Ltd, Bristol
Printed in England by Clays Ltd, St Ives plc

Warner Books
A Division of
Little, Brown and Company (UK) Limited
165 Great Dover Street
London SE1 4YA

Joanna I of Naples was the most beautiful and accomplished woman of her time. She is also remembered as a cold-blooded murderess and a woman of the lowest morals. Perhaps history has been too harsh in its judgement. This is her story.

JOANNA'S FAMILY TREE

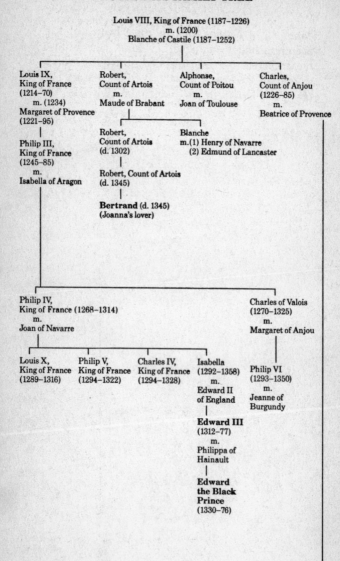

Louis VIII, King of France (1187–1226)
m. (1200)
Blanche of Castile (1187–1252)

Louis IX,
King of France
(1214–70)
m. (1234)
Margaret of Provence
(1221–95)

Robert,
Count of Artois
m.
Maude of Brabant

Alphonse,
Count of Poitou
m.
Joan of Toulouse

Charles,
Count of Anjou
(1226–85)
m.
Beatrice of Provence

Philip III,
King of France
(1245–85)
m.
Isabella of Aragon

Robert,
Count of Artois
(d. 1302)

Blanche
m.(1) Henry of Navarre
    (2) Edmund of Lancaster

Robert, Count of Artois
(d. 1345)

Bertrand (d. 1345)
(Joanna's lover)

Philip IV,
King of France (1268–1314)
m.
Joan of Navarre

Charles of Valois
(1270–1325)
m.
Margaret of Anjou

Louis X,
King of France
(1289–1316)

Philip V,
King of France
(1294–1322)

Charles IV,
King of France
(1294–1328)

Isabella
(1292–1358)
m.
Edward II
of England

Philip VI
(1293–1350)
m.
Jeanne of
Burgundy

Edward III
(1312–77)
m.
Philippa of
Hainault

**Edward
the Black
Prince**
(1330–76)

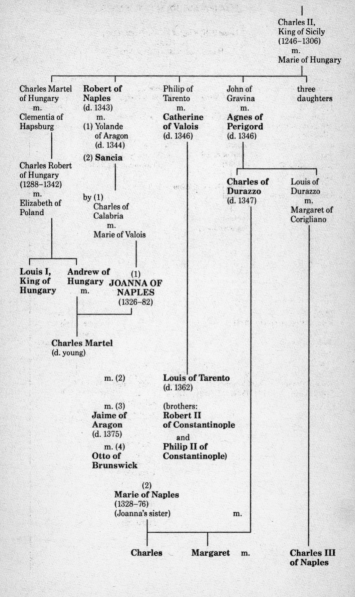

Charles II,
King of Sicily
(1246–1306)
m.
Marie of Hungary

Charles Martel
of Hungary
m.
Clementia of
Hapsburg

Robert of
Naples
(d. 1343)
m.
(1) Yolande
of Aragon
(d. 1344)

(2) Sancia

Philip of
Tarento
m.
Catherine
of Valois
(d. 1346)

John of
Gravina
m.
Agnes of
Perigord
(d. 1346)

three
daughters

Charles Robert
of Hungary
(1288–1342)
m.
Elizabeth of
Poland

by (1)
Charles of
Calabria
m.
Marie of Valois

Charles of
Durazzo
(d. 1347)

Louis of
Durazzo
m.
Margaret of
Corigliano

Louis I,
King of
Hungary

Andrew of
Hungary
m.

(1)
JOANNA OF
NAPLES
(1326–82)

Charles Martel
(d. young)

m. (2)

Louis of Tarento
(d. 1362)

m. (3)
Jaime of
Aragon
(d. 1375)

(brothers:
Robert II
of Constantinople

and

m. (4)
Otto of
Brunswick

Philip II of
Constantinople)

(2)
Marie of Naples
(1328–76)
(Joanna's sister)

m.

Charles   Margaret   m.   Charles III
of Naples

PROLOGUE

M y inquisitors surrounded me with sinister stares. Their eyes were all I could see of them, for each man wore a black cowl which entirely concealed his face and neck, while their garments were of a likeness, and the only light was provided by two guttering torches set in sconces on the walls. My guards stood at the back of the room by the locked door, and I was alone in the centre of the stone floor, bare-footed and wearing no more than a shift, as if I was at the very least a penitent. I was equally well aware that these men had the power to command me to the rack, or worse.

But I had been exposed to such misfortunes before, and survived. Nor had the catastrophes of my life affected my beauty, which had surmounted even middle age. Besides, I was consumed with grief and a sense of injustice. I would defy them to the very grave.

'Your mistress is dead,' one of the priests said. 'She has paid the penalty for her life of crime. It but remains to be decided what should be done with her creature. How say you, woman, are you guilty or not guilty of being an accomplice in those awful deeds?'

I tilted my chin the better to look him in the eye, and tossed my head, my still-golden hair falling about my ears and down my back. 'If Her Grace was guilty, then no doubt so am I. But my crime has never been more, or less, than that of acting the faithful servant to a woman I admired, and now mourn.'

The priests exchanged glances, then their spokesman said, 'Tell us of the Queen, and yourself, that we may judge.'

I was happy to do so.

CHAPTER 1

My early years are of interest only to establish how I, an Englishwoman, came to be in Italy at all. I was born in the Year of Our Lord 1325, in the town of Lincoln, in eastern England. My name is Richilde Benoit. Richilde is taken from the male, Richard, which was the name of my father. And Benoit is, of course, a French name. That is because my ancestor crossed from Normandy with the Great William. But he married a Saxon lady, and this habit persisted throughout the next eight generations, so that I reached the age of ten without knowing a word of true French.

My father was a prosperous man, as had been his fore-bears. Unlike most of them, however, he was also a pious one, who daily thanked God for his remarkable good fortune, in being so wealthy as to be one of the King's creditors – he had been presented at court – in possessing perfect health, and in having fathered four fine children, two girls and two boys. It never seemed to have occurred to him that what the Lord giveth, the Lord can also take away. And all too often does.

When dear Papa was forty, and I ten, he determined to fulfil an ambition he had possessed for years, and make a pilgrimage to the centre of the Roman Church, and there kneel before the Holy Father himself. It may be supposed that our destination was therefore Rome, for Papa was determined that the entire family should accompany him.

1

However, going to Rome in 1335 was a waste of time; the Holy Father we recognised had betaken himself to Avignon in the south of France, where, a Frenchman surrounded by French cardinals, he felt considerably safer than on the banks of the Tiber. Yet my father conceived that journeying across France, then on the verge of open war with England and civil war with itself, would be more dangerous than taking a sea voyage round Spain and through the Straits of Gibraltar. In this too he was being heedlessly optimistic. I can only say that if this was the gravest mistake he ever made, it was also the last.

We thus took ship, my father, my mother, my elder sister Constance, my elder brother Richard, my younger brother Henry, and myself. Henry was a year younger than myself, Constance was sixteen, and Richard fourteen. If I say so myself, we made a remarkably handsome family, all yellow-haired, with well-shaped features and even better-shaped bodies. At least, Constance had a very well-shaped figure. I was still too young. But this was my fortune, and her misfortune. For Father's mistake was in considering the free companies of France to be more dangerous than the freebooters of Algiers. Our ship was taken.

Father was killed in the fight when the pirates boarded. Richard my brother was not so fortunate and, being seized and bound, was stripped and used as an object of desire by his captors, the Moors having decidedly ambiguous tastes in profane matters. So while Richard was breached from behind, Mother was being breached from in front. It mattered little in the end, as upon the crew tiring of them they were both tossed over the side.

Constance might have fared better, but for a singular circumstance. Like us all she was seized and dragged, screaming as loudly as her vocal chords would permit, before the pirate captain, who could not help but be impressed with her beauty. He wished to discover more, however, and my sister was stretched across a barrel while her skirts were thrown about her head, her long white legs were parted to their fullest extent, and the captain and several of his more senior compatriots delved between, with eye and finger. They were disappointed in what they found, and a few minutes later Constance had also been stripped naked and was lying beneath one of the crew while others made as free as possible with whatever parts of her body they could reach.

Since that unhappy day, as I gained experience in such matters, I have come to understand that, incredible as it may seem for a sixteen-year-old girl who had led a sheltered life, Constance was not a virgin. As to how and where she had surrendered that precious aspect of femininity by the age of sixteen I cannot offer an opinion – I am certain my father and mother did not know of it. In the event, she had every reason to regret her lapse from propriety before she followed Mother and Richard over the side.

Happily, my hymen was intact. Well, what would you expect of a ten-year-old child? Not that I enjoyed being spreadeagled across the same barrel and explored in a manner I had never considered possible. But to my relief I was not submitted to any of the maltreatment meted out to the rest of my family, and was instead taken below and shut up in a cabin. Henry was shut in another, close by, and we were able to speak to each other, but I was never to see him again. We were separated shortly after our ship was captured, and again my later experiences led me to suppose he was taken to Algiers and there castrated and made a eunuch in some prince's harem. No doubt there are worse fates. Being dead is one of them.

It may be felt that I have related the destruction of my family with some callousness. It happened a very long time ago, and I have seen too much murder and mayhem since. But at the time I was distraught with grief, and even more with loneliness and apprehension, as I had no idea what was to become of me. I was also at an age to be concerned more with physical discomfort than mental anguish – but in this regard was soon reassured, as I was fed three meals a day and no attempt was made to harm me in any way. Quite the contrary, there was invariably a man placed in my cabin to make sure I could not harm myself.

I was not left long in any doubt about my fate. Only two days after being captured by the corsairs I landed in Trapani, which is a seaport in the west of the island of Sicily, and was taken ashore in the dead of night, wrapped in a white linen robe which concealed me entirely. It appeared that the Algerine was known to and accepted by the people of this town, and had done business with them for some time. Thus no sooner had the captain laid eyes on me and ascertained that I was a virgin than he discerned a sale for me, which would not involve my being placed on the public block; this would mean that he would recoup my value the more quickly, and without having to share my price with any slave dealer.

His cupidity was equally another stroke of fortune for me. It set my feet upon the path I was to tread for the rest of my life, although I was yet unaware of it. And if from time to time I have been forced to doubt that this was indeed fortunate, I do not think I would really change any one of the things which have befallen me, even if I could.

My then feelings were limited to my immediate experience, which was startling enough. I found myself in a private apartment in a private house, with a man and three women, swarthy enough but not Moorish, as well as the pirate captain, while my finer points were discussed. The Sicilians were easily impressed by my long, straight, golden hair, my fine features and, above all, my large blue eyes.

There were other aspects of me which also had to please them, of course, and so I was stripped again and examined, this time by the women, both as to my virginity and in a search for any blemishes which might disfigure my body. There were none of these, and the good ladies

4

pronounced themselves pleased by clapping their hands. Gold was exchanged by the men, and I had become the possession of a Sicilian merchant.

But not yet a slave. Signor Albani was indeed a merchant, but in my case a go-between. If the pirate captain had known immediately where he would find a buyer for someone of my age and complexion, Signor Albani had known immediately where he might discover a profit on the transaction. But first, I had to be groomed. That meant that I had to learn Italian, and that my manners had to be improved. I had always supposed my manners to be perfect – Mother had been a strict disciplinarian – but it now appeared that she had been positively lax in important matters.

I was taught to walk and sit with a book on my head so that my neck, back and shoulders never varied from the perpendicular; to arrange my legs beneath my skirt so that there was never a trace of gaucheness; to use my fan, which became a language in itself; to play the lute and to sing – I was fortunate in possessing a high, clear voice. I was given books to read in Italian – I had naturally never been taught to read English.

The arts I was required to learn were all those of the boudoir and the salon. Mother had been used to instruct me in the kitchen, at home in Lincoln, and to assure me that a woman's true happiness lay in providing good food for her husband. In Trapani I was never allowed into the kitchen, which was reserved for menials.

I was, however, made to attend church every day, for early morning mass and for confession, and for instruction by the priest, who regarded the English version of Christianity with some suspicion, but was reassured by my ready acceptance of his point of view.

I was also taught the pleasures of the bath. In England we had bathed every Saturday night throughout the summer, and not at all during the winter months. In the warmer Mediterranean climes I discovered that everyone

5

was required to bathe at least every other day. This frightened me in the beginning, as I could not help but suppose it unhealthy, but I soon learned to enjoy it.

And all the while I learned Italian.

I was also taught French, by a neighbour who spoke the language fluently; this struck me as odd at the time, but I was soon to be enlightened. In any event, soon the least familiar of my three tongues was English, for I never heard it spoken.

Best of all, I was dressed. In England, although my father had been reasonably well-to-do, only the nobility truly dressed well. For a common merchant, or his lady, to do so was frowned upon. And indeed, for much of the year our principal concern was to keep warm – for the rest it was to keep dry. In Sicily, where it seldom rained and the temperature seldom dropped below a comfortable coolness even in the depths of winter, all was elegance. My cotehardie was of silk, and tailored with tippets and fitchets – no girdle was required. But for walking abroad my girdle rested on my hips, and my cotehardie was shrouded beneath a flowing, pleated skirt, while my mantle, in blue velvet, drooped from my shoulders to my ankles. I considered myself the perfect lady while I was still a child.

It must be remembered that I was only ten years old, although I was eleven by the time my education was regarded as completed. Admittedly I was a bright and exceptionally intelligent girl, but I had just suffered a great catastrophe and an even greater bereavement, and thus I was given to inattention and sometimes even rudeness. This was punished most severely, as if to remind me that despite all I was still an inferior being. The instrument used was a thick leather strap which was known as a ferrula, and which had the property of causing a most painful stinging sensation when applied to the bare buttocks, while leaving no blemish upon the skin. My beatings were administered by Signora Albani, in the presence of her sister and her companion, who were required to hold my arms as I knelt across the bed, shrieking my lungs away to no avail.

Thus, if my physical comfort and cleanliness and my education were on a considerably higher scale than anything I had known even in my father's comfortable Lincoln house, I was yet being forced to live a totally loveless, and indeed friendless, existence. I possessed no toys, and no one of my own age with whom to play. Often I looked down from my garret window at the happy Italian children romping together, and wept, for I was never allowed near them.

At that time, I was aware only of my misery. On reflection, now that I am older, I realise that the coldness of heart of which various gentlemen have accused me was a natural result of this unnatural upbringing, and of the events which were to crowd upon my life even before I attained the age of twenty.

After six months Signor Albani decided I was ready for the next step in my career, and I was escorted across the island to the great seaport of Palermo, whence he and I took ship for the even greater seaport of Naples.

I was naturally apprehensive of again risking the Barbary pirates, but Signor Albani assured me that I was in no danger in this sea, between Sicily and the mainland, because pirates never ventured into it. He also told me that Naples was ruled by the House of Anjou, and that he was taking me to commence a lifetime of service to that famous House.

I did not believe him.

The journey, made over a flat calm sea, would have been enjoyable, but for the fact that we were travelling on a large galley, which was, indeed, the only manner of vessel which could reliably cross such a windless ocean. The galley was very comfortable, for those who, like myself, were accommodated aft. It was less so for the hundred and fifty oarsmen, who were all condemned criminals, Signor Albani assured me, and sat naked, chained to their benches, and would remain there until they lacked the strength any longer to pull an oar, when they would be tossed overboard and their places taken by other unfortunates. Signor Albani did not appear to draw a parallel between this treatment of unhappy humanity by the Christian Sicilians and the fate meted out to my family by the Moors. He enjoyed standing at the rail of the raised after-deck looking down on the men, and encouraged me to do so also.

No doubt he considered this a part of my education, as I had never seen a naked man before, and indeed the spectacle interested me, but was not enjoyable, both because of the obvious misery of the wretches, and because of the offensive smell which rose from the benches and shrouded the entire ship – for these men never left their seats for an instant, and thus performed their necessaries as they sat.

I also could not help but reflect that I was no less a slave than they, and as yet I had no concept of my ultimate fate.

Which lay in Naples. There is a saying: See Naples and die. The poets choose to consider this an apt description of the beauty of the place, whereas I now know it truly refers to the noxious fevers which are prevalent in the south of Italy, and equally to the dark and desperate nature of the people who inhabit this fairest corner of the earth.

But the poets are not entirely wrong. The Bay of Naples can have few superiors for beauty in the entire world, especially when approached from the sea. To the north it is guarded by the islands of Ischia and Procida, which lie off the headland of Cape Misena. This headland is low-lying, although Ischia rises several hundreds of feet.

To the south there is the fabled isle of Capri, behind which is the headland of Sorrento, and this is high and splendid. Better pens than mine have written of Capri, and more sensual natures enjoyed its manifest charms, for it was here that the Roman Emperor Tiberius spent much of his time, by repute, in sexual dalliance with a variety of young boys and girls.

My own experiences convince me this tale is not at all false.

Capri is the first part of the bay the voyager from Sicily sights, and it sets the scene for what follows, because long before the island emerges above the horizon, one is staring at a huge, distant peak, capped with a circle of cloud, which is immortalised in song and story. Vesuvius not only dominates the Neapolitan landscape. In its beautiful exterior, which so successfully hides the tremendous angry passions that lie in its heart, it typifies the Neapolitans themselves.

The city lies on the northern side of the bay. It is a huddle of houses amidst which rise several noble palaces and churches, and is dominated on the one hand by the Mole, the arm of the harbour which the Neapolitans are pleased to use for their promenades, and on the other by the Castel Nuovo, the New Castle, built by Charles I of Anjou, the man who, nearly seventy years before my arrival, appropriated the Kingdoms of Sicily and Naples as his own. Sicily soon escaped him, after an unfortunate incident known as the Sicilian Vespers, but the Angevins continued to hold sway in southern Italy – their Kingdom stretched north nearly to Rome, and encompassed the entire south of the peninsula. The Angevins owned many other fiefs as well, not least being that very city of Avignon in which the Pope presently resided.

Naples is a colourful and indeed bright city. Therefore the awful aspect of the Castel Nuovo looms the more grimly. It is large and dark. The walls are thick and high and turreted, the drawbridge unassailable. It must be remembered that men could scarce recall when last the Kingdom of Naples had been ruled by a native prince: for centuries it had been the prize of Romans, Normans, and Germans, before the coming of the House of Anjou, who indeed seemed to combine in their talents, and their vices, aspects of all of their predecessors. Charles I had no doubt felt the need of a bastion which could resist the angry mob.

His descendants certainly needed it.

The drawbridge was lowered once Signor Albani identified himself, and we were escorted into the interior of this prison-like palace which was to be my home. My master was apparently well known in the castle, for without question we were led across the great courtyard, past the barracks and stables and kitchens, through growling dogs and scattering chickens, while watched by a variety of men and women, and admitted into the inner keep, and, soon after, the apartments of the royal residence itself.

I was lost in admiration of the drapes and carpets, the cloth-of-gold which was everywhere, the magnificently uniformed guards and majordomos, and thus did not immediately pay attention to the fact that our perambulation had ceased, and we were in a small chamber, facing a woman. The reason for this is simple: the woman in question did not match her surroundings. She was tall and strongly built, in early middle age, richly dressed and not unhandsome, but her features revealed more cunning than majesty, and her manner was totally lacking in that regal bearing I would have expected on such a stage.

Of her power, however, there could be no doubt. Signor Albani, having bowed so that his feather brushed the floor, explained how he came into possession of me. The lady bent a severe gaze upon me, and then beckoned me closer. 'Indeed, Albani,' she remarked. 'You have done well. My precious charge will love this toy, and she will smile upon me. You say the creature speaks Italian?'

'Like a native, Donna Filippa.'

'And French?'

'Equally so, Donna Filippa.'

'What is your name, child?' asked Donna Filippa, in the latter language which was normally used at court: the Angevins were, of course, themselves French.

'My name is Richilde Benoit, may it please you, my

lady,' I answered as I had been taught.

'She even has a French name. That is capital,' cried Donna Filippa, clapping her hands. 'Roberto, my pet, what do you think of her?'

I had not previously observed the boy, who lounged by the narrow window looking out over the harbour. He was somewhat older than myself, perhaps the same age as my brother Richard would have been, and, like his mother, was tall and well built. His complexion was remarkable, however, for it was distinctly dark, and his features, if bearing some of the characteristics of Donna Filippa, were none the less unlike any I had ever seen before: his lips were thicker than normal and his cheekbones more pronounced, while his hair possessed an unusual curl. But he was undoubtedly handsome, if, I felt even then, untrustworthy.

He advanced towards me. 'She is a pretty thing, Mama,' he agreed, and took some of my hair to strand through his fingers. 'What a pity this is not truly gold.' And he gave it a tug.

I would have kicked him had I not been hampered by my heavy gown, and also by my understanding that he was the master here, and I the servant.

'See my steward, Albani, and be paid,' said Donna Filippa, rising. 'And you, Richilde, come with me.'

I glanced at Signor Albani, who gave a somewhat sad smile. 'I shall not behold you again, Richilde,' he said. 'I will pray for your prosperity.'

It seemed to me that I had already attained that as I followed my new mistress down another resplendent corridor, and through a doorway into a quite magnificent chamber, from which there issued, as we approached, the sound of girlish laughter.

'Kneel,' commanded Donna Filippa, 'to the Duchess of Calabria, heiress to the throne of Naples.'

There were four girls in the room. Two of them were older than myself, and, I thought, older than their brother

Roberto, for that they were his sisters was obvious at a glance: while they were certainly attractive, their features contained the same heaviness as his. The third girl was hardly more than a child, and although clearly destined for great beauty, seemed rather frightened of my entrance.

The fourth was a year younger than myself, as I soon learned. But I would have knelt before her even had I not recognised her to be the heiress in question. This then was my first meeting with Joanna of Naples, to whom, for close on fifty years, I was to be friend, confidante, attendant and, sadly, accomplice. Had I, indeed, at that moment understood what dreadful adventures lay before me, I might well have dashed to the open window and thrown myself into the moat. And yet would I surely have regretted forgoing the intimate friendship of the most remarkable, as well as the most unfortunate, woman who ever lived.

I have no need to describe Joanna's beauty, which was renowned the length and breadth of Europe – and which she possessed even at ten years of age. It was in the strongest contrast to my own. Where my hair was long and yellow, hers was longer and of an utterly raven hue. Where my features were perhaps too big and too bold, hers were small and exquisite. Where my mouth was wide and given to smiling, hers, no less wide, was firmer and perhaps less generous. Where my chin was rounded, hers was pointed. And where my eyes were large and blue, Joanna's were huge, and black as midnight, and yet luminous and indicative of the bottomless recesses of her mind; they could warm as no fire has ever done, but they could equally chill like twin blocks of ice. And they were but the drapes that concealed a seething heart.

Of our bodies I will not now speak, as we were both children, yet were we both splendidly formed, and clearly destined to turn men's heads.

'Rise,' the Duchess said, her voice a trickle of warmth, yet possessive of all the majesty Donna Filippa lacked.

12

'Her name is Richilde,' Donna Filippa now explained, 'and she is from England. She was brought to me by Signor Albani, and I knew at once that she would make a splendid companion for you.'

It occurred to me that this speech somewhat lacked the respect one would have expected in addressing a duchess. But Joanna did not appear to notice.

She continued to gaze at me. 'Do I need a splendid companion, signora?' she asked. She might have been twenty instead of ten.

'Indeed you do. One of your own age,' Filippa admonished. 'Marie is too young, and Aurora and Benita will soon be too old.'

The two mulattoes, for such they were, giggled. Marie, I later discovered, was the Princess's younger sister, who was then eight years old.

Joanna shrugged. 'So be it, nanny. She will be my playmate.'

Thus it was done.

Joanna was far from being as indifferent to my presence as she pretended, for she was as desperately lonely as myself, despite all the pomp and the perpetual company with which she was surrounded. In part this was due to her precocity, for her mind had been fashioned almost from birth for her future role as Queen of Naples; her father had died when she was an infant, and from that moment childish matters had been put aside in favour of learning and politics. While, as a future queen, her domestic situation had also had to be determined at this early age, and my new mistress and playmate was already married.

The marriage had not yet been consummated, of course, but her husband, Prince Andrew of Hungary, who was both younger brother to the future king of that great country – Louis – and also the Princess's cousin, had been brought from Buda some two years before my arrival to celebrate his nuptials, and to take up residence in Naples in the hope that he would cease to be a rude Hungarian and become instead a refined Frenchman.

This ambition had not yet been achieved when I met the Prince. Nor was it ever. Andrew was well built and undeniably handsome, and he was just a year older than his wife. But his manners were uncouth and his temper uncertain, even then.

To compound matters, he had been accompanied from Buda by a retinue of Hungarian nobles, older than himself, to be sure, but hardly men, and yet with modes of behaviour which disgusted the Angevin court. Worst of all, he was never to be encountered without his confessor, a Dominican priest named Robert. This man was ugly in every way. Red-haired, red-bearded, misshapen both of feature and form, he was an affront to the beauty which was the Angevin glory, and his mind was no less twisted.

To be fair to the rascal, in regarding the Court of Naples as the most debauched in Europe he was doing nothing more than reflecting universal opinion. And in determining that Donna Filippa di Cabane, Joanna's nurse, governess and foster mother, was the most debauched person in that court, he was merely revealing a sound knowledge of human nature – he could not have *known*, then. Yet in their hatred for one another, which was obvious to me on the occasion of their first meeting in my presence, and the resulting rivalry, which the Dominican presumed he was bound to win in the end, as Andrew would always need a confessor while Joanna would soon cease to require a nurse, lay the seeds of the horror that was soon to encompass us all.

The hatred of nurse for confessor, and indeed of Neapolitan for Hungarian, was not lost upon Joanna. At ten, going on eleven, she had of course no knowledge of the requirements of the marriage bed. Neither did I. But she understood that her life was to be no bed of roses. Perhaps

14

she also understood, even then, that Filippa and her children were more interested in their futures than in hers, and, while she loved her younger sister, regarded her as too much of a child to be treated as a confidante. Equally at the other end of the scale: although King Robert and Donna Sancia adored their granddaughter, and equally valued her as their heiress, they were too remote for her to love with any passion.

Thus her loneliness, which I had been chosen to alleviate.

It took us some time to achieve any mental intimacy. Joanna was every inch a princess, and was used to treating inferiors with a cool disdain. In the beginning, when we threw a ball to and fro or dressed our dolls or compared our childish drawings, her attitude was one of contemptuous superiority. However, it is not possible to share one's entire life with another and not rapidly discover either hate or love.

My naturally sunny disposition, added to my beauty, which grew with every day, made me, happily, difficult to hate, and besides, I was the slave, she the mistress. Thus as I laboured to please, she unconsciously lowered her guard.

We were thrown into complete physical intimacy from that first day. 'You will never leave the Duchess's side for an instant,' Donna Filippa commanded. I now appreciate that this was all part of her plan, to awaken the Princess's obvious sensuality to her own advantage, but at the time it was merely an exciting adventure to us both. We shared our baths, and we shared Joanna's bed, sleeping in each other's arms. We were both naked.

I attended to her toilette and brushed that lustrous hair, and she would draw her fingers through mine. She asked me about my past, and wanted to hear the tale of the pirates and the demise of my family, and if I would never have dared ask about her family, she gradually told me

15

something of their history. Equally, she confided her fears for the future as well, yet without any apprehension that she would be unable to deal with the problems which would confront her as the youthful queen of the most turbulent people on earth.

We went abroad together, riding palfreys, to watch the hunt, at which sport Joanna's husband excelled even as a youth, and to which he was passionately devoted. We got drunk together when the huntsmen returned. They got drunk even more quickly. The Hungarians got drunker than anyone else. And Brother Robert glowered at us, so that I could not doubt that he had associated me in his mind with Filippa, and regarded me as her creature.

If this thought frightened me, I could at least take comfort from the reflection that I served a future queen, while his master was but a future consort.

There were of course less pleasant aspects of my existence. I was required to taste the Princess's food, which was no hardship: I did not apprehend the possibility of poison. But I had another duty to perform, that of the Princess's whipping girl. Joanna might have the mind and bearing of a future queen, but she was still a little girl, who had her moods, and even her tantrums, when she would hurl crockery at the nearest object. On these occasions it was my fate to kneel on a chair, my arms clasped around it, my skirts raised and tucked into my girdle, while Donna Filippa applied a cane to my buttocks. This was painful and humiliating, the more so when Roberto happened to be present, which was too often. And it lasted until Joanna, not myself, had suffered enough, when she burst into tears – I would long have been shrieking my lungs out – and begged her nurse's forgiveness, and the whipping ceased. If she was in one of her intransigent moods and refused to surrender, I suffered accordingly.

Yet I loved her. I love her still. And I was forced to watch her life begin to disintegrate before my eyes.

*

16

At this stage in my narrative, I feel bound to make an important point: I have no place in history. My name will be found in no learned books. This is the fate of the servant. But the events I am about to relate, every one, are attested by other witnesses, and cannot be denied. This should be remembered, for there are times, when I think back over them, that I find even myself wondering whether it was all some hideous nightmare. Alas, the briefest perusal of the appropriate pages of history will reveal that it is all true.

Let us begin by considering this House of Anjou. It should not be confused with that earlier house, of which Henry II of England is the most famous scion, and which delivered England into the hands of the Plantagenet Dynasty, which still rules that sceptred isle.

The title, Count, and then Duke, of Anjou, a French appanage, lapsed after Henry and his fire-eating sons had become so thoroughly English, and was not revised until early in the last century, for the fourth surviving son of Louis VIII Capet, King of France.

Louis's eldest son, Louis IX, is fondly remembered as Saint Louis – from having, somewhat unsuccessfully, twice taken the Cross – and from him and his wife, Margaret of Provence, are descended the present rulers of France; his great-granddaughter, Isabella, was married to the father of my own late sovereign lord, Edward III of England, and spent the last part of her life languishing in prison for the misdeeds of her lover, Mortimer.

It is possible to see in the history of this family the curse of heaven.

Louis VIII's second son was Robert, Count of Artois. He married Maude of Brabant, and their daughter Blanche married as her second husband the English Prince Edmund of Lancaster, thus, like her second cousin, becoming involved in English affairs. Count Robert's son, also named Robert, perpetuated the Artois line, and elected to follow the fortunes of his uncle Charles, to the cost of his descendants, as will be seen.

Louis's third son, Alphonse, Count of Poitou, is of little account – Poitou itself has remained in English hands for most of my lifetime – but his fourth son, Charles, was a man of distinction. Born in 1226, he was created Count of Anjou and Provence on his twentieth birthday, and soon after accompanied his brother on the Seventh Crusade, a disastrous affair which culminated in the rout of the French army and the capture of the two royal siblings.

They were ransomed, as had been our own King Richard a generation previously, but the event had a vastly different effect upon their characters. King Louis returned to France and devoted his life to improving the lot of his people. His brother, having surveyed the chaos obtaining from one end of the Mediterranean to the other, resolved to achieve an empire for himself.

The means were to hand. The Emperor, Frederick II Hohenstaufen, known to his contemporaries as *Stupor Mundi*, or The Wonder of the World, because of his learning and unending talents, had recently died. Now Frederick, if undoubtedly one of the greatest men to walk the human stage, had also been a profoundly independently minded one, particularly in matters concerning his prerogatives. Thus throughout his life he was at loggerheads with the Papacy. He was excommunicated no fewer than three times, on one occasion for not going on a crusade when he had promised the Pope to do so, and on another for going on a crusade without the Pope's permission!

To make the situation more disagreeable to the Pontiff, Frederick's crusade was the most successful ever undertaken – and did not cost a life in battle. Landing in Palestine with a huge army, the Emperor summoned the Sultan to a conference, at which the two most powerful men in the world agreed to be friends, part of the price of such friendship being the free and unmolested admission of Christian pilgrims to Jerusalem and the Holy Places.

To Rome this smacked of dealing with the devil!

Obviously, while the Pope could thunder denuncia-mentos and issue bulls of excommunication as often as he liked, to confront such a man with force was out of the question. But when Frederick died at the early age of fifty-six in 1250, Innocent IV saw the opportunity for revenge. He promptly launched what was, in effect, a crusade against the Emperor's sons, Conrad and Manfred. Manfred was illegitimate, but both these young princes were worthy of their father, and thus a Papal champion was needed.

He was eventually found in Charles of Anjou.

But recently released from Saracen captivity, Charles's ambitions were ranging on a scale unsuspected by the Curia. He had already secured himself, by treaty with Baldwin II, domination over the throne of Constantinople: he married his daughter Beatrice to Baldwin's son Philip, who was an imbecile. Now, at the Pope's request, he was to undertake the reduction of Sicily, long the stronghold of the Hohenstaufen. Frederick had made Palermo into the fairest city in Europe, and Charles undoubtedly saw it as the capital of a Mediterranean empire which would stretch to the Bosphorus. Both Papal and Angevin ambi-tions meant a great deal of bloodshed, but this is a pastime to which popes and princes have always been addicted.

Charles was equal to his task. Conrad died before he could raise an army, and Manfred promptly defeated the Papal forces and had himself crowned king of Naples and Sicily. This naturally encouraged Innocent's successor, Alexander IV, to support Charles even more vigorously, and at Benevento in 1266 Manfred died in battle against his rival, and Charles became king in his place.

There remained Conrad's son, a sixteen-year-old youth named Conradin, not unworthy of bearing the banner of the Hohenstaufen into battle. Unfortunately he was no match for Charles, and following his defeat at Tagliacozzo, he was publicly decapitated. European opinion was shocked by this regal murder, but there was no condemnation from Rome, and Charles was confirmed as King of Sicily and Naples.

Yet Charles had already sown the seed of his own failure. His harshness had indicated to all the world that he was too dangerous to be allowed to pursue his course unchecked, and even the Papacy rapidly turned against him. More serious, as he was now the first soldier in Europe and unlikely to be defeated by any new Papal champion, his tyranny antagonised his subjects, and they too sought his overthrow. They had to hand a native princess, Constance, Manfred's daughter, who had been married to Pedro III of Aragon.

The Spaniard was delighted to have the opportunity to add Sicily to his dominions, which already included the Balearics, but not so anxious to have to face Charles in battle. A plot was therefore hatched. It came to fruition on Easter Monday, 30 March 1282, at the hour of Vespers, when the Sicilians rose and slaughtered every French man, woman and child they could lay hands on. Some two thousand perished in Palermo, and many more elsewhere. The resultant war dragged on for twenty more years, but the Angevins were eventually driven from the island and were left with only the Kingdom of Naples.

Here they made themselves secure and, in time, even loved. This was the achievement of Charles's grandson, Robert of Naples, who succeeded to the throne in 1309 on the death of his father, Charles II, and came to be regarded as the most perfect knight in Christendom. This was in part because he staunchly supported the Pope in everything, or perhaps the reverse was true. The Great Schism which still divides the church occurred in 1305; the Pope took refuge in Robert's appanage of Avignon, and the two men remained close associates. But Robert was equally a famous soldier and a patron of the arts; it is said that the great Petrarch himself refused to accept the crown of poetry from the hands of anyone but the King of Naples.

Robert I was still on the throne when I arrived in his palace.

The question may well be asked, how suited is a perfect knight to be a successful king? Obviously one would have supposed that such a man as Robert would have secured the future of his dynasty no matter what misfortunes the future might hold. This was not so. The Angevins ever carried the will to self-destruction within them.

Robert's father, Charles II, had married a Hungarian princess, Marie, the daughter of King Stephen V of that country, and the sister-in-law of the unhappy Byzantine Emperor Andronicus II, who was torn to pieces by a mob.

These were wild times.

The eldest son of Charles and Marie went to Hungary to pursue his fortunes with his mother's family. He died young, but his son, Charles Robert, or Carobert as he was known, became ruler of Hungary in 1310, being elected to the throne after an interregnum had followed the death of the last male Arpad. This Carobert married Elizabeth of Poland, daughter of the great Vladislav IV, and carved for himself a vast empire in the centre of Europe. He was still ruling when I reached Naples.

Carobert and Elizabeth had two sons, which is where the tragedies which were to overtake us all had their roots. The elder boy, Louis, would obviously succeed his father as King of Hungary. The younger, Prince Andrew, was the husband of my mistress.

The problem was that Carobert felt that Naples was also rightfully his – a point of view I may say he passed on to his children. Strictly speaking, of course, he was absolutely correct; he was the son of the eldest son of Charles II.

One might have supposed that ruling Hungary, and

effectively Poland as well even if he left the title of King to his son, would have been sufficiently arduous. Unfortunately our Good King Robert, being so perfect a knight, was afflicted by an importunate conscience. Even if no opposition had been raised at the time to his taking the throne of Naples in the absence of his elder brother, he yet felt he was an usurper. This feeling grew when his son and heir, Charles, Duke of Calabria – the title always borne by the Neapolitan heir – died young, as I have related. Following this misfortune, Robert came to the conclusion that all wrongs might be set right by marrying his granddaughter – now heiress to the throne – to his grandnephew. As I have said, here was a recipe for disaster. Apart from the differences in temperament and background between the two children, to which I have already alluded, Robert was now advanced in years, and it seemed clear that there would have to be a regency when he died.

But Robert compounded error upon error by neglecting to consider the feelings of the rest of his family – who were extremely numerous. Of his three sisters, Blanche had been married to Jaime II of Aragon, and Lenore to Frederick III of Sicily – another Spanish prince – in an attempt to end the enmity between Spain and Naples. Margaret had married Charles of Valois and departed in her turn to mother another line of French kings.

These ladies could only watch from afar and weep for their homeland.

But Robert had also had two younger brothers. The elder of these had been known as Philip of Tarento, and he had married Catherine of Valois. Now Catherine was the daughter of Charles of Valois by Catherine of Courtenay, and Catherine of Courtenay was the daughter of that Philip, Emperor of Constantinople, to whom Charles I of Anjou had married his daughter Beatrice.

That Philip and his wife were second cousins is of less importance – my readers will have gathered from even this diversion into the affairs of a single family that just about every prince and princess in Europe was at best a second cousin of every other, which no doubt accounts for the high proportion of viciousness and imbecility amongst these exalted personages – than that, through her mother, Catherine could lay claim to the crown of Constantinople. The Byzantines had sunk so low that this crown was worth precisely nothing, yet Philip called himself Emperor and, following his death, which occurred some years before I appeared in Naples, his wife continued to use the title of Empress.

And I may add, she studiously cultivated the arrogant demeanour of an empress, too.

She had four children. Her daughter Margaret married Edward Balliol and disappeared into the highlands of Scotland. But each of her three sons, Louis of Tarento, Robert and Philip, who were both known as of Constantinople, considered himself to have more right to marry the Neapolitan heiress, and wear the crown as her consort, than any barbarous Hungarian.

Graver yet were the claims of Charles of Durazzo, son of King Robert's youngest brother, John of Gravina, who, if the heir of the youngest branch of the family, happened to be older than his cousins, and regarded himself as far more capable than they.

These young men, all possessing the Angevin looks and talents, I met during my first weeks in the palace, even if they were hardly aware of my existence other than as a new toy with which they could play. Not one of them was yet twenty, and they possessed all the high-spirited arrogance of healthy youths who also know themselves to be princes of the blood.

Also present at most of these teenage gatherings was Robert of Artois, only a year older than myself, and the descendant of that Count of Artois who had been Charles I's elder brother. He had as much claim to the throne as any of his cousins, but was the least assertive.

Every one of these young men left no doubt as to his feelings for Joanna: they adored her.

Of them all, my favourite was Prince Louis of Tarento. Sixteen years old, he was already a famous knight in the lists, and his handsome, laughing face was in the strongest contrast to the frowns of his cousin of Durazzo.

The butt of the princes' jokes was too often Prince Andrew, and in this could be discerned a source of future discord, presuming that Andrew would one day be King Consort of Naples. But yet, the wildest of boys often grow into the most sober and sensible of men. That this often happy gathering grew into a pack of mad dogs was due to one thing only: the passions of their beautiful cousin-who-was-to-be-their-queen. And those passions were to be shockingly aroused by the woman to whom Joanna and Marie turned as nurse, governess, preceptor, and even mother – Filippa di Cabane.

The rise and fall of this hoyden would make a good subject for a tragedy. She was born in that same little Sicilian seaport of Trapani where I had come ashore, and thus Signor Albani was an old acquaintance. A laundry-woman, no more, she was married to a fisherman, but contrived to abandon him and discover herself at the court of Naples, where by her persistence and ability she became laundress to the royal family.

As a reward for her services, her husband having conveniently died, she was given in marriage to a certain Raimondo di Cabane, a no less remarkable personality, for he was a Negro slave, raised to eminence by his master, whose name he adopted, and on whose death he soon far surpassed in the extent and success of his business dealings. He in turn so impressed King Robert that he was raised to the rank of Grand Seneschal of the kingdom.

One might suppose that a laundrywoman had here climbed to heights dizzy enough to satisfy even the most rampant ambition. But not Donna Filippa. Her second husband also dying, she contrived to remain in the palace, now as nursemaid to the two princesses, the daughters of Charles of Calabria's second wife, Marie of Valois.

The Duke having already died, Joanna was now Duchess of Calabria, heiress to the throne. Her mother now also died, to the distress of King Robert and his second wife, Donna Sancia. It does not seem to have occurred to them that people in the vicinity of Donna Filippa had this facility of dying when they became irrelevant to her advancement. Indeed, they could conceive of no better solution to the problem of the upbringing of their granddaughters than to place the little girls entirely in the hands of the faithful Catanian laundress.

Which is undoubtedly what Donna Filippa had had in mind from the beginning.

Thus was born the most evil conspiracy in history. For Filippa, understanding both the King's age and her charges' innocence, recognised that she had within her grasp the very kingdom itself.

Her plans had not yet reached fruition when I appeared on the scene. They were, however, fully formed. Joanna and Marie were already entirely in the mental power of Filippa and her two daughters, Aurora and Benita. The more sinister figure of her son, Roberto di Cabane, the youth who had pulled my hair on my first day in the palace, remained at this time in the background.

Mental domination was all that the Catanian had so far considered practical. The two girls had not reached puberty, and King Robert was in excellent health. It was his decision to reverse the past by bringing together the two branches of his family that aroused a sense of urgency in Filippa's breast.

The marriage entailed that her principal charge would be taken away from her as soon as she was considered sufficiently nubile to consummate her union. That might

25

have been a serious but not irreparable blow to the nurse's dominion. What made her ultimate defeat almost certain was the presence, and the enmity, of Brother Robert.

It thus happened that when I arrived in Naples, at eleven years old hovering, like the Duchess, on the edge of womanhood, Filippa was already anxiously awaiting the day when she could carry her foul designs a stage further, and hopefully make Joanna her slave forevermore.

At the time I was quite unaware of my new mistress's intentions – I naturally regarded Donna Filippa, who had actually bought me, as my mistress rather than Joanna. Joanna was my friend, and I hers. To be sure, I fetched her food, not she mine, and I bared my backside when chastisement was required, for either of us. That is what a whipping girl is for. I endeavoured to share her joys, and her concerns as well, for Joanna, if unable to discern any more loving person in the world than Donna Filippa, was yet, for all her youth, aware that the world was filled with demons, with whom she would one day have to cope.

And yet, the innate sweetness of her nature, combined with her natural intelligence, which matched my own, would I am sure have overcome every obstacle and made her one of the most revered names in history. But for the Catania.

The plot which this dreadful woman concocted, in the secrecy of her own heart and mind, was a simple one. She understood too well that beneath Joanna's calmly beautiful exterior there lurked all the passions of her race and her heritage – but unsuspected to exist by the Princess, because of her youth and innocence. It was Filippa's intentions to mine this molten ore, and bind it entirely to herself. She had no doubt that once a personality like Joanna's was introduced to the pleasures of the flesh she would never be able to renounce them. And she was, alas, right. Joanna's story is that of a continuing battle between

26

the good and evil sides of her nature. In extenuation, I have to remind you that the good she was born with, the evil was induced. But like any poison lacking an antidote, it soon overwhelmed the healthy body.

Why was not I that antidote? How I wish I could have been. But I was only fourteen years old when the plan was put into effect. And besides, I was one of the instruments the Catanian was determined to use.

As I have mentioned, Donna Filippa was simply awaiting the right moment, which was the onset of puberty. For two years Joanna and I enjoyed each other's company, and that of our young friends and admirers, blissfully unaware of the fate hanging over us.

Even I did not lack admirers. The princes made free with my person, as they could not do so with Joanna's, and I was often pinched and tossed until I was black and blue, without any greater emotion than that of tearful laughter when the pain was severe.

Their grooms equally looked at me with interested eyes, but like the Princess, I was still too young to understand what such interest might entail. If some of the questing fingers aroused within me feelings which were as disturbing as they were exciting, these were no different to the feelings Joanna and I on occasion aroused within each other.

Such is the innocence of youth.

The decisive moment arrived in the summer of 1339, when in the same week Joanna and I began to menstruate, she being, it must be remembered, a year the younger.

This was naturally a moment awaited with eager anticipation by the whole court, as it would permit a consummation of the Princess's marriage. However, it was also necessarily an event known in the first instance only to Donna Filippa, her daughters, Joanna, and myself, and the Catanian was determined to conceal it for as long as was necessary – Joanna was only thirteen, and no one would be concerned about her failure to reach maturity for another year.

'This is best,' Filippa explained. 'Because it will give me time to complete your education. It is a terrible thing to go to a husband unaware of what lies in store, of what should be expected, and of what should be rejected. It is my duty to acquaint Your Grace, in whose care I have laboured day and night these past dozen years, with the final, and most important, facet of humanity: the sexual relationship between man and woman. Fortunately, I have a willing volunteer. Aurora, my dear, admit your brother.'

To my astonishment, Roberto di Cabane had been waiting in the adjoining chamber, and now he was brought in, looking a trifle hot, to be sure.

'Roberto, my darling boy,' Filippa said. 'I have a boon to ask of you.'

'Anything, dearest Mama,' he agreed.

'Would you be so good as to demonstrate to the Princess the act of love, my son?'

The wretch had clearly been instructed beforehand as to his reply. 'It would be my great pleasure, Mama.' He bowed, and then straightened again. 'But with whom?'

His sisters clapped their hands. It should be mentioned that the two mulatto girls, now in their late teens, had both been advantageously married, Aurora to the Count of Terlizzi, and Benita to the Count of Morcone, men considerably older than themselves.

'Why, with Richilde, of course,' Filippa said. 'Is she not here for that very purpose?'

Joanna here clapped her hands as well. 'That would be capital,' she cried.

Like me, she was of course quite ignorant of what was involved, and supposed it was going to be some fine new game. Well, perhaps she was right, even if with every move it filled me with more apprehension.

It began well enough. 'A man approaches his beloved,' Filippa explained. 'So. And kisses her hand.'

Roberto did so to my hand, and caused me to suppress a giggle of embarrassed pleasure; he had grown into a most handsome boy.

'Time passes,' Filippa said, 'and your lover seeks more. Supposing he is favoured, he may be granted more.'

Roberto held my hand, ran his fingers up my sleeve, and caressed my bodice. I had of course been touched here before, ostensibly by accident, in the course of my rompings with the princes, and never failed to enjoy the resulting sensation. But on this occasion I was for the first time aware that the sensation extended to the person touching, as well; the masculine dress of the day consisted of hose worn beneath a doublet, but the doublet did not descend beneath the thighs, and a quick glance assured me that something was happening inside Roberto's hose. I had noticed this also before when romping with the princes, and I had been tossed from arm to arm, but had never deduced cause and effect, as it were.

Now I began to feel frightened.

'See the colour in those pale cheeks?' Donna Filippa cried. 'Now her heart is lost, and she agrees to the ultimate. We will adjourn to the bedchamber.'

Off we went, myself and Roberto hand in hand, Joanna and Filippa following, Aurora and Benita behind with Marie, who was now eleven and beginning to reveal as much precocity as her sister.

I still had no concept of what was about to happen to me.

'Let us assist the lovers to bed,' Filippa commanded. Her daughters promptly seized me and in a trice had stripped me naked. This astonished me, as no one had ever lifted a hand to assist me to undress before, and besides, it was the middle of the morning. Moreover, I was distressed to be thus exposed to the gaze of Roberto, especially after he had made free with my person. But I may say that at fourteen I was already almost a fully grown woman, and feared comparison with no one for shape of breast or belly or leg.

My embarrassment was compounded when Roberto was alike divested of his clothing by his eager sisters. My later knowledge of this diabolical family leads me to suppose that this was not the first time they had thus enjoyed themselves, and even that incest was not a word unknown to them.

Like myself, however, Joanna and Marie had never beheld a naked man close to, and Roberto was at once handsome and aroused. The princesses both exclaimed with pleasure, and wished to inspect his marvellous – and huge – appendage. This Filippa allowed them to do, permitting them to touch and caress it, which seemed to increase its size, as Roberto himself seemed to swell with pride and anticipation.

Although certainly interested myself, I waited patiently, still unaware of my true part in the proceedings.

I was not kept in ignorance for very long. The two countesses proceeded to stretch me upon the bed, and made free with my body, kissing my mouth and stroking my breasts, and allowing their hands to wander between my legs. 'The better to prepare you,' they told me.

Certainly the excitingly strange sensations I had earlier experienced returned in greater measure, but all suggestion of pleasure ended when Roberto proceeded to kneel between my thighs, and I realised that I was about to be lanced by his enormous weapon.

I screamed, and tried to sit up, but the countesses held my shoulders to keep me flat on the bed, and Filippa herself had hold of one of my legs. With the other I could still kick, but Joanna and Marie now decided to take part in the game, laughing happily as they grappled with the waving limb, and, so secured, I was deprived of my maidenhead.

The pain was intense. I conceived a violent hatred for Roberto, who was kissing my face and mouth with great intensity while he surged back and forth within me, seeming to be slitting me from arse to tit. When he was

30

finished I was a welter of sweat and discomfort. But the other ladies were delighted, and congratulated their hero. Only Joanna was slightly concerned at the blood on the inside of my thighs and staining the coverlet, but Filippa assured her this was perfectly normal.

'There are, of course, several other ways to accomplish the act of love,' she announced. 'I know of at least thirty.'

I was the only one who apparently did not feel that it had been an act of love.

The deed completed, I was allowed to wash and dress myself. Joanna and Marie wished to see it done again, but Filippa explained that Roberto had given his all for the moment, and that we should have another lesson tomorrow.

Certainly, and greatly to my relief, his lance was entirely broken, or perhaps crumpled would be a better description. But he was tremendously pleased with himself, I think more at having been allowed to display himself before the princesses than at having raped me.

His mother had scored an absolute triumph, as she well knew. It mattered not to her that I had been reduced to trembling tears, or that my respect for her had been stripped away to leave nothing but disgust. I was unimportant. For Joanna had been utterly intrigued by what she had witnessed, and, having been aroused but not sated, or even disgusted, as had I, she could think of nothing else.

That night as we lay together she asked me over and over again how it had felt, and even sought to repeat some of the sensations, as best she could with her fingers. This comforted me, but it also frightened me. I knew already what the outcome had to be. As did Filippa, undoubtedly.

When we gathered again the following morning for a second lesson, Joanna declared that on this occasion she would accept no instruction other than what could be practised on herself.

Now I must say again that neither Joanna nor I, and of course certainly not Marie, had been taught anything of sexual matters. We had no concept of the cause of pregnancy. Our menstrual periods had been dismissed by Filippa as a curse women had to bear. We knew nothing of the importance of virginity – the cause of what had happened to my sister was still a mystery to me. We only knew that we had discovered a marvellous new plaything, and an exciting new game.

I still hold my head in wonder at the risk Donna Filippa took, with such calculated confidence. Had a word of what was happening in the royal nursery reached the King and Queen, the nurse would have found herself upon the scaffold even sooner than she ultimately did. But of course, no word did escape. Filippa had bound her charges too closely to her, and knew that young girls do not naturally make confidantes of their grandmothers, especially where that grandmother was herself a stepgrandmother. And so Joanna, dear, darling, beautiful Joanna, exposed her naked white body to the lust of Roberto di Cabane, found blood upon her own thighs, and became a woman at the age of thirteen.

This tremendous step taken, Filippa tightened the bonds. A woman of much learning in the matters of the body, she proceeded with caution, but determination. Having been deflowered, I was cast aside, except for various demonstrations. I would be lying did I not admit that, once the initial pain was forgotten, I found Roberto's ministrations delightful, and regretted that I was not the sole object of his affections. But his interest, directed by his mother, lay solely in the Princess.

Over the next few months, on days which I now know were carefully calculated by Filippa, Joanna was entranced by her lover in a succession of different ways. Within a fortnight they were being closeted privately in her bedchamber, and there she gave herself up to every variety of caress and adoration, a majority of them unrecognized by the Holy Church. I know this, because she told me what was done to her, and what was done by her at her master's behest, and was wont to demonstrate her new-found art, or have me attempt to repeat Roberto's expertise. Our intimacy grew. But her love for Roberto grew faster.

The Catanian of course had certain steps to take, apart from ensuring against Joanna's possible pregnancy. Secrecy was essential to her plan. And the secrecy had to be maintained without permitting the princesses to understand the depravity into which she had led them. The risk was that, having discovered Roberto's special asset, they would seek it elsewhere, in the hose of those princes who still came to our apartments to frolic. Filippa put a stop to these visits, announcing that now Joanna had reached a certain age childish games were behind her. This greatly impressed King Robert and Donna Sancia, as to the seriousness with which she took her responsibilities. While she impressed upon the princesses, and upon me, that a man's particulars were never to be mentioned, or caressed, without a precise invitation.

We were bewildered, but obedient. In any event, from Roberto we received invitation enough.

It was now time for the Catanian to take her plan a stage further. 'We must inform His Majesty, Your Grace, that you are ready to consummate your marriage with Prince Andrew, and live with him as man and wife.'

'You mean he will be allowed to make love to me?' Joanna demanded.

'That will be his right,' Filippa agreed. 'Of course, I doubt he will be as accomplished or as loving as Roberto ...' She stroked her son's head, for the youth by now was almost as permanently to be found in the royal bedchamber as myself; Joanna was insatiable.

'Then I shall inform Grandpapa that I do not wish the marriage to proceed,' Joanna declared.

33

Filippa appeared to be aghast. 'My dear girl, you cannot do that. Your marriage was celebrated at the cathedral.'

'But it has not yet been consummated,' Joanna insisted, triumphantly. She had learned a great deal during the past few months. 'Thus it has no validity. Nor can it ever be consummated, now. I belong to another. I belong to Roberto.'

'You belong to your husband,' Filippa said severely. 'He may not be the man either you or I would have chosen for you, but he is your husband. And you are a princess, and the future Queen of Naples. You have responsibilities which you cannot evade, and which you have already gravely compromised. Do you not realise that you have committed a great crime?'

'I?' Joanna's tone was imperious.

'You have yielded your virginity to a man, out of marriage. You have committed adultery. You have compromised yourself beyond hope of salvation, should this ever become known outside these four walls.'

Joanna stared at her in amazement – but also in alarm.

I was shivering.

'Were your grandfather ever to know of it,' Donna Filippa continued, pressing her point home, 'you would be confined in a convent for the rest of your days. While your faithful friends, myself, Roberto here, and my two daughters … why, even Richilde, would all be sent to the stake.'

My knees gave way and I sat down, for the first time in my life unbidden, in the presence of the Princess.

But Joanna had also seated herself, involuntarily. 'Then we are lost. I am lost. And it is your doing, signora. You have betrayed me.'

'I, betrayed you, my dearest girl? I love you better than I love myself. But I am a weak woman. When you told me you desired my son, I could not resist you.'

It is still incredible to me, but we both remained unaware that she had engineered the whole thing.

34

We were still but children.

'Of course you are right, dearest Mama,' Joanna cried, bursting into tears and throwing herself into her nurse's arms. 'But what are we to do?'

'Do you not think I have studied the matter?' Filippa demanded. 'I have lain awake night after night, trying to discover a solution. But there is none, save secrecy. You must go to Andrew, and be his wife.'

'But I love Roberto,' Joanna wailed, leaving Filippa's arms for those of her paramour. He stroked her hair and murmured encouragements into her ear.

'I know you do, my pet,' Filippa agreed. 'And you will continue to do so. Andrew will not be here all the time, whereas, if you wish it, Roberto and I will be here always, as we are now. And when the Prince is absent ...'

'Oh,' Joanna said. Even her ardent nature balked at the thought of sharing her bed with two men in rapid succession.

'It is your only hope of happiness,' Filippa pointed out.

Joanna considered. 'But,' she said at last. 'I will not bleed. He will know that I am not a virgin.'

'I will attend to that,' Filippa said. 'On the night you go to him, your servant, Richilde, will carry, concealed in her girdle, a tiny sachet of fresh blood. During the night, after he has penetrated you, you will break the sachet and allow the blood to stain your thigh and the sheet. Thus will your reputation be maintained.'

Joanna freed herself from Roberto's embrace, and walked to the window, to look down at the harbour and the sea beyond for several minutes. He waited, silently. No doubt Filippa realised this was the critical moment.

I was merely terrified.

Joanna turned, and gave a sad smile. 'As you say, it seems I am an adulteress even before I am a bride. Can we really maintain such a subterfuge, good Mama?'

'If we all swear to trust each other, and believe in each other, and never to betray each other. And,' she added, almost as an afterthought, 'if we swear that we shall always be together.'

'Yes,' Joanna said. 'We will swear.'

And we did, the countesses and Marie joining in the ceremony.

Thus did Donna Filippa di Cabane appear to seize control of the crown of Naples. I say appear, because the best, and worst, plans can go awry. Donna Filippa was to be betrayed . . . but from a quite unexpected quarter.

In the beginning, everything turned out as she had prophesied. The news that Joanna was now a woman was conveyed to King Robert, who was delighted. He caused the bells to be rung and himself visited our apartments to congratulate his granddaughter. I do not think I was the most terrified person present, by any means, but Joanna appeared as the soul of dignified eagerness to begin her adult life.

Messengers were sent galloping to Buda, to inform King Louis and the queen mother; King Charles had recently died. There was a great feast and enormous celebrations. Even Brother Robert was seen to smile. He assumed his moment of triumph had arrived.

And before the feasting was over, the young couple were closeted in Joanna's bedchamber.

Here I attended my mistress, and secreted the precious phial beneath her pillow while her husband was distracted. This he easily was by finding himself alone with two beautiful females. Indeed I swear the drunken youth was uncertain which of us to mount first, and so I beat a hasty retreat and left Joanna to cope as best she could.

It may be asked, how did Donna Filippa know that the marriage would not immediately be a success, and lead Joanna to turn her back upon Roberto and all that had happened before? The Catanian's judgement, on all matters save only one, was never wrong. She knew that

36

her son was a past master at the art of love, as she had taught him herself, and at the most important aspect of the art of love, that of arousing and then satisfying the woman – a procedure too often ignored by senseless men – for a woman, once so captured, will remain loyal, and in love, for as long as the man wishes.

She had also discerned, which was simple enough to do, that Prince Andrew was a man who regarded women, even a future queen, as his inferiors, placed upon earth solely for his pleasure. In this she rested her trust, and she was proved entirely correct.

Joanna played her part to perfection, allowed him to enter her, and broke the sachet of blood as soon as he was asleep. Next morning the bed was carefully examined, by Donna Sancia, Donna Filippa, and Brother Robert, and the marriage was pronounced consummated. There was more ringing of bells, and more messengers were despatched to Buda bearing the joyful news.

Recovered from his nuptials, Andrew promptly summoned his lords and went hunting. Joanna remained in her private apartments, where we attended her with apprehensive expectancy.

'He is a brute,' she declared. 'Vulgar and unpleasant. And smelly,' she added. 'He did no more than kiss my cheek before he was forcing himself into me. Then he fell asleep. I have never been so humiliated in my life. Oh, my darling Roberto!' She took him in her arms, and the rest of us tactfully withdrew.

Outside, the Catanian for the first time dropped her guard before me. 'Now is the Princess entirely ours,' she told her daughters. 'Our future is assured.' Then she stared at me. 'Your future is bound with ours, Richilde,' she said. 'Remember that. Utter a word out of place, to either the King or Princess Joanna, and I will see that you are broken on the wheel.'

I understood then, for the first time, that the Princess had

37

been caught in a snare. But I did not know, for I was too young, how much catastrophe would arise from it. My position was a precarious one. If I was sure of my own love for Joanna, I had no certainty of her love for me – at least when opposed to her criminal passion for Roberto di Cabane. I was equally aware that if I was Joanna's maid, I was Donna Filippa's slave, and that she was fully capable of carrying out her threat – while there was not a hand in the entire kingdom would be raised to prevent her.

If I felt that we were all sitting on top of a volcano which was but waiting to explode, I could do nothing save wait myself, and pray, and I could at least watch my Princess's happiness as she went to her Roberto, sweeping away the tears of frustration and disappointment which accompanied her to and from Prince Andrew's bed.

Thus matters continued for some two years, until Donna Filippa's triumph turned to ashes. The agent who brought about this calamity for the laundrywoman was her own son.

CHAPTER 2

For three years Filippa di Cabane had her way, with nothing but fortune to look forward to. On the surface, all was well in the Kingdom of Naples. The Duke and Duchess of Calabria created a public impression of devoted marital bliss. King Robert and Donna Sancia were the happiest of grandparents. Friendly messages came and went between Naples and Buda. There was peace on every side.

Only those at the heart of the conspiracy knew what a perilous and deceitful path was being trod. Prince Andrew suspected nothing. If Joanna was undoubtedly undemonstrative in his bed he accepted it as but a woman's part. He was himself not overly interested in playing the husband – except for the public gaze in order to establish quite firmly that he was the future King of Naples – performed his conjugal duties perhaps twice a week, and devoted the rest of his time to hunting. Which suited Joanna well enough.

It did not, however, suit Brother Robert, who was a sorely confused man. The intimate of his master, he well understood Andrew's nature. Equally well could he discern Joanna's, and that she would forever lie there supinely beneath her husband and smile her thanks when he dismounted seemed out of character.

He suspected nothing of the truth, of course. But he feared for the future, the more so as, despite his

39

remonstrations, Joanna steadfastly refused to dismiss her nurse and her family, and insisted they retain their apartments within the castle. The Dominican therefore brooded, without arriving at an answer to the riddle which confounded him.

Equally confounded were those erstwhile playmates of my mistress, and princes of the blood. None of them had doubted for a moment that the consummation of the marriage between their beloved Princess and the rude Hungarian would also mean the end of the marriage in all but name, and the despoiled and disappointed heiress would then look for a man truly capable of satisfying her nature. Louis of Tarento, Robert of Constantinople, Philip of Constantinople, and perhaps even Charles of Durazzo, all dreamed of filling that need, regardless of the dangers involved. While Bertrand of Artois never saw the Duchess of Calabria but he broke into a heavy sigh. And yet, so far as they could discover, their idol had immediately become a happily married woman, who would bestow on no man more than a friendly smile.

Within the Catanian camp, as it may be called, all was contentment. We ladies gathered every morning for our sewing and gossip, and as soon as it was ascertained that the Duke and his Hungarians had departed for the hunt, Joanna retired to her bedchamber and was there joined by Roberto, to emerge an hour later smiling and sated.

She had at this stage little else to do, as her grandfather still regarded her as too young to be involved in affairs of state.

The only member of our group who immediately suffered following Joanna's marriage was myself. I had entirely ceased to be of importance. Joanna's desire for childish caresses was now submerged beneath her lust for Roberto, I had served my purpose as regards Donna Filippa, and, to make matters worse, the Catanian had begun to suspect that I regarded her as an evil influence on my mistress.

40

The wonder of it is that she did not immediately put me up for sale. Perhaps she suspected that, for all her apparent indifference, Joanna still entertained some regard for me. And it was in Filippa's nature to approach every problem in a tortuous fashion. Rather than risk a confrontation with the Duchess, she sought to undermine any affection that remained between us by the simple expedient of introducing a new confidante into the royal bedchamber.

'It is most unseemly that your toilette and private moments should be shared with a slave who is also a foreigner,' she told the Princess. 'You should have a companion of better background, and Neapolitan. I know the very person.'

And so Donna Cancia was introduced into our midst, to bring doom and destruction upon us all.

Donna Cancia was a year older than myself, so two years older than Joanna. She was also, very rare in a Neapolitan, a blonde. No doubt Donna Filippa had my own colouring in mind when making the selection. Our complexions apart, however, we had nothing in common. Even Cancia's hair was curly where mine was straight. Her face was rounded, like that of a mischievous monkey, where mine was calm and a trifle long. Our bodies were equally voluptuous, but we put them to different uses.

Our principal difference, however, lay in our characters. Mine was of a grave and reflective cast; Cancia bubbled like heated wine. No sooner had a thought entered her shallow head than she had to implement it, heedless of the consequences. Undoubtedly she was a delightful companion for her irresponsible gaiety, the more so as her nature was as sensuous as Joanna's. She had not been in our midst a month before she had seduced the Count of Terlizzi. Not that this concerned the Countess, who was of course Donna Aurora; she was already sharing the bed of some other noble. Such was the court of Naples in 1340.

41

Donna Cancia's arrival seemed to complete the Catanian's triumph. She appeared entirely as Donna Filippa's creature. I was thus relegated even farther from the royal presence, was left with the most menial tasks to perform, from sweeping the floors to emptying Joanna's chamber pot, and received seldom a smile for my efforts. If I found some solace in the company of the grooms and footmen who from time to time were required to invade our feminine presence, I am surely not to be blamed.

It was in the summer of 1342 that I became aware of a change in Joanna. The cause was Roberto di Cabane.

This young lout lacked the character for the high station, that of royal lover, to which he had been elevated by his mother. His background, which, after all, was that of the son of a slave and actually lower than my own, and his personality, which a life of fortuitous but unrelieved prosperity had caused to become impossibly arrogant, alike unfitted him to hold the adoration of a woman such as Joanna. And yet he did, simply because of his proficiency in the art of love. Joanna had known no other able to match him – as she had known only her husband apart from him – nor did she seek one.

Yet she was a royal princess, and a future queen, and she could not help but resent the harsh words and careless manner with which Roberto often humiliated her. I watched her weep, at once with anger and shame, on more than one occasion. And yet I dared not interfere. This was a low period of my life. Others were to be more dangerous, more physically unpleasant, but the loss of Joanna's intimate friendship, however temporarily, was the hardest cross I ever had to bear.

Mistreated as she was by her lover, Joanna had no recourse. But Donna Cancia did. This scatterbrained harlot suddenly found ambition. She could see as well as myself that Joanna was miserable, and, unlike myself, she felt herself able to provide a remedy. She had replaced me as Joanna's intimate, and could speak to her as a friend, as I had done when we were children.

Nor did she have anything to fear from the possible vengeance of Donna Filippa. Unlike me, she was not a slave. As for whether she should have felt gratitude to the Catanian for having introduced her to the corridors of power in the first place, I can only say that gratitude was not an emotion that ever took a high place in the breast of Donna Cancia.

'To be loved,' she said one day, 'oh, it is the most blessed state in which a woman can find herself. Am I not right, Your Grace?'

The three of us were alone, busy with our needlework. Roberto had satisfied himself and departed, as had the countesses and their mother, sure that Joanna could be left in the care of Cancia – unaware that Cancia was preparing to betray them.

'To be loved,' Joanna sighed.

'Are you not loved, Your Grace?'

'Am I, Cancia?'

'I can assure you that you are, Your Grace. By every man in Naples. And by some more than any others. But how dare I speak of love, when Your Grace wishes to speak only of Roberto di Cabane?'

'Is that what I wish, Cancia?'

'You do not wish to speak of your lover?'

'My lover?' Joanna laid down her needle. 'Can you suppose that? Oh, he is the lover of my body. For the rest ...'

'He is a wretch!' Cancia declared, somewhat jumping the cue she had herself set up. 'Oh, the foul monster, so to distress my lady.'

'Alas, good Cancia, he is also, as you say, my lover and my master. My life is his.'

'Must it be so?'

Joanna gazed at her.

'You seek love, Your Grace. It is understood that you

cannot find it in the arms of your husband. But can you any longer find it in the arms of a brute like Roberto?'

Joanna sighed some more. 'Have I any option?'

'You have many, Your Grace. But you have one more than any other. I know of a man who loves you more than life itself. Who would never do more, or less, than worship you, as he does now. Who would give ten years of his life to be allowed to enter your bedchamber, and who would there serve you as no man, not even Roberto, can ever have done.'

'You speak of a god?'

'I speak of a cousin, Your Grace. Your cousin.'

Joanna frowned at her. 'I have many cousins.'

Cancia glanced at me, sitting demurely in a corner, head bowed. But she, like everyone else, considered me of little account. Besides, she knew that she was going to need an accomplice to carry her plan to fruition. 'I speak of Bertrand of Artois.'

Joanna's head jerked.

'Is he not twice as handsome as the blackamoor?' Cancia asked. 'Is he not four times as gallant? Is he not eight times as gentle, and twelve times as much in love with you? And is he not a hundred times better born?'

'Bertrand,' Joanna said, softly. 'Could I but believe ...'

'Believe, Your Grace. Believe! But give him the opportunity to prove himself.'

'Bertrand,' Joanna said again. 'If I thought it could be managed ...'

'It will be my responsibility,' Donna Cancia assured her. 'Richilde will assist me.'

My mistress and I had taken another step on the path to hell.

Introducing Bertrand of Artois, when the time came, into the Princess's bed was no difficult matter. The Castel Nuovo was riddled with secret passages and secluded corridors, which were familiar by now to both Cancia and myself

– for, as she had warned, I was required to play my part.

I was indeed the only person Cancia dared trust. The danger lay in exchanging Bertrand for Roberto without immediately causing a storm which would betray all of us to an unthinkable fate. That such a fate actually did lie in store for most of us never crossed our minds. Such is the optimism of youth!

The situation was complicated by Joanna's reluctance to be parted from her present lover, who, however unwelcome he had become, yet satisfied her needs, for another, as yet unproven, until such proof could be provided. So that, while Donna Cancia acted as the go-between, and Bertrand of Artois wrote tender love notes which were secreted by the Duchess, and read between the three of us with much pleasure during our private hours, some time elapsed before Joanna announced herself ready to try the experiment.

On this day she endured as usual the caresses of Roberto, while Bertrand and I lurked in a secret corridor just outside the royal bedchamber. The young prince was in a state of high agitation, and could scarce keep his hands off me. I did not reject him. He was a prince, and a handsome boy, and I knew that he had to be in a condition of undoubted ardour when he bared himself to my mistress. But in fact, so excited did he become from fondling my breasts that I was afraid we might lose all before he ever reached the Princess, and I was heartily relieved when Cancia stole along the corridor to find us, and beckoned Bertrand to follow her.

I did also, into Joanna's bedchamber. Roberto had of course left, and the Duchess was alone, and, although partially concealed beneath the covers, clearly naked. And on this occasion, equally clearly unsated.

Bertrand bowed, with difficulty owing at once to his awe at seeing so much beauty awaiting him and to his condition as a result from dallying with me in the passage. Cancia and I curtsied.

'I understand that you would speak with me upon a privy matter, cousin,' Joanna said softly.

Poor Bertrand was speechless, and could do no more than glance at us.

'Leave us, ladies,' Joanna commanded. 'And be sure I am not disturbed until I ring.'

We curtsied again, and withdrew. Now indeed was the most dangerous part of the proceedings. But our domestic affairs had fallen into a set routine, and we did not apprehend the return of either Filippa or her son until it was time for dinner. They regarded Joanna as so utterly theirs it never crossed their minds to wonder, knowing as they did how the Duchess amused herself after leaving her husband's bed, how she might amuse herself after Roberto had left *her* bed. Thus we sat, and sewed, not speaking but occasionally glancing at each other and smiling, for at this moment we were entirely united, until the bell rang.

We returned to the bedchamber, and found Joanna aglow from head to foot, with love and sated lust. Bertrand seemed somewhat dazed, but entirely happy. It was my business to escort him back along the secret corridor and during our journey he muttered to himself, or perhaps to me, 'I love her,' over and over again.

There now only remained to complete the second half of the conspiracy. Next morning Joanna at last permitted herself to take offence at one of Roberto's importunities. Even if Cancia and I were aware of what was going to happen, we were yet alarmed by the vehemence of the Duchess's anger, as her voice rose from behind the bedchamber door.

Roberto naturally tried to reply in kind – he had no more wit than that – and the quarrel grew louder. Donna Filippa hurried in, together with her daughters. Cancia and I were spectators, to witness our mistress, clad only in a sheet, sitting up in bed and pointing her imperious finger at the door.

'Your Grace,' Filippa protested. 'Whatever can be the matter?'

'Your son has insulted me once too often, signora,' Joanna declared. 'I will see him no more.'

Filippa was thunderstruck, and gazed at Roberto.

'I did nothing more than—'

'Be quiet, wretch,' Joanna told him. 'I wonder I do not send you to the gibbet.'

Even Roberto's dark complexion paled, and his sisters clung to each other in terror.

Their mother was more equal to the occasion. 'Do that, Your Grace,' she warned, 'and we are all condemned.'

Joanna gave her a haughty stare. 'I am the Duchess of Calabria,' she announced. 'Only His Holiness can ever condemn me.'

Which was true enough, but her words had Cancia and myself emulating the two countesses and clutching each other's hands – no Pope was needed to condemn *us*.

'However, signora,' Joanna said, icily, 'I am too generous to forget that you have been the preceptor of my childhood, that once I called you mama. I will do so still. But I will not again permit your son to enter my bedchamber.'

Filippa bowed her head. 'Are you also dismissing my family and myself, Your Grace?' she asked in a low voice.

'We swore an oath to remain true to each other,' Joanna reminded her. 'I am not in the habit of breaking oaths, signora. My proscription applies only to your son as regards my bedchamber.'

'As Your Grace pleases,' Donna Filippa agreed, and escorted the crestfallen Roberto from Joanna's presence.

We were not so dim as to suppose we had won any sort of a victory. If the Catanian had been taken aback by this sudden disruption of her plans, Joanna's temporising had indicated to her that the Duchess understood the dangers of her own position. Thus relieved of any fear for her person, or those of her children, Filippa soon got her brain working again, and with her shrewd knowledge of human nature and, above all, Joanna's nature, she very rapidly deduced the reason behind the Duchess's amazing volte-face.

Once that was done, it did not take her long to establish who had replaced Roberto in Joanna's affections. This we had feared would be the case, and we expected recriminations and even threats. To our surprise, these were not forthcoming. The Catanian appeared to accept her fall from power with equanimity, happy only to be able to retain her position as Joanna's governess.

I alone found this suspicious. Joanna was once again head over heels in love, with her Bertrand, and Donna Cancia, totally unsuspecting that Filippa might have any idea that she had played a part in the transference of the Duchess's affections, resumed her madcap ways. But I could feel the undercurrents, and I knew that the Catanian and her brood were but awaiting their opportunity to regain their dominance over my mistress.

I also could not help but feel that the Hungarian faction was at least partly aware of what was going on. Prince Andrew, certainly not. He had even less wit than Roberto. But his valet, a Neapolitan named Tomasso Pace, and Brother Robert could not help but know that Joanna found very little joy in her husband, and yet was often in a joyous mood. It seemed to me that even a valet and a Dominican priest must eventually be able to arrive at the truth of the matter.

What would happen then did not bear consideration.

But before they gave any evidence of having done so, we were distracted by the event we had all been awaiting for some time: King Robert was taken ill, and word spread through the kingdom that he would not recover.

Indeed, the King's final illness ran a very rapid course. No sooner was he put to bed than the two princesses were in

48

constant attendance, all thought of amatory dalliance forgotten, while the rest of us proceeded about our duties with long faces and no doubt busy minds. Mine certainly was. But that the various princes, and the Hungarians, were less interested in the dying King's misfortune than in what was going to happen after his departure from this earth was very evident.

I suspect this preoccupation with the future on the part of his family even communicated itself to the King, for on the third day after he had been taken to bed, the entire brood was summoned to his chamber. There was such a crush in there one or two extra were not to be noticed, and Cancia and I took our chance to sneak in at the back and thus oversee the proceedings. Needless to say, Donna Filippa and Roberto di Cabane were also present, hidden at the back, like ourselves.

I doubt there has ever been, before or since, such a gathering of the Royal House of Anjou in one room. Or of the Neapolitan nobility. By the King's bed there stood his wife, Donna Sancia, and his two granddaughters, the Duchess of Calabria and the Princess Marie. Prince Andrew of Hungary stood next to his wife, and held her hand; the ghastly visage of Brother Robert could be discerned in the gloom behind them.

Charles of Artois, Court of Aire, the King's first cousin, stood with his son Bertrand; the young man bent his gaze upon Joanna and her husband, alternating guilty love with equally guilty hate.

Charles of Durazzo stood with his mother, the Dowager Countess Agnes, and his two younger brothers, Ludovico, Count of Gravina, and Robert, Prince of Morea.

Catherine of Constantinople was accompanied by her three sons, Louis of Tarento, Robert of Constantinople and Philip of Constantinople.

Americ, Cardinal of St Martin des Monts, the Papal Legate, stood at the foot of the bed. Behind him were the three greatest nobles of the realm: Don Philip of

Cabassole, Bishop of Cavaillon, Vice-Chancellor of the kingdom; Philip of Sanguineto, the Seneschal of Provence, one of the King's appanages; and Godfrey di Marsan, Count of Squillace, the Grand Admiral.

And many others.

Once all were assembled, and the clearing of throats, shuffling of feet, and rustling of dresses had somewhat abated, the King signalled his doctors, who were also in attendance, and they raised him up the bed, propping him there with pillows.

It took him a few seconds to catch his breath, during which time I took in the scene, which was truly awe-inspiring. It was late evening, and the torches and candles threw shadows in every direction, now illuminating, now concealing. The huge tester bed with its cloth-of-gold counterpane and drapes was in the very centre of the room, and the flickering lights played constantly on the pale, ravaged features of the famous monarch who lay there, fighting for breath. The faces around the bed were a study in seriousness, mingled with fear, and anger, and contempt, as each man, and each woman, too, considered his or her situation at this moment of great change in all their lives.

At last the King felt strong enough to speak. 'I have gathered you here,' he said, 'that you all, my family and my friends, may hear my last words, and obey them, on penalty of my everlasting curse. I die before my time, before my beloved granddaughter ...' he smiled at Joanna, 'is truly ready to assume the crown of this blessed land. I therefore charge you all to make it your duty to see that Queen Joanna is accorded your total support, and that such support is also given to her husband, Prince Andrew.'

It was no doubt unfortunate that the remark concerning Prince Andrew came rather as an afterthought, and that he had been referred to as 'prince' rather than 'king', where Joanna had been designated 'queen'. Instantly there was a shuffling of feet and a fresh interchange of glances.

'To my great joy,' the King continued, 'my dear wife, Donna Sancia, although it is her wish to take the veil and retire to her own convent, has agreed to remain as Queen Dowager for one year after my death. She will therefore be able to advise the Queen in the performance of her duties during that time, and assist her to bear the heavy burden of responsibility which will be hers.' He smiled at his wife, who stood with her arm round her step-granddaughter.

'Now as to my Will,' the King continued, and made a sign to the Vice-Chancellor, who thereupon unrolled a lengthy piece of parchment, and began to read, in sonorous tones.

'I, Robert, by the grace of God, King of Sicily' – for the Angevins had never given up their lost title – 'and Jerusalem, Count of Provence, Forcalquier and Piedmont, vice-regent of the Holy Roman Church, do hereby name and declare as my sole heiress to the Kingdom of Sicily, on both sides of the Pharos, as well as to the counties of Provence, Forcalquier and Piedmont, Joanna, Duchess of Calabria, elder daughter of the late Most Noble Signor, Charles, Duke of Calabria, of illustrious memory.'

The Vice-Chancellor cleared his throat. 'And I do name and declare the nobly born maiden, Marie, younger daughter of the said late Duke of Calabria, my heiress to the County of Alba and to the valley of Grati and the estate of Giordana, with all the castles and dependencies appertaining thereto; and I direct that the said Marie shall receive the aforesaid territories from the said Duchess and her heirs, but only on this condition, that if the said Duchess shall choose to allot to her illustrious sister, or those having her rights to the premises, the sum of ten thousand ounces of gold, by way of compensation, the said county and other territories shall continue to be vested in the said Duchess and her heirs.

'And I further direct and desire, for sufficient reasons known to myself alone, that the said Marie shall give her hand in marriage to the Most Illustrious Prince Louis,

51

King of Hungary. But if any obstacle should arise to this marriage, by reason of the marriage contract entered into and signed between the King of Hungary and the King of Bohemia for his daughter, I hereby doth direct that the said Marie shall give her hand in marriage to the eldest son of the most puissant Jean, Duc de Normandy, eldest son of the reigning King of France.

'I do further desire and direct that the counties of Forcalquier and Provence shall be united to my kingdom, indissolubly and for all time, under the dominion of a single person, and as an inseparable domain, even though there may be several sons and daughters, or under any other conceivable circumstances, such a union being absolutely essential for the mutual safety and welfare of the kingdom and the said duchies.'

It will be observed that the poor fellow was labouring under the delusions which are said to accompany the approach of death, in supposing that he could so delineate the future 'for all time'.

'I do further direct and desire,' continued the Vice-Chancellor, 'that Donna Sancia, with the Reverend Father Don Philip of Cabassole, Bishop of Cavaillon, Vice-Chancellor of the Kingdom of Sicily, and the illustrious lords Philip of Sanguineto, Seneschal of Provence, Godfrey di Marsan, Count of Squillace, Admiral of the Kingdom, and Charles d'Artois, Count d'Aire, as her co-adjutors, shall be governors, regents and guardians of the said Andrew, and the said Joanna and Marie, until they shall independently have attained the age of twenty-five.'

There was a moment's silence when the reading of the Will was finished, and then the King, who had lain with his eyes closed, now opened them again, and said, 'Let he who denies my wishes burn forever. I make this your charge, Louis of Tarento ...' he flung out his arm with sudden strength, and the handsome young man stepped back, taken by surprise. 'And yours, Robert of Constantinople.' The pointing finger moved. 'And yours, Philip of

Constantinople. And yours, Charles of Durazzo.' The hand dropped, and fell to the bed, and the King's eyes closed.

For a moment all supposed that his last effort had been too much, and he was dead, but a moment later his eyes opened again, and he looked at us in turn. Then he said, 'Now swear allegiance to your Queen.'

Instantly the great nobles bowed their knees and their heads as they swore. They were followed by the princes of the blood. These were led by Charles of Durazzo, who, kneeling before Joanna, said, 'To you, my Queen, do I tender my homage,' at the same time casting a scornful glance at Andrew which could leave his meaning in no doubt.

The oaths taken, the King said, 'Now leave me,' and we filed out, each to hurry away to his or her private consideration of the matter. Andrew, indeed, did not even attend the Duchess that night, as he sat up making plans with Brother Robert.

Joanna herself was distraught, and hardly slept. Before dawn the bell tolled the death of the King, and the Council of Regency knocked on the door of our chamber to inform the Duchess that she was now Queen of Naples, while in the streets the shouts of 'Long live Queen Joanna!' rang again and again, feebly contended against by the Hungarian shouts of 'Long live King Andrew!'

All was bustle for the next week while the King's funeral was prepared. In the warm southern climes there is little encouragement to have even the greatest of monarchs – despite embalmment – lie too long in state, and King Robert was interred on the seventh day following his death, in the church of Santa Clara, which he had himself founded, and where were to be found two columns said to have been part of Solomon's temple in Jerusalem, brought to Naples by the piety of the King. Here he was laid to rest beside the altar, and beside, too, his dead son, Charles of Calabria, while the choir chanted a *Te Deum*, and the assembled people of Naples wept for the passing of a great and wise man, who had also been their King.

We returned to the Castel Nuovo in a downcast frame of mind. The funeral itself had been an awesome reminder of the futility of human greatness. But for those of the Queen's party there was also the daunting prospect of what lay ahead. Indeed, the first meeting of the Council of Regency was held immediately. And was immediately attended by discord. No sooner had the three nobles, Donna Sancia, and Queen Joanna taken their places, than Prince Andrew appeared, accompanied by Brother Robert and several of his Hungarian friends, notably including a murderous lout named Conrad of Goltes, and demanded a place at the table for the Prince. In vain did the Bishop of Cavaillon point out that this had not been provided for in the late King's Will, and that Andrew's place must await the decision of his wife after she had been crowned.

The Hungarians refused to accept his fiat, and the meeting broke up with nothing achieved save a determination on the part of the Bishop to have the coronation carried out as soon as possible.

Joanna was exhausted and tearful when she returned to her bedchamber, and equally mutinous. 'I shall not have him in here tonight,' she declared. 'I shall not.'

'Well, of course, Your Grace, as you are in mourning ...' Donna Cancia agreed.

'But I must have solace. Fetch me Bertrand.'

Even madcap Cancia was aghast. '*Now*, Your Grace? It will soon be supper time.'

'Now,' Joanna declared. 'I could not exist another second without the comfort of his arms.'

'And if the Prince should come?'

'Send him away.'

Cancia and I exchanged glances. Yet Joanna was the Queen, and had to be obeyed. I was despatched to find Bertrand, who was as taken aback as any of us by the unexpected summons so soon after King Robert's death, but was nothing loath to obey the royal command; he had not been alone with Joanna since the onset of her grandfather's illness, ten days previously. I therefore escorted him along the secret corridors and introduced him into my mistress's waiting arms. That done, Cancia and I withdrew to the antechamber, and picked up our sewing. We had not been there five minutes however, before we heard the sound of approaching feet, and a moment later the door was opened, and there stood Prince Andrew and Brother Robert.

'I have been remiss,' the Prince announced. 'I have quarrelled with my dearest wife, when she is in deepest mourning for her grandfather. As am I.' He frowned at us. 'Where is Her Grace?'

We had both risen at the intrusion, and now we both curtsied. 'Queen Joanna has retired, Monsignore,' Cancia explained, speaking with considerable calm; my heart was bouncing like a ball.

Prince Andrew smiled. 'Then I shall go to her, and seek her forgiveness in her arms.'

He stepped towards the door, and I muttered a quick Hail Mary, certain that our last moment had come.

But Donna Cancia, whatever her faults, did not lack courage. She sprang in front of him. 'Monsignore, Her Grace has taken a sedative powder, and wishes to rest. She has left the strictest instructions that she is not to be disturbed. I pray of you, if you would not anger her the more, to return when she has awakened, and is rested. Then I have no doubt she will receive you with a smile.'

Prince Andrew hesitated, irresolute as ever.

'What, woman, would you come between a man and his wife?' growled Brother Robert.

'Queen Joanna is my mistress,' Cancia said severely. 'I will obey her to the grave, Father. And as she is fast asleep, I cannot be coming between Prince Andrew and herself. The moment she is awake I shall inform her that Monsignore wishes to call upon her.'

'You take too much upon yourself, woman,' Robert insisted.

'I would as soon not have another quarrel, good Father,' Andrew said. 'We will withdraw, signorina. But I expect to hear from my wife after supper.'

Cancia curtsied again, and I did also. The door closed, and we gazed at each other. Then Cancia revealed that she had not been as calm as she had pretended by folding me in her arms and hugging me most tenderly.

'Should we warn Joanna?' I asked.

'Time enough for that. She is engaged in amatory intercourse. To interrupt such pleasure would be a sin. And no doubt incur her wrath. There is time enough.'

Optimistic harlot! She picked up her sewing, as did I, and we were promptly again interrupted by the door opening. This time we were aghast to find ourselves gazing at Donna Filippa and Roberto di Cabane.

I realised at once that we were lost. Undoubtedly the Catanian, with that devious and remorseless mind of hers, had been awaiting such a moment as this ever since her fall from favour. Presumably she had kept the royal apartments under the closest surveillance until she saw her chance.

I also observed that she carried with her two rolled parchments, as if she were about to present a petition. Or was it to be an ultimatum?

'Signora,' Cancia said, ready to resume battle. 'How good of you to call. Alas, Her Grace has retired for a rest.'

'I must see the Queen, now,' Donna Filippa announced, without responding to the greeting.

'Signora, Her Grace has taken a sedative powder and is fast asleep. She has found the events of today too wearing to be borne.'

'Do not give me any of that nonsense, Cancia,' Filippa said. 'I intend to see the Queen.' And she marched for the bedroom door.

'Signora!' Cancia threw herself in front of the invader,

and was promptly seized by Roberto and lifted out of the way. I attempted to grapple with the scoundrel from behind and received an elbow in the stomach which left me winded on the floor. Before we could act further, the inner door had been opened, and Filippa was in the bedchamber.

I scrambled to my feet in despair, peered past the Catanian and Roberto, who had crowded in behind his mother ... and gazed at Joanna, sitting up in bed, the sheet held to her throat, her cheeks pink, her magnificent hair scattered on her shoulders – but quite alone.

Filippa was taken aback, which proved that she knew Bertrand should have been in the room. And I immediately understood where he was, for the poor fellow, startled into losing his breath, was too obviously concealed behind the drapes at the head of the bed: they moved to and fro with a regular betrayal.

Filippa naturally noticed this phenomenon as well, nor could it be explained by a breeze whispering through the bedchamber – the windows were closed.

Joanna, unfortunately, was not aware of what was happening behind her bed, and allowed her eyes to flash fire. 'How dare you, signora?' she demanded. 'How dare you enter my bedchamber unbidden?'

Filippa gave a deep curtsy, and Roberto, who had also observed the fluttering drapes, bowed. If I had long hated the pair of them, I could at that moment have slain them both. They had my mistress in their power, and meant to use that power.

'I humbly beg your forgiveness, Your Grace,' Filippa said. 'My son and I but wished to reassure ourselves that you have not been overcome by the events of the day.'

Joanna's gaze softened. 'Should I not have been overcome?' she asked. Her expression hardened again as she gazed at Roberto, who was staring at her. 'I wish only to be left in peace to rest.'

Filippa curtsied again. 'Of course you must rest, Your

Grace. But, before we take our leave, I would crave a small boon of your generosity.'

'Speak,' Joanna commanded, unaware that she was caught in a vice from which there was no escape.

'My dear son,' Filippa said, 'who for so long enjoyed Your Grace's favour, and is now cast out from the warmth that emanates from your person, is sadly aware that, lacking rank and fortune, he is the laughing stock of the court. Can Your Grace truly be so hard-hearted as to condemn him to a life of servility, he who has already served you so hard and so well?'

'He may have a pension,' Joanna conceded.

'My son has little use for money, Your Grace. It is a title he seeks, that he may hold his head high in the company of other men.'

'A title? What manner of title?' Joanna's voice was like an icy torrent.

'We had thought of Count of Eboli.'

'Count of Eboli?' Joanna shouted. The title was one of the highest in the land, although it happened then to be vacant. 'Are you insane?'

'It would be but a small reward for the hours of pleasure my son has brought to Your Grace,' Filippa protested. 'I am sure no one would begrudge the honour you would thus bestow. Why, I have no doubt that Prince Andrew himself – he is still in the castle, by the way – would agree, were I to summon him here, that you had done nothing more than justice.'

Joanna stared at her, and realised that Bertrand's presence was known. Her glare was so imperious that Cancia and I held hands, fearing an outburst which would condemn us all. For if Andrew were to return, and discover Bertrand ... he would have all the rights of an outraged husband.

Filippa met the Queen's anger with equanimity. She knew the strength of her position. As did Joanna. Slowly the marvellous black eyes clouded. 'Very well, Donna

Filippa. As you put it so plainly, I will give consideration to your request. I promise to bring it before the Council of Regency when next it meets.'

Filippa was not going to fall into that trap. 'I have the letters patent here, Your Grace,' she said, unrolling one of the two parchments she carried in her hand. 'All that is required is your signature.'

The anger was back in Joanna's eyes, but she spoke in a low tone. 'I have not the power to create anyone count without the agreement of my regents.'

'Stuff and nonsense, Your Grace,' Filippa declared, reverting to the role of nurse and governess. 'You are Queen of Naples. You have the power to do anything you choose, always providing,' she hastily added, 'that you keep within the laws of the land and those of the marriage bed. I have no doubt at all that Prince Andrew, were he summoned here now, would agree that the sooner you begin to exercise your prerogatives as queen the better for the kingdom.'

Joanna's gaze was positively vituperative. Without another word she extended her hand, and the parchment was given to her. She looked at me, and I provided her with her quill, hastily dipped, and a book – her Bible – on which to rest the offending parchment as she wrote her name. My heart bled for her at that moment, even as I vowed vengeance on the Catanian. I need not have worried; the wretched woman, by her intrigues, was steadily building her own funeral pyre.

But right now she was the mistress of all she surveyed. 'I thank Your Grace,' she said, regaining possession of the signed decree, and waving it to and fro until the ink had dried. 'My son and I will always be in your debt.'

'Then leave my presence,' Joanna said, still speaking in a low voice. 'And do not ever return, unbidden.'

'As Your Grace wishes,' Filippa agreed. 'There is but one more small matter ...'

Joanna's head came up. 'You go too far, signora.'

Filippa bowed. 'It is a political matter, Your Grace. The Count of Eboli feels that he has much to offer your kingdom, and yourself. He is not the sort of man to rest on his laurels and play the fool, as do so many young men.' She glanced contemptuously at the trembling drapes. 'He seeks an appointment where he may serve Your Grace with the loyalty which is his alone.'

'He may have a commission in my army,' Joanna said. 'And I will discover him a war in which to fight. And perhaps even die on my behalf. Would that not be most satisfactory ... to his honour?'

Filippa did not respond to the macabre joke. 'The Count seeks a more purposeful way of serving Your Grace. The office of Grand Seneschal of the Kingdom has been vacant now for some years ...'

'Now I know you are insane,' Joanna snapped. 'That ...' she bent a withering stare on Roberto, 'Grand Seneschal!'

'You seek to insult my son, Your Grace. Was not his father Grand Seneschal before him? It is a measure of our late King's regard for my husband – may God bless both their souls – that the post has not been filled since my husband's death. But it should be filled. And who better to do so than the son of the previous holder?'

'Then would he ever be in my councils. And yourself, no doubt, signora. I cannot consider such a situation.'

Filippa bowed her head again. 'I cannot help but regret Your Grace's decision. And as it is such an important one, I am sure you would wish to reconsider it. To discuss it, perhaps, with your husband. Roberto, chase behind Prince Andrew and tell him that not only is the Queen now ready to receive him, but wishes to discuss a matter of the greatest importance.'

Roberto moved to the door, and was checked by the Queen. 'Wait!' she commanded, while the drapes behind her positively shivered.

Roberto waited, his hand on the knob.

60

'I have not the power to create any man Grand Sene-schal,' Joanna said. 'I will recommend the appointment to my council.'

'You have the power, Your Grace,' Filippa insisted, and thrust forward the second parchment. 'You have but to sign your name a second time.'

Joanna looked at her, and had I been the Catanian I would have felt a chill on my heart. But the laundry-woman gave no sign of apprehension, and the hand which held the paper was steady.

'Is this the last of your demands?' Joanna asked, her voice no more than a whisper.

'The last, Your Grace,' Filippa assured her.

Joanna looked at me, and I dipped the quill again. The Queen wrote her name a second time, and handed the parchment back to Filippa. The Catanian smiled, and curtsied. 'I wish Your Grace a good night's sleep,' she said, and left the room, together with her son.

The door had hardly closed when Bertrand leapt from behind the drapes. 'Fiends!' he gasped. 'I shall go behind them and seek a quarrel with Cabane. I will cut him down and trample on his foul remains.'

'No.' Joanna held his arm. 'Then would our secret be out. Our guilty secret, Bertrand. We must be patient, and await a more propitious moment for our revenge.'

He hesitated, and as always was lost when he looked upon his beloved. Cancia and I breathed a sigh of relief, that the crisis was for the moment over. But that our mistress was deeper than ever in the toils created by her own nature could not be doubted.

And further crisis was waiting to descend upon us. Joanna had to act the Queen, as she was the Queen, and although she was allowed a month of seclusion and personal grief for her grandfather, on the fifth Sunday following his death it was necessary for her to appear in public, and take mass at the Cathedral of San Giovanni, her patron saint, as although I may refer to the Queen by her English appellation of Joanna, the name in Italian is rendered as Giovanna.

The occasion was made one for a political rally. When Donna Cancia and I, wearing our new black habits, had prepared the Queen, of course also dressed in black – her sideless surcoat trimmed with velvet, the sombreness of her garb relieved only by the gold fillet encircling her brow and her white silk gorgette – and we were descending to the courtyard where Prince Andrew and Brother Robert waited, there was a great noise.

The drawbridge had already been lowered for our exit; now across it rode Prince Louis of Tarento and his brothers, Charles of Durazzo and his brothers, and a host of other Neapolitan nobles, prominent amongst them the Counts of Terlizzi and Morcone. These men were armed and armoured, as if riding off to war, and they surrounded the Queen with loud shouts and the clash of weapons.

'What means this, monsignores?' Joanna demanded, looking at Charles of Durazzo as the natural leader of the turbulent mob, as he was the eldest of the princes. 'Are we invaded?'

'We have come to escort Your Grace to worship,' Charles answered, raising his visor and bending low in the saddle.

'Why, monsignores, how very charming of you,' Joanna said, giving each man one of those special smiles of hers which would have conquered any heart not made of stone. 'Am I in any danger?'

'We have come to honour our Queen,' Charles declared in a deep voice, and placed his horse on Joanna's right hand as she mounted, astride of course, as this was a few years before the side saddle was introduced into western Europe, while Louis took his place on her left.

'Way there, make way for Prince Andrew,' bellowed Brother Robert, but he was jostled aside as Louis's two brothers took their places immediately behind the Queen.

'Forward,' Charles commanded, and the cavalcade began to move, the Queen in front, her cousins to either side.

'I do think a place should be found for my husband, Charles,' the Queen protested.

'You are the Queen of Naples,' Charles reminded her, fiercely. 'The people wish to see their Queen. Not some Hungarian lout,' he added as an afterthought.

Joanna acquiesced. I know from my own relationship with the Queen, which far surpasses in intimacy that enjoyed by any other person, living or dead, that she was not a weak character. Once her mind was made up she was inflexible. But she often appeared weak by her readiness to accept direction where she was not yet herself decided. Although in this case there can be no doubt that Prince Charles was touching a very responsive chord.

And so we rode out of the Castel Nuovo and into the streets of Naples, where vast crowds had assembled, and where the shouts for the Queen sent the seabirds soaring away from the Mole. Our assembly was a large one, consisting as it did of both Hungarians and Neapolitans, but the Hungarians were crowded to the back, as was their Prince. As a slave, I also had to find my way behind all the nobles, and although I could not understand the barbarous tongue spoken by Andrew's companions, it was not possible to mistake their anger.

Which grew during the service. By the time the Queen and her admirers emerged the Hungarians were boiling with fury, and a chance word caused the ensuing set-to. Fists were raised and whips were used. Even some swords were drawn. Charles of Durazzo immediately took charge of the Queen's person, and with an escort of his own retainers forced his way through the fracas. Cancia and I were happy to take advantage of the support of some more of Charles's men-at-arms to escape harm, and we careered into the safety of the castle, Charles immediately commanding the drawbridge to be raised.

Joanna was quite overwhelmed by the disturbance, and was pale and panting as we escorted her to her apartments, where, a few moments later, Charles himself joined us. 'They are insufferable,' he commented.

'They were piqued, as I suggested would be the case,' Joanna corrected him. 'But I am most grateful to you, cousin, for returning me here so safely. Now I would be even more grateful if you were to withdraw that I might rest. Besides, I am sure my other cousins could use your assistance.'

'They can take care of themselves, Your Grace,' he assured her. 'And I would willingly leave you to rest. But there are matters of vital importance which need to be discussed, and immediately.'

'What matters?'

Charles glanced at Cancia and myself. 'Matters which can be known only to yourself and myself, Your Grace.'

Joanna also glanced at us, and shrugged. 'Leave us, ladies.'

We curtsied. But we had both understood Joanna's look, for she was a mistress of the art of conveying her true meaning by her eyes rather than her words. So although we left her company, we immediately hurried to that secret corridor which gave access to the bedchamber, and by that means virtually re-entered the royal presence, being able to kneel at the door and hear every word that was spoken in the other room.

'He is undoubtedly the most hated man in Naples,' Charles was saying when we had settled ourselves.

We understood of whom he was speaking, of course, and our surmise was confirmed by the Queen's reply.

'However, he is my husband,' Joanna said. 'And must be treated as such.'

'Your people will never watch him crowned their King, Joanna.' In private, Charles appeared to feel he need show no respect save that of one relative to another.

'I understand that. I do not propose that he should be crowned,' Joanna said.

64

'Yet will he always be at your side, associated with your decisions. I doubt the people will accept that either.'

'My people will accept whatever I tell them to accept,' Joanna announced, somewhat contradicting her earlier remark. 'Especially if you also tell them the same thing, cousin.'

'And if I do not tell them the same thing?'

There was a brief silence, and we could imagine Joanna giving him her most imperious stare. But her voice was composed. 'Then you would no longer be my most trusted friend, Charles.'

'I would be more than that, cousin.'

Another brief silence.

'You must explain your words, cousin,' Joanna said. 'And I beg of you, be careful what you say, lest I have to consider treason to have been uttered.'

'Would you accept the word, avenger?'

'Have I then been done an injury?' Joanna's voice was perfectly calm, but it was easy for us, trembling ourselves, to imagine the emotions that must be seething in our mistress's heart and brain.

'You are done an injury every time that Hungarian lout enters these chambers,' Charles declared fiercely.

'And you would challenge him in the lists?'

'He would refuse me,' Charles said. 'There is a more certain way.' We heard the rasp of steel, and clutched each other's hands. Had the madman dared to draw his poignard in the presence of the Queen?

Apparently he had. And she shared our sentiments. 'You are mad,' Joanna told him. 'Put it away.'

'You have but to say the word,' Charles said, and we heard the slither as the dagger was returned to its sheath. 'And I would make you a free woman.'

'My God, that my own cousin would suggest murder to me,' Joanna said. 'A free woman? To marry you, you mean?'

The scrape of a shoe suggested that Charles was bowing.

'Much as I would be honoured by such a union, sweet cousin, I fear that there are many, including perhaps God Himself, who would find that not to their liking, especially after such a deed as we contemplate. Besides, I doubt our characters, so alike as they are, could ever live together in domestic bliss. I would only ask for the hand of your sister. I would never interfere with your prerogatives as Queen of Naples. My only desire is to be named your heir.'

This time the silence was longer. We could only imagine the expressions that might be crossing the Queen's face. At last she spoke, her voice laden with emotion. '*We* contemplate? Foul wretch! This projected deed had its birth in your own evil mind. Marry my sister to you? I would sooner send her to a convent. Disapproved by God! He would strike us dead with a thunderbolt. Become my heir? You? Never! I shall bear my own heir.'

Silence.

'You would do well not to make of me an enemy, sweet cousin,' Charles said in a low voice.

'Be content that I do not call my guards and have you imprisoned for treason,' Joanna told him. 'You would bring dishonour upon us all. And devastation upon our kingdom. Do you not realise that King Louis would immediately seek to avenge his brother? With all the host of Hungary?'

'Have we no army of our own? I will command your army for you, Joanna.'

'You will never command my army, Charles. You are the foulest wretch who ever walked this earth. I order you from my presence, and I forbid you ever to enter it again, without my express invitation.'

Silence.

Then the Prince said, 'As you have made it so, Your Grace; if I cannot be your trusted friend, then I shall be your implacable enemy.'

We heard the outer door close, and instantly opened ours.

Joanna was almost unrecognisable, her cheeks pink, her breathing laboured, her whole body as if afflicted by an intense pain. It needs to be remembered that she was no more than sixteen years of age.

'You heard?' she demanded.

'Every word, Your Grace,' Cancia told her.

'And we would willingly give evidence against the Prince, Your Grace, if it should please you,' I volunteered. For us both, although Cancia did not look very happy at the prospect.

Joanna shook her head. 'It would be futile and dangerous. Charles has too many friends and spies in the city. Once a charge was brought against him, he would have you both murdered.'

A prognostication which quite changed my ardour for his downfall.

'No,' the Queen continued, 'if he wishes to be my enemy, then he shall be my enemy. At least we know where he stands.'

She thus affected to shrug off the unhappy interview with her cousin, but I could not help but be alarmed when Charles of Durazzo could be seen paying open court to Prince Andrew and his Hungarians. I felt that the hypocrisy of a man who could propose murder in one breath and in the next fawn upon his intended victim must be obvious to all. It was not, apparently, to the Hungarian camp; they welcomed the Count of Durazzo as a formidable ally.

It did seem, however, that Charles was backing a loser. The Council of Regency, which, as I have mentioned, was composed of the highest nobles in the land, having considered the matter at some length, and understanding that Joanna was in agreement with them, came to the conclusion that it would be injurious to the health and prosperity of the Kingdom to have Prince Andrew crowned as King-Consort. They therefore put in hand the preparations for the coronation of Queen Joanna, at which ceremony

Andrew would take his place simply as husband of the Queen, and in the meantime all decrees and documents emanating from the Castel Nuovo were issued and signed in the name of the Queen alone. Joanna was actually reluctant to take this extreme step, and was persuaded to do so, not by the Council of Regency, but by the famous lawyer Andrew of Isernia, a close friend of the late King, and a man she trusted absolutely.

These decisions naturally enraged the Hungarians, principally Brother Robert, who ranted and raved before the Council, to no effect, of course, and encouraged Andrew to assert himself in his own name, with the result that the Prince bestowed honours and wealth upon a certain John Pipino, Count of Altamura, one of the most disliked men in the Kingdom.

Meanwhile Brother Robert wrote letters to Hungary belabouring the mistreatment of his royal master and beseeching King Louis to come to the aid of his brother.

This naturally Louis could not do, except by invitation or as an act of war, and war upon another Christian state could not be considered without the sanction of the Pope, who was Joanna's own tenant. The Hungarian cause was therefore at an impasse. But we were apprised that Andrew's mother, Elizabeth of Poland, was on her way to visit Naples, and discuss the situation with her son and daughter-in-law.

This prospect caused consternation, as this princess – who was known as the Queen of Poland although she had never actually ruled her native land – had a formidable reputation. She was the daughter of the great Ladislas, who after many wars and tribulations had restored Poland to the dignity of a kingdom, from which she had sunk following the Mongol invasions of the previous century. Ladislas was undoubtedly a mighty warrior, but with many Germans, Hungarians, Lithuanians and Russians casting greedy eyes upon his beleaguered country, he would not have achieved his ambition but for the support of the Papacy. It was this thought that taxed us.

Elizabeth's visit, however, passed off very well. She was naturally overjoyed to see her son, from whom she had been separated for some considerable time, looking well and hearty, and Joanna put forth her best efforts, even permitting Andrew to return to the royal bed during the occasion of his mother's sojourn in Naples – he had been barred from such intimacy following the Sunday morning fracas.

There were fiestas and entertainments, boat rides to Capri to visit the Grotto, and jousts. The arrival of the Dowager Queen, coinciding as it did with the elapsing of the six months' mourning period for King Robert, proved an ideal occasion for the Neapolitans to let loose their emotions with the gusto which only the hot-blooded can truly do.

To add to the enjoyment of the Queen's stay, she and Donna Sancia proved the best of friends. During the six weeks that Elizabeth spent in Italy the clouds of threatening violence that had hung over the city since the King's death seemed to dissipate, and Naples was again a laughing, happy place.

But eventually she had to leave. And with her went our joy. Nor, it was plain, had she been quite as deluded as she had sometimes appeared. She spent many hours closeted alone with Brother Robert, and undoubtedly heard the other side of the story. Joanna, Donna Sancia, and the Council of Regency had all assured her that while it would undoubtedly be dangerous, given the present mood of the populace, actually to crown Andrew king, and that in addition they could find nothing in King Robert's will suggesting that such had been his intention – which was not altogether true – the Prince would yet be granted all the rights and privileges of a monarch, would stand always at the Queen's shoulder and be associated with her in all things.

Elizabeth expressed her understanding and her gratitude

... but on the day she left Naples she gave her son, in the Queen's presence, a curiously wrought ring.

'This talisman has been in our family for many years, dear Andrew,' she said, embracing him. 'I give it to you now, to safeguard your life and person. Wear it always, and you can never die from either poison or steel.'

With which curious statement she embraced the dumbfounded Joanna in turn, and took her departure.

We were at a loss to understand the Queen of Poland's apprehensions. It was inconceivable that Charles of Durazzo, who was now giving a splendid impersonation of Andrew's dearest friend, could possibly have let slip his erstwhile ambition to murder the Prince. Nor could Andrew's life, surrounded as he always was – save when actually in the Queen's bedchamber – by his faithful Hungarians, be in danger from any common assassin. While he surely had enough sense not to enter the lists with any of the royal princes.

If I had lost some nights' sleep as I realised, following Joanna's interview with her cousin, that she had not once rejected his solution to her problem on the grounds that murder is a mortal sin, but had refused Charles solely because of the danger of the enterprise and her disinclination to put herself in his power and make him her heir, that was a personal nightmare and not one shared by Donna Cancia. Cancia certainly did not consider murder a mortal sin. She belonged to that happy band who believe all things are possible – where a Pope can be found to provide absolution.

Can it be that the very real loathing Joanna felt for her husband made itself apparent to the Queen of Poland? But even so, she cannot possibly have felt that the Prince was in danger from his wife. I certainly discounted such a possibility. Nor would he had been, but for Andrew's own folly, which penetrated that deep, noble, but passionate nature of Joanna's so deeply as to threaten the one thing

70

she held more dear than herself and her prerogatives – the life of whichever man happened to be her chosen companion of the moment.

The departure of the Queen of Poland, as I have said, left Naples, for a brief period, a tranquil, happy city. Alas, it was a brief period, before true horror crowded upon us. Because it was in this last blessed sunset of her family that Donna Sancia, after the year she had promised her dying husband, withdrew from our society and entered the convent of Santa Clara, which she had herself founded some years previously, and whence, she no doubt hoped, she could watch the successful reign and growing happiness of her granddaughter. The scene she did have to watch drove her to her grave within another year.

It was as if her departure from the stage had removed the last restraint controlling the seething passions of her family. Only a month after the convent doors had closed upon the Queen Dowager, the Castel Nuovo was utterly distracted by the discovery, one morning, that the Princess Marie had disappeared.

I must again remind my reader that I am recounting fact. For it may seem incredible that such a crime could take place in the midst of a royal castle which was also an impregnable fortress. Yet the Princess had gone, and with her, her two most trusted handmaidens.

For the palace, of course, and the castle, was never barred to the comings and goings of the royal princes. Everyone knew at once who the perpetrator of the abduction had to be, and what his purpose had to be, as well. Joanna clenched her fists until her nails bit into her palms, as she stared from her window across the bay. 'The wretch,' she said. 'The foul wretch.'

Now it may seem even more incredible that, knowing where her sister was and who was keeping her in captivity, and who had undoubtedly already robbed the girl of her maidenhead – which, unlike Joanna's, had been jealously

71

guarded – the Queen did not summon her army and march upon the palazzo of Charles of Durazzo – it was more a castle than a palace, but was only a few streets away – and tear it down and the Prince with it.

The plain fact of the matter was that she dared not. Charles had made himself so popular with the people of Naples, by means of the lavish disbursements of his enormous wealth, that Joanna had no idea which of her captains were in his pay and which in hers.

I had supposed she might be able to turn to Louis of Tarento, who also commanded a considerable following in the city, but he too had been estranged by her temporising over the matter of the Hungarians. If Louis was too noble a soul ever to contemplate murder, he also had the spirit of a warrior, and would have had the Queen expel her husband, seek an annulment of the marriage from the Pope, and place her trust in her cousins – one of whom, no doubt himself, she would then marry – when it came to facing the wrath of Louis of Hungary.

The Queen was therefore helpless, and had to content herself with offering a reward of three thousand ducats for any information leading to the restoration of her sister, knowing full well that no one would dare claim the prize.

But there was another reason why she did not act. She and Marie had never been close. As children they had been deliberately kept apart by the machinations of Donna Filippa, but there was also a considerable difference in character between them. Marie had always been gay and smiling, careless of tomorrow when she could enjoy today. In Joanna's heart there lurked a suspicion that her sister might be continuing that practice in captivity.

Undoubtedly Charles of Durazzo was a handsome young man, who could be charming when the mood took him or necessity demanded – and equally undoubtedly he would be playing upon the girl's imagination; she was only just fifteen, with heady thoughts that one day she could be queen, as her sister was undoubtedly barren ... with him as her consort.

There was even the consideration that Marie's abduction might not have been an abduction at all, but a flight. That the pair were first cousins was not regarded as an impediment; they were royalty, not common people, and it was understood that royalty did not obey the common laws. All that would be required was a dispensation from the Pope, and this was in fact all that Charles was waiting for.

Thus, while Cancia and I wailed and tore our clothes, as was expected of us, and Bertrand muttered threats and half drew his sword before letting it slip back into its scabbard, as was expected of him, the Queen remained calm. More disturbing, this event brought about a partial reconciliation between Joanna and the Catanian. Filippa was constantly present. As Grand Seneschal of the Kingdom, Roberto was also present. No one could have been more sympathetic than the laundrywoman and her son. Roberto declared that Joanna had but to say the word and he would himself tear down the Durazzo palazzo.

Joanna accepted their sympathy and offers of assistance as if there had never been a quarrel between them. She was undoubtedly marshalling her forces behind her ... but against what? Or whom? For she still made no move against Charles of Durazzo, still continued to rule her way, now growing more into her role of Queen, and giving every promise of being a good, if not a great, ruler of her people, as she went amongst them, enjoying their huzzahs, sympathising with their problems, receiving deputations in the Castel Nuovo. Her apparent confident patience, as she grew into an eighteen-year-old girl, was the amazement of all. But it is possible that she already felt she was in possession of a weapon which would put all of her cousin's machinations at naught.

Charles, meanwhile, celebrated his triumph. A month

after Marie's disappearance, during which time the great doors of the Durazzo palazzo remained firmly locked, these doors were opened to a fanfare of trumpets, and, the papal dispensation having been received, Charles and his bride rode to the Cathedral of San Giovanni to celebrate their marriage. So secretly had Charles's negotiations with Avignon been carried on that the city, and the Queen herself, were taken by surprise, and the marriage was a fact before anyone truly realised what had happened. Besides, it had undoubtedly already been consummated.

There was thus no interference with the happy couple, as they rode to their home, which was thrown open to the populace for feasting and drinking. Joanna revealed enough of the ordinary woman at least to feel curious as to the state of her sister's mind, and thus I was despatched to mingle in the throng, gain admittance to the palazzo, and observe what I could. I will admit that I was intensely nervous. Charles might never have truly deigned to notice me on his visits to the Castel Nuovo, but I had no doubt my face was familiar to him. And disliked by him, as belonging to a creature of the Queen.

The truth of this assumption I was to discover, horrifyingly, in the not too distant future.

However, on this occasion my reconnaissance was untroubled by recognition or arrest. I easily gained access to the palazzo, ate and drank with the rest of the common herd, and was vouchsafed several close glimpses of the bride. I have to say that she looked as pink-cheeked and healthy and contented, and indeed, happy, as any other bride. Perhaps she was drugged. Perhaps she had merely taken too much wine when in a state of excitement. But I was forced to report to the Queen that her sister did not look as if she had in any way been coerced.

'Faithless girl,' Joanna commented. 'Well, let her enjoy her marriage while she may.'

'And if she should bear issue, Your Grace?' Cancia asked.

74

Joanna laughed, for once with genuine good humour. 'She is welcome to enjoy her child as well,' she said.

A week later, the cause of the Queen's contentment was obvious. She was pregnant.

Singularly, all three of us bosom companions discovered our pregnancies in the same month. But it seems only Joanna had previously suspected her condition. Cancia and I were too bound up in the affairs of our mistress to concern ourselves over a trifle like a missed month.

Two, of course, was a different matter.

Every child needs a father, and this is sometimes difficult to provide. Donna Cancia had no problem. She declared the father to be the Count of Terlizzi, and the Count was pleased to accept responsibility for the deed: he had had no success in impregnating Aurora di Cabane. Aurora herself was pleased, as was her mother. They were all one happy family, regardless of Cancia's deviousness over the dismissal of Roberto.

Joanna's situation was a little more complicated. But of course there could be only one possible father for a royal prince, and besides, as Joanna had foreseen, her prospective son – or daughter – would quite put an end to Charles's dream of succeeding to the throne by right of his wife. Andrew was delighted, even Brother Robert smiled, and messengers were sent galloping to Buda bearing the glad tidings. We could only pray that the future king, or queen, of Naples, would not be born with Bertrand of Artois' somewhat long nose, or his amber eyes; something possessed by neither the Queen nor her husband.

My situation was the most complicated of all. It is not my intention to allow my personal affairs to intrude upon this story, which concerns greatness far above any station to which I might aspire, but naturally I did not spend all my time in attendance upon my mistress, nor, nowadays, was I ever required to share her bed, which post was reserved for Donna Cancia when it was not filled by either

Bertrand or Andrew. I thus had a considerable amount of time to myself, principally at night, while being always surrounded by the sensuous atmosphere which pervaded the court of Naples.

Thus there were actually three contenders for the position of my child's father. One was the Queen's coachman, Caesare, who was a large and able fellow, old enough to be my own father.

The second was actually Prince Andrew's valet, Tomasso Pace. I did not like the lout, but I was forced to spend many an idle hour in his company while his master and my mistress engaged in sexual conversation, and servants will follow the example set by their betters.

The third was one of the Queen's personal bodyguards, Alberto Cogni. He was tall, handsome, and young. He walked like the prince he was not, and loved, I am sure, as no prince could.

When I told Joanna that Alberto was the father of my child, she was delighted. She summoned the young man to her presence and gave him the happy news. He was considerably taken aback, but was too overawed by the Queen's obvious pleasure to argue the matter.

'I cannot, of course, permit one of my maids to marry,' Joanna told him. 'Nor am I willing to release Richilde from her duties – she is far too valuable to me.'

Quite apart from my knowledge of the secrets of the royal bed.

'But I wish you to know, Captain Cogni,' Joanna continued, 'that you will be rewarded and promoted, and will have access to both mother and child on a reasonable basis.'

Alberto bowed and withdrew. I obtained permission to hurry behind him, and drew him into an alcove in the corridor outside the royal apartment.

'Have you no kiss for your wife?' I demanded.

'I have just been told you cannot be my wife,' he pointed out.

I kissed him anyway.

'Our child will have no name,' he said sadly.

'Nonsense. I will call him Alberto. He will look like you. And one day, why, we will be permitted to marry. I have no doubt of that.'

'Suppose Alberto is a girl?' he asked, more gloomily yet.

It was not the first time I had observed that a lover cuts a much less gallant figure when he discovers he is also going to be a father.

Incipient motherhood is possibly the happiest condition a woman can know, at least in its earliest stages. For not less than three months after the discovery of pregnancy there is no external evidence that one is actually two, and one is aware of fulfilling the greatest of natural functions.

This state of bliss does not last. Few states of bliss do. In the case of pregnancy, it is confounded by the distortion of one's figure, is followed by much pain, and after another brief period of bliss while one is feeding the babe – supposing it is born alive – one's life is rendered a turmoil by the infant's problems, whether those be of health or character.

Still, as the three of us were only just two months gone we should have been blessed with another twelve weeks of contented contemplation of the stirrings in our wombs. It was not to be. Indeed, the storm, which had been brewing for ten years, was about to burst, with frightful violence, over our heads.

It rages still.

Hardly had the news of the Queen's pregnancy been announced, and the rejoicings begun to abate, than Joanna was required to do homage for her crown to the Papal Legate, Americ, Cardinal of St Martin des Monts. This was because Naples was regarded as a Papal fief, the Pontiff having originally bestowed it on Charles I following his quarrel with, and excommunication of, the House of Hohenstaufen.

77

This great occasion took place in the church of St Clara, where the Queen's father and grandfather lay buried. Joanna, clad in the royal chlamys, and with the crown on her head, knelt before the high altar and took the oath of fidelity from the Legate, with all the princes of the blood, including her husband, gathered behind her.

There was a huge and glittering assembly, dominated by the retinue of the delegation of Avignon, made up of the Archbishops of Pisa, Bari, Capua and Brundisium, together with Father Hugolin, Bishop of Castella, and Philip, Bishop of Cavaillon, the Queen's chancellor, and it was undoubtedly the most profound moment of Joanna's life to that time.

Yet even it was marked by angry glances, and even words, exchanged between Hungarian and Neapolitan. But still, Joanna's position appeared to be secured by the ceremony.

Alas, it was hardly more than a week later that one evening Bertrand of Artois stumbled up the secret passageway into Joanna's chamber, and there collapsed into a chair.

He was so faint and trembling that the Queen commanded me to pour a goblet of wine for him, while she herself knelt beside him and held his hand; Cancia was absent.

'Whatever is the matter, my dearest sweet?' she asked.

'Have you not heard the news?'

'What news?'

'No doubt Prince Andrew will himself bring it to you, when he has savoured it sufficiently.'

'Then give it to me now,' the Queen suggested, with admirable patience. 'So that it may be old and stale when he does.'

'This news can never be old and stale,' Bertrand said bitterly. 'A letter has arrived from Avignon. From His Holiness himself.'

'Saying what?' Joanna demanded, commencing to frown.

'Insisting that Prince Andrew of Hungary be crowned King of Naples beside you.'

Joanna started to her feet in consternation. 'We have not asked His Holiness for an opinion.'

'No,' Bertrand said, more bitterly yet. 'You have not consulted His Holiness about anything. Perhaps you should have. Your cousin has not been so remiss.'

'My cousin?' Joanna's hands clasped her throat. 'Charles of Durazzo?'

'Who else?'

'He has written to the Pope?'

'He did the next best thing. He wrote to his uncle, who is also your uncle, and mine – Cardinal Charles de Perignon. The Cardinal has the Pope's ear, as you must know. And Charles of Durazzo has always been his favourite nephew, as you must also know. This is the result. You have been too confident of your position, my sweet Joanna. And now we are undone. I at the least.'

Joanna took a glass of wine herself. 'The wretch,' she said. 'One day I will be avenged upon him. But what has he truly achieved, save to discomfort me? You make too much of the matter, Bertrand. I will accept that I have been careless in not applying to His Holiness for a ruling in my favour before anyone else could enter a plea against me. But what real difference can it make? Andrew will be King of Naples. And my husband. He is already my husband. He is an indolent, careless husband. I anticipate that he will be an indolent, careless king. I will still rule.'

'As king, my dear, innocent girl, he will hold powers of life and death over his subjects.'

Joanna's frown returned. 'What do you mean?'

'I mean that Andrew is a man of long memories, and much more knowledge than you suppose. And he may be indolent, but he can act when he chooses to do so. He has already done so.'

'Tell me.' The Queen was now definitely agitated.

'Last night, within one hour of the Pope's letter arriving

79

in Naples, Andrew of Isernia was murdered.'

'Andrew of Isernia? He is one of our most eminent lawyers. How could this happen?'

'He was cut down in the street, after a provoked quarrel, by Andrew's bravo, Conrad of Goltes.'

'My God!' Joanna cried.

'That is but the beginning,' Bertrand said. 'Andrew of Isernia is known to have advised Your Grace against crowning Prince Andrew. He is only the first on the list of those your husband counts as enemies. The Prince has composed a proscription, of all the men who have harmed him or insulted him in any way. The common herd will be dealt with immediately. Those of noble, or perchance royal, blood will live until his coronation. But they will die none the less.'

'Of royal blood?' the Queen whispered.

'Indeed. There is at least one prince of the blood on his list.' He stared at her. 'Myself.'

The Queen took a step backwards, and, supposing she was about to swoon, I started forward to catch her. But she did not fall. Instead she stood quite still for several seconds, gazing at her lover, while her face settled into an expression I had never seen before, and had no wish to see then.

It was at that moment I knew Andrew's own death warrant was sealed.

CHAPTER 3

I was naturally the last person in the Queen's entourage to know what was going on. This was because, as a slave, my mistress did not consider I should be privy to such a terrifying concept as the murder – or execution as she would have preferred to call it – of her husband.

I was deeply grieved to be utterly excluded from the secret meetings which now began to take place, deep in the recesses of the palace, the more so when I discovered that these enclaves included Donna Filippa and her son, and both her daughters and their husbands; Joanna was reaching back to her childhood confidantes to prepare the dreadful deed she contemplated to save her lover – Bertrand also naturally attended these conspiratorial huddles – but I knew that Filippa and her entire brood were about as reliable as a bucket with a hole in it.

Also involved was no less a person than Catherine de Valois, Empress of Constantirople, the Queen's aunt – like everyone else, she had her own plans afoot, of which ridding Joanna of her husband and leaving her a desirable widow was the most important aspect to a mother with three eminently marriageable sons – as well as at least one member of the Council of Regency.

My pique was increased when I realised that Donna Cancia was also of the magic circle, from which I was excluded. Cancia, indeed, was very fond of reminding me of how she knew the innermost workings of the Queen's mind, while I did not.

However, I now know that my exclusion from the conspiracy was the most fortunate event of my life. Had it been otherwise, had I indeed been one of the plotters, I would not now be writing these words – my bones would long ago have been scattered along the Neapolitan seashore, suitably racked and burned.

For almost from their first meeting, the conspirators were betrayed, by my erstwhile lover, Tomasso Pace.

It may seem very foolish of my mistress and her friends to have included in their most private conversations the valet of the man they were about to kill. But it turned out that Tomasso had always been in the pay of Donna Filippa, and hated the Hungarians, and especially Brother Robert – who was wont to beat him with a stick – as much as anyone. This hatred was genuine, and Tomasso did not betray Joanna to her husband. While, with his ready access to the Prince's chambers, and his pre-knowledge of the Prince's activities, as well as the trust in which Andrew held him, he was a very important part of the plot.

But he was none the less a disastrous inclusion. For he had a friend, to whom he owed a favour, and this friend, a lawyer named Nicolas di Melazzo, soon suspected that Tomasso had a great secret – he no doubt boasted of it much as Cancia did to me – and very rapidly wormed it out of him.

None of the Queen's party was aware of this. Even less were they, or poor Tomasso himself, aware that Nicolas di Melazzo was in the employ of Charles of Durazzo. Indeed, the unhappy lawyer owed Charles his life for escaping the consequences of a serious crime, and to safeguard the future of his wife and children was prepared to go to any lengths to serve his patron. Charles had actually, it later transpired, told Melazzo to approach Tomasso and discover everything that was happening in the royal apartments of the Castel Nuovo. No doubt he was sure he would turn up something he could use to his advantage, beyond the sure fact that Joanna had exchanged Roberto di Cabane for Bertrand of Artois as a lover, and equally no doubt he was anxious to be informed about the Queen's reaction to the news that he had managed to secure a Papal decree for the coronation of Prince Andrew.

What he did turn up was something he could never have anticipated in his darkest midnight hour. The Queen, who had rejected his cousinly offer to dispose of the Prince because it would entail placing herself in his power, was now actually planning to carry out the murder herself, with a much less able bunch of henchmen. While the henchmen themselves included such famous men as Bertrand and his father, the Count of Aire; Godfrey di Marsan, Count of Squillace, the Grand Admiral – both these members of the Council of Regency; the Counts of Terlizzi and Morcone and Catanzaro, all sworn enemies of the House of Durazzo; and, even more important, the Empress of Constantinople, who equally regarded him with aversion; in addition, of course, to Donna Filippa and her brood. I can well understand that Charles could hardly believe his good fortune; here was the Queen and her most intimate associates playing directly into his hands.

For he had no intention of doing what you or I might have done, and warn the Prince of his danger. Andrew's life meant nothing to this dark man. His intention was to allow the Queen to carry out her crime, because then she and her principal supporters would be utterly in his power. With her guilty and deposed, perhaps even executed but certainly disgraced, Joanna's crown would have to pass to her child, under the regency of her sister – and her sister's husband. It may be accepted that he had no intention of allowing the babe to survive childhood.

He therefore did nothing but listen to the reports that Master di Melazzo took to him. And of these reports, only one mattered: the names of the people who attended the secret meetings. The absence of my name from the list prepared by the wretched lawyer undoubtedly saved my life.

Joanna, meanwhile, unsuspecting the sword which was hanging over her head, proceeded with her plan. It may well be asked, what manner of woman was this eighteen-year-old girl who could so calmly, and with such determination, plot the death of her husband? And how could I spend the rest of my life as her faithful servant after the completion of so hideous a deed?

I can only answer that she was a Queen, brought up from birth to believe there was no check to her imperious will; that she was an Angevin, the great-great-granddaughter of Charles I, who had feared neither God nor man nor devil when his passions were roused; that her passions had been roused, continuously, from the age of fourteen; and that she was in love, and when Joanna loved, it was with every fibre of her molten personality. And for my part, I loved her.

Indeed, had she turned to me, my approach to the problem would have been entirely straightforward, and a great deal of subsequent misery might have been avoided. But she did not approach me, and the absurd band of conspirators she did surround herself with were inept, and too concerned with fantasy to deal in fact.

They were confounded from the beginning by the presence of the talisman. Wearing it, and it never left his finger, Andrew could neither be poisoned nor stabbed – according to his mother. As I have already indicated, had I been involved I would certainly have voted for testing out the efficiency of the talisman before turning to other means, but this simple solution was apparently rejected out of hand.

A man who can neither be pierced nor poisoned can therefore only die before his time in one other way: suffocation. This was the method chosen, regardless of the dangers involved in attempting to strangle a large, powerful, and vicious man, habitually surrounded by guards.

As I was not in the conspiracy, I had no idea what had been decided. I only observed that my mistress seemed more settled in her mind than she had been since the dreadful news of Bertrand's planned execution had been broken to her. I also observed that she became more friendly towards her husband, and welcomed him to her apartment far more often than in the past. This seemed a natural thing to do, for news had reached us from Hungary that his father, Charles Robert, was very ill and not expected to live. It would, indeed, have saved a great deal of misery had Andrew considered it proper to go to his father's bedside. But he had no intention of leaving Naples for a moment, and thus continued on his way, dreaming of the power that was soon to be his, and totally unaware of the fate hanging over him.

It is in the nature of conspirators, however, that they find it difficult not to impart their knowledge to their intended victim, and Joanna did this to Andrew, one day soon afterwards.

The Prince was, as usual, lounging by the window in the royal boudoir, alternately looking out at the people promenading the Mole and the ships in the harbour, and then at his wife, who was engaged in threading a most magnificent silken cord, while Cancia and I, in the far corner, applied ourselves to our needlework. At last Andrew remarked, 'You are so industrious, my dear wife. It is pleasing to the eye. But I had supposed your talents should be turned towards creating something for our child. I cannot make out what you are doing with such diligence.'

Joanna held up the cord, which was then about six feet long. 'It is a cord, Monsignore.'

'I can see that, Joanna. But its purpose escapes me.'

Joanna gave a ghastly smile. 'Why, Monsignore, it is to hang you with, of course.'

The Prince took this as a jest, and laughed heartily. I had but to look at Joanna's face, and then Cancia's, to know that she had just told him the exact truth.

I thus came into possession of the secret by my own wit and understanding. If I was horrified, it was at the thought of the magnitude of the crime and the risks it involved rather than any fear of God's law. I admit this frankly. I had no reason to love Andrew or any of his people, who had made free with my person often enough when it amused them to do so. But I understood the dangers into which my Queen was marching – and carrying all her people with her.

Not being privy to the plot I was not informed of the intended denouement. But again, I was able to guess what was planned when, the following week – the silken cord now being completed and twelve feet long and very strong – Joanna announced that she intended to accompany her husband to the hunt, which on this occasion was to be between Capua and Aversa. This was unusual, to say the least, and an absurdity when she was pregnant. It was equally an absurdity for Cancia and me, but we had no choice but to go along.

The Queen of course did not actually mean to ride behind the hawks. Instead her intention was to join her husband at the Convent of San Pietro, just outside Aversa, where he would retire when his day's sport was completed. But even this would involve a ride of several miles, which is the method recommended by most medical men for bringing on a miscarriage when it is deemed necessary. I therefore realised that Joanna was carrying out another part of the plot, and realised it even more when we reached the convent to discover not only that Bertrand of Artois also intended to spend the night there, as well as Roberto di Cabane and the Counts of Morcone and Terlizzi, but that the guards were entirely Neapolitans of the Queen's own retinue – my Alberto was amongst them.

The arrangements had all been made by Roberto, in his

capacity as Grand Seneschal, and he had carried out his requirements to the last detail. It did not occur to this simple buffoon to remark upon a singular fact – that for the first time in several months, Charles of Durazzo was not accompanying his bosom friend Andrew to the hunt. He had cried off on the grounds of the illness of the Princess Marie, offering the Prince the use of his best falcon in his stead. No one found this the least suspicious.

When Andrew arrived, he was naturally accompanied by his Hungarians, and he and Brother Robert were somewhat taken aback to discover all the arrangements already completed. But Joanna was so vivacious that night, so lovingly tender to her husband, that all suspicions were quickly allayed. She had ordered a great feast prepared for the Hungarian nobles, and these worthies, who enjoyed eating and drinking even more than wenching, and possibly even more than hunting, fell to with great spirit. Needless to say the wine had been drugged, and by midnight the entire troop was fast asleep. Even Brother Robert, who enjoyed his wine as much as anyone, was caught in the trap and snoring as loudly as the rest.

The convent sank into darkness. The good friars occupied a wing at some distance from the royal apartments. These were guarded by Neapolitans, and, if they were not privy to the plot, they were subject to certain instructions. Thus it was that at two in the morning, they admitted into the antechamber outside the Queen's bedroom six men: Bertrand of Artois, Roberto di Cabane, the Count of Morcone, the Count of Terlizzi, Tomasso Pace, and someone I did not know, a late addition to the number of conspirators, but who I later learned to be Nicolas di Melazzo himself – for Charles of Durazzo had insisted that he actually take part in the murder, the better to betray his accomplices later. That this would mean his own death on the gallows he was apparently prepared to accept – his patron had promised to care for his wife and family, whereas if he had refused, they too would have suffered an unthinkable fate on account of his previous crime.

The gullibility of the Queen's party in, at this late stage, admitting a new face to their councils, on the sole grounds of being a friend of Tomasso's, defies understanding.

Now the Queen was fast asleep, so far as anyone knew, in her bed, with her husband beside her. Thus Cancia and I were sleeping in this very antechamber, and my first reaction on awakening to find six desperate men standing above me was to scream. Cancia put a stop to that by clapping her hand over my mouth and drawing me into her cot beside her, where she held me tightly. 'Do not utter a sound,' she whispered in my ear.

I panted with apprehension, but I did not have long to wait. Tomasso Pace, this man who had held me naked in his arms as Cancia was doing at that very moment, and who was, so far as anyone not in the plot was aware, the faithful servant of the Hungarian Prince, now knocked on the inner door and called, 'Master, master, it is time for the hunt.'

A moment later the bedchamber door was opened, and Andrew stood there, as naked as the day he had been born, with a poignard in his hand. 'Tomasso?' he inquired. 'You must be mistaken. Cancia? Richilde? Where are you ...' as he blinked in the darkness.

He had not finished speaking when Bertrand, who had been standing behind the door, slammed it shut with his foot, and in the same instant dropped the fatal noose around the Prince's neck. The shock caused Andrew to drop his dagger, which was fortunate for the murderers, for the most tremendous struggle now ensued. Andrew was only one against five – for Master di Melazzo took little part in the contest – but he was a large and strong man, as well as a determined and courageous one.

He also had a loud voice, which he used to the fullest advantage. 'To me!' he bellowed. 'Help me, my Hungarians, I am beset! Conrad of Goltes, to me!'

His shouts reverberated throughout the convent. They certainly reached the friars, who preferred to remain safely in their cells. Equally they reached the Hungarians, but none was awake. And equally they reached the guards, but they were under orders that in no circumstances were they to approach the Queen's apartment that night.

And they certainly reverberated around the room in which the struggle was taking place, while the seven men staggered to and fro, each of the assailants trying to gain a grip which would pin Andrew down and allow Bertrand to tighten the noose, while Andrew fought with the fury of a man who knows he has been betrayed. Their stamping feet brought them up against the cot in which Cancia and I were huddled, and over we went in a flurry of arms and legs, only with difficulty extricating ourselves as we crawled for shelter.

The Prince now tried to regain the supposed safety of his bedchamber, where not only the Queen but his sword would be waiting, but Nicolas di Melazzo thrust his own dagger through the bolts to prevent him, while the others resumed their assault. The struggle and the noise lasted for several minutes, and then its course took the heaving group of men against the outer door of the chamber, which opened on to a high balcony. This door gave way before so much weight, and the antagonists stumbled into the open air, where Andrew's shrieks grew even louder. But he was now becoming tired, and at last Bertrand was able to tighten the noose. Cancia and I listened in horror as the shrieks became gurgles, and then gasps, and then faded altogether, and the only sound was the heavy breathing of the murderers. At least, I listened in horror. Cancia listened with growing excitement of a quite perverse kind, which left me feeling that I had been in the arms of a man.

'Make the cord fast, here,' Bertrand panted.

There was a sliding, slithering sound.

'Now,' Roberto snapped, and there was a kind of 'thrumm'.

We could control our curiosity no longer, and crept to the door to look out. The end of the cord had been secured to one of the balustrades, and Andrew's body thrown over the rail. Our mistress had done her work well, and the cord had not snapped from the sudden weight; it hung, and Andrew's lifeless body swung, to and fro, beneath the balcony.

It might have been expected that the assassins, or at least Bertrand, would have now reported the success of their awful deed to the Queen, but instead, scarce deigning to give us two naked girls a glance, they ran from the balcony and took horse.

Cancia and I looked at each other, and then at the dead Prince, and then returned inside our chamber and closed and locked the door.

'They will say he committed suicide,' Cancia whispered.

I preferred not to comment. 'They' would have to be demented not to see the evidence of Andrew having been forcibly put over the rail. 'Should we go into the Queen?' I whispered in turn.

'She is asleep, and should not be disturbed,' Cancia said. Clearly this was her night for fantasies. I did not see how anyone not drugged and within half a mile of the convent could have failed to be disturbed by the racket. However, I followed her example and resurrected our cots before lying down again, my heart pounding, my mind seething, any chance of sleep gone – and in fact as I laid my head on the pillow I heard a cock crow.

But it was half an hour later before Joanna called.

'Richilde,' she said. 'Cancia. Come to me.'

It was some solace that she had thought of me first in this dire moment. We opened the door and went in. The Queen sat up in bed, and when Cancia had scraped the tinder and lit a candle, we could observe her bloodless cheeks, her staring eyes, her heaving breasts.

'Is it done?' she asked, in a low voice.

'It is done, Your Grace,' Cancia said.

'Oh, God,' she murmured, and buried her face in her hands. 'The noise ...'

'Has aroused no one, Your Grace,' Cancia assured her, with her invariable optimism.

'Bertrand ...?'

'Has left, together with the others.'

The Queen inhaled, for so long I feared her lungs would burst, and then released the trapped air in the most doleful sigh I ever heard.

'Shall I raise the alarm, Your Grace?' I asked, anxious to help her.

'God forbid!' she gasped. 'No! Bolt the door. Bolt the door and come to me.'

I could not help but feel this was a mistake, but she was my mistress. Thus I obeyed, and the three of us huddled beneath the covers, still warm from the body of the dead Prince.

Within a little while there were shouts from the garden below, and soon after we heard voices calling for the Queen. It was now becoming light, and we looked at our mistress for instruction. But she merely held us closer, her eyes tight shut. Another few minutes passed, and then there was a knock on the door. 'Your Grace,' a man said. 'This is the Prior speaking. Madame, there has been a great tragedy. Madame, your husband is dead.'

Joanna gave a great shudder, but uttered not a sound; her fingers on my back were like talons digging into my flesh.

'Madame,' the Prior said, more urgently. 'What is your pleasure that we should do with your husband's body?'

Still Joanna made no reply, and they seemed to go away again. But then there were other voices, asking the same question, and seeming to pray at her door. And now there was a growing hubbub as more and more people gathered to stare at the dangling corpse of the intended King of Naples.

'Joanna,' I said. It was the first time I had ever addressed her by her name, but in this awful situation we were all equals. 'We must do something, or they will eventually break down the door and we will be exposed to the mob.'

'They will tear us to pieces,' Cancia moaned, her ardour quite spent.

Joanna appeared to stir herself with an enormous effort. 'You must summon my guard, Richilde,' she said.

'Me, Your Grace?' In my alarm I remembered my station.

'Of course. Is not your husband one of them? Summon them, and tell them to prepare a litter, and bring it here.'

'I have no clothes, Your Grace. My clothes are in the other room with the monks.'

'Then wear mine,' the Queen commanded. 'And make your escape, and fetch my guards.'

And so I donned the habit of the Queen, and departed by a side door which led into a private corridor. From here I was able to gain the staircase, panting with fear. People saw me, and called out, uncertain whether I was indeed the Queen, for I kept my head covered, but before they could catch hold of me I was in the guard quarters and folded in Alberto's arms.

He was in a sombre mood. 'There will be a great to-do about tonight's work,' he said.

He was given to understatement.

'Nevertheless,' I told him, 'as we are the Queen's servants, we must carry out her wishes, and quickly.'

He agreed, and sent four of his men to fetch a litter and the horses. When all was prepared, I went boldly back up the main staircase, accompanied by six mailed guardsmen. The monks and the spectators parted before us – the Hungarians fortunately were all still too woozy to understand what was going on – and we arrived at the door of the Queen's bedchamber, where I made myself known.

Joanna and Cancia were dressed by now, and heavily veiled, as was I. The three of us hurried down to the litter, no one being quite sure which one of us was actually the Queen, if any, and we were carried off, riding through the mob, which muttered but as yet was indulging in no violence. A few hours later we were safely inside the Castel Nuovo, and the drawbridge had been raised.

If safety was available to us anywhere in the world. The affair had been utterly botched, and no one could have any doubt as to the guilty. But even the guilty were affected. We had not been in our apartments more than a few hours, and told a horrified Donna Filippa and her daughters what had happened, than Bertrand arrived. He came by way of the secret staircases into the Queen's chamber, and I was there when the guilty lovers stared at each other.

It might have been expected that they would throw themselves into each other's arms for mutual succour, and Joanna was certainly ready to be so comforted, but Bertrand gazed at her as if she had been a monster, and it was plain from his expression, and indeed his visage, which had seemed to age twenty years in a night, that he realised the awfulness of the deed he had committed, for love of this woman ... and that that love was not going to save him from the consequences of his deed.

'What news, my love?' Joanna asked.

'News!' He threw himself into a chair, and covered his eyes. 'The body has fallen, and lies on the ground.'

'Has no one taken it away?'

'No one has touched it,' he shouted. 'It has not even been covered. It will lie there and rot.'

'But ... the Hungarians ...'

'Have fled for the border, in fear for their lives.'

'Then what have we to fear, dear Bertrand?' the Queen asked, a slight note of impatience entering her voice.

93

'The wrath of God,' the miserable youth moaned, and got up, going immediately to the door.

'Where are you going?' Joanna demanded.

'To my father's estate at St Agatha. He is already there. He wishes me at his side.'

'But I wish you *here*,' Joanna snapped, stamping her foot.

'We are damned,' he said. 'Damned! I am of no more use to you, Your Grace.' He banged the door behind him.

Joanna stared at us in angry consternation. Cancia gave a peal of laughter. 'Damned!' she shouted happily. 'Yes, we are all damned!' She went to the table and poured herself a goblet of wine, drinking it so hastily that the red liquid spilled on the bodice of her gown.

'I do not think that is at all seemly, Cancia,' Joanna said severely.

Cancia gave another peal of laughter. 'What will you do, poor damned Queen? Will you summon your guards and have me flogged? How can you be sure I will not confess all, and your part in this damnable affair?'

'Do you not suppose they know?' Joanna asked, her voice quiet but filled with ice.

'They may suspect, dear lady. But no, they dare not know, or say. Because that would be treason. You would have to be accused by someone not afraid to die. Like me.' She poured herself another goblet of wine.

Joanna glared at her for several seconds, then turned to me. 'You'll attend me, Richilde,' she said.

My heart bled to see the awful trap in which she had placed herself, but her humiliation had hardly begun. We had not gained the bedchamber when the apartment doors were thrown open to admit Donna Filippa and Roberto, who had clearly recovered their nerves.

'All hail, great Queen,' said the Catanian.

Joanna gave her a look which should have shrivelled her to a skeleton, but the laundrywoman was in no mood to be crushed by a glance. 'There are things to be done, Your Grace.'

94

'Yes,' Joanna said. 'I must go into mourning.'

'Black is your best colour. But first, there will have to be a funeral.'

'When someone reclaims my husband's body.'

'Ha ha. Some wretch will do so, eventually. It will be a great occasion. You will permit me to ride at your side, I trust?'

'You, signora?' Joanna demanded.

'Am I not your dearest friend? Your mentor? Your very mother? There is another matter. We shall need clothes, to look our very best for the gaping throng.'

'Have you no clothes already, signora, suitable for such an occasion?'

'I was speaking of new clothes, Your Grace. You would not have my daughters and me, or the Grand Seneschal, disgrace your procession? No no. Two hundred ducats will suffice.'

'Two hundred ducats?' Joanna echoed.

'I have the order here,' Filippa announced, unrolling one of her dreadful parchments.

Joanna glared at her, then snatched the parchment and carried it to her escritoire, signing it with a flourish. 'Now leave me,' she said, in a quiet tone but one filled with emotion.

Filippa bowed, as did Roberto. 'No doubt I will think of something else we need, Your Grace. When I do, I know that Your Grace will immediately provide it, because of the generosity of her heart ... at least towards those who know her secrets. Good day to you, Your Grace.'

She glanced at Cancia and myself, and left the room.

Joanna also looked at us, and then sat down, her hands on her lap; I think she was then for the first time realising that she was doomed.

I would have comforted her, had not there been another summons at the door. Joanna turned quite pale, but before she could give any instructions, Cancia had thrown the door open, to admit the Empress of Constantinople, looking as imperious and ill tempered as ever. 'What, Your Grace?' she demanded. 'Sulking?'

Joanna stood up. 'I am mourning my husband, madame,' she said coldly, using the French form of address to the French empress.

'A husband mourned is one soon forgotten,' Catherine declared. 'God knows I have experience of these matters. It is time to look to the future. To your next husband.'

'Madame, I beg of you. Prince Andrew is not yet cold.'

'He is cold enough. And you are a defenceless girl who needs a strong man at her side.'

'No doubt you have already found such a man,' Joanna snapped.

'I have. My son Robert. He is of your own age, and of your own blood.'

'Robert?' Joanna cried. 'He is my first cousin. It will not be legal.'

'That is an irrelevance. His Holiness will provide the necessary dispensation. And Robert adores you. I have already spoken with him.'

'You have ...' for a moment Joanna was speechless. Then she said, 'Madame, Prince Robert is not your eldest son.'

My heart leapt, for Louis of Tarento would have made the Queen a splendid champion.

Catherine understood what Joanna meant. 'I have spoken with Louis as well,' she said. 'The boy is a romantic fool. He has told me that it would be unseemly to approach Your Grace on such a matter at such a time. Robert has no such scruples.'

'And do you not suppose I have scruples?' Joanna demanded. 'I honour Prince Louis for his forbearance. I can consider no remarriage until I have mourned my husband for six months.'

'Joanna,' said the Empress, dropping all pretence at deference, 'you will marry my son. He is not yet a party to the information I possess. None of them are. And in the coming days you are going to need their support, and the support of every strong right arm you can find. Were I to reveal to my sons the truth of Prince Andrew's death, you would find them ranged against you, and I doubt you could withstand so much. Thus in six months' time you might find yourself no longer a Queen. So give me your hand as my future daughter-in-law. I but seek a betrothal at this point. I understand no marriage can take place until you have been widowed for six months, and we must obtain that dispensation from His Holiness. All I require from you is permission for Robert to take up residence in this castle, so that all the world will understand that you are betrothed, and that he be allowed into your presence once in every day. So, give me your hand.'

How I wanted Joanna to refuse the harridan. I knew this Robert. He had the mind of a boy, and would be as much protection for my mistress as a shield made of straw. I also saw that the Empress was attempting a colossal bluff, for how could she tell the 'truth of Prince Andrew's death' to her sons without revealing her own part in the affair?

But I could communicate none of these truths to Joanna, and sadly I saw that she was too distraught to see them for herself.

The Queen hesitated, then sighed, and extended her hand.

'What could I do?' she moaned, when we were at last alone. 'Marriage to Robert ... marriage to anyone, is an abhorrent thought to me at this moment. Were I not Queen I should take the veil. I am the most wretched creature on earth. Those that I had supposed I could trust ...' she bent a scornful glance at Cancia, who was still guzzling away, 'are set to betray me for their own ends. I am utterly alone in the world.'

'I am at your side, Your Grace,' I reminded her.

'Oh, Richilde, my dearest Richilde,' she said. 'Without you I should go mad.'

That night I was readmitted to the royal bed for the first time in several years, but it was a poor night for me, as Joanna suffered the most terrible nightmares, tossed and turned, and finally kicked me on to the floor. I bore it all with patience, as I could understand my mistress's feelings – I shared some of them. And we both knew our ordeal had not yet truly begun. For the next day Prince Andrew's body was brought to Naples.

This was the work of Charles of Durazzo, who was now ready to begin his carefully concerted plan to bring down the Queen and all her intimates.

He pretended to have heard of the events at the convent by chance, as it were, and immediately rode over there, where he was 'horrified' to discover that, lacking instructions from the Queen, Andrew's body remained lying naked at the foot of the balcony. Charles immediately had the corpse gathered up, and conveyed to Naples with great pomp. It was taken directly to the Cathedral, where vast crowds gathered to see the man whom the Pope had directed to be their King.

Here too gathered those of the Hungarians who had not fled, and to these Charles looked when he stood beside the catafalque, and shouted, 'Nobles and commoners, here lies the body of our King, cruelly murdered and then abandoned. I tell you all, I will never rest until I have discovered the perpetrators of this foul deed, and have punished them without pity and without remorse, but with implacable anger, regardless of their rank or station. I call upon you all to join me in this sacred task.'

It will be noted that the crafty scoundrel took care to make no accusations at this time. He knew full well that his creature would provide all the proof necessary, and that then he could reveal a proper horror and indignation that his Queen should have despatched her own husband.

The mob responded with a mighty roar, in which the voices of the Hungarians rang loudest. 'Vengeance!' they shrieked.

The noise reached us in the Castel Nuovo, as did the reason for it, and Joanna was in a state of such agitation I feared for her reason. Indeed, it now approached us, and with trembling voice she ordered the castle to be placed in a state of defence, expecting the outbreak of civil war at any moment.

My gallant Alberto marshalled his guards, and prepared to do battle, while we poor females peered from the windows at the approaching throng. They were led by Charles himself, and he now demanded admittance.

'Let the rascal in,' said the Empress Catherine, who had hurried to her future daughter-in-law's side. 'Let us hear what he has to say.'

'Him alone,' Joanna warned.

The drawbridge was kept raised, but a postern gate was opened, and through this, by means of a boat in the moat, Charles was admitted to the royal presence, where he surveyed both the Queen and her aunt, and their ladies, as might a conqueror.

'Your Grace,' he said, bowing so low his feather touched the floor. 'A sorry business. I well understand that your grief has prevented you from appearing in public, or even attending to the matter of your husband's body. I have been happy to act in your stead, as your brother-in-law, and your heir.'

'My heir?' Joanna demanded.

'Am I not? I am the husband of your adoring sister. Will she not succeed to the throne should you, a hapless widow, die without issue?'

'I will have issue,' Joanna declared. 'It is in me now.'

Charles smiled. 'It will be many years before your babe, supposing it is not stillborn, can possibly rule Naples. The people demand assurance that their lives and property will be protected by a ruler who will be worthy of the name.'

'You concern yourself too much with affairs of state, nephew,' Catherine remarked. 'Joanna will rule Naples to the satisfaction of all, nobly assisted by her new husband.'

'Her new husband?'

'Exactly. My son.'

'Your son?' For just a moment Charles lost his aplomb, and how I wished that Catherine might have been able to utter the name of Louis of Tarento, for there was a warrior before whom even Charles of Durazzo would have had to tremble. 'You have three sons, aunt.'

'My son Robert.'

Charles stared at her, then threw back his head and uttered a peal of laughter. 'That puling boy?'

'He is a prince of the blood, of higher rank than yourself,' the Empress flashed.

'But still a boy. And effeminate with it, if I may offer an opinion, ladies. In any event, the people consider myself to be the only true heir to the throne, and the only worthy protector of our unfortunate Queen. They are gathered outside the castle now, as you have no doubt observed. It is their wish that I be created, this instant, Duke of Calabria, as heir to the throne. They have already called me by that illustrious title. They will not be denied.'

'You claim too much,' Catherine snapped.

'I claim what is mine by right,' Charles insisted, and looked from her to the Queen. 'It is I who have been called upon, by the people, to discover and punish the murderers of Prince Andrew – regardless of rank or station. Do you not suppose I have already begun my investigations, and reached certain conclusions?'

Joanna paled, and even the Empress, proud Valois though she was, had little immediate answer to such a threat. She was, however, a mistress of dissembling. 'Perhaps, my child,' she suggested to the Queen, 'in view of the turbulent state of your kingdom, it would be best to choose Charles as your heir – until such time as your babe is strong enough to grasp the sceptre himself.'

'Yes,' Joanna gasped. 'Until.'

Charles smiled, and bowed, and accompanied the Queen to the ramparts to be hailed as the new Duke of Calabria, while the populace cheered.

He had, it seemed, accomplished his purpose. He was soon to discover differently.

For Catherine of Valois was no woman with whom to trifle. 'Foul wretch!' she declared, as soon as the Duke of Calabria had withdrawn. 'He seeks to parade himself above us, does he? Above me and my son! I will bring the rascal down in weeping horror, my child. Do not fear for that.'

'He is so strong,' Joanna moaned. 'He commands so much allegiance amongst my subjects. I tell you, Aunt, I have a growing wish to give him what he most wishes, the kingdom, and retire to a nunnery.'

Catherine was appalled, when she was foreseeing herself, as Queen Mother, becoming the real power behind the throne. 'You have a sacred duty to be Queen of Naples,' she announced. 'You cannot surrender such a responsibility to the threats of an upstart. Leave Charles of Durazzo to me. I will ...' she considered. 'I will have Louis challenge him in the lists.'

'No!' Joanna screamed, revealing in that instant where her heart truly lay.

Catherine frowned at her. 'Do you not suppose my son would despatch Charles as he might the meanest peasant?'

'I know he has the skill, and the strength, dearest Aunt. But in the lists ... who can tell what the merest mischance may cause to happen?'

Catherine pinched her lip. 'Yes,' she said thoughtfully. 'Yes. It is a pity. I should enjoy seeing that rascal naked and bleeding at my feet.' She sighed. 'Well, then, I know of a substance ...'

'No,' Joanna said again, more calmly. 'I will not have

him poisoned. I have committed sufficient crimes in my life.'

And she was not yet twenty.

'Your Grace,' Catherine said severely. 'How may I deal with this wretch if I am not allowed to destroy him?'

It was at this moment that Cancia, who had as usual been drinking, gave a merry peal of laughter. 'Why, madame,' she trilled, 'there is more than one way to skin a cat.'

'That girl should be whipped,' Catherine suggested. 'She is drunk.'

'Hear me, madame,' Cancia protested. 'And if you do not like my proposal, then will I bare my arse without hesitation. You seek to destroy Charles of Durazzo. But madame, death is often a release. Is it not better to have him live in torment?'

Catherine's reply to this riddle was to go to the corner of the room and select a stout cane from amongst the walking-out sticks to be found there.

Cancia did not seem disturbed. But then, Cancia would not have been disturbed had she indeed had to yield to a caning.

'Tell me, madame,' she said. 'Who is the person in all this world to whom Charles is most devoted? Indeed, who is the only person in this world to whom he is devoted? It is most certainly not his wife.'

'It is his mother,' Catherine snapped.

'I will not have my Aunt Agnes harmed,' Joanna said.

'Not a hair of her head, Your Grace,' Cancia said. 'But were we to sow discord between Charles and the Duchess, would we not thereby make him the most miserable man in the kingdom? Hear me, great ladies. The Dowager Duchess of Durazzo has been suffering for some weeks from a fit of depression. I have heard this from her ladies.'

'That does not surprise me in the least,' Catherine remarked. 'She must be aware of her son's ambitions. Equally must she be aware that those, like Icarus, who fly

102

too close to the sun are liable to have their wings burned.'

'The fact remains, madame, that she is depressed, as would be a woman with much on her mind. Now, great ladies, consider this: suppose the cause of her depression was the discovery that she was pregnant?'

Joanna and Catherine stared at her in consternation, while even I could not follow Cancia's drift.

Joanna put my thoughts into words. 'Agnes of Durazzo?' she cried. 'She is the most chaste widow in the kingdom.'

Joanna was in error here; Agnes of Durazzo was the *only* chaste widow in the kingdom, certainly in society.

'That may be, Your Grace,' Cancia argued. 'But consider this: how does a surgeon usually determine pregnancy? Is it not by analysis of the lady's water? Have we three ...' she allowed even me the courtesy of a glance, 'not between us sufficient impregnated water to convince the most determined sceptic that the lady from whom it issues is with child?'

Joanna gazed at her with her mouth open.

'I would willingly offer mine,' Cancia continued.

Joanna looked at Catherine, still catching flies.

But the Empress had ceased to frown. Instead she clapped her hands in delight. 'How splendid,' she shouted. 'It will drive Charles from his mind to suppose his mother is *enceinte*. Oh, the villain, he will never sleep again. But ...' the frown returned. 'How may the substitution be made? If a soul outside this room ever learns of it, we are again subject to blackmail.' It was her turn to glance at me, as if wondering whether it might not be a good idea to reduce our numbers immediately.

'No one will know of it, outside the room, madame,' Cancia promised. 'I am already friendly with Alice of Salerno, who is one of the Duchess's ladies. I will become more so, and as Charles is now heir to the throne, it will seem natural. I will visit the palace of Durazzo, and laugh and play games, and drink wine. Thus, in the course of a very short space of time, I shall receive a natural call. If, great ladies, I cannot insert my chamber pot beneath the Duchess's bed in place of hers, then shall I count myself a miserable failure. Once that is done, the merest hint to Charles as to the cause of his mother's depression will have him summoning his surgeon.'

'Truly, Cancia,' Catherine said, 'you are a woman of great resource. Were you my daughter, I would be proud of you.'

And so it was agreed.

I hasten to say that Joanna was as disturbed as myself by the whole idea. For neither Catherine nor Cancia had given a thought to the distress they were going to occasion Agnes of Durazzo, a most blameless lady. In the event, their plan to make Charles the most miserable of men succeeded beyond their wildest expectations, and beyond Joanna's and my most doleful apprehensions. Cancia duly substituted her water for that of the Duchess, and saw to it that an anonymous note found its way into the hand of the Duke of Calabria.

After that, we could only judge circumstances by events, for what took place was a closely guarded secret within the palazzo. Cancia did gather, however, from her friend Alice, that Charles, having been approached by his mother's physician, who felt bound to disclose the dreadful situation of the Dowager Duchess, first of all refused to believe the fellow, and when he was convinced that the physician was telling the truth, flew into the most dreadful rage.

Nothing further was heard from the palazzo for over a week, and no one was allowed in or out. At the end of that time, it was announced that the Dowager Duchess had been taken ill and died, as had the surgeon attending her.

Naples was plunged into mourning for the departure of an honoured lady. Joanna was plunged into despair, for there could be no doubt that Charles had murdered his mother, whether by having her opened to discover the truth of the matter, or by poison – we later discovered that it had been poison, which had also been forced upon the physician, to prevent the truth of the matter ever being known. As of course it never could be. Catherine's and Cancia's revenge was a very barren victory.

Catherine, indeed, appeared to feel remorse for what she had done, and now began to go out of her way to be sympathetic to the unhappy duke, and his no less miserable duchess, for Marie, surrounded as she was by intrigue and anger of which she understood nothing, was now, like the rest of us, pregnant. Catherine's fawning, in which she included her son Robert, would have been laughable in any other circumstances – it reminded me of Charles's own fawning upon Prince Andrew, when he had first been rebuffed by the Queen. Nor, it was evident, was Charles the least taken in by this pantomime.

However, Catherine's hypocrisy served a very useful purpose and gave rise to a most singular turn of events. As the Empress and Robert now removed themselves from the Castel Nuovo for much of every day, paying court at the palazzo of Durazzo, Joanna and her ladies were left very much to themselves, and we were able to contemplate our navels, which yet remained flat enough, but which we knew would soon begin to grow. It was in these circumstances, with the furore of the murder of Prince Andrew seeming to subside – we were innocent enough to suppose that the storm had blown itself out, leaving us in safety – a most remarkable occasion arrived.

We were one morning concerning ourselves with needle-work and fantasies as to our respective children, as ladies will, in the privacy of Joanna's boudoir, Catherine and Robert having betaken themselves to Charles as usual, when we heard the creak of the drawbridge being lowered. I was despatched to discover from whom Alberto was taking orders, as it was not the Queen, and thus observed, riding across the bridge in all the panoply of a knight off to war, none other than Louis of Tarento, who was accompanied by half a dozen squires, also armed.

It will probably not have escaped my readers that this man was my favourite member of his sex, and I was immediately all of a twitter, the more so as he commanded the bridge to be raised behind him. Alberto looked at me, and I gave a quick nod. I did not know Prince Louis's purpose. I could only hope. And perhaps even pray.

The crane was in place to assist him to dismount, and he was divested of his armour by his attendants, who then adjusted his clothes; he retained his shirt of mail and his richly decorated tabard, as well as the flat iron cap he wore inside his helmet. Then he looked at me. 'Take me to your mistress,' he commanded.

I formed the opinion that he was in the grip of a most powerful emotion, but curtsied, and led him into the royal apartment, heart pounding as I listened to his boots at my heels. At the door of Joanna's boudoir I curtsied again. 'You will permit me to acquaint Her Grace with your presence, monsignore,' I said.

'I will acquaint her myself,' Louis announced, and opened the door.

There was a chorus of delicate screams from within, and I followed the Prince inside to discover both Joanna and Cancia on their feet, needles poised like swords, staring at the handsome knight who had so rudely invaded their presence. And if outside I had felt he was aroused, he was now barely holding himself in, that was very obvious.

However, he possessed sufficient self-control to bow. 'Your Grace,' he said.

'Monsignore?' Joanna's voice was quiet, but that she too was powerfully affected by this pleasant surprise could not be doubted. 'What means this abrupt invasion of my privacy? Are you not aware that I am betrothed to your brother?'

Louis straightened. 'I would have come before, Your Grace. I have spent many a sleepless night, wrestling with my soul, my conscience, and my heart. Now I know that I cannot let you wed another. I cannot live without you, my dearest Joanna.' And he fell to his knees again, this time to seize her hand and kiss it.

I could have clapped my hands for joy, and Cancia did do so, while Joanna stared at her favourite cousin in a mixture of amazement, delight, and sadness – for she was well aware of the difficulties that would make such a desirable match all but impossible to achieve.

'Have you no words to give me, no hope?' Louis asked her, still holding her hand.

'Alas, dear, dear Louis,' she said. 'While I can think of no man with whom I would rather share my bed, I am already betrothed, as I have reminded you. To your brother.'

'That puling boy?' Louis demanded, as contemptuously as Charles of Durazzo.

'Your brother,' Joanna repeated, and added, more to the point, 'the son of your mother.'

'They acted while I was distraught,' Louis claimed. 'Their haste was indecent. I will not permit it.'

Joanna gazed at him with love in her eyes, and when Joanna had love in her eyes she was indeed the most beautiful woman in Europe. 'Would you defy your mother?'

'I would defy God in His heaven, Your Grace, to attain you.'

'No blasphemy, I beg of you,' Joanna protested. 'Well, then, let us put our situation to the Empress when she returns.'

'I cannot wait that long, Your Grace,' Louis said, rising to his feet. 'Nor would it be wise. My mother is a woman who does not like to be crossed, and she possesses a devious mind; she would very soon find a way to separate us, and keep us separated. We must face her with a *fait accompli*.'

'Monsignore,' Joanna said. 'We can hardly hurry down to the cathedral and beg the archbishop to marry us. Quite apart from the unseemliness of such an action, there have been no banns, and we lack papal dispensation for our mutual blood.'

'Your Grace,' Louis replied, 'while I am aware that a marriage needs to be consecrated in heaven, and that a marriage between us will require the approval of His Holiness, there is a further requirement which, if not fulfilled, renders even such consecration and such approval null and void. But which, if fulfilled, leaves the consecration as but a formality, to be undertaken at a convenient moment, and which makes it impossible for Papal approval to be withheld.'

Joanna stared at him, while blood gathered in those pale cheeks, and her breast started to heave. 'Monsignore, what are you proposing?' she asked. As if she did not know, well enough. Certain Cancia and myself understood his meaning; we were both holding our breaths.

Nor was the Prince loath to spell it out. 'I am proposing, dearest Joanna, that we consummate our marriage on the instant, and worry about the formalities afterwards.' He frowned. 'You have not permitted my brother such a privilege?'

'Heaven forbid!' Joanna exclaimed.

'Then there is no obstacle remaining.' He beckoned me. 'Undress me, Richilde.'

I fell to with vigour. It seemed to me that both the Queen and I were going to have a pleasurable half hour, whatever storm might afterwards break. But Joanna still felt called upon to protest.

'Monsignore,' she said. 'I am *enceinte*.'

'I will not harm the babe,' he promised. 'I may even improve his wellbeing.'

Joanna bit her lip, and looked at Cancia, who began to unfasten the Queen's dress. I was working well at my own task, and despite my unfamiliarity with such items as mail shirts and codpieces, soon had my lord as naked as any woman could wish. Cancia was performing the same

108

duty for Joanna, and then we stood back, panting, and aroused ourselves as we gazed at the two most beautiful people in the kingdom, at their most beautiful, for Louis was in an even greater state of agitation now than before. A moment later they were in each other's arms, and a few moments after that Louis had swept the Queen from the floor and carried her towards her bed. At which point common decency commanded that Cancia and I withdraw, much as we would have liked to stay.

I would not care to suppose how Cancia amused herself for the next hour, but I know I hurried off to find Alberto, and play the valet for him as I had for the Prince. Alas, we commoners are seldom considered by Fate as she pursues her inconsiderate way, and we had barely coupled when we were interrupted by the sergeant of the watch, who informed us that Prince Robert of Constantinople was approaching, with his mother and his retinue.

'What's to be done?' Alberto asked.

'He must be refused entry,' I replied without hesitation.

'Refuse the Prince entry? He is our future king.'

'The situation is fluid,' I told him, pulled on my shift, and in such *déshabillé* ran back to the royal bedchamber. I am not likely ever to forget the sight that greeted my eyes, of my Queen seated astride her lover, her magnificent hair flopping this way and that in time to her head as her whole body surged in the ecstasy of orgasm. I did not dare interrupt so precious a moment, as it was clearly a mutual one. Fortunately, these matters are usually short-lived, and no sooner had Joanna collapsed in a welter of sweat and semen than I made my presence known, and the subject of my anxiety.

Joanna sprang from the bed, hands clasped to her throat. 'Oh, my God!' she remarked.

Louis began pulling on his clothes. 'I will deal with the matter, my dearest wife,' he assured her, and left the room. I followed, shift flying, and Joanna was behind me, scarcely more modestly dressed. We watched from a window, while Louis appeared on the battlements above the drawbridge.

Robert was already in a fine fury at being refused entry to what he now considered his home. 'Wretches,' he was shouting at the guards – who included my Alberto in their ranks. 'Lower this bridge instantly, or I will have you all hanged like dogs.'

He did not immediately perceive his brother, but Louis now replied, 'They are acting on my instructions, Robert,' he said quietly. 'I did not wish to be interrupted.'

'Interrupted?' Robert bellowed. 'Interrupted while doing what?'

'I have been pledging my troth to Her Grace the Queen,' Louis explained.

Had he possessed some infernal machine and dropped it from the battlements he could not have caused more consternation. The mob, which had as usual quickly gathered at the possibility of an altercation involving their betters, gasped, while Robert looked about to have a fit.

His situation was not improved by what Louis next had to say.

'I know you will wish to congratulate me, Brother,' he continued. 'Her Grace has accepted my troth, and indeed, our marriage has been consummated.'

More sensation, and Catherine rode forward to be at her son's side. 'Are you out of your senses?' she demanded.

'On the contrary, Mother, I have come to my senses,' Louis said. 'Will you not offer your blessing upon the Queen and myself?'

'Foul wretch!' Robert screamed, drawing his sword and waving it. 'Betrayer of our blood! Come down from those walls and meet me face to face, if you dare.'

'Willingly,' Louis agreed, and left the battlements. But Catherine of course could not permit her sons to duel, especially as the event could only end in Robert's death. She spoke urgently to her younger son. Joanna and I, holding each other's hands, watched as Robert glared at his mother, and reacted so violently that their horses clashed and the Empress was all but unseated. But then, as the drawbridge began to lower to permit Louis to leave, Robert turned and galloped off, undoubtedly to the palazzo of Durazzo.

We cared naught for his destination, however, merely hugged ourselves with delight at his departure. Unfortunately, it was now necessary to admit the Empress, who stood before the pair of lovers like some avenging fury.

'I know not what to say,' she said.

'You have but to bless us, sweet Mother,' Louis told her. 'And admit that you would have preferred this arrangement to any other from the beginning.'

Catherine of Valois shared the weakness of every woman in the kingdom: she could no more look upon the countenance of Louis of Tarento and frown than she could fly. And she was his mother, who would yet, she was realising, achieve her ambition of being the power behind the throne.

'Dear Louis,' she said. 'Dear Joanna. I would be an unnatural wretch were I to cavil at your so evident happiness. I but fear the wrath of your brother ...'

Louis made a gesture of contemptuous dismissal.

'And of Charles of Durazzo,' Catherine continued. 'To whom Robert has undoubtedly fled for support.'

'Do you think I am the least afraid of Charles, madame?' Louis demanded.

'Of course I do not. Nor would I fear for you, could you meet him sword in hand. But Charles fights with other weapons. And alas ...' she sighed. 'He has too many other weapons with which to fight.'

Louis, of course, knew nothing of the conspiracy to murder Prince Andrew, and clearly did not understand his mother's meaning. I, alas, understood it too well, and if Joanna affected to enjoy her husband's confidence, and Cancia gave one of her merry peals of laughter, I felt as if an icy hand had taken hold of my heart.

111

CHAPTER 4

For a season we were happy. As nothing seemed to be evolving from Charles of Durazzo's hatred, or Robert of Constantinople's anger, we allowed ourselves to be lulled into a false sense of security. We did not understand that the wheels of justice grind very slowly, especially where royalty is concerned. There can be no doubt that even before Joanna's marriage to Louis of Tarento, Charles had submitted to Avignon the evidence he had gathered, and was awaiting only the official command of the Pope to proceed against the murderers.

But His Holiness had a great deal to consider, the most important being, naturally, how he might best benefit from this sorry affair. In this regard he could not help but consider that he was an exile from the tumult that was Rome, and was, as I have mentioned, no more than a tenant of the Crown of Naples.

Clearly, with a view to his own security, it mattered a great deal to the pontiff who occupied that throne, and he thus had to weigh the personality of Charles of Durazzo, who sought it, a prince who, however innocent – at least in the matter of Prince Andrew's death – and indeed worthy of a crown, was also a man of strong passions and the most unmitigated arrogance, against that of Joanna, who held it, and who, however guilty, was still not yet twenty-one, a pliantly beautiful young girl, and one who, if saved from the awful consequences of her deed, would necessarily prove grateful to her benefactor. These cogitations occupied the Holy Father for some time.

Time we put to good use. Joanna duly gave birth to a handsome son, whom amidst great rejoicings she named Charles Martel, after Prince Andrew's father, no doubt in some hope of appeasing King Louis of Hungary, Andrew's brother, who remained a brooding shadow on the northeastern horizon.

Cancia duly gave birth to a son, named John, or Giovanni, and promptly got herself pregnant again, as usual by the Count of Terlizzi.

I gave birth to a daughter, whom I named Lucia, and Alberto and I drank a bottle of wine together.

Marie, Duchess of Calabria, also gave birth to a daughter, whom she named Margaret.

Catherine, Empress of Constantinople, and mother-in-law of the Queen, stalked the Castel Nuovo, and indeed, all Naples, as if she were the Queen herself.

Her son Robert sulked.

Her other son was soon reconciled to Louis's coup.

Louis himself played the role king-consort to perfection, riding amongst the people with his visor lowered so that they might admire his handsome, smiling face, distributing presents, jousting in the lists, and making my mistress the happiest woman on earth. A fulsome, ebullient man, he even found some time for me when Her Grace was indisposed, to my great gratification. But, like Joanna, I did not again conceive, no doubt fortunately.

Donna Filippa of Catania blossomed in a manner second only to the Empress, and her son Roberto swaggered about his duties like the veriest bravo.

The people cheered their Queen and were happy.

And Charles of Durazzo shut himself up in his palazzo and waited for word from Avignon. This arrived in the middle of June, 1346.

At this time, and in view of the momentous, not to say

earth-shattering events which were to overtake us during the next two years, it may be of advantage for me to delineate the picture presented by Europe, and indeed the world, as the fourteenth century approached its middle.

If we properly accept that the centre of the world is situated in Rome, we find that the Papal States are shrunk to a very small enclave in the centre of Italy, and, of course, as I have mentioned, the popes themselves had found cause to flee the turbulence of the Roman mob and seek refuge in Avignon, where, as will be related later, they were forced to confront the hardly lesser peril of the ambitions of the French monarchy, but where they could appeal for the support of their landlord, who was now their landlady, the Queen of Naples.

Naples itself occupied the lower third of the peninsula, but, again as I have related, Sicily had been lost to the Angevin family, and was part of the Kingdom of Aragon, ruled at this time by King Pedro IV, a man who was facing rebellious barons at home, but was certainly a major factor in Mediterranean affairs.

North of Rome, there had arisen several duchies, or republics, call them what you will. Siena, Florence and Genoa were unashamedly republics; Milan, Mantua, Ferrara and Savoy took the more aristocratic path, and Venice was Venice, an accumulation of ambitious pirates prepared to defy pope and layman in their quest for empire and wealth.

Of these places, it is only necessary to note that Florence was in a condition of financial collapse; Milan was controlled by three villainous brothers named Visconti, and the rest were regarded by most sensible human beings as irrelevant ... not altogether correctly.

Moving north from Italy brings us to the Holy Roman Empire, which was at this time claimed by the Emperor Louis IV, of the House of Wittelsbach. His claim was, however, disputed by a prince known as Frederick the Handsome – why entirely escapes me – of the House of

Habsburg. Frederick had been supported by the Papacy, and although the civil war he had inspired had long since collapsed in a welter of blood, the Pope and the Emperor were still mortal enemies.

If we move due north from the Empire, we find that Denmark was being ruled, and well ruled, by Waldemar IV, whose daughter Margaret was to unite all Scandinavia. But at this time Sweden was a separate country, ruled by Magnus II, a nonentity, whose nickname was Smek.

If we now turn west, we come of course to the British Isles. Of these, Ireland was in its habitual state of anarchy, Scotland was hardly better off under the rule of David II Bruce, son of the great victor of Bannockburn, but a quite incompetent king, while England was beginning its march to glory behind its youthful monarch, Edward III. I must be frank and admit that in the spring of 1346 the eventual outcome of this march was difficult to discern. Our King, having come to the throne in what had best be described as murky circumstances, had elected to go to war with France, over an issue I shall prefer to discuss later, when, owing to matters beyond my control I became involved.

Thus far, Edward had managed to gain a great naval victory off the coast of Flanders, at Sluis, and ravaged northern and eastern France to no great effect; his immense victory at Crécy was to come later in this very year of 1346, but this was not an event anyone could foresee in the spring. At that moment, it was the news that he had repudiated his debts to the Florentine bankers which was on everyone's lips, and which was contributing in no small degree to the turmoil in Italy.

France was being ruled by Philip VI, a cousin of our Edward, who actually had no legitimate claim to the throne at all. Again, I shall enter into this tangled web of legal and illegal argument in its proper place; for the moment it is only necessary to observe that Philip was a Valois, and therefore a close relative of Joanna's aunt Catherine. And about as unscrupulous.

The Iberian Peninsula continued to be split up into several small kingdoms. I have already mentioned Aragon. Castile was under the rule of the valiant Alfonso XI, who a few years earlier had gained a great victory over the Moors at the River Salado, and was firmly established as a national hero. This business with the Moors – trying to get as much of Spain as possible back out of their hands – naturally occupied most of his time. On the far side of the peninsula Portugal was ruled by Alfonso IV, known as the Brave, although the soubriquet may have been more properly earned in the bedchamber, for his court was a scandal, bedevilled principally by his son and heir's infatuation with the beautiful Inez de Castro.

South of the Tagus, the Moorish kingdoms reigned supreme.

Thus Western Europe. If we turn east, we will discover that John of Luxemburg, King of Bohemia and son of the late Emperor Henry VII, was busily dying, to be succeeded by his son Charles I. The Swiss were as usual revolting against their Austrian masters. The Poles were ruled by Casimir III, known as the Great, Lithuania by some heathen named Olgerd, Russia by a Tatar puppet named Simeon. Most important to us, of course, was the Kingdom of Hungary, where Andrew's brother Louis was fast establishing himself, and whence we had to anticipate some friction in the near future.

Surrounding the Christian enclave of Europe were vast, dark masses. Not only southern Spain, but all the southern shores of the Mediterranean Sea, were in the hands of the Arabs, as my unhappy family had found out to their cost. No doubt fortunately for Europe, the Arabs, while paying lip service to the authority of the Caliph of Baghdad, much as we Christians paid lip service to the authority of the Pope in Avignon, were continually engaged in a series of internecine squabbles amongst themselves, again entirely in the manner of Christendom.

Far more sinister, and threatening the entire continent,

was the burgeoning might of the Ottoman Turks. These fierce horsemen from the steppes of Central Asia had destroyed the Seljuk Empire and had for some years been nibbling away at the vast possessions of the Byzantine Emperor, John V. In this they were assisted by the disunity within Byzantium itself, and indeed only the previous year Ottoman forces had been invited to cross the Bosphorus to assist the army of John Cantacazune, who was opposing the Emperor in civil war.

We could only hope and pray that these events, so close to his eastern border, would occupy the mind, and the army, of King Louis. In this we were wrong, to the cost of both ourselves, and, as it has turned out, of Europe.

The Papal Bull, which was dated 2 June, was actually directed to Bertram de Baux, Count of Monte-Scaglioso, Lord Justiciary of the Kingdom, and commanded him to proceed with the utmost vigour against those found guilty of Prince Andrew's murder, His Holiness at the same time pronouncing anathema against them.

This news caused a great consternation, as might be supposed, especially as Bertram let it be known that he was already in possession of the names of two of the conspirators. Joanna all but fainted when she heard this, and the rest of us were all in a twitter, the more so as Prince Louis was quite unaware of the cause of our agitation, and could make nothing of it.

We in turn were unaware that Clement had added a secret note to his Bull, for the eyes of Bertram alone, which commanded him that under no circumstances were the Queen or any of the Princes of the blood to be charged or even implicated: His Holiness would punish them in his own good time and fashion. Had we known this we would have been less terrified.

As it was, Joanna was in no state to attend the preliminary hearing, so I went in her stead, obliged to abandon my domestic duties and the care of the young Prince and my own darling Lucia, to both of whom I was nursemaid – I had indeed given the little boy my own teat when his royal mother was otherwise engaged, as I am mammarily very well endowed and perfectly able to accommodate two hungry mouths at the same time – to mingle with the throng which crowded the great courtroom, on which a platform had been raised, where sat all the high nobles and dignitaries of the Kingdom, both Louis and Charles amongst them, looking most severe.

Into the hall were marched Tomasso Pace and Nicolas di Melazzo. This was as to be expected, as they were the least able to pronounce their innocence with any conviction, but it is now clear to me that Master de Baux had undoubtedly been in conference with Charles of Durazzo before convening the proceedings, as – in view of his secret instructions from Avignon – how else could he be certain that the two accused would not shout the name of the Queen before anyone who would listen?

Clearly Nicolas di Melazzo was Charles's creature, but in the interim Tomasso had clearly been equally suborned, and the two men promised a quick and hopefully painless death were they to speak as commanded – as against the horrifying tortures to which they would otherwise be subjected, and which would most certainly involve their families as well.

In this, of course, Charles was himself being duped. He had every intention of bringing down the Queen, and while he had agreed readily that it would be unseemly to have her accused by two commoners – who would hardly be believed in any event – he had no doubt at all that when those whom his servants were going to accuse were shown the iron and the rope, the Queen's implication would come as a matter of course, and from the mouths of her nobles and intimates. In this he was reckoning without the judicial skill of Bertram de Baux.

The two accused pleaded their innocence in the first instance, not unnaturally, knowing full well that they

118

would in any event be commanded to undergo the preliminary torture as a test of the truth of their claim. They were thus removed to the public square, but as they left the court, I observed Nicolas give Charles a meaningful stare, to which the Duke of Calabria replied with a brief nod. I did not then understand the meaning behind the exchange, but I now realise that the lawyer was but seeking confirmation of his instructions, and confirmation also that the Duke would abide by his bargain to protect his victim's wife and children.

Then I was running as hard as anyone to gain the square to witness the spectacle, for it is a lamentable fact that the human senses are more stirred by the prospect of seeing another suffer than from any other cause. I arrived panting, and having to share the square with it seemed everyone else in Naples, all anxious to watch the two unfortunates torn limb from limb.

In the centre of the square a gallows had been erected, and from this ropes were suspended by the hooded executioners. Their intention was not, of course, to hang Tomasso and Nicolas; such a method of execution was considered too simple and painless for miscreants, and in any event they had not yet been sentenced. But they were, as a preliminary to their future punishment, to undergo the ordeal of the strappado, in which the victim's wrists are tied behind him, and attached to a rope; this rope is then hoisted to whatever height is desired by the executioner, and let fall again. The resulting jerk can cause extreme discomfort from a few feet; can entirely dislocate both shoulders from a few feet more; and can tear a man's arms out of their sockets from an extreme height. The gallows this day was certainly high enough to accomplish this last effect.

But it was all play acting. Tomasso had no sooner been attached to the fatal cord than he announced that he would change his plea to guilty, and confess everything. This caused a great to-do, mainly of disappointment, as

119

the mob found itself robbed of its entertainment. Indeed, the spectators surged forward as if about to take matters into their own hands. I went with them, partly because there was no way I could stop myself being carried along by the human wave, and partly because I was in a quandary, as, not being in the confidence of Bertram de Baux, I could foresee the most dreadful consequences were Tomasso really to reveal all.

Perhaps I had some idea such as begging him to keep silent for love of me, no matter what suffering was thereby involved – I was very young and given to romantic notions. However, the guards were numerous enough to repel the riot, and the two prisoners were both hurried away, by different streets. I decided to follow Tomasso, and, as the crowd lost interest and dwindled, found myself almost alone. Almost. My companion was none other than the Count of Terlizzi, who had with him four of his servants.

'You are after the same game as I, Richilde,' he said. 'But you may leave it to me.'

I had no idea of what he was speaking, and could only wait and watch, as a moment later we caught up with the soldiers.

'Hold there,' said the Count.

Naturally they obeyed so high a nobleman.

'I would speak with this fellow,' Terlizzi said.

'I am ordered to take him back before the Justiciary, monsignore,' the sergeant protested.

'And so you shall. But I would speak with him first. I am instructed by the Grand Seneschal.' His brother-in-law, of course.

The sergeant hesitated, and bowed to authority. 'As you wish, monsignore.'

'I will not be long,' Terlizzi assured him. 'It so happens that this house we are coming to belongs to me, and is at this moment empty. I will just take the prisoner inside for a moment.'

The wretch had timed his intervention to a nicety.

Tomasso did not seem to like this idea. 'I beg of you,' he said to the sergeant. 'Take me to the court.'

'But monsignore wishes a word,' the good sergeant said, clearly confused.

'Inside with him,' Terlizzi commanded his men, who immediately seized poor Tomasso and bundled him into the house. Before I could draw breath the Count had seized my arm and taken me inside as well.

'Monsignore,' I protested. 'I have business elsewhere.'

'This business will not take but a moment,' Terlizzi repeated.

'Richilde,' Tomasso begged. 'Intercede for me, Richilde.'

I was as confused as the sergeant. I could not believe that Terlizzi would dare murder a man who was, so to speak, under the protection of the court, especially when there could be no doubt as to who would have done the deed. And while I was still wondering what it was best to do, the Count acted.

Tomasso, in speaking at all, had made a most dreadful mistake, for now the Count's servants pulled his mouth wider – his hands were still bound behind his back – and squeezed his lower jaw to force him to stick out his tongue, which was then seized. He made a horrible choking sound which changed to an even more horrible howl of anguish as Terlizzi, with a single movement, whipped a razor from his pocket and severed the protruding piece of flesh.

To do this he had to release me, and I needed but one look at Tomasso's ghastly expression, and at the blood frothing from his mouth, to know that I had to get away, and quickly. I darted for the door and regained the street, where the soldiers gazed at me curiously.

'Stop that girl,' Terlizzi commanded, appearing in the doorway.

But I was already past them and running for my life, only pausing at the corner to look back. While the sergeant had other matters to consider.

'Where is my prisoner, monsignore?' he demanded.

'Why, my servants are bringing him now. I have finished my business with him. The poor fellow appears to have bitten his tongue.' Whereupon he set off after me. But I gained the Castel Nuovo before him, and there I supposed I was safe.

Not a bit of it. I was immediately sent out again, to act once more as the Queen's ears, although I told her that it was quite impossible for Tomasso now to denounce anyone. And so it proved. I took my place with the common folk, staring across the courtroom at Terlizzi, who gazed back with a bland expression.

'Now, Master Pace,' said Bertram de Baux, facing the unhappy valet. 'You have promised to make a full and true confession of your part in the murder of Prince Andrew of Hungary, and to establish to the court's satisfaction the names of your accomplices in this dreadful deed. I charge you to speak.'

Tomasso certainly tried. He opened his mouth, but all that issued was a mess of blood and a most unhappy sound. Bertram stared at him in astonishment, as this was not part of the carefully constructed plot between himself and Charles of Durazzo.

'How now,' the Justiciary shouted. 'Speak plain, fellow.'

But try as he might, Tomasso could utter no coherent sound.

'The fellow has lost his tongue,' cried Terlizzi. 'Ha ha ha.'

The laughter became general, and Bertram frowned in frustration.

But now a quiet voice spoke. 'May it please the court, monsignore.'

Heads turned, and the laughter died away as Nicolas di Melazzo stepped forward, his guards at his elbows.

'You may speak, Master di Melazzo,' Bertram said.

'I wish to confess, monsignore, my part in the foul murder of Prince Andrew.'

Consternation.

'Confess, you say?' Bertram feigned surprise. 'Confess? Will you name your accomplices in this terrible deed?'

'Willingly, monsignore.'

'Then do so.'

'Tomasso Pace.'

The spectators growled ominously, as this was obvious.

'The Count of Aire.'

Sensation, and more head turning, but the Count was not in court.

'His son, Bertrand of Artois.'

This was expected, in view of the implication of the father.

'The Counts of Squillace, Mileto and Catanzaro.'

More sensation, as Godfrey di Marsan, Count of Squillace, was of course Admiral of the Kingdom as well as a member of the Council of Regency. He sat, indeed, only a few feet from Bertram de Baux, and stared at Nicolas as if he would have struck him dead with the ferocity of his expression – but he did not move. Mileto and Catanzaro had, like Charles of Artois and Bertrand, prudently absented themselves from the court.

'The Counts of Morcone and Terlizzi,' Nicolas continued.

These two scoundrels gazed at each other in dismay, and Terlizzi made to rise, but the guards on the doors had already drawn their swords.

'Their wives, the Countesses of Morcone and Terlizzi.'

'Foul wretch!' Morcone shouted.

'Continue,' Bertram commanded.

'Donna Filippa di Catania.'

Shouts from the crowd. Donna Filippa was not universally popular.

'Her son, Roberto di Cabane.'

Even louder shouts, for Roberto's arrogance had caused him to be disliked even more than his mother.

'And the woman, Donna Cancia di Reggio.'

123

Bertram de Baux gazed at him. 'Were there no others?'

Nicolas met his gaze. 'No, monsignore. On my oath as a Christian.'

And he was about to die. We can but remember that he had agreed to perjure himself for the sake of his family.

'Very well. You are to be congratulated on your honesty,' Bertram said, blandly. And then pointed. 'Arrest the Count of Squillace, and also the Count of Morcone and the Count of Terlizzi.'

The three men were pinioned before they could attempt to escape.

'I will issue warrants for the arrests of the other named persons,' Bertram announced. 'Master di Melazzo, you and Master Pace deserve well of this court, and I am therefore disposed to leniency. Yet do you stand self-confessed of the crime of murder. Your sentence is that you be taken straightaway to the town square, and there hanged by the neck until you are dead. Bailiffs, carry out the sentence.'

Tomàsso gave a dreadful groan, but Nicolas uttered not a sound. He knew he was indeed receiving a merciful end compared with what was going to happen to his fellow conspirators.

It may have occurred to the impartial onlooker, like myself, that in hanging the accuser before giving any of the accused an opportunity to challenge their denunciation, Monsignore de Baux was stepping outside the accepted tenets of justice, but with the Papal Bull safely in his pocket he was a law unto himself, and of course he had no intention of ever allowing the case to be discussed in open court.

I was now in a considerable dilemma. My duty to my mistress demanded that I hasten back to the Castel Nuovo to warn her, and her ladies, of the sword hanging over their heads. But my duty to my own instincts called me to follow poor Tomasso to his last appointment; he was, after all, an erstwhile lover.

My instincts won, as I reflected that Louis of Tarento had been in court, and, if apparently struck dumb by Nicolas' amazing revelations about such a plot devised by the Queen's own intimates, would soon enough recover and return to inform, if he could not warn, his wife of what had happened.

Thus I ran with the crowd, as Tomasso and Nicolas were stripped and tied to the tails of two horses, thus to be dragged through the streets, bumping and twisting, and bleeding as the stones cut their exposed flesh.

The crowd jeered and hooted, as was their wont, but I was silent, as I stared at the miserable valet, his all flapping in total humiliation, and remembered those occasional evenings we had spent in each other's arms. The poor fellow continued to moan and shriek, unable to articulate. Nicolas remained silent, his eyes tight closed; fortunately his wife and family were not present.

But Charles of Durazzo was, riding in the company of his men, gazing at the lawyer from beneath frowning brows. And then searching the crowd. To my horror, his gaze alighted upon me, and he continued to stare at me for some seconds, obviously reflecting upon the singular fact that I alone of the Queen's intimates had not been named a conspirator by his spy – and turning my knees quite to water.

Then he looked away, for the procession had reached the square, where the same gallows and the same ropes awaited it. The proceedings now were more speedy. Nooses were placed around the necks of the two men, their hands being still bound behind them, and they were hoisted from the platform, while the crows cheered. Their faces turned blue, while their penises rose – as will happen when a man is hanged; I shudder to consider the fate of a woman. But their kicks gradually dwindled, their manhood subsided, and they died.

I reflected that they were only the first two victims of the conspiracy.

*

Poor Tomasso dead, I hurried back to the Castel Nuovo as fast as I could, to find all in a turmoil. I arrived, indeed, almost at the same time as the soldiers sent by Bertram de Baux to arrest Donna Filippa and her brood. There was no denying an authority based on a Papal Bull, and my Alberto had already lowered the drawbridge and permitted the Justiciary's men to enter.

They proceeded straightaway to Joanna's apartments, where Filippa and her daughters, as well as her son, had gathered to hear what a totally confused Prince Louis had to tell them. They were still indeed shrieking their horror at the arrest of Morcone and Terlizzi when the guard arrived, myself at their heels.

Everyone stared at the sergeant, as he read out the names of those under arrest. Then Filippa threw herself at Joanna's feet. 'You must save us, Your Grace,' she begged. 'Only you can do so. And, Your Grace, you have no choice.'

She raised her head as she spoke, to leave no doubt as to the threat her entreaty contained. But Joanna was utterly struck dumb by the catastrophe clouding about her, and the sergeant was in no mood to wait. Donna Filippa was seized and bound like the commonest malefactor, as were her children. Roberto had made the error of attending the Queen unarmed, and was helpless. His sisters screamed their outrage at being manhandled by the rude soldiery. Only Cancia merely smiled. But she had been at the bottle again, and besides, being pregnant, she knew she would survive awhile yet.

Filippa, realising she was going to receive no aid from the Queen, turned to the Prince. 'Monsignore,' she cried. 'We are your wife's servants. We are her responsibility, monsignore. You must save us.'

But Louis was frowning. 'If you are indeed guilty of so hideous a crime, then you deserve to be punished, signora,' he replied sternly.

'But monsignore, you do not understand. You ...'

My heart lurched, as I assumed she was about to reveal all. The sergeant however, had been given his orders by Master de Baux, and before Filippa could say another word a cord had been tied around her mouth, leaving her only able to splutter. The same fate befell the other four, and they were marched off to their dungeon.

The door had barely closed when Joanna gave a little sigh and sank into a chair.

'Quickly, Her Grace has fainted,' Louis snapped. 'Fetch some wine.'

I obeyed, and fed her strong liquids – I felt in need of some myself – while her husband patted her hands.

'I well understand,' he said, 'the shock you must be experiencing, my dearest heart, to learn that you have harboured such vipers in your bosom for so many years. Be sure they will be punished, my own dear wife.'

'Yes,' Joanna said faintly. 'Yes. I really am not well, monsignore, and would retire, if you will permit it.'

'Of course. Shall I send another lady to you?'

'My faithful Richilde will suffice, monsignore. I thank you.'

He left us, and we fled into Joanna's bedchamber, where we hugged each other and the Queen wept most copiously down my neck.

'What am I to do, my dearest friend?' she asked.

'There is naught you can do, Your Grace,' I told her, 'save deny their accusations, when they are made. No one will accept their words against that of the Queen.'

'But they are being punished for carrying out my wishes,' she moaned. 'I cannot just abandon them.'

'Such apparent coldness is a necessary part of being a ruler, Your Grace,' I insisted. 'You are greater than they, because you were born greater. You cannot carelessly plunge into the depths with them. What of your kingdom? Did you not conceive of Prince Andrew's death in order the better to protect your people from the excesses of the Hungarians?'

I doubt that had entered her head at the time, as she had then been concerned only with protecting her own person and that of her lover from the excesses of a single Hungarian, but my exhortation seemed somewhat to calm and relieve her, and I pressed on.

'What of Charles of Durazzo? Would you abandon the kingdom to him?'

'The wretch,' she said, informing me that I was gaining the day.

But I had several more cards to play. 'What of your child, who looks to you to inherit this great office? Will you abandon him? What of Bertrand of Artois, who hides with his father in St Agatha?'

Here I made a mistake, for Joanna frowned. 'Do not mention that faint-hearted poltroon to me,' she said.

I hastened to retrieve my ground. 'Well, then, what of Prince Louis, who loves you more than life itself?'

'It is he who most troubles me. When he learns of what I am accused ...'

'Then will his love be put to the utmost test, Your Grace. I have no doubt it will triumph.'

'If only I knew ... Richilde, should I not go to him now and confess all, and throw myself on his mercy?'

'No, no, Your Grace,' I cried in alarm. 'You must deny, and deny, and deny again. And I will support your denial.'

She hugged me. 'You are the dearest friend I ever had, Richilde. Sometimes I think you are the only friend I ever had. With you at my side I feel strong enough to face tomorrow. But oh, Richilde ... what will tomorrow bring?'

Neither of us slept a wink that night.

Of course the Queen was in no danger at all, thanks to Master de Baux's instructions from Avignon. She was not even in any danger from her husband's consideration of the whole affair, for Louis's love was so great that not even the considerable circumstantial evidence available to suggest that Joanna must at least have been aware of the plot, even if not an actual conspirator, could affect his mind. He did not even find it suspicious that his mother – who with Joanna was the only one involved not yet accused and arrested – should now have left the Castel Nuovo, which she had virtually adopted as her home, and retired to her real home, there to take to her bed with an affected illness.

But we knew none of this, and so at dawn the next morning I was as usual despatched by my mistress to oversee the proceedings, and bring her early warning of any fresh impending catastrophe.

The questioning had been carefully arranged by Master de Baux. It was to take place on board a galley, moored just off the beach, ostensibly so that no attempt could be made to rescue the accused, but in reality so that no spectator could hear what any of the conspirators might say. Additionally to this end, a stout palisade had been erected on the beach, to hold the concourse back from the water, and there was indeed a great concourse. It seemed that every man, woman and child in Naples had assembled to witness the torture, such being the sad inclination of most of us.

Amongst the throng, needless to say, was Charles of Durazzo, splendidly horsed and accoutred, and accompanied by a great retinue of knights and men-at-arms. Today was to be his triumph, as he did not doubt that on the Queen being accused of the murder of her husband by one of her erstwhile accomplices, he, as heir to the throne, would be immediately ordered to arrest her, and this he undoubtedly desired to do more than anything else in the world.

He too had not reckoned with the devious cunning of Bertram de Baux. At eight o'clock, punctually, the gates of the prison were opened, and the four men and three of the four women accused of this heinous crime – Cancia, being pregnant, was not to be exposed to the torture at this time – were brought down to the beach. I was informed by one of the gaolers that they had been confined together during the night, and I shudder to imagine what must have been the tenor of their conversation, and indeed their thoughts, as they gazed upon each other during the midnight hours, and reflected on the terrifying fate which awaited them. Certainly in the cold light of day their faces appeared pale and drawn, and their expressions most pitiable.

Not that they excited any pity in the hearts of those who had assembled to witness their destruction. The mob applauded to see Roberto di Cabane, swarthy and angry of visage, Godfrey di Marsan, aged and trembling, and the Counts of Terlizzi and Morcone, no less terrified and shivering, emerge from the gateway in their shirts, to be hurried through the crowds to stand quivering upon the beach.

The noise grew even louder when Filippa and her two daughters, reduced to their shifts, were similarly led forth. I am bound to confess that I howled myself as loud as any of my companions. This was partly because not to do so might have suggested I sympathised with the miscreants, and indeed I did do so, but it was also partly because all of these people had ill used me in their time, and equally because I saw them as dangers to my mistress and wished only to see them dispatched.

Like Charles of Durazzo, however, I was keenly aware that the moment of crisis had arrived. The prisoners' arms were bound behind them, but there was no restraint upon their tongues, and indeed Filippa, at the least, turned round to face the crowd, and endeavoured to address us. I say endeavoured, for amazingly, no coherent sound could escape her lips, only a high-pitched and totally desperate yammer, and while we still pondered this remarkable lack of articulacy, the prisoners were conveyed up the gang-plank and on to the deck of the galley.

Now the crowd surged right up to the palisade, carrying me with them, and all but broke it down – and crushed me

130

to death – in their anxiety to witness the dreadful deeds which were about to be perpetrated. For the question to be used was that of the chair, than which there can hardly be anything more unpleasant for tender skins to suffer.

This device is a stout iron armchair, comfortable enough to regard from a distance. However, both seat and arms are studded with iron prongs, as well as iron collars and cuffs to restrain the victim, while his ankles are similarly secured to the front legs. Sitting still on these sharp prongs is an impossibility, but of course every movement only makes the discomfort worse, and can soon lead to a penetration of the skin, or one of the natural orifices of the human body, which is followed by extreme discomfort.

Even this, however, is but the beginning of the torture. For underneath the chair, and a part of it, is nothing less than an iron stove, which can be filled with heated coals to make the seat above, prongs and all, red hot. This was the fate which now awaited these erstwhile playmates of mine.

The first to suffer was Roberto, whose shirt was removed and whose naked body clamped into the chair. The fire had already been lit, and his wriggles and screams were dreadful to see and hear, the more so as heat, in the first instance, has an elevating effect upon the male genitals. The crowd roared its pleasure at the spectacle, while Roberto shrieked no doubt a dozen confessions. Yet strange to say, as with Donna Filippa a few minutes before, he seemed incapable of uttering any coherent word.

He did not have to endure his agony very long, as after only about two minutes he was deemed to have admitted all and was removed, to lie writhing and trembling upon the deck while his brother-in-law, the Count of Terlizzi, was inserted in his place.

This worthy, who had so proudly cut the tongue from the mouth of my poor Tomasso, was a shivering jelly of terror before he even reached the chair, and his screams were louder than Roberto's but equally as unintelligible.

131

No doubt it was the sight of Terlizzi, and the memory of Tomasso, that first aroused a dreadful suspicion in my mind, that Monsignore de Baux had taken a leaf from his victim's book, as it were. My suspicions were well founded, as I later learned. Bertram had not removed the tongues of his prisoners: that would have been too blatant an indication that he feared their confessions. He had, however, caused a fishhook to be attached to each tongue, a sufficiently unpleasant concept to be sure, so that although each could scream to his or her heart's content, and a glance into their mouths would reveal no trace of mutilation, yet were they incapable of uttering any sound which could be recognised as a word.

And so they suffered, one after the other, not excluding Filippa and the two countesses, girls not greatly older than myself, forced to expose themselves to the jeers of the mob and to endure the heat of the fire while the prongs ate into their flesh. By the time they too were thrown to the deck to continue writhing in agony I was quite faint, but the crowd had grown even more barbarous, partly because even this insensate mass was beginning to gather that it had in some manner been duped of hearing the confessions, but more certainly because it was now announced that as the accused had all admitted their guilt, there was no need of a further trial and they would all be executed the following day.

Which would, of course, present yet another stirring spectacle.

The prisoners having been returned to their dungeon, unable to stand and still groaning and screaming in their continued agony, my objective was to regain the Castel Nuovo just as rapidly as possible, both to acquaint the Queen with what had happened, and to have a glass of wine, or perhaps a bottle of wine, and try to shut out the horrid scene I had just witnessed.

But there was another in the crowd who had been as confounded as I by the inability of the prisoners to accuse the Queen, and who, like myself, had slowly come to understand that they were being prevented from doing so. Charles of Durazzo was not the man to be so cheated of his prey, and as I pushed my way through the excited people I became aware that he was seeking me, standing in his stirrups to oversee the throng.

Naturally I redoubled my efforts to gain safety, but in doing so wandered down a side street which was deserted save for three men. These blocked my path, and I realised they were my enemies.

I turned to run the other way, and found myself in the embrace of three more men, who had apparently been following me, and were well equipped for their task, as they produced a black cloak which they dropped over my head before I could draw breath, and which was then secured tightly round my waist, leaving my head and arms completely encased. I was then lifted from the ground, thrown across someone's shoulder, and carried off.

My position was indecorous – the man's arm was round the back of my thighs to keep me in place – unpleasant, as his shoulder ate into my stomach, dangerous, as I had great difficulty in preventing myself from sucking the material of the cloak against my nostrils and thus suffocating, and frightening, as I could not imagine what terrible fate might be in store for me.

My journey, however, was not a long one. Gates clanged open and then shut, voices spoke, hardly discernible to me inside the cloak, and I felt myself being carried downwards. There were more questions and commands, another door opened and shut, and I was unceremoniously pitched to the floor, which was of stone and very hard.

The cloak was then taken from my head, and I was able to look around me. I did not like what I saw. I was in a dungeon, beneath, I could not doubt, the palazzo of Durazzo, and there were three men standing over me.

They wore black hoods, and were of a very sinister cast. Of an even more sinister cast, however, were the various

133

objects which the room contained, illuminated by the two torches which guttered from their sconces on the walls. I could not make out everything, although I could have no doubt that they were all unpleasant, but my attention was most certainly drawn to the rack, which in this instance was composed of a high, stout ladder leaned against the far wall, at the foot of which were the drum and wheel which would draw the victim's body beyond its natural limits.

I swallowed, and sat up, and crossed myself, while the men watched me, and had reached my knees when an inner door opened, and Charles himself entered.

'Praying?' he inquired.

'Should I not be, monsignore?' I asked, as boldly as I could, even if I suspected that within a few minutes I should be shrieking my lungs away.

'I doubt it will do you much good,' he remarked, coming closer. 'But you remain on your knees for the time being. I have some questions to put to you.'

'Questions I will willingly answer, monsignore, providing I know the answers. There was no necessity to have me abducted and manhandled.'

'You think not? And will you answer me truthfully, my pretty slave?'

'As God is my witness,' I assured him. I had no doubt that He would forgive me any slight misdemeanours.

'You were at the shore,' Charles said. 'I saw you there. What thought you of those events?'

'My heart bled for those poor people, monsignore.'

'As it should, when you could soon be sharing their fates.'

'I, monsignore? I am accused of nothing. I am guilty of nothing.'

'Ha! We shall soon discover the truth of that. Did it not occur to you that those felons were unable to speak?'

'Nothing occurred to me, monsignore, save to wonder at their agony.' If one believes in a forgiving God, one must

134

give Him something to forgive, from time to time.

Another long stare. Then he said, 'You are the Queen's creature.'

'I am her servant, monsignore,' I corrected.

'She confides in you, all things.'

'Would that were so, monsignore.'

'Don't fence with me, Richilde. You know of her guilt.'

'Of her guilt, monsignore?'

'Of the murder of her husband. You were there. You remained secreted in her chamber for several hours after the deed. I have this on the authority of the monks themselves.'

'Indeed I was there, monsignore. And terrified out of my wits. As was Her Grace. We shared the opinion that the assassins meant to take our lives as well, and so remained in her bed until we thought it was safe to venture forth.'

'You dare to lie to me?'

'I dare only to speak the truth, monsignore.'

It is axiomatic that when one begins to lie, one must do so with utter conviction, and, if necessary, a constantly growing repertoire.

'We shall see,' Charles said. 'We shall see.' He pointed at his minions. 'Put her on the ladder.'

I opened my mouth to protest, but was seized so roughly I could not speak. My clothes were torn from my body in a most indecent way, the scoundrels finding every opportunity to handle me in even my most private places, and then I was carried to the rack. I endeavoured to fight them, but they were far too strong for me, and indeed my feeble wriggling seemed merely to amuse them.

One of the men climbed the ladder before me, and the other two held me up, so that the rope could be secured to my wrists. A turn of the pulley and I was suspended there, for all the world like a side of beef. My toes immediately found one of the lower rungs to take some of the pressure from my wrists and shoulders, but before I could enjoy this temporary respite my ankles were brought together and also secured. I dared not look down, but I knew that I was now attached to the wheel itself, and that the next time the pulley turned, I would endure excruciating agony.

In this position, the most unpleasant any human being can find himself or herself in, but the more so for a woman when entirely in the company of men, I attempted to prepare myself for the coming ordeal, and found myself staring at Charles, who had come round beneath the ladder, where it leaned against the wall, to look at me through the rungs against which I was resting. And indeed he was doing more than just inspecting my face, for the rest of me was of course clearly visible save for the half dozen inconsequent slats of wood.

Charles had never seen me naked before, and I was conscious that he liked what he was looking at.

'It would be a tragedy to destroy so much beauty,' he said. 'Come, confess to me your mistress's guilt. You will set it down on paper, and will be exempt from punishment yourself. I give you my word on this. More, I will make you my slave in turn. You will find ministering to me vastly more enjoyable than ministering to Joanna, I'll wager.'

'I can never desert my mistress, monsignore,' I said. Even had I been prepared to do so, I knew that his promises were worth so much air; once I had made a written accusation against Joanna, the sooner I was dispensed with the better, so that I could never change my testimony.

If I was to die in any event, there seemed little point in compromising my honour as well.

'Do you suppose you can defy me?' Charles asked. 'You, a chit of a girl, and a slave into the bargain? Tickle her up,' he told his minions.

I did not know what he had in mind, and was taken by surprise when a cane slashed across my buttocks. For a moment I was too surprised to utter a sound, then the pain seemed to sear right through my groin, and I threw back my head and screamed my loudest. My cry seemed to inspire the scoundrels, and I was hit I think five more times – after the first two I lost count. Suspended as I was, from both ends as it were, there was no way I could avoid the blows, although I attempted to do so by twisting my body from side to side, all the while screaming my lungs dry.

These contortions seemed to please Charles greatly, and indeed he put his hands through the rungs to hold my breasts while I seethed to and fro.

After the blows ceased, the pain continued, and tears flooded down my face, half obscured by my hair, which had also flopped in front. This was now removed by Charles' hand, quite tenderly, so that he could see me the better.

'Are you ready to reconsider?' he asked. 'You have but to sign the paper. I will write down all that is necessary.'

'My mistress is innocent of any wrongdoing,' I sobbed. 'As am I.' Thus telling at least half a truth.

His fingers twined in the hair he had just been stroking, and he pulled it, and my face, through the rungs. 'Stupid girl,' he said. 'Do you not realise I can destroy you?'

'I will put my trust in God, monsignore,' I said, managing to reduce my tears to a sniff; I would undoubtedly need them again shortly.

'God,' he sneered. 'He has no compassion for murderesses.' He snapped his fingers. 'The pear.'

One of the robed men hurried forward with a small object, and I caught my breath, for I recognised it. It was indeed shaped like a large pear, but was made of two pieces of wood, which fitted closely together when in repose, as it were, but were connected by a steel spring, which was worked by a simple key that protruded from the bottom of this fearsome fruit. When this key was turned, the two halves of the pear were gradually forced apart – they could be separated to a width of some six inches.

The principal use of this horrid device was for gagging;

137

introduced into the mouth and then expanded, it would hold the jaws so far apart that any sound other than a gurgle at the back of the throat would be impossible.

However, I knew that it could also be used for more destructive purposes, as the mouth is not the only orifice in the human body; inserted into the anus or the vagina, and then opened to its fullest extent, the pear could leave its victim incapable of performing any natural function for a very long time, if not forever. As it was surely not Charles' intention to prevent me from speaking, I therefore feared the very worst, and found myself trembling like a jelly as he held it in front of my eyes.

'Now,' he said, having observed my reaction. 'Do you wish to suffer the pear? I do assure you that a brief visit from it will ruin all of your prospects for future joy. Would you not prefer to sign the statement I have prepared?'

I was in a terrible predicament. I knew the Queen was guilty, and further to defend her was to risk the loss of all my attributes as a woman, which, after all, was all I had to sustain myself. And yet I also knew that I must defy this vicious creature, that it would be better to live without comfort for the rest of my days rather than surrender to him, and see the only person on earth who had ever dealt me pure kindness condemned as a murderess.

'I cannot accuse an innocent person,' I said. 'I will not.'

He stared at me, then reached through the rungs and squeezed my breasts most angrily, causing me to cry out again in pain. Then he said, 'Prepare her.'

The preparations necessary to insert the pear are perhaps more unpleasant – they are certainly more humiliating – than receiving the dread object itself.

Charles' minions busied themselves about my body, which, it must be remembered, was already quite naked, with great glee. My ankles were released from the rope holding them to the rung, so that my knees could be carried, one at a time, as high as possible without actually bending my back, one to each side of the ladder. Ropes

138

were then secured under my knees and to the rungs above, to hold them in position. Other ropes were passed around my thighs, where they joined my body, and these were secured to the outer edge of the drum and drawn tight. Then two more ropes were attached to my ankles, and similarly secured.

So there I was, hanging by my wrists and knees, but with my thighs and ankles pulled down to leave me trussed like a chicken ready for the oven, while my thighs were at the same time being pulled so far apart that I more resembled a frog on a windowpane.

In this position, while I was virtually unable to move, every aperture in my body was extended as wide as possible ... including my mouth, as, assuming I was about to be destroyed, I felt nothing was to be lost in again screaming my loudest.

Charles had moved round to the back of me to oversee these proceedings. Now, through my screams, I heard him telling his people to leave. Clearly he did not wish to share the pleasure of inserting and expanding the pear with anyone. A moment later the door had clanged shut and the Duke of Calabria and I were alone. I could of course twist my head – it was the only part of me that could move – but I could not see behind me, and indeed I was reluctant to discover just what he intended. I abandoned screaming, because I had run out of breath, and kept trying to tense my muscles to resist any attempt at entry, but with no success as they were so distended, and thus awaited with trembling horror the inserting of the wooden tormentor.

When I felt his hands on my buttocks I screamed again, and a moment later, as his fingers explored my privities. Now I knew the orifice he intended to assault, and found that prospect even more horrifying than the alternative. Then I felt the pear itself. However, it was different to what I had expected, although hard enough.

It embedded itself in me, and I was expecting, in an

agony of mental torment, the slow expansion which would forever rob me of the joys of the flesh – when I realised that I was actually enjoying the joys of the flesh at that moment, that the pear was made of flesh itself, and that Charles of Durazzo was grunting and sighing into my hair, in which he had twined a hand to help sustain himself on the ladder, but which was pulling my head back so as nearly to break my neck.

The wretch, so to mistreat a helpless woman, especially if he did intend to torture me afterwards.

But for the time being he was totally occupied with thrusting and gasping, and it was a brief period before he flooded me with wet heat, and then subsided down the ladder, leaving me seething with dissatisfaction and concerned about the coming moments.

For several moments nothing happened at all. Then I felt him on the ladder again, and my limbs were released and fell back into place. I thus hung from my wrists, but he now grasped my feet and placed them on the appropriate rungs, so as to take the weight from my arms, and then released those arms themselves. I wrapped them around the ladder to prevent myself from falling, while I massaged them together, for the returning blood was like a succession of pins being thrust into my flesh.

Thought was beyond me.

And perhaps Charles as well. 'You are a faithful slave,' he remarked. 'Too faithful to serve such a creature as your mistress. But as you have chosen her, return to her. Only remember that when she falls, as fall she will, you will tumble at her side. Now begone.'

Prophetic words, but none I was prepared to notice at that moment. Still unable properly to grasp that all my organs remained in one piece, I descended the ladder and with trembling fingers picked up my gown. I dared not look at him. Indeed, I had no wish to. My thoughts were entirely concentrated upon gaining the street before he changed his mind or revealed that he was but playing a trick upon me. But a few moments later I was hurrying for the Castel Nuovo just as fast as my shaking legs could carry me.

It was of course necessary to relate my adventure to Joanna, who had been beside herself with worry as to my fate when I did not return in time for dinner. I gnawed a cold chicken bone and gulped down some wine while explaining what had happened to me. She was intensely interested, and made me recall every single thing that had occurred, being most keen on ascertaining whether Charles had any skill as a lover.

Well, as to that, I could not tell her more than that he was well endowed and impatient. For the rest he had revealed absolutely nothing of the lover and a great deal of the lusting brute.

'Oh, the wretch!' the Queen exclaimed. 'And he is my appointed heir. That can never be.'

It seemed to me that she was jealous ... of a slave? But I was also alarmed, as I concluded she was again plotting murder – and Charles of Durazzo was a very different kettle of fish to Andrew of Hungary.

'But those poor people,' Joanna continued. 'Louis has told me how they suffered and shrieked, but made no denunciations, of anyone. No one can understand it. Neither can I, however much I am relieved by it. Can I have misjudged Filippa and Roberto all of these years? Are they truly my faithful friends?'

I let her suppose so, as it seemed important to her. For my part, I had no desire ever to leave the castle again, or at least until my senses should have recovered from their assault by the Duke of Calabria.

I was also concerned lest Alberto should learn of my experience, for he was a confoundedly jealous fellow and might well have offered his services to the Queen for some dark deed if he became aware that I had been raped.

But truly, a slave has no rest, and at dawn next morning

I was aroused from the bed I shared with my precious Lucia by Joanna herself.

'I must learn of their final moments,' she told me.

'Will not the Prince attend the executions?' I asked.

'No doubt, but Louis conceives that I am a young and innocent girl whose ears are not to be assailed by tales of horror.'

This was a natural error for the Prince to make, for Joanna, especially in *déshabillé*, as she was now, certainly looked like the youngest and most innocent girl in the world. As well as the most beautiful. I sighed, and set out to obey my mistress's command, aware that I was going to have my senses assailed all over again.

It is an unfortunate fact that the human animal is the most savage in existence. What is even more unfortunate is that man endeavours to conceal this consuming lust for death and destruction beneath a veneer of culture, of religious justification, of mock pity.

While all the time intending to make his victims suffer to the utmost of his ingenuity.

People of course vary in their attitudes to these matters. In England, I may claim that we are as humane as any. The miscreant found guilty of treason is sent to be hanged, to be sure, but he is taken down before death. He is then stretched upon the floor of the gallows and his privities cut off, his stomach slit open and his intestines exposed. This is no doubt as painful as it is humiliating, but no sooner is this done than his head is cut off as well. The subsequent quartering of his body and its exposure in various parts of the kingdom is surely meaningless to him however distressing it may be to his relations. And – this is an important point – this unfortunate end is never perpetrated on a female. Of course it is impossible to remove that which does not exist, but for the rest it would still be an unhappy end. In my country, however, respect for feminine modesty is still regarded as worth preserving.

Female criminals are hanged or burned, or, if they are great ladies, beheaded, without any of the unseemly exposure of their persons men are forced to suffer.

Not so in Naples, or indeed, I have heard, anywhere in the warmer climes. Indeed, it seems to me that the Neapolitan attitude to execution indicates some serious religious doubts, as the principle appears to be that the victims must be made to suffer as much as possible on earth just in case Lucifer is in a merciful mood when they reach the other side.

There is another aspect of the situation in these southern climes which is disturbing. It will have been noticed that Donna Filippa and her cohorts were being sent to execution without the semblance of a trial, upon the deposition of a single witness, Nicolas di Melazzo – who had himself been a party to their conspiracy – and without a word being offered in their defence by any of the many learned lawyers who abounded in the city.

In England this would have been impossible. No testimony would have been accepted without independent support, and the accused would have had the right to challenge, through their advocates, the evidence against them before a jury of twelve of their peers. Whether this would have availed them anything of value I cannot say. But they would have had that privilege.

Bertram de Baux had here acted as accuser, judge, and jury, safe in his possession of the fatal Bull. And so without, due to his precautions, having actually uttered a word in their defences, or even being allowed to deny the crime of which they were accused, the seven victims were dragged to their dooms. In fact there were eight, for the long arm of the law had also reached out to snatch Raimondo Pace, brother of my poor Tomasso.

Joanna despatched me from the castle at dawn, so that I should be able to oversee the entire proceedings. But she might as well have let me sleep in until mid-morning, for it was noon before the gates of the prison swung open. By then the crowd, and there were many thousands present, animated at once by the heat of the sun and by their desire to see the once mighty fallen – as well as by the consummation of a vast quantity of wine – were so many ravening beasts, and when the victims did appear they were greeted with a roar which sent the seagulls soaring away from the Mole.

First appeared a triple row of horsemen, in full armour, with visors lowered and lances at the rest. Then came the carts containing the victims, who lay, stripped and gagged, with their hands bound behind their backs, so as to leave them helpless before the black-hooded torturers, two of whom accompanied each cart, with orders, as I have indicated, to cause their victims the maximum misery before the pyre was reached. This had already been lit, and great clouds of smoke were seeking the skies above Naples, accompanied on their way by the cheers of the crowd.

The first cart contained Donna Filippa di Cabane. Her legs were also bound, and she lay on her belly, and, thus helpless, was scourged by her two tormentors, with iron-tipped whips, blow after blow, so that blood flew from her lacerated flesh and even through the gag she uttered the most heart-rending shrieks.

In the second cart were to be found the Countesses of Terlizzi and Morcone, both delightfully attractive damsels only a few years older than myself. Moaning and squirming with terror, they were greeted by the crowd with even louder shouts of approbation than their mother, especially when it was observed that their punishment was to be even more severe. For the two men in the cart with them were armed with razors, with which they proceeded to slice portions of flesh from their fair victims, and throw them to the crowd. This was horrifying in the extreme. The bloodthirsty mob soon began to dictate which dainty morsels they most preferred, and when a sliver of nipple or buttock was hurled at them they fought like mad dogs to obtain such a memento of the day's work. Several times I

144

was jostled to the ground, in close proximity to one of these dreadful, bleeding scraps of flesh, as the human animals about me fought for their possession.

So thoroughly was the work done that there seemed little chance that the two girls could still be alive by the time they reached the pyre, on which their mother's body already lay. But when their bleeding carcasses too were cast into that living hell, they yet moved and shrieked. For the ultimate torture still remained to be endured; having deliberately been lit early, the fire had now ceased to smoke, and was nothing but a vast barbeque of glowing coals, so that the miserable carcasses were roasted alive.

The men who followed were similarly maltreated, save that instead of being sliced their flesh was torn with red-hot pincers. The Counts of Terlizzi and Morcone, Godfrey di Marsan, Raimondo Pace, and Roberto di Cabane, my very first lover, saw their manhoods reduced to blistered scabs, as indeed was every other portion of their bodies. Like the women, they screamed and howled, save, I must record, Roberto, who kept sternly silent, even though the executioners paid him especial attention. So much so that I swear he was dead before ever reaching the glowing charcoal.

The crowd remained around the fire for several hours, dancing and chanting, until the flames were finally extinguished, water thrown upon the ashes, and they could rush forward and seek what bones they could find as mementoes of this terrible day. Long before this I had taken myself back to the Castel Nuovo, to tell the Queen what I had seen. Joanna listened in silence, but sweat broke out upon her brow as she realised that, but for the protection granted her by her royal blood, she could have suffered as terrible a fate.

Nor had she yet been absolved by the Pope, to whom, indeed, she had not yet dared apply.

So she shuddered, and held me to her breast, and said, 'Let us pray that the business is now ended.'

As if such a business could ever be ended.

CHAPTER 5

I ndeed, we still had a great deal on our minds. Now that the furore of the trial and execution of the conspirators was behind us – with the exception of Cancia, of course, who remained languishing in gaol to await her fate after the birth of her child – Joanna wrote to Avignon begging His Holiness to exonerate her from all connection with the crime. But we could not forget that Clement had not yet responded to the joint appeal made by Prince Louis and the Queen for an indulgence to permit their marriage to be acceptable to the Church.

These were worrying matters. More immediately to our concern were affairs in Naples. Charles of Durazzo might have so far succumbed to the temptations of my flesh as to let me go, but I was in any event of no account in the great issues to be decided. Charles remained Joanna's appointed heir, and in seeing her emerge free and untainted from the murder of her first husband, he conceived that he had been balked of his prey as well as his rightful position – in more ways than one, for I will swear that Charles would have given a great deal to have his beautiful cousin suspended before him as I had been.

Perhaps he still dreamed of that. Certainly he dreamed of the crown of Naples. And if that crown was not to be his by default, then he determined it would be his by force. He began what was nothing less than a planned takeover of the city. Armed men in his retinue and wearing his colours appeared in all the streets, browbeating the citizens: the only redress was the palazzo of Durazzo – those who sought the Queen's protection suffered the more for it.

This was intolerable, but Charles's men were so numerous the Queen herself had no redress. Fortunately, she was now married, at least physically, to a soldier who was also in every way a man. Louis of Tarento sallied forth at the head of the palace guard, my husband at his shoulder, and confronted a group of men-at-arms wearing the colours of Durazzo. The skirmish was brief, and Louis and Alberto returned in triumph. But the next day they were challenged by a much stronger party, and forced to retreat to the castle.

'My God, my God, we are lost,' Joanna wailed. 'Oh, to have my cousin, and my own sister, treat me so.'

I doubted that poor Marie had any say in what was happening, but kept that opinion to myself.

'Lost, never,' Louis declared. 'Charles has taken the trouble to recruit an army. Well, then, we must do the same. Then we shall see.'

'An army, monsignore, requires money with which to pay for it,' Joanna said dolefully. 'I have none to spare.'

'Ha,' snorted Catherine of Valois, for she had re-appeared in our midst to assume her position as mother of the future King of Naples, now that all those who could bring her down, save only her niece-cum-daughter-in-law, had been safely disposed of. 'You need money? I shall get you money.'

'You, dearest Aunt?' Joanna cried in surprise, for it was well known that the house of Constantinople and Tarento was, to put it mildly, strapped.

'But give me half of your guard, Joanna,' Catherine declared. 'And I will return here before very long with all the riches you can possibly wish.'

And this she did. It was only after her triumph that she told us how it had been accomplished – no doubt she

147

feared that to have done so before setting out might have caused the Queen to demur.

For Catherine's plan was nothing less than to sack the castle of St Agatha, where Charles of Aire, and his son Bertrand – the Queen's erstwhile lover and almost certainly the father of her child – who were of course as guilty a pair of conspirators as Catherine herself, had taken refuge, and from the strong battlements of which they defied all, even Charles of Durazzo. Whether they could have defied the papal anathema is another matter, but they were princes of the blood, and thus definitely excluded from the jurisdiction of Bertram de Baux.

They were not, however, safe from the vicious wiles of Catherine of Constantinople. It must be recalled that this fearsome woman was a Valois, a family which ruled in France with every aspect of ancient tyranny. That, as a Valois, she was also a cousin of Charles and his son – by blood as much as marriage – might well seem to make her crime more heinous – but she was not a woman to let family relations stand in her way.

Charles and Bertrand were naturally taken aback to find their refuge surrounded, not by soldiers of Durazzo, but by those of the Queen herself, and more, to discover in their midst, and apparently in command, the woman who had been the life and soul of the conspiracy. Heralds were despatched to discover the meaning of this demonstration, but Catherine, who was a mistress of the art of dissembling, disavowed any hostile intent towards her dear cousins, claimed that her escort was for her own protection in these parlous times, and but begged an interview with Charles to discuss matters of mutual urgency. As she knew he was confined to his chair with gout, she magnanimously offered to enter the castle and speak with him, accompanied only by her steward, Nicolas Acciajuoli, and ten soldiers.

Charles was naturally relieved to learn he did not have a war on his doorstep, and equally naturally he understood what these matters of mutual urgency had to be. The drawbridge was therefore lowered, and Catherine and her escort were greeted by Bertrand of Artois in person, to be escorted into the presence of his father.

Catherine, a most attractive woman when she cared to exert herself, now threw herself at Charles' feet, and bewailed the fate which had overtaken them. The Count was concerned, and at the same time flattered, that the Empress of Constantinople could think of no one better than himself to approach for a discussion of the situation.

Catherine had a great deal of discussing to do. She could talk the hind legs off any donkey. Thus her visit to Charles gradually extended from a few days into a week, and then into a fortnight. During this time, the weather becoming somewhat inclement, the whole of her force was insensibly admitted into the castle, no one by now having the slightest suspicion of what she intended.

When her entire company was assembled, this dreadful woman threw off the mask. Accompanied by her men, she entered the Count's apartment, herself seized him by the throat while her cohorts presented their swords, and rudely demanded to be told the locality of his treasure – for it was well known that Charles of Aire was a very wealthy man – on pain of being murdered on the instant.

Charles, an elderly fellow infirm in health, was so taken aback by this assault that he could think of nothing better than to fall on his knees and beg Catherine at least to spare the life of his son, who had not yet recovered from the black mood that had followed the murder of Prince Andrew.

This Catherine graciously consented to do, on being given custody of the treasure of Artois. The poor old count showed her where the treasure chest was kept, and a few minutes later Catherine was plunging her arms to her elbows into caskets of pearls, and diamonds and rubies of incalculable value, as well as many other precious and semi-precious stones gleaned over several generations from the dealings of Charles, his father and his grandfather, with Eastern potentates, as they had served the original Charles of Anjou.

The Count now ventured to remind Catherine of her promise.

'His life your son may have,' Catherine told him. 'But not his liberty. He will spend the rest of his life in a dungeon in my castle of Malfi.'

The Count was so stricken by this news that a couple of days later he was found dead, his lips covered with blood-flecked foam to suggest that he had had a fit. Bertrand did not long survive his father; on learning of the Count's death he hanged himself from the bars of his dungeon.

Thus two more of the malefactors perished.

Catherine hurried back to Naples with her ill-gotten gains, and we were also permitted to enjoy the splendour of the heaped jewels. Indeed we were glad to see her. For the most terrible tidings had afflicted us in her absence: Charles of Durazzo, despairing of gaining the advantage over the Queen's party without assistance, had had the temerity to send messengers to Buda, to summon the martial array of King Louis of Hungary, perhaps the most formidable monarch in Europe at that time – I have mentioned that it was in this very year our own Edward III laid claim to the title of the first soldier in Christendom by his victory at Crécy, but this battle had not yet been fought.

Louis indeed had been in quandary since the death of his brother. The ties of blood, to which were added the tears of the Queen of Poland and the curses of Brother Robert, cried out for him to avenge the murder. But to go to war without the sanction of the Pope was to risk excommunication. For a while therefore he had held his hand, being assured from Avignon that the murderers would all be brought to justice. He had in any event been dissatisfied to learn that only the common herd had suffered, for he had his suspicions. Now these suspicions were confirmed by Charles of Durazzo.

Enraged, Louis wrote to the Pope and demanded justice against this 'murderous adulteress' – his words – who sat on the throne of Naples flaunting her evil beauty to the world. Clement, who was pursuing a policy of his own of which we were soon to become aware, replied in a softer tone. He conceded that there had to be grave suspicions concerning Joanna's part in Prince Andrew's death, and he further heartily condemned her immoral behaviour since that sad event, but he reminded King Louis that as the Pope is the fount of all truth and goodness, it was quite impossible for him to take action without the most irrefutable proof that the Queen was indeed guilty.

His Holiness, a very busy man, had undoubtedly forgotten that he had commanded the execution of the only people who could have provided such proof, and equally that towards those unfortunates he had behaved with very little truth and even less goodness.

He had also, it seemed to Louis, left the matter open-ended, almost inviting the injured brother to secure, if he could, the proof of the Queen's implication in his brother's death. This was of course absolutely true – His Holiness was steadfastly pursuing his master plan, which he now saw developing entirely as he had foreseen. For Louis, sure that he would not now incur the Papal wrath, set his vast army in motion. Had he led it against the infidel Turks, who were at that very moment beginning their long and successful invasion of Eastern Europe, it might have served history better. He might even have lost his head, as so many of his descendants were to do when endeavouring to stem the tide of the Crescent.

Instead, he marched on Naples. With total success. Joanna was terrified out of her wits, and hastily despatched a letter to her erstwhile brother-in-law, swearing her innocence – like me she had a sublime faith in the forgiveness of God – and begging him to abandon his warlike demeanour.

151

King Louis' reply was brief and disappointing. 'Madame,' he wrote, 'your disorderly life, and your assumption of executive power; your neglect to avenge the death of your husband upon his murderers; your subsequent "marriage"; and the very fact of your seeking to excuse yourself, are sufficient proofs that you were party to that foul deed.'

This epistle sent Joanna into a further paroxysm of fear and despair. Prince Louis, of course, was of a mind to face the foe with all his martial panoply. Unfortunately, this was not a practical solution to our problem, as his panoply mustered less than half the Neapolitan army, the rest being in the pay of Charles of Durazzo, and no one knew which way that particular cat was going to jump.

While we were in a twitter, Catherine of Valois took control, as was her wont, and, as it turned out, for the last time. She was a woman who always went straight to the heart of any problem; if Naples was doomed without the allegiance of Charles, then Charles's allegiance we would have to claim. She persuaded Joanna that there was no alternative, and Joanna, suitably dissembling, although she confessed to me in the privacy of her bedchamber her horror of the deed, agreed to a private meeting with her cousin, in the inner garden of the Castel Nuovo.

There she forswore her own infant son, and formally accepted Charles as heir to the throne. It may be supposed that none of the four people present, myself included, had anything less than total reservations regarding this sacred pact.

Catherine certainly reflected that Charles, should he be defeated by Louis of Hungary, would cease to be a problem, while should he be victorious, he would merely have to be acknowledged until further steps could be taken – she had no intention of allowing her son, and any offspring he and Joanna might have, to be ousted from his proper inheritance.

Joanna's thoughts were of a similar cast.

Charles clearly had every intention, once he had repelled the Hungarian invasion, of assuming at least a regency immediately.

And I had no doubt at all that the wretch – after all that had happened between us he allowed me nothing more than a glance, so anxious was he to get at the business in hand – was going to come to a bad end.

This was to happen sooner than I had expected. For the moment, our problem seemed solved, as Charles and Louis united their forces and marched off to give battle outside the town of Aquila, which was already flying the Hungarian flag.

The evening before our heroes went to war was, as may be imagined, a violent mixture of the sad and the lubricious. It was the first time that Joanna and I were to be separated from our husbands for any length of time, and none of the four of us could estimate what trials might lie ahead, or even if we should ever meet again.

Thus we repaired to our respective chambers to kiss and couple to our hearts' content, until certainly Alberto and I were both sated, and lay together in sweat- and semen-stained exhaustion. It was while in this delicious condition that I was aroused by a shout from my mistress's chamber, which was but a door away from my own.

I was out of bed in an instant, fearing that some catastrophe had happened, and giving a cautious knock to Joanna's door.

'Richilde!' the Queen cried. 'Is that you? Enter!'

I hesitated while I arranged my composure; so hastily had I left my bed that there was in fact nothing more than this to arrange, save that I might pull my hair back from my forehead and shoulders; but then, Prince Louis was no stranger to my femininity.

Thus braced, I opened the door, and gazed at the Queen and her husband.

They were both as naked as I, and therefore entrancing to behold, for they were two of the most beautiful people I have ever seen. Equally they looked as amatorily tousled as Alberto and myself. But equally it was obvious that some point of difference had arisen following the expenditure of their passion.

To my concern, I realised that they were both regarding my nether regions with considerable interest. I have always been proud of my beauty, and between navel and knee I would set myself against any woman in the world, although naturally I would have preferred to do so against a man. Nor, owing to the sad circumstances of my life, even at that early age, have I ever suffered from excessive modesty, and certainly not prurience. If the Queen and Louis were still unsated and wished jointly to assail my body I could but reflect that I was their servant, and must submit to their desires.

However, it now became apparent that they were not admiring me, or even desiring me. Joanna thrust out a long white arm, her finger pointing, and demanded, 'Well?'

Prince Louis got out of bed, a splendid sight. 'Alberto!' he bellowed. 'Alberto!'

'Your Grace!' I gasped. For if I was prepared to expose myself to the royal gaze, I could not conceive of royalty exposing itself to the gaze of a common captain.

The same thought obviously occurred to Joanna, who pulled the sheet around her shoulders, quite ineffectively.

Alberto hurried in, having dragged on his breeches, and carrying a drawn sword, no doubt assuming that some treason was afoot. Now he also stopped in consternation at the sight which met his eyes.

'Alberto! Your wife is not wearing the instrument!' Louis said.

We all looked at me, myself included. Instrument?

Alberto was flushing. 'I had not yet broached the subject, monsignore.'

'You have had an hour to do so,' Louis accused.

'Yes, monsignore. The fact is ...' Alberto gave me an anxious glance.

The fact was that my dear husband was far more afraid of me than of any armed and armoured foe.

'Instrument, husband?' I inquired, speaking as softly as I might.

'Instrument?' Joanna echoed, somewhat more brusquely.

Louis sighed. 'You have sorely compromised our situation, Alberto,' he said. 'But now ... fetch them in.'

Alberto departed back to our bedchamber, while Joanna and I exchanged messages with our eyes.

Alberto returned, carrying in each hand a most peculiar garment, resembling a pair of the drawers men wear when they wish to go swimming in the presence of ladies. That is to say, the garment was designed entirely to encompass and conceal the pubic area of the wearer, leaving apertures for the legs, with a belt to be tightened to make it snug.

But what divided these drawers from any we had ever previously seen was that they were each made of meshed iron.

Our husbands looked at us, at each other, and then at us again. The room was entirely silent, and yet filled with unspoken comment.

'They are recommended by the Holy Church,' Louis ventured.

'Indeed?' Joanna commented.

'They are made of the highest workmanship,' Louis pointed out. 'And are, I am told, most comfortable. In addition, they provide great peace of mind, to both wearer and husband.'

'And considerable inconvenience,' Joanna suggested.

'Not so, Your Grace. If you will examine these cunningly arranged apertures, you will observe that no call of nature need be impeded.' He seized one of the chastity belts from Alberto's hand and carried it to the bed to be examined.

155

When faced with a situation demanding decision, Joanna was seldom hesitant. In fact it can be averred that too often she was a shade *too* decisive. In this case, she realised that the two men whom the pair of us loved more than any others were desirous that we should incarcerate our private parts until their return, and that if we did not humour them they should depart most unhappily – and they had a war to fight and win.

Yet she remained a woman. 'Do you, then, fear for our chastity, monsignore, in your absence?'

Louis was quite tongue-tied with embarrassment. 'The Holy Church ...'

'Recommends these unnatural garments,' Joanna agreed. 'Well, who am I to gainsay the Holy Church. But, monsignore, will you and Captain Cogni also be wearing such garments?'

'I ...' Louis looked at Alberto for assistance.

'It is not possible to ride a horse, Your Grace,' Alberto protested. 'So restrained.'

'Ah!' Joanna said. 'Of course. Very well, Captain. Now, will you insert your wife, so that we may see how it is done?'

So there I was, forced to thrust my legs through the apertures, following which Alberto settled the iron mesh securely around buttock and groin, and then drew the belt, which lay on my hips, just tight enough to make it impossible for me to slide the garment past my thighs. There was a buckle in this belt, which contained a lock. Into this lock my husband now inserted a small key, which he turned with a click, and then stood back to admire his handiwork.

'Is that not comfortable, my dear wife?' he inquired.

Well, I am bound to admit that in this first instance it was not *un*comfortable, as it was a warm night and the metal was cool. But the humiliation of it ...

'Who retains possession of the key?' Joanna asked, still speaking very softly.

'The husband, Your Grace,' Alberto explained, nervously.

'Ah,' Joanna commented again. 'Well, then, Captain, my thanks for your demonstration. You may now withdraw. Richilde, you will assist monsignore.'

Thus we incarcerated the Queen.

Joanna, Catherine of Valois and myself stood at the window of the Castel Nuovo to watch the martial array, the glittering lances, the fluttering pennants, the gleaming armour, the prancing war horses, the gaudily clad esquires, the leather-jerkined crossbowmen, the priests and the farriers and the wagon masters, the women and the children, the dogs and the cattle, the fowls and the sheep and the pigs, which make up the components of an army marching off to war. It was a great and solemn occasion, as well as splendid and invigorating, for every man, as he passed our window, turned to look at the Queen and utter a great shout of loyalty. Joanna glowed with pride and beauty, and that night we attended the cathedral to pray for the success of our armies.

Following which a most singular event occurred. We returned to the castle, supped as usual, and Catherine of Valois departed to her bed. Next morning Joanna and I, curled in each other's arms as was our wont whenever Prince Louis was otherwise engaged, were aroused by one of the Empress's terrified ladies. In *déshabillé* we ran to Catherine's chamber, and there found her stone-cold dead. There was no evidence of any foul play, nor even of any discomfort upon those frozen features, while her ladies swore that she had not called out.

She had simply died.

We buried her immediately, with little pomp, as the country was at war, and her sons were all absent with the army. And truth to tell, when we regained the castle, Joanna and I, both dressed in sombre back, gazed at each other for several moments, then threw back our veils, poured each other a goblet of wine, drank, and embraced.

'She was a dreadful woman,' Joanna said. 'I do not know how she mothered such a son as my own dear prince.' Then she fell sombre again. 'Oh, to know how he is faring at this moment,' she said.

The Queen and I actually had a more pressing concern at that moment: how to rid ourselves of our unwanted encumbrances, and yet be able to don them again when news of our husbands' return was posted.

This requirement therefore precluded the use of axe or sword, even had such a concept been acceptable, in view of the areas of soft white flesh which lay immediately beneath the belt. We thus had to put our heads together.

'Spinelli!' Joanna decided.

She could not have made a better choice. Antonio Spinelli was her private secretary, and therefore entirely to be trusted. He was, of course, a man, which involved a certain risk, but he was past forty, and Joanna and I, just coming up to half of that age, were at a stage of our lives when we could presume he had long lost the sexual urge.

Youth is a time of folly.

Master Spinelli was duly summoned to the royal apartments, and the door was securely locked upon the three of us. Whereupon Joanna explained our situation. She did this without the slightest blush, although my cheeks were burning before she had finished. And were about to burn some more.

'Hm,' Spinelli commented, revealing no other emotion. 'Hm. What is required, Your Grace, is a substitute key.'

'That will be capital,' Joanna agreed. 'Can you make such a key, Antonio?'

'Of course, Your Grace. But ... it will be necessary to take a wax impression of the lock.'

'I understand,' Joanna said. 'Richilde!'

What are slaves for, but to undertake the functions the

mistress does not wish to have to carry out herself? It was therefore necessary for me to lie down on the floor, my skirts pulled to my waist, while Spinelli knelt beside me, and warmed his wax over a candle, in more ways than one, because of course I was totally exposed to his gaze – those apertures intended to permit the bodily functions to proceed unhampered were obviously of sufficient width equally to permit the human gaze to enter, unhampered.

However, the good secretary gave no immediate sign of his proximity to the fount of all enjoyment, save for a slight quickening of his breathing, and a slight trembling of his hand, which caused one of the drops of wax to fall upon my stomach, and me to give a shriek of alarm.

Extracting the wax key, without damaging it, took a good deal longer, and the knave found it necessary to insert his hand inside the belt, while I sucked my belly in as far as I could, and fiddle around for some time before he obtained what he wanted.

Joanna was kneeling on my other side to oversee the proceedings, and clapped her hands for joy when Spinelli announced that he had obtained a perfect specimen, and would return the next day with the key. This he did. The magic metal was inserted into my lock, and a moment later I was free, and the belt itself undamaged.

'Splendid!' Joanna cried. 'Oh, you will be well rewarded, Antonio. Now leave us.'

Spinelli bowed, and withdrew, but not, as it turned out, very far; the rascal suspected what was going to happen next.

Joanna was quite panting with excitement, for if, at this early stage of her life, she had not yet developed the promiscuity which marred her later years, and was solely the result of disappointment in love, I believe she felt the constraints of the belt even more than I – after all, she was a queen. No sooner had Spinelli closed the door behind himself, therefore, than she hoisted her skirts to her waist, and commanded me to release her.

This I attempted to do. But the key would not fit her lock as well as mine.

We gazed at each other in consternation. But there was nothing for it. Spinelli had to be recalled, and Joanna had to submit herself to his examination. Now the poor fellow was positively agitated. Like almost everyone who found himself, or herself, in close proximity to the Queen, he had fallen desperately in love with her. To have her stretched, virtually naked from the waist down, before him was clearly nearly too much for him. I had to assist him in applying the wax, and even so Joanna was forced to shriek in her turn as some of the molten material spotted her flesh.

However it was done at last, I tenderly massaged my mistress back to comfort, the key was produced, and we were both free. This left our minds open to a consideration of how indeed our husbands might be faring.

We had every reason to be concerned, for Louis – with whom of course was my own dear Alberto – was faring very badly indeed. In fact, we all were, although we were not then aware of it. Louis of Hungary, having been granted a free passage through northern Italy by the various pusillanimous states which might have endeavoured to block his march, entered the Kingdom of Naples by way of Puglia. The recent events in Naples – to which must be added ancient hostilities aroused by Charles of Anjou when at his mightiest – had indeed encouraged the northern Italians to applaud the Hungarian army, and two gentlemen of Verona, brothers named Alberto and Martino della Scala – ever to be remembered with infamy – went so far as to supply a regiment of three hundred horse to King Louis' already overwhelming strength.

This was ill news. Worse was to follow. Joanna had persuaded the Papal Legate to accompany her army, and attempt to dissuade King Louis, in the name of the Pope, from advancing further. King Louis naturally refused to be so intimidated, pointing out that His Holiness was aware of his intention and had not himself forbidden it. This fact, of course, the Legate well knew, and there seems little doubt that, acting on instructions from Avignon, he used the occasion of this meeting to give the invader certain information regarding the disposition of the Neapolitan forces.

Our Prince Louis had indeed arranged his people well, to disrupt the passage of the River Volturno at Capua, thus blocking the obvious road for the Hungarians to follow. But apprised of this, his evil namesake turned aside, secretly made his way through the Alife and Morcone Mountains, and arrived at Benevento while our hero of Tarento was still emplaced at Capua.

This was catastrophe; the Hungarian army was already within a day's march of the capital. There was panic in every direction, and Joanna had no choice but to follow the advice tendered by the Legate, who had hurried in advance of King Louis, that she should flee without waiting to consider what might happen next.

To find herself in chains at the feet of Louis of Hungary was of course not a fate the Queen could contemplate, and so we took the Legate's advice, accompanied by only a few attendants and but one counsellor, the faithful Spinelli, in a Provençal galley which providentially – it belonged to the Pope – happened to have been in our harbour for some days, as if fearing, or awaiting, such a misfortune. Thus the Queen of Naples delivered her baby son, her faithful servant, her faithful servant's infant daughter, and most of all, her own sweet white body, and mine, into the clutches of His Holiness the Pope of Rome. Without even the protection of a chastity belt, for those obnoxious garments we allowed to fall into the sea as we boarded.

At this stage it would be best to complete the story of Louis of Hungary's dramatically successful campaign. Apprised of the Queen's flight by the cunning Legate, and understanding that a Hungarian army lay between them and their own soldiers, the elders of Naples promptly sallied forth and offered the conqueror the keys of the city. His victory was absolutely bloodless, at this point, if we exclude one or two peasants he hanged along the way after his soldiers had raped their wives and daughters. This is, after all, the natural concomitant of warfare. I have often considered what fun we women would have did we compose the armies. Think of the men we would have to disport ourselves with.

I digress. The news of the Queen's flight and of the surrender of the city also rapidly reached the Neapolitan camp, and caused consternation, as may be imagined. Immediately the various captains deserted the flag to see if they could make their peace with the invader.

Prince Louis himself galloped back to Naples, unbelieving that his wife had fled, only to discover the awful truth. Undismayed, and still full of love, he sought to follow her. But there was no ship left in the harbour, and the Hungarians were at the gates. Still Louis refused to be downcast or afraid. Taking but four companions, amongst them my Alberto and the faithful steward Nicolo Acciajuoli, he boarded an open rowing boat and in this put out to sea.

His namesake gave him no further thought, assuming him certainly drowned. But Louis survived, and actually reached Pisa, a very long way up the coast. There he went ashore before resuming his journey, overland, for Avignon.

In acting thus he was maintaining his reputation for daring and gallantry. His allies also maintained their known characters: Charles of Durazzo and Robert of Constantinople determined to throw themselves on the mercy of the conqueror.

They found him at Aversa, for although he had sent his troops to occupy Naples, Louis was in no hurry to lose himself in that tumultuous city while he had foes abroad. But now these foes had either fled or come to him, and in the very place where his brother had perished. He must have counted himself a happy man.

Charles and Robert had at least had the sense to leave their younger brothers in the relative safety of Naples. But now their host, for such Louis appeared to be in the generosity of his greeting, inquired as to the whereabouts of the young princes. Nor would he accept their excuses, which varied from ill health to pressing duties, with the result that the junior members of the House of Anjou were duly summoned to the conqueror's presence. While Louis continued to reassure them all that his quarrel was with the Queen, and that he was their friend.

This was balm to the ears of Charles who undoubtedly now reckoned that, the Queen having fled, she had also forfeited the throne – and that Louis would bestow it on his faithful ally. In this he was acting the fool, but Charles was given to this. Certainly he should have known better, for I have it on the best authority that after he had finished feasting with the King, he was visited in his quarters by Lello of Aquila and the Count of Fondi, who warned him that Louis was determined upon his execution. Charles refused to credit this and ordered them from his presence.

Thus the next day he again presented himself, with his brothers and cousins, before the King. And was once again invited to dine. This sumptuous meal was held in the very room where Prince Andrew had supped on the night he was murdered, but even this sinister coincidence seems to have escaped Charles. He was, I understand, warned yet again to fly while he had the chance, by Lello, who was serving, and once again ignored the warning, preferring to bask in the glory of the King's smile, and enjoy his food and wine and splendid plate and cutlery, and, no doubt, reflect to himself that with all the other conspirators dead or disgraced, he was on the verge of the triumph he had so long sought ... when Louis stopped smiling.

Sitting opposite Charles, the King suddenly threw out

his right arm, and, pointing, shouted, 'Wretched man, vile traitor! How dare you sit at my table when you are the being I most hate on all the earth?'

Charles goggled at him in consternation, quite taken aback by the fury of the onslaught.

'Do you suppose I am unaware of your many machinations to secure the throne of Naples for yourself?' Louis shouted. 'Do you suppose I am unaware that when you could have saved my brother's life by a timely warning you allowed matters to take their course?'

Charles fell to his knees in terror, as did his brother and cousins.

'Do you think,' demanded King Louis, 'that I am unaware that you marched with my namesake, this so-called husband of the murderess, in arms against me?'

'Monsignore,' Charles stammered. 'I am innocent. I swear it. I would have warned Prince Andrew, who was my dearest friend, of the plot against him, could I but have got here in time. As for marching against you, monsignore, I was commanded to do so by the Queen, and could do nothing more than dissemble until I could gain your presence.'

'You lying wretch,' Louis declared. 'Yet these are but little crimes. You are guilty of a much greater one, that of marrying the Princess Marie, whose hand was given to me on his deathbed by her grandfather.'

'Monsignore,' Charles begged. 'Have mercy upon me, I ask of you. I did not know you seriously wished the Princess for yourself. Monsignore ...'

'Take them away,' Louis commanded his principal officers, Stephen Vaivode and the Count of Zimic.

Charles and his brother and cousins were imprisoned for that night, and next morning the younger princes were despatched under guard for Hungary, where they were to spend many years as captives.

Charles himself, however, was sentenced to be executed on the very spot where Andrew had breathed his last.

Taken to that terrible balcony, before the assembled army, a sword was driven into his breast, his head was cut off, and his body thrown to the ground to be left unburied for three days, as Andrew's had been.

It is said he died a gibbering wreck.

King Louis now proceeded to Naples, refusing the homage offered him by the elders, and entering the city as a conqueror. And one bent on vengeance. His anger was no doubt increased by his inability to lay hands on the Duchess of Calabria. Marie concealed herself in a convent before the arrival of the Hungarian army, and thence made her escape disguised as a friar, with her children and but a single woman attendant. It is impossible for me to suggest what plans Louis had for the miserable girl – he had a wife of his own – but it is safe to say that had she fallen into the hands of the conqueror her lot would have been an unhappy one.

Although ours might have been happier!

As it was, the people of Naples now had to pay for the escape of the two princesses, as well as for their own treachery in so readily attempting to replace them. Louis' first act was to have Donna Cancia brought before him. She had languished in prison for some months, and had been delivered of her second child. But Bertram de Baux had not proceeded against her, and it is possible that she might have escaped with her life but for the Hungarian invasion. For Louis was not the man to be softened even by a pretty face and a full figure, and Cancia still possessed both. He commanded her to die as her fellow conspirators had, and the next morning she was taken in the sinister cart to the town square, suffering as had the Countesses of Terlizzi and Morcone. To her credit, Cancia died as she had lived, laughing to the end, herself indicating the choicest portions of her body to the knives of the executioners.

An even worse fate befell the Count of Catanzaro, who

was also accused of being one of the conspirators, and who, having fled the prosecution of Bertram de Baux, made the mistake of returning to the city in the hopes of making his peace with King Louis. This unhappy fellow was broken on the wheel, the most horrible of all fates, for the living victim, after every last bone in his body has been shattered with an iron bar, is then raised on the wheel in this unhuman state to be eaten alive by the birds.

In Catanzaro's case the punishment was made the more frightful as Louis commanded the wheel to be studded with razors before the wretched victim was bound to it.

My own experiences in Naples convince me that the populace no doubt enjoyed these ghastly spectacles as much as they had those of the previous year, and might have gone on doing so, had the victims been limited to those of noble birth. But now Louis' insensate fury began to encompass people from all walks of life. Anyone who had served, in the most casual capacity, any of the known conspirators, was adjudged guilty. Even the baker who had baked their bread was hauled away to execution. The good people of Naples had all had their doubts about the Queen's innocence, and they had supposed they were but exchanging one monarch for another. Now they discovered that they had exchanged a young and beautiful and essentially pleasant young woman for a harsh and brutal tyrant. There was little they could do to alter matters back again while the enormous Hungarian army, which mustered some twenty thousand men, dominated the city, but their thoughts began to drift across the sea to their erstwhile queen. And soon, as we shall see, they were to be visited by a foe far more terrible than even the Hungarians.

Meanwhile, Joanna and I and our children had landed at Nice. The voyage from Naples took five days, in the most perfect weather and without the sight of a hostile sail. And in Nice we were greeted with enthusiasm. The good people of Provence had never before seen their duchess, as was

Joanna's title in this appendage she had inherited from her grandfather, but, like all the world, they had heard a great deal about her. Now they clustered to behold her, and decide for themselves whether or not she was a black-hearted murderess. One look at that pale, marvellously contoured face decided them in her favour. They shouted their huzzahs, held fiestas and tournaments and surrounded her with joy.

Several of the gallants, no doubt despairing of ever obtaining a smile from the Queen, even bent appreciative glances on the tall, yellow-haired, and – dare I say it – not greatly less lovely young woman who was constantly at her side.

For the Queen was quite unable to share in the merry-making which went on around her. Her heart indeed was heavier than at any previous time in her tumultuous life. To the guilt which was wearing her down had to be added the catastrophe of having been forced to flee her throne, the uncertainty as to whether her husband was alive or dead, and the very real certainty that she must now throw herself on the mercy of a pope who had not as yet revealed himself to be anything of a friend.

I shared her feelings, on a lesser scale to be sure, but I too had been driven from my home, and I equally knew not whether my husband was alive or dead. We spent much of our spare time sighing in each other's arms.

Still, it was reassuring to feel that we were amongst friends, and thus we received a rude shock when we reached the gate of the city of Aix, after a triumphal journey across the rolling Provençal countryside. The magistrates of Aix duly opened their gates to their suzerain, but there was no enthusiasm in either their expressions of welcome or those of the citizens.

'They are overawed by your majesty, Your Grace,' Spinelli ventured to suggest.

I did not agree with him, and felt even more apprehensive as we approached the Château Arnaud, where the

Queen was to stay during her sojourn in the city. Here were assembled all the nobles, in a double line, through which we walked, while they bowed low before the Queen. But no sooner had Joanna, Charles Martel, Lucia and myself, with Spinelli, passed through them than they closed ranks behind us to shut off the rest of our party.

'Your Grace,' Spinelli muttered, as we were ushered inside the building, 'I very much fear we are prisoners of this municipality.'

'What am I to do?'

'At least seek to learn by whose order.'

Summoning her courage, Joanna requested an interview with the Chief Magistrate, and on his arrival asked when would arrangements be completed for the continuance of her journey to Avignon. The worthy fellow replied that he did not know, as they were in fact awaiting instructions from His Holiness. At which Joanna assumed her most imperious look, and demanded to know whether she, or the Pope, was their rightful ruler.

The unhappy magistrate bowed lower yet, and begged Her Grace to understand that she was at once loved and respected by everyone in Aix, and that there was no doubt of their allegiance, but that they all, Her Grace included, owed a greater allegiance to His Holiness, and it was this greater allegiance they now felt obliged to acknowledge.

This was of course merely another way of saying, yes, you are prisoners, and was most unsatisfactory. The next few days were quite disturbing, as for all the honour and respect paid the Queen by the nobles and magistrates of Aix, we never knew, and neither did they, when they might be summoned to bind Joanna with chains and deliver her to the awful judgement of the Supreme Pontiff; the recent examples of that judgement were too fresh in our minds for comfort.

Had we but known, there were stout hearts and able tongues even then being exerted on our behalf. Louis of Tarento, as I have recounted briefly, managed to make a landfall in the neighbourhood of Pisa, a fortunate occurrence for us all. For here was this gallant knight, now bereft of all his fortune save his sword, and accompanied by only half a dozen faithful companions, cast adrift in a hostile world. Fortunately, Louis had chosen his devoted band with care. As I have mentioned, it included Alberto, who was willing to die sword in hand at the side of his master. More important, it also included that advocate, Nicolo Acciajuoli, who had served the Empress so well, and had now transferred his allegiance whole-heartedly to the only one of Catherine's sons still at liberty. And this Nicolo had an even greater gift to offer than loyalty; he had a brother, Angelo, who happened to be Archbishop of Florence, and a man of importance in the eyes of Avignon.

To Florence therefore the little band took themselves, and found a ready ally in the good prelate. He clothed and fed them, and then took them himself direct to Avignon. Louis was by now aware that Joanna was restrained in Aix, but on the advice of Angelo Acciajuoli opted to apply directly to Clement rather than to attempt a rescue with but a handful of followers.

This was a happy decision, for the Archbishop was really very well favoured by His Holiness, who equally could not help but be taken by the handsome and open features of the young prince, so cruelly separated from his wife and stepson. Louis indeed later confessed to us that he approached the papal throne with considerable apprehension, but Clement, whom he was meeting for the first time, raised him with his own hands, and welcomed him – as King of Naples! Those of us like myself, who, through force of circumstances, have been compelled to adopt a somewhat cynical view of life, even at the highest level, will naturally conclude that in doing this Clement, who never performed a single act that was not intended to be for his eventual advantage, was here allowing history to repeat itself. As, a century before, Charles of Anjou had grown too far too fast, so was Louis of Hungary now engaged in the same alarming process. To have acknowledged him as King of Naples by right of conquest would have left him the most powerful monarch in all Christendom, and this Clement was not prepared to consider: better Louis of Tarento – as his faithful lieutenant – than Louis of Budapest.

Whatever the machinations of the papal mind, this was all to our advantage. Of course we knew nothing of what was happening, confined as we were in the Château Arnaud, and a strict confinement it was. Four of the Provençal ladies were introduced into our midst as Joanna's attendants, in place of those she had brought with her from Naples, and these harridans were nothing less than gaolers and spies. One of them was with the Queen during every waking hour, watching her every move. They would have liked to be with her at night as well, having sent me away, but this Joanna absolutely refused to permit; it was only during the midnight hours that we could share our fears and, occasionally, our hopes.

But that we were in dire straits could not be doubted. Until, without warning, the Archbishop of Aix requested an audience with the Queen, and, on being admitted, set about, with every expression of humble reverence for her majesty, to explain what had been happening.

'We earnestly desired not to alarm Your Grace in any way,' he said, 'and thus did not allow you to understand the considerable danger in which you had inadvertently placed yourself by entering our city. The fact is, Your Grace, that but a few days before your arrival, we received an intimation from the King of France that he intended to award Aix as an appanage to one of his younger sons.'

He paused, and Joanna, who could dissemble with the best of us, permitted herself to say, 'The wretch!'

This would indeed have been a high-handed act, but not necessarily an illegal one, for Joanna held Provence, and the cities therein, not in her own right as Queen, but as Duchess: Provence and Naples might be united in the

Anjou family, but for political matters they were separate entities. Provence had been granted to Charles of Anjou as his appanage more than a hundred years earlier. Thus bestowed by the French crown, it remained legally French, and so Philip VI was in this affair Joanna's liegelord.

The war which was at this very moment being carried on between my own England and France was a result of the English King, Edward III, also having possessions for which he was expected to yield homage to the French king.

Joanna, alas, was in no condition to go to war.

'I wish you to believe, Your Grace,' avowed the worthy prelate, 'that the people of Aix would have died rather than deliver your fair city to the French, but the responsibility of having you in our midst when a French army might be marching upon us was a severe one. We thus endeavoured to conceal your presence while we sought assistance, and this assistance, I am overjoyed to inform Your Grace, has now been provided from the greatest of all sources. His Holiness himself has guaranteed your safety, and desires only to entertain you at his court in Avignon, where, he wishes you to know, your husband is already in residence and anxious to kiss your hand. In these joyous circumstances, we of Aix must accept that we can no longer impose upon Your Grace to remain with her loyal subjects, as we understand how anxious you must be, not only to be reunited with your husband, but to visit His Holiness. Thus your horses are saddled and await your pleasure.'

Here I feel compelled to pause a moment in order to translate the above mumbo-jumbo into plain English for my more innocent readers.

What the Archbishop had said was:

The Pope has claimed you as his prisoner.

He already holds your husband as a hostage for your surrender.

In these circumstances we are desperately anxious to see the back of you just as quickly as possible.

Joanna understood this as well as I, but she had no choice other than to obey the Papal summons, and, besides, she was equally desperate to see Louis again, although I doubt she was considering requiring him to kiss merely her hand.

I of course was then unaware that my dear Alberto was also at Avignon, but I was no less anxious than the Queen to face the Pope and achieve some definite settlement of our unfortunate situation. So off we set, on a remarkable journey, which confounded our expectations.

Avignon, as is well known, lies on the River Rhône, above the cities of Arles, Beaucaire and Tarascon. But the river itself flows at such a tumultuous speed it was necessary to proceed across country, and even crossing the bridge below the city was a hair-raising experience. The journey from Aix took several days, but at last the towers of the Papal enclave – which, it should be remembered, belonged to Joanna – came into view, dominated, indeed, by the huge square tower of the Papal Palace itself.

Long before we gained the city, however, we were encompassed by splendour, Joanna being greeted at once as Queen and suzerain by the population. Outside the gates waited Louis of Tarento himself, clad in shining armour. At the sight of her husband Joanna uttered a great shriek of joy and all but fell from her palfrey. Endeavouring to assist her, I also nearly slipped from my saddle as I observed, at our lord's shoulder, Alberto, whom I had feared dead.

The knights were surrounded by a clutch of red-coated cardinals, whose presence somewhat diminished the ardour of our first greetings. But these were but a fraction of the host awaiting us. We were met and escorted by pages dressed in the most dazzling of garments, who erected above the Queen's head a canopy of scarlet velvet, embroidered with the emblem of the fleur-de-lys in gold thread and surmounted by waving plumes. Handsome youths and beautiful girls walked before us, their brows garlanded with flowers, singing Joanna's praises, while when we passed through the gates, Louis now proudly riding at the Queen's side as did Alberto at mine, we found the houses decorated as for a national holiday, and the streets crowded with people come to see and to cheer. Above all rang out the chorus of the bells, as every church in the city gave forth its joyous peal. How I wished those wretches such as Roberto di Cabane and Charles of Durazzo could have beheld us in our hour of triumph. Well, perhaps they did, looking up from the fiery furnace.

Our way took us to the Castle of Avignon, the Papal residence, at the head of the steps to which awaited the Pontiff himself.

It may be remembered that some ten years earlier I had left England with my unfortunate family to undertake a pilgrimage to the Holy City. My father's hope, then, had been perhaps to obtain a distant glimpse of God's vicar; in my wildest dreams I had never expected to come face to face with the man himself – albeit this was a different vicar to ten years previously.

Over the last century, indeed, the Papal position had undergone a variety of harassing vicissitudes. In an earlier chapter I have recounted how, having raised Charles of Anjou as a rival to the sons of Frederick II, the popes had then been forced to find a counterweight to their erstwhile champion, as he in turn grew too powerful. This was successful, but it meant an ever-increasing involvement of the Holy See with secular and political matters, and once involved in the backstairs art of diplomacy and treachery, the men who stood as God's representative on earth necessarily found themselves regarded by their subjects more and more as just men, with no guarantee of spiritual purity to make them better than other men, and, worse, even less guarantee of spiritual protection when the going got rough.

The epitome of this new situation was Pope Boniface VIII, of the Gaetani family, who was Pontiff from 1294 until 1303. Handsome and vain, arrogant and domineering, lecherous and ambitious, he briefly bestrode the European world like a colossus, caring nothing for the enemies he raised to left and right as he pursued his triumphant path, which had two goals: to secure for all time the temporal power of the Papacy, and the financial power of the Gaetani.

Boniface reached his zenith in the year 1300, when he celebrated a Papal jubilee on a scale of unequalled splendour – without perhaps pausing to reflect that this was the end of the thirteenth century of Christendom, which could possibly be interpreted as an ill omen.

In fact, his days were already numbered. His long contest with Charles of Anjou, which had appeared to end in victory, had alienated too many of the crowned heads of Europe, who saw their own positions trembling should they fall foul of Rome, if any Pope with a snap of his fingers could summon armies to march against an over-successful monarch. More especially, and fatally, Boniface had made an enemy of Philip IV of France, who was not only a cousin of Joanna's great-great-grandfather, but was also ruler of a nation which was just beginning to rise to glory, and had not yet been forced into the disastrous course of waging war against England. Philip, known as the Fair – on account of his complexion rather than any nobility of spirit – raised the banner of revolt against the secular ambitions of the Papacy, and, listing every crime of which Boniface was known to be guilty – and quite a few which were mere rumour – demanded that the Holy Father be taken to France for trial.

This unprecedented proposal was of course ignored by the Pope, who hurled anathema against the French King. But Philip belonged to that small group of men for whom the anger of heaven, at least as interpreted by mortals like themselves, held no terrors. Having defeated the Papal army, he sent two of his willing servants, Guillaume de Nogaret and Sciarra Colonna – the Colonnas being sworn

174

enemies of the Gaetani – to arrest Boniface in his retreat of Agnani and bring him to Paris.

The attempt at abduction was unsuccessful, the Italians rallying around their Pontiff, but not until the two agents had broken into the Papal apartments and laid hands upon the vicious old man, treating him with every form of contumely, which even included relieving themselves upon his trembling supine body. They then fled, but they had accomplished their purpose, for Boniface never recovered from the humiliation to which he had been exposed, and soon died.

This event, as may be supposed, set all Christendom to wondering what would happen next. That a pope could be so treated without direct intervention from Above was unthinkable ... but there was no such intervention. A new pope, Benedict XI, was hastily elected, but he was not even able to reach Rome, such was the anarchy throughout Italy, and contented himself with excommunicating all those who had taken part in the Agnani affair.

This proved equally fatal to him, for he was dead within a year, and few doubted that he had been poisoned, or that the deadly draught had been arranged from Paris.

Ambitious as are most cardinals to achieve the ultimate height available to them, this sad trend revealed a total lack of candidates to replace Benedict. The worthy prelates indeed debated for ten months before choosing one Bertrand de Got, Archbishop of Bordeaux, who was reputed to be a bitter enemy of Philip's.

But it was immediately revealed that Bertrand had merely been dissembling – or more likely was merely determined to stay alive – and on ascending the Papal throne as Clement V, he displayed a willingness to co-operate with the French monarch. There was much toing and froing, and lengthy legal discussion, the upshot of which was that Philip was exonerated of crimes against the Church, and Boniface was exonerated, posthumously, of his crimes against man and nature. Philip then proceeded, with Papal approval, to destroy the Knights Templar, a very wealthy organisation, while Clement, unable to return to Rome because of the continuing anarchy there, but unwilling to remain in territories ruled by the French King, secured the permission of Robert of Anjou, Joanna's grandfather, to establish a 'temporary' court at Avignon. This was in 1308, and it will therefore be seen that this court had endured thirty-eight years when we arrived there.

In that time Clement had been succeeded by John XXII, who had in turn been replaced by Benedict XII, and on Benedict's death in 1342, the very year in which all of our own misfortunes had begun to gather, the cardinals had chosen as their head a certain Pierre Roger.

Born in Correze in 1291, Pierre had entered the Church, become in succession abbot of the Benedictine monasteries at Fécamp and then at La Chaise-Dieu, Archbishop of Sens in 1329, and of Rouen in 1330. It will be seen that he was therefore a Frenchman, and even more, a French churchman, from the toes of his shoes to the top of his head. Becoming Pope as Clement VI, he set out on a career of reckless aggrandisement of his office and the new Papal city, which outdid even the progress of Boniface. Palaces arose in and around Avignon like mushrooms, and the splendour of the Papal court became a byword. Not everyone approved. Critics spoke of the 'Babylonian Captivity' of the Church, and sneered at the Pope's claims to be called Clement the Magnificent. This carping he could afford to ignore. What he sought was a consolidation of his position, and towards this end he had been working with infinite patience from the moment Joanna had ascended the throne of Naples and thereby become his landlady.

This handsome, smiling fifty-five-year-old prelate was the man before whom we now knelt in supplication, and if we were at the moment unaware of it, I have no doubt at

176

all that the principal thought in Clement's mind was: everything comes to he who waits.

'Your Grace,' the Pope said, himself raising Joanna by the hands, and clearly drinking in her sensual beauty with every one of his own senses. 'It is an honour and a privilege to welcome you to Avignon, your very own city.'

'Oh, Holy Father,' Joanna confessed, 'if you knew for how long I have wished to find myself in your presence.'

Greetings are nearly always a tissue of lies in any event. It was now necessary to get down to the nitty gritty.

'I but wish the occasion could have been a more fortunate one,' the Pope commented.

'I but seek justice, Holy Father,' Joanna replied, gazing into his eyes. 'But rest assured that I am prepared to atone for any crime of which I may be found guilty.'

The Pope returned her gaze, and it was clear that they had reached a preliminary understanding.

Clement smiled. 'I am sure a suitable penance can be devised to wipe every stain from your character, Your Grace,' he said. 'But grave charges have been laid against you, and it will be necessary for you to appear before the assembled cardinals to explain your situation.'

Joanna bowed her head. 'As Your Holiness wills it,' she agreed.

'But there is naught for you to fear,' Clement reassured her. 'I give you my word on that.' He now allowed his gaze to play over the rest of us, and, I discovered with some sensation of alarm, it came to rest on me for several seconds. 'And these are your children?' he inquired, gently if incredulously.

'This is my son, Charles Martel,' Joanna said, offering the little boy. 'The little girl is the daughter of my most trusted lady, Richilde Benoit.'

'Indeed.' Clement barely glanced at my Lucia in favour of myself. 'She has a striking colouring.'

'She is from England, Your Holiness,' Joanna explained.

'And is your most trusted confidante, you say. Come forward, girl.'

My knees touched each other as I stepped away from Alberto's side and knelt before the purple robe. And felt the Papal fingers under my chin as he raised my head. 'Truly striking,' he remarked, his gaze drifting from my face down to the bodice of my gown. 'Perhaps you will share your mistress's penance.' Then he released me, and I was allowed to retire to Alberto, a prey to some very disturbing thoughts.

But for the moment all was sunshine and light. Joanna's party was escorted to apartments in the palace of Cardinal Napoleon des Ursins, and here we were permitted truly to greet our beloved husbands, and re-introduce them to their children, and to the joys of the marriage bed. This was a happy evening, and if perhaps all of us remained aware of the cloud still hanging above our heads, we refused to permit it to interfere with our simple pleasures. The ultimate pleasure, indeed, that of wrestling naked in the arms of our respective lovers, was all that either the Queen or I at that moment desired.

They apparently felt the same, for no mention was made of the missing chastity belts.

We awaited the judgement of the Pope, but Clement appeared in no hurry to place Joanna on trial before the cardinals. This was in part because these reverend gentlemen had to be assembled, and not all were close to Avignon. But equally, I have no doubt, as His Holiness undoubtedly knew the verdict he wanted, it was necessary to make sure that every cardinal understood exactly how he should vote at the time, regardless of what evidence might be presented. Some of them clearly required more persuasion than others.

We were happy enough to be left in this relative security

178

after the events of the past year, even if Joanna from time to time sighed for her poor family and indeed her people of Naples, still held firmly beneath the foot of the conqueror, whose terrible deeds of vengeance now began to be widely known.

And were confirmed in part by the arrival of Princess Marie of Durazzo, who, it will be recollected, had escaped Louis dressed as a friar, and accompanied by two little daughters and her son Charles, who was still hardly more than a babe in arms.

Would that he had perished on the journey.

Indeed he nearly did so, for the Princess had endured a series of remarkable hardships, not unattended by danger, before gaining the safety of Avignon, where she knelt in the most humble supplication before her sister.

Joanna had ample cause to believe that Marie had betrayed her in her support of Charles of Durazzo's outrageous ambitions, but such emotions were for the moment forgotten in her concern at beholding her sister, a penniless widow, fleeing a common foe. She raised Marie and took her into her arms, and promised her that the pair of them would face the tribulations which awaited them together.

Meanwhile, as she could not be Queen of Naples, Joanna busied herself with being Duchess of Provence. This was both on account of her nature, which could not bear to be idle, and as a deliberate act of policy, for she was determined to illustrate to Clement how good a ruler she would be were she but given the chance.

Avignon, as I have indicated, had become the very centre of the Christian universe since the Holy See had been removed there from Rome. It was very difficult to do business at any level, one could not marry or give birth, one could not even properly die, without the blessing of the Church upon the enterprise. To humble folk this blessing was at the dispensation of the parish priest, or for those slightly higher up the social scale, the local bishop.

For those who dealt in great affairs or had great ambitions, however, it was necessary to treat with the hierarchy, and if one was going to sit down with an archbishop or a cardinal, one had to find one's man, and this was easier done in the Holy City than in a diocese, the great men of the Church preferring to live as much as possible in the shadow of their master.

Equally, it followed, that if one was going to journey to Avignon to plead one's cause before one's archbishop, it made sense, if possible, to go even higher, and seek an audience with the Pope himself.

The result of this was that Avignon was by some distance the busiest and most cosmopolitan place I have ever experienced. The streets were constantly thronged, with people of every possible description. Proud prelates rubbed shoulders with Muslim Arab merchants; famous soldiers with anxious Jews; Spaniards with Italians; Frenchmen with Hungarians; Englishmen with Scandinavians; poets with monks; clowns with scholars. All of this was very good for business. The innkeepers made fortunes, as did the meat vendors and wine sellers. But man does not only eat and drink and sleep. He fulfils a fourth function, more enjoyable than all the others put together, and without which none of us would be on earth at all.

This special function requires, as a rule, a special service, that provided by women. My Joanna might have dallied as her fancy took her or as she was directed, but if we except Roberto di Cabane, at this early stage of her life neither desire nor direction had ever lowered her gaze beneath that of a royal prince. And even I, a humble slave, would permit myself only to know the best available. But to cater to the sexual needs of the multitude that thronged Avignon, women in vast numbers were required, and women who would sleep with a Tatar if the price was right. Thus to the kaleidoscopic crowd I have described above must be added another multitude, that of prostitutes, who also earned fortunes from the ready purses and even readier lusts of this itinerant population.

Indeed, understanding how necessary they were, and confident in their numbers, the courtesans of Avignon were the most forward, noisy, and aggressive of any in the world.

This situation distressed Joanna. Her own morals, at least in regard to those feelings popularly supposed to arise between the legs, might have been utterly corrupted at a very early age, but at this time at least, her passions were always indulged in strict privacy, and, as I have mentioned, with men who aspired to her own class. The sight of women openly flaunting their bodies and calling out their prices for various services at every street corner was abhorrent to the young Queen, as lowering the whole dignity of her sex.

She therefore, as Duchess of Provence and thus ruler of Avignon, promulgated an ordinance which cleared these unfortunates from the streets, and forced them to live together in a single large house.

This house, known to all by the red lantern suspended outside its door, was open for business every day of the year save for the last three of Holy Week – although its doors were always closed to Jews – but the men who entered, and there was a constant stream as may be imagined, were also strictly controlled as regards lewdity or obscenity. The whole was overseen by an abbess specially appointed to be mistress of the prostitute population. It may have been supposed that the Queen would have had some difficulty in discovering a good woman prepared to undertake so onerous and surely distasteful a duty, but on the contrary – it was a matter of turning the eager nuns away.

This undertaking of Joanna's was the first of its kind anywhere in the world, I have been told, although it has since been copied elsewhere. It attracted a great deal of discussion, and a good many varying opinions. Most men were in favour of it, as it meant they stood less chance of having their pockets picked while they humped, or indeed of becoming diseased, as the abbess was required regularly to inspect her charges.

The prostitutes themselves did not like it at all, and spread abroad a scurrilous rumour that they were being confined so that the Queen could have the pick of the men in Avignon for herself.

But, most important, the good matrons of the city assembled to pay their tribute to their Duchess for cleansing the streets of these vermin – as they described the hard-working young women of the town – an acclamation which could not fail to be noticed by the Pope.

For the hour of Joanna's trial was approaching. Clement, with his usual sense of ostentation and personal glory, was busy assembling judges from all over Europe, although everyone was well aware that the only judge who would matter was the Pope himself. However, his preparations were now interrupted by ambassadors from Louis of Hungary, demanding that the Queen be condemned for the murder of his brother. This spurred Clement to action, and so Joanna was required to take her place in the Papal palace and convince the world of her innocence.

This was quite the most solemn and magnificent occasion at which I have ever attended. The trial took place in the great courtyard of the palace, over which awnings had been erected, and at the far end of which Clement himself sat upon a lofty throne, raised high above the rest of us. To the left hand of the Pontiff sat the purple-clad cardinals, their chairs arranged in a semi-circle. Behind the cardinals were arrayed all the bishops, vicars, canons, deacons, archdeacons and every cleric who could be found.

At their feet stood the ambassadors of Louis, the accusers of the Queen.

Facing the serried ranks of the church, also on a raised

dais, but not so high as Clement, was a throne for Joanna and space for her attendants, amongst whom of course was myself. But we did not make our appearance until everyone else was seated. For to either side were now assembled all the ambassadors of foreign powers, all the great captains and merchants who were in the city. Truly I conceived that we were being placed on trial before the whole world, nor could I doubt that were the Queen to be convicted, I would be intimately associated with her descent into hell.

But Joanna, now that the moment of truth had arrived, was strangely unafraid. Her face was pale but her demeanour truly that of a queen, as, dressed in sombre black, she entered the courtyard on the arm of her uncle, the aged Cardinal de Perigord.

Joanna had now lived in Avignon for some months, and it is probable that almost everyone present had obtained at least a glimpse of her during that time, yet as she appeared in the arena – for it was hardly less than that – a great sigh rippled through the huge concourse, and I will swear that it was at least partly caused by desire. Joanna was but twenty years old, her beauty untarnished by the slightest blemish, but rather made the more awesome by her expression, by the glow of her magnificent eyes, the slight parting of her crimson lips, the delineation of her perfect body as she advanced to her chair, and bowed to the Pope.

As I gazed at those eager faces, young and old, and reflected that should the Queen be condemned, there might not be lacking sufficient swords drawn in her defence yet to carry the day, I was struck by one youth in particular, and indeed he was a youth, younger even than ourselves. He was a handsome fellow, with the most splendid chestnut hair and a strong face as well as body. I inquired of his name from one of the Queen's Avignon attendants, and was informed that he was Jaime of Aragon, Infante (which is the Spanish word for Prince) of

Majorca, and a scion of the Royal House of Aragon. Here, I thought, is a true defender of my lady.

I was unaware, then, that one of my unsuspected talents was the gift of prophecy.

The assembly was hushed into silence as Joanna, having taken the oath, began to speak. I have suggested that this was the Moment of Truth. It was, of course, more in the nature of the Moment of Lies, as had Joanna confessed all not even her admirers could have saved her. But she denied any knowledge of the conspiracy to murder her husband, weeping as she spoke, and leaving every man convinced. This was easily done, although I could not help but feel that had her arbiters been women instead of men she might have had a far more difficult task.

The crux of the matter was those fearsome hours when instead of rushing to her husband's side and calling for vengeance upon his assassins, the Queen, with Cancia and myself, had huddled in her bed. To many such behaviour seemed to confirm her guilt. But this charge Joanna refuted with as splendid a display of acting as I have ever witnessed. Eyes burning while tears stained those magnificent cheeks she told her audience of her terror at the realisation that her husband had been murdered, of her fear for herself and her faithful attendants – at which point she allowed me the courtesy of a glance, and, having been provided with a large onion which I had concealed in my kerchief, I was able to join her in copious tears while I worked my features into a state of great anguish.

But by now the tears were fairly general, and increased as Joanna reached the climax of her remarkable peroration, throwing her arms wide as she turned half from the Pope to her audience, and in a strong, clear voice bewailed her fate, and begged for assistance and protection against the usurper of her throne, the man who had murdered her relatives and was so cruelly oppressing her subjects.

When she ceased speaking, and allowed her arms to fall to her sides, there was a moment's silence, in which my heart thumped most painfully. Then my fears were set at naught by the roar of approbation which rose it seemed from every throat, by the hundreds of swords which were whipped from their scabbards and thrust skywards. I watched the Hungarian ambassadors, who, witnessing this spontaneous demonstration of support for the Queen, looked at each other in dismay, and then without a word rose and left the courtyard. And indeed, Avignon, by the shortest route.

Clement watched them go, and waited for the noise to cease. Then he said, 'Good Queen, you have right royally this day placed before us the facts of your husband's sad death, and your own experiences. It but remains for me to give judgement as regards your accusers, and yourself. This I will do tomorrow morning.'

Joanna gazed at him in some concern, as did I, and there was a rumble of disapproval from the spectators, who were by now determined that the Queen was the most innocent woman in the world. But the Pope was dismissing the court, and there was nothing for it but to withdraw, our apprehensions returning, and redoubling, as, when we were about to leave the stage, a black-robed priest sidled into our midst and said, 'His Holiness requires a private audience of Your Grace in order that he may clarify one or two outstanding matters before pronouncing judgement on your case.'

'A private audience?' Joanna breathed, glancing in agitation at her husband.

'I shall be at your side, dearest heart,' Louis declared.

'With respect, monsignore,' the priest said, 'His Holiness has specifically stated that he wishes to interview the Queen alone, save that she be accompanied, for propriety's sake, by a single handmaiden.' His eyes searched the royal party, but I already knew whither he was looking, and my knees had turned to water. 'Her confidante, the Englishwoman, Richilde Benoit.'

Joanna looked at me, and I looked back at her. We did

not speak, but we both understood what was in the other's mind. And yet, having faced so many dangers together, we gained a certain confidence from confronting this latest prospect hand in hand, as it were.

'We shall prepare ourselves,' Joanna said.

'I am instructed to convey you to the Papal apartments without delay,' the scurvy knave insisted.

Joanna sighed, and turned to her husband. 'I shall join you as soon as I may, beloved knight,' she said. 'And I will bring you the sweetest of presents, the blessing of His Holiness upon our union. Never fear.'

I contented myself with squeezing Alberto's hand, and then hurried behind my mistress, who was accompanying the priest. Neither of us spoke, nor did we even look at each other, because we both knew that all that had gone before had been but play acting; the true reason for the Queen's presence in Avignon, and the true settlement of the affair of Andrew of Hungary, was about to be revealed to us.

We entered the palace by a small doorway, were led along a series of dark passageways and up equally dark and narrow staircases, and then emerged into a splendid reception chamber, hung with drapes representing the stations of the cross, well carpeted, and at the same time light and airy, for there were several windows, set high in the walls to be sure, but admitting the afternoon sunlight even if not permitting us to see out.

'You will wait here, if you please, Your Grace,' the priest said, and withdrew.

There was no one else in this room, at the moment, and so Joanna and I were at last able to draw our breaths.

'Your Grace,' I said, 'I am afraid.'

'Do not be,' Joanna said, revealing a greater knowledge of human nature than I possessed. 'Had Clement meant to condemn us, he would have done so in open court, to prove his greatness. As to what he wants of us, we must bow to his wishes.' She glanced at me. 'And remember, that even if he is a pope, he is still a man. I suspect this is what disturbs him.'

Her words disturbed me, for they seemed to smack of blasphemy, but before I could offer an opinion another door, on the far side of the chamber, opened, to admit Clement, and another priest. This grey friar was already known to us; his name was Pierre, and he was the Pope's private secretary and confidant.

Joanna dropped to her knees at the Pope's entry, and I followed her example.

'You may rise, Queen Joanna,' Clement said. 'And bid your handmaiden do likewise.'

We stood before him, and he lowered himself into a carved wooden chair, Father Pierre standing at his shoulder. 'What a charming picture the pair of you do make,' Clement remarked. 'One so dark, the other so fair, the couple so beautiful. And so deadly.'

My knees struck each other so hard I felt sure they were bruised. Whether Joanna suffered a similar misfortune or not I do not know; her voice was strong, with only the faintest of tremors.

'Am I accused of perjury, Holy Father?'

'What is perjury, compared with murder?' Clement asked. 'But would you seek God's forgiveness, you must confess all of your crimes.'

Joanna gazed at him for some seconds, while I already felt the bite of the executioner's knife. Then the Queen asked, 'And does God forgive all crimes?'

'His forgiveness is infinite, my child,' Clement replied, 'where true repentance is shown.'

'Then may I beg His indulgence, for having acted as a woman and a queen, in taking steps to rid myself of a foul wretch who battened upon my body and would have battened upon my kingdom.'

I gasped for breath, but Clement inclined his head, gravely.

187

'Foul wretch, indeed. Do you also confess to perjury?'

'In the interests of my people, I would commit any crime, Holy Father. And I consider it in the interests of my people that I should rule over them, not an usurper.'

'Do you also confess to adultery?'

'Where a marriage is loveless, Holy Father, a woman of spirit and feeling must needs find solace where she may.'

Clement studied her for several seconds, then he nodded. 'I am not sure that you have not just put forward a better defence than your tearful one of this afternoon. And is your handmaiden equally guilty of these crimes?'

I gave the Queen a beseeching look, but of course Joanna would not desert me. 'Richilde is entirely innocent of any knowledge of my late husband's death, until after the event, Holy Father.'

'But you cannot absolve her of the other crimes.'

Joanna bowed her head. 'She has been a slave, Holy Father. And has thus been sinned against more than she herself has sinned.'

'You make a worthy advocate, Your Grace. But still, I have here a hideous confession. God knows that you acted, perhaps as you claim, in the best interests of your people as well as yourself. And I know that He will be disposed to be merciful. Yet murder, and adultery, and perjury, cannot be allowed to be committed without due penance.'

'I have said that I am willing to submit to any penance Your Holiness may require,' Joanna said in an even voice.

Clement's eyes narrowed. '*Any* penance, Your Grace?'

Joanna gave a little sigh. 'Save that of renouncing my kingdom, yes.'

Clement smiled at her. 'Then rest assured that you will be forgiven. Penances may take many forms. There is the simple one of praying to the Lord, or in your case, the Holy Mother. There is the more severe one of suffering physical pain and humiliation in atonement of one's crime. And there is the sublime one of donating a portion of one's wealth to the Holy Church. In a crime of this gravity, atonement necessarily requires all three.'

He continued to gaze at the Queen as he spoke, and his face was becoming flushed with excitement. I was still too terrified to decipher his true meaning, but Joanna, although the younger of us, was already far older in the ways of the world.

'I understand this, Holy Father,' she said, still speaking in a low voice.

'Then your first penance will be that you pray to the Holy Mother ten times every night for the rest of your life.'

'I will do so, Holy Father.'

Clement looked directly at me for the first time. 'Your handmaiden will also perform this penance, for the rest of her life.'

'She will, Holy Father,' Joanna promised on my behalf.

'The second penance is that you will be whipped until you bleed, that you may atone for your crime with your own blood.'

I caught my breath at the very idea, but Joanna merely inclined her head; this time she did not speak.

'The penance will be performed here and now,' Clement said. 'It will be a private affair between us four.'

He was now in the grip of a considerable emotion, his breast heaving and his breathing hard.

Joanna turned away from him to face me. 'Assist me, Richilde,' she said.

Mind spinning, I hurried forward. As Joanna had so truly prophesied, even the Pope was merely a man, and given to a man's urges.

But how many of a man's urges?

My fingers slipped on the fastenings of my lady's gown, and indeed Joanna did most of the undressing herself. But she was not heavily encumbered with underclothing in the heat of a Provençal summer, and in hardly five minutes she was stripped to her shift, whereupon she turned to face her master again.

'The whipping must be administered upon the bare

buttocks, Your Grace,' the wretched man pronounced, and now he was positively panting with desire, for Joanna, clad only in a thin shift and with her black hair tumbling down her back, was a sight to drive men mad – as it had already driven more than one into that unhappy state.

But that was nothing to be compared with the sight of Joanna naked, for now she slipped the shift from her shoulders and let it settle about her ankles before stepping out of it. Clement rose from his chair as if drawn at the end of a string.

'So young, so beautiful,' he muttered, pinching his lip.

I dared not look at Father Pierre, who was certainly in the same state of arousal.

'I grow cold, Holy Father,' Joanna said, her voice equally chill, although it remained quiet.

'Then I shall make you hot, Your Grace,' he promised. 'Kneel, on the chair.'

Joanna obeyed and wrapped her arms around the back.

'The cane, Pierre,' Clement commanded.

Father Pierre hurried to a chest against the wall, which he opened, revealing several choice canes. One of these he whipped back and forth, slashing the air with a most dreadful sound. It seemed to me that as she listened, without turning her head, Joanna's body quivered from head to toe. It was, indeed, a most terrible position for a queen to be in, but worse was to follow.

I had anticipated, and I am sure Joanna had shared my opinion, that her chastisement would be of a cursory and nominal nature. A few light blows across the naked buttocks, to satisfy the male lust of the Pontiff ... but no: he laid into her with a vicious energy which took my breath away. Nor was he content with a mere six strokes, but delivered twelve with all of his strength, so that at the end of it my royal mistress was indeed bleeding.

Joanna bore the first few blows with great fortitude, but the tears began soon enough, and although she forbore to scream, I could see her knuckles, which held the back of the chair, whitening with the force of her grip. Indeed, when the whipping was finished, she remained motionless for some seconds as if glued to the chair, and then seemed to uncoil herself, and without a word or a glance at any of us – her cheeks were flaming – picked up her shift and put it on.

I now received a tap on the shoulder from Father Pierre. 'It is your turn, mademoiselle,' said the rascal.

Here it may be worth our while to pause and register our amazement at the power by which the Holy Church controls our minds no less than our bodies. Heaven knows I am not an innocent; circumstances have conspired against me in this regard. But I have no doubt that Heaven will, in due course, exact a suitable penance for my misdeeds – there was no necessity for me to submit to an hors d'oeuvre, as it were, any more than there had been for Joanna. We were both some twenty years younger than either Clement or his henchman, we were both strong girls, and I have no doubt we could each have dealt either of them such a buffet as to lay them unconscious on the floor.

Instead I merely submitted, because he was the Pope and I was the slave. What fools we mortals be.

As I was not a queen, I saw no reason to preserve my dignity in these surroundings, any more than in Charles of Durazzo's dungeons, and thus screamed my head off at the very first stroke of the cane, my voice rising in crescendo at every other of the twelve, a noise I maintained for some seconds after the caning ceased.

The Pope, meanwhile, sank into the chair, looking utterly exhausted, which did nothing for Joanna's temper. In tones which dripped ice, she asked, 'Are we now permitted to leave, Holy Father, as our penance is completed?'

'Completed?' Clement sat up. 'There is yet the matter of a donation to the Church.'

Joanna glared at him. 'I have no doubt that you will inform me of what you have in mind, Your Holiness.'

'Indeed, Your Grace. I think, to secure absolution for your crimes both now and in the hereafter, it should be a donation of such size and magnificence that only a Queen could support.'

'Yes?'

'I was thinking of this great city in which I reside as your tenant. It is surely unseemly that God's vicar upon this earth should be placed in the position of having to pay rent.'

Joanna was struck dumb by his effrontery, coming on top of his other excesses. It was some seconds before she said, 'You wish me to give you Avignon?'

Her tone was such that even Clement realised he might have pushed her too far. 'I was considering a suitable cash adjustment,' he explained. 'After all, I may bestow upon you every right as Queen of Naples, but unless that rascally Hungarian obeys my diktat, you may have to drive him out. For that you will need an army, and to raise an army you will need money. Where are you going to get sufficient, save from my coffers? In return for my financial, and spiritual, aid I should think Avignon would be a suitable quid pro quo.'

Had looks been able to kill, there would straightaway have had to be an election for a new pope.

Once again Clement understood that one step backwards might assist the giant step forward which was his ambition. 'I can also aid you in another form, Your Grace, by awarding your sweet husband the Order of the Golden Rose, and by officially pronouncing him King of Sicily and Jerusalem. Not to mention Naples. What more could Your Grace desire?'

The inclusion of Louis in the papal beneficence did much to calm Joanna's anger. But she was still displeased. 'How much?' she asked.

'Ah ... fifty thousand florins?' Clement ventured.

'You are amusing yourself, Holy Father. For Avignon? A hundred thousand.'

'Well, I might go to sixty.'

'Ninety,' Joanna said, 'and not a penny less.'

'Eighty,' Clement replied, 'and not a penny more.'

My mistress might just have been whipped, but her mind was as sharp as ever; she knew she would not improve on the last figure. She dropped to her knees and bowed her head.

'Holy Father, it is my wish to atone for my crimes by presenting the Curia with the city of Avignon, in perpetuity ... and in consideration of the sum of eighty thousand florins. To be paid in cash.'

CHAPTER 6

The pain and humiliation felt by Joanna and myself after our mistreatment by the Pope was of course considerably assuaged by his absolution and his promise of a Papal Bull demanding the immediate withdrawal of Louis of Hungary from Naples, together with the large amount of money the Queen now had at her disposal. These items even consoled our respective husbands as they kissed the red weals on our bottoms and muttered threats.

'They are best forgotten,' Joanna insisted. 'It is to the future we must now look.'

Louis of Tarento and Alberto immediately commenced discovering where galleys, and men, could be hired, without waiting for the Papal Bull actually to be promulgated. But they had barely started on their quest, when news of a most singular nature arrived from Italy: Louis of Hungary had stolen out of Naples in the dead of night, with the main part of his army, and disappeared over the Apennines.

We gazed at each other in relief at hearing this, but at the moment it was amazement which dominated in our minds. 'My people have driven him out?' Joanna asked, ever an optimist.

'Only by their prayers, Your Grace,' the messenger told us. 'But the Hungarian army, Naples, all Italy, perhaps the entire world, has been visited by a most virulent sickness, called the Plague, which has people dropping dead like flies.'

'My God!' Joanna cried. 'What can it be?'

'As to that, Your Grace, no man may know. Undoubtedly it is a visitation from God for our sins. But it is a peculiarly horrible sickness, which first of all manifests itself in a swelling in the armpits and the groin, following which it runs a very rapid course, and terminates in an agonising death.'

'And it is fear of this sickness that has driven the King of Hungary from Italy?' Prince Louis asked, somewhat contemptuously: he certainly feared no sickness himself.

'His soldiers were dying in great numbers, monsignore. But he has not yet given up possession of the city. There is a garrison in the Castel Nuovo, commanded by Corrado Lupo, and it is presumed that the King means to return.'

'The devil,' Louis muttered, while Joanna turned pale.

'We must act with haste,' declared Master Acciajuoli. 'But you must not endanger yourself, Your Grace, at least until our way is clear, and we are certain that the people of Naples are prepared to rise and reject the invaders forever. Do you therefore allow me to precede you, as your envoy, and ascertain the true state of affairs.'

This gallant offer Joanna was happy to accept, and so we remained in Avignon as guests of the Pope – who smiled upon us most charmingly whenever we happened to encounter one another, which was often enough – while Louis and Alberto continued in their task of raising both a fleet and an army, as it now seemed that, plague or no plague, these would be necessary.

Meanwhile Acciajuoli, equipped with the most formidable weapon in the world, a Papal Bull, departed for Italy. It was necessary for him to proceed with caution, however, and so he went first of all to the only castle in all Naples which had not surrendered to the Hungarian host, that of Melzi, which as it happened was commanded by his own son, Lorenzo. We may imagine with what happiness these two most faithful servants of our Queen embraced.

Lorenzo was able to assure his father that the Neapolitans had become heartily weary of the exactions and executions visited upon them by the Hungarian monarch, and that they awaited only the word that their Queen was willing to return to them – and forgive their betrayal of her – to unite behind her. This was good to hear, but Master Acciajuoli was a cautious fellow, and preferred to discover the truth for himself. He thus visited every town and city in the kingdom before finally appearing in Naples itself. This journey was not unattended by danger, and indeed discomfort, for the plague seemed to be intensifying its grip upon the countryside, and many a community shut its gates and posted armed guards on its walls, to prevent any itinerant, who might be a carrier of the dread disease, from entering.

But Master Acciajuoli, armed as he was with both the Papal Bull and his position as Queen's Ambassador, always prevailed, and always won the hearts of his audiences, too, as he told them of the Queen's marriage with Prince Louis having been legalised, of the Papal absolution as regards her involvement in the death of her first husband, and of the great benefits which would accrue to the Kingdom following Joanna's reinstatement.

His welcome was greatest in Naples, although he had to enter the city clandestinely because of the Hungarian garrison. Thus thoroughly reassured, he hastened back to Avignon, and told the Queen that her birthright awaited her.

By now Louis and Alberto had raised a considerable fleet, as well as a formidable force of mercenaries anxious to serve so beautiful and, at the moment, wealthy a mistress. We thus sailed on 10 September 1348 from Marseilles; the Duchess of Durazzo accompanied her sister, as did our children, and of course the faithful Acciajuoli and Spinelli.

*

As it would have been too risky to attempt to force the harbour of Naples itself, which was dominated by the castle, still in Hungarian hands, Louis made our landfall at the little seaport of Santa Maria del Carmine, at the mouth of the Sebeto River. No sooner were our sails sighted than a crowd began to gather, and on entering the small harbour we were surrounded by a tumultuous multitude of people, all cheering themselves hoarse. Such a welcome had Joanna weeping with gratification, but it rapidly became apparent that the people did not only see her as their rightful ruler, and their deliverer from the Hungarian yoke, but, being simple peasants for the most part, they also saw in her their deliverance from the foul pestilence with which they were afflicted.

This was indeed horrifying. Parts of the town were barricaded and patrolled by armed guards; no one was allowed to leave, and no one outside the barricade apparently had the slightest desire to enter. We gathered that those were the quarters where plague had been discovered in one of the houses.

'But they cannot exist without help,' Joanna protested.

'They are beyond help, Your Grace,' declared the mayor.

'They are my people,' Joanna insisted. 'I cannot permit them to die in lonely misery. Break down that barricade immediately.' She turned to her confessor. 'Father Anselm, you will accompany me to minister to those poor people.'

The good priest gulped. 'I, Your Grace? Alas, I have but this minute twisted my ankle. To walk upon it is the purest agony.' And he certainly gave a convincing display of hobbling in great pain.

Joanna gave an impatient toss of the head. 'Then you will accompany me, as ever, my faithful Richilde.'

Being not so quick-witted as the priest, I could not immediately think of a sound reason not to obey. But as we were escorted to the barricade I managed to whisper,

'Your Grace, do we not take an unnatural risk?'

'Nonsense,' Joanna declared. 'Who ever heard of a queen dying of the plague?'

To be sure, I had not. However, it did occur to me that the reason might be that queens, by the very nature of their positions, are more easily able to avoid sources of contamination. And in any event, only one of us was a queen.

But there was nothing for it; the soldiers were removing the barricade.

'You will not enter that pestilential place without me,' Louis now declared.

'Dearest monsignore,' Joanna said, resting her hand on his arm. 'Would you permit me to accompany you into battle?'

'Well, of course not,' the bewildered hero said.

'Then permit me to fight this demon with my own weapons. I would not have us both exposed to danger.'

Which indicated that she was at least sensible of the risk she was taking.

The barricade dismantled, we made what might best be described as a preliminary descent into hell. Nor is the simile ill chosen, for mingled with the noxious odours which immediately assailed our nostrils was that of woodsmoke, and our first sight was of some people attempting to burn dead bodies on an open fire. This was sufficiently unpleasant, but the living creatures were more so, for they wore rags and clearly had not washed for some time, nor, from the way their ribs and other bones protruded through their skin, was it obvious when last they had eaten.

They stared at the two elegantly dressed ladies suddenly introduced into their midst with total disbelief, not unaccompanied by lust, so that I feared we might well be in danger of losing more than our lives – not, of course, that actual loss would have been involved in either of our cases. But Joanna walked straight up to them, and said, 'Do not be afraid. I am your Queen.'

They gaped at her, and then fell to their knees about her, crying out their gratitude for her visit, and seeking to kiss her hand or even the hem of her gown. Others similarly besieged me, but when I would have taken to my heels I looked at the Queen, standing there with calm and beautiful majesty, and felt I could do nothing less, although I was certain the dread disease was already taking hold of my body.

Joanna's courage was remarkable. When I thought of the young girl trembling in my arms following the murder of her husband, or when we learned that Louis of Hungary was marching upon us with all his panoply, I realised that my dear friend had, no doubt because of all these misfortunes, succeeded in growing up, and was now every inch the Queen she had been forced to become so prematurely.

I was still concerned, however, at the way in which she continued to expose herself, and me, to the dangers of contamination. For, surrounded as we were by every putrid odour that can be imagined, she insisted upon entering the miserable hovels of these unhappy people, and examining the sick for herself.

This was another horrifying experience, for in addition to the unsightly swellings at groin and armpit, the complexions of those in extremis had taken on a very swarthy hue, and this aspect of the disease has caused it to be known as the Black Death. Nor could we doubt the reports we heard of its virulence. Several people died while we were with them, and we were assured by their distraught relatives that four days was the normal course of the illness. Were the victims still alive on the fourth afternoon, then his or her survival was assured. But these happy circumstances were rare.

The ravages of this foul pestilence will be remembered by many still living. It has been deduced that perhaps one person in three succumbed in Europe during the three years or so that it raged. An unbelievable figure. Nor has the most learned physician yet discovered its cause – it seems obvious that it came to Europe from Asia and who knows what noxious vapours may cling to that mysterious continent? – or has advanced a satisfactory reason why it suddenly ceased, beyond the logical one, that in a short space of time it destroyed every human being susceptible to it.

It did, however, have certain characteristics, which have been observed by the medical profession, and which have explained events which might otherwise appear miraculous. The principal one of these characteristics was that it was a disease of the heat. In the northern climes, in my own England, where I have learned it raged with as terrible effect as anywhere else, it virtually disappeared during the winter months. And even in sunny Naples, with the onset of the cooler time of the year, its incidence dropped away virtually to nothing aided by the fact that it was an intensely cold winter throughout Europe.

From this we, and especially Joanna, obtained a great benefit. For it will be remembered that the Queen had been hailed as a redeemer, come to rid her faithful people of this dread misfortune – a reputation enhanced by her boldness in plunging into an area in the grip of the plague – and that she had arrived on Neapolitan territory towards the end of September. As regards Santo Maria del Carmine, she took immediate steps, forced the reluctant population to break down the barricade permanently, to convey food and drink to the stricken people, and to commence the proper disposal of the dead.

She supervised this work herself, with her faithful servant ever at her side, and reluctant as the townspeople were to expose themselves, they could not help but follow the example set by their Queen. That we lived in a state of terror is obvious, and every night Joanna and I examined each other for signs of the dreaded buboes, or swellings. To do her justice, Marie assisted us as best she could. We sent our children to a monastery in the country, where we hoped they would be safe, and we removed our menfolk from the scene of danger by sending them to fight against the Hungarians in Naples. This may seem an odd remedy, but there can be no question that a Hungarian lance was not a hundredth part as dangerous as infection by the Black Death.

And, within a month of Joanna's arrival, the incidence of the plague commenced to decline, so that by Christmas it was virtually non-existant. That this happened throughout Naples was a signal for great rejoicing; the Queen was after all a deliverer. That it equally happened throughout Europe, even in lands such as Hungary filled with deadly enemies of Naples, was ignored: news travels slowly. And that it happened when the weather was unseasonably cold was unobserved.

That it happened at all was not an unmixed blessing for us, as I shall now relate.

From Santo Maria del Carmine, Joanna and I and our entourage removed ourselves to the palace of Signor Ajutoris near Porta Capuana, this being regarded as the safest place for the Queen's person until the outcome of the war was determined. For all this while Louis and Alberto and their soldiers were reconquering our fair land for our fair lady.

Master Acciajuoli was given the task of clearing Naples itself of the enemy, and here he revealed as much talent as a soldier as he had as an advocate: General Lupo was soon forced to evacuate the Castel Nuovo, leaving half of his men behind as prisoners. Meanwhile Louis and Alberto pursued a victorious course in their round of battles and sieges, one by one reducing the other Neapolitan strong-holds in which Hungarian garrisons were maintained. It therefore seemed, as the new year progressed, that our affairs were truly on the mend. Alas, catastrophe was again at hand.

One of the problems of employing mercenary armies is that such men are fighting not for honour or patriotism, but simply for pay. They are thus always liable to desert the flag if their wages become in arrears, and they are equally prone to exchanging one flag for another, if a higher offer for their services is made by the opposing general.

Now it so happened that Louis of Hungary had also found it necessary to employ mercenary forces in raising his army to the strength required for a successful invasion of Naples in the first place. These foreign troops, mostly German, had composed the major part of the garrisons left behind when the Hungarian host had found it necessary to retreat. They now surrendered en masse to Louis of Tarento, and cheerfully took up arms again in Neapolitan colours. This immediately vastly increased both our army and our prospects, and the commander of these mercenaries, a brute named Warner, rapidly made himself the essential second-in-command to our gallant Prince, in which capacity he was given more and more responsibility.

No one guessed that the lout was all the while negotiating with the Hungarian viceroy, Lupo, who was still maintaining himself in the field.

Equally, no one knew that Louis of Hungary, brooding in Buda, was observing the apparent disappearance of the Black Death from Italy, as it had already disappeared from Hungary, and concluding that the pestilence had sped its course, once again mobilised his army.

Thus suddenly two tremendous shocks overcame our fortunes, and at an awkward time, for no sooner had Joanna and I mutually celebrated the onset of our second pregnancies, than we learned that General Warner had surrendered himself, his army, and the town of Corneto where he had been positioned, to Lupo, whom he was once again determined to serve, and almost in the same breath that Louis of Hungary had disembarked with a vast army at Manfredonia, and had already seized Trani, Canosa and Salerno; he was now besieging Aversa.

This terrible news was slightly alleviated by the

gallantry of the defenders of that town, who numbered only five hundred men, but were commanded by the splendid Giacomo Pignatelli. The Hungarian monarch was disposed of no fewer than ten thousand horse and seven thousand foot, and yet could make no impression, and indeed, leading one assault himself, received an arrow wound in the foot.

The result of this was that he determined to starve the garrison out. Our problem was how to relieve it. For with the desertion of Warner we lacked the men to face the Hungarian army in the open field. With his usual gallantry, Prince Louis issued a challenge to his namesake to settle all by single combat between the pair of them, but the Hungarian was not such a fool as to match himself against our hero's strong right arm. Meanwhile Renaud de Baux – a brother of the Grand Justiciary – assembled a fleet of galleys in Naples harbour, just in case our cause again reached such a state as to necessitate flight.

This indeed was the course our destiny now followed. Aversa surrendered when it was starving, and the Hungarians marched against Naples itself. Needless to say, history repeated itself, and the good citizens sought to make what terms they could with the conqueror. As it happened, his harsh response resolved them after all to resist him for as long as they could, but this unexpected spirit was too late for us: we had already embarked.

It was only when we came again to port that we became aware of another singular and horrifying event.

Marie of Durazzo, the Queen's sister, had spent the time since our return at the Castello del Uovo, south of Naples, anxious to preserve her three small children from the risk of contamination by the plague, and having little to offer her sister in the ruling of the country: truth to tell, for all the kindness and sisterly love Joanna showed her sister, she could no longer bring herself entirely to trust her. In these circumstances, out of sight and out of mind, and in the alarums and excursions which had attended our return, she had been somewhat forgotten, but of course Joanna would not abandon her to the mercy of Louis for a second time, and considered that she could do no better than send Renaud de Baux himself to bring her safely to embarkation.

The story of what happened we heard later, from the lips of Marie herself. She had been informed of the sad state into which the kingdom had again fallen, and was packed and ready with her babes, awaiting only the escort necessary to join her sister. When the approach of Renaud de Baux was observed, she was utterly relieved of her fears, and sought only an immediate departure. Imagine her consternation, then, when Renaud entered her private chamber, accompanied only by his son Robert, and his chaplain, and informed her that he must exact a certain condition, or he would abandon her.

Marie could not believe her ears. 'Has not my sister sent you?' she demanded, her voice trembling with a mixture of fear and anger.

'Your sister, the Queen, is no longer in a position to send anyone anywhere,' the rascally fellow informed the Princess. 'She and her husband have already fled. She is once again a fugitive, and this time she will never regain her throne. But if you do not accede to my wishes, you will become the victim of Louis of Hungary. I have heard it said that he means to expose you to his soldiery, and allow each man in turn to have his way with you.'

Marie was reduced nearly to fainting by the possibility of such a fate, and, clasping Renaud's hand, begged him forthwith to remove her and her family beyond the reaches of the Hungarian monster.

'That I shall do, madame,' he assured her. 'And at the risk of my own life if need be. Providing only you agree to my requirements.'

'Which are?' Marie could be quite as haughty as her sister when she deemed the occasion right.

'That you wed my son, this instant. My chaplain will perform the ceremony.'

Marie confessed to us later that she supposed she had gone mad to have heard such a proposal made to her, at such a time, and from such a man, who had not a drop of royal blood in his veins.

She took refuge in anger.

'You insolent wretch,' she snapped. 'How dare you make such a proposal to the sister of your Queen? You had best pray that I agree to forget your words, and attempt to atone for them by your devotion to duty.'

Renaud merely bowed. 'Then I will bid you farewell, madame.' And he went to the door, his son and the priest, neither of whom had spoken a word, at his heels.

This time Marie could not believe the evidence of her eyes, rather than her ears.

'Would you abandon me?' she shouted.

Renaud turned to look at her.

'Be thankful, madame, that I do no more than that,' he said. 'I am indeed tempted to avenge here and now the insults you have just hurled at me. But I will be content to leave that vengeance to the King of Hungary. I will imagine you, kneeling at his feet, naked and bleeding, and praying for mercy. They say he does not know the meaning of the word.'

Marie dropped to her knees. 'Then see, I beg you, proud lord. If not for myself, then for my children. Will you not at least take them to safety?'

'You should have thought of your children, madame, before spurning my good offices.'

Marie here thought that her heart would burst with horror. Yet she still supposed that she could appeal to reason, and understanding, and humanity.

'But I do not love your son,' she moaned. 'I have never seen him before this day. I know nothing of him. How can you, brother to our minister of truth and justice, dare to contemplate such a crime as this?'

And then, seeing that Renaud's face remained stern and unbending, she turned to the boy himself.

'For God's sake, good Robert,' she said. 'I am a widow and a mother. What beauty I had is sadly fading before the exigencies of my life. Have you no true love to whom you wish to turn? Have you no softness in that young heart of yours? I beg of you, but dissuade your father from his foul purpose, and I will honour you above all men for the rest of my life.'

But the youth was a true son of his father. If he did not dare look the Princess in the face, he could yet mutter, 'I am bound to obey my father's wishes, madame.'

In desperation, Marie turned to the priest, who had thus far been a silent witness of her terrible predicament, but one look at his face assured her that he intended to remain silent, until called upon to pronounce the dread words. Thus she stared at the three men, and they stared at her. Marie later confessed to us that she was at that moment tempted to rush to the window, and throw herself into the sea, but could not bring herself either to abandon her babes or kill them with herself.

This pregnant pause was interrupted by a growing tide of noise, which, as it approached, could be discerned as the sound of people running and shrieking their fear. They seemed mainly women, who screamed, 'Fly! Fly! Fly! God has abandoned us! The Hungarians are in the city!'

Marie's daughters joined in the screaming, as did Marie herself feel like doing. Instead she gazed at Renaud, who gave her a brief bow.

'We have tarried long enough,' he said. 'I will bid you adieu, fair Princess. Certain it is that I will never see you again.'

'Wait,' Marie said, her voice calm. 'If I must sacrifice myself to save the lives of my children, then so be it. I will wed your son.'

'Then let us make haste,' Renaud said.

The young couple knelt before the infamous priest, and

a moment later were pronounced man and wife.

'Now let us flee this place,' Marie said, when the ceremony was completed.

'Not so fast, daughter-in-law,' Renaud said. 'The marriage has yet to be consummated.'

She gazed at him in horror. 'You expect me to undergo that, now? There is no time.'

'There is time enough for that,' Renaud assured her. 'It does not take more than a few minutes, and I promise you that your husband is eager. Is that not so, Robert?'

The dreadful youth was already removing his breeches to prove his father's point.

Renaud gestured to the bed. 'Do you prepare yourself, madame.'

Marie was once more close to fainting with the shame of it, but she endeavoured to keep some of her wits about her. 'My ladies ...'

'Are unnecessary. It is a simple matter of hoisting your skirts. I shall assist you.'

'No,' she gasped. 'Never!'

'Then do it yourself, or the marriage is null and void and we will take our departure.'

Poor Marie crawled on to the bed and arranged herself, with her skirts about her waist. Nor was she to be spared the slightest indignity, for Renaud and the priest remained, one standing on either side of the bed, while the infamous young man humped her. As the Princess later told us, so unprepared was she, either mentally or physically, for such an ordeal, it was as painful as her first night with Charles of Durazzo.

The marriage consummated, Renaud gathered his people and the fleet put to sea. This villainous fellow had of course a great many plans afoot. His concept was that he should abandon the Queen at sea, flee past her, gain Provence, and there announce that Joanna was dead and Naples lost forever, and that the Duchess of Calabria was therefore now also Duchess of Provence, which meant, as she was his daughter-in-law, that he would effectively be ruler of that country; he had no doubt that he could repel Joanna when she eventually appeared.

However, God in His own way truly punishes those who transgress His laws. Sometimes He appears to take a very long time to do so, to be sure, and tries our patience, but in the case of Renaud de Baux retribution was short and swift in coming. His squadron encountered a fierce storm, and far from being able to make Marseilles, felt compelled to seek shelter in the port of Gaeta. Imagine his consternation when he beheld, already in the port, the main part of the Neapolitan fleet, with Joanna and Louis, and myself, on board.

We of course were not aware of the drama which had taken place after we had left Naples, and were simply overjoyed to sight the rest of our fleet, bearing, as we knew, the Duchess and her children. We hurried on deck to greet them with acclamation, and it was some minutes before we realised that the ships were behaving oddly, to say the least; instead of entering the harbour in all haste to escape the blustery wind, they were clustering in apparent confusion beyond the Mole.

Only later did we learn that Renaud was attempting to persuade his sailors to keep the sea. He began by ordering them to do so – as soon as he had identified our vessels at anchor – but when they demurred on account of the weather, he fell to entreaties. However, they insensibly wore closer and closer to the securely moored ships of the Queen's fleet, while we studied them, until suddenly we witnessed Marie herself emerging on deck and running to the rail, looking at us, and screaming, even above the howl of the wind, 'Help me, Louis! Help me, my nobles! Slay these villains who have perpetrated such a dastardly outrage upon me.'

Without hesitation, Louis and Alberto, followed by several of their boldest knights, climbed into a small boat

208

and put out. They rowed with all their strength against the wind, while Joanna and I cheered them on, and gained the side of Renaud's galley. Before anyone could stop them they had clambered aboard, and Marie was telling them her story.

'Foul wretch!' Louis declared, and without further ado ran Renaud through and despatched him. He then, assisted by Alberto, placed the infamous Robert and the even more infamous priest in chains, and brought them, as well as Marie and her children, safe to the Queen's galley.

Distressed as we were at this sad occurrence, and confounded by the weather, which was preventing us from reaching any port from which we could lay plans for the future, a mood of depression could have been excused us. But amazingly, we were about to recoup all of our fortunes, at least in a purely material sense. For in our absence, as Marie told us, the Hungarians had indeed dashed upon Naples, but so anxiously that they quite exhausted themselves, and more important, their horses. Witnessing this sorry procession of men and beasts, so far removed from the typical appearance of a conquering host, the citizens of Naples hastily recovered their courage, manned the walls, and shouted defiance at the enemy.

Taken aback by this, and no doubt weakened by his wound, Louis of Hungary was prepared to call a truce, and await an improvement in his health and his fortunes. But this of course was not forthcoming. With the arrival of warmer weather, which occurred early in the new year, the plague made its reappearance, and he was forced to realise that the game was up.

Negotiations were therefore undertaken, with the Pope as intermediary, and eventually a treaty of peace was arrived at by which Louis agreed to abandon his claims upon Naples, and his determination to avenge his dead brother, in consideration of the payment by Joanna of three hundred thousand florins.

This sordid end to the Hungarian's loudly pronounced campaign was no doubt dictated by his own financial straits, as he had now been keeping an army in the field for a very long time, by the fear of the Black Death, and by the pressing necessity to start thinking about Hungary, and the steady encroachment of the Turkish hordes. And indeed it must be said that he used his time well in the east, at one time ruled Poland as well as his own country, extended Hungarian influence far and wide, and finally ended his days known as Louis the Great.

We might have our own opinions as to the worthiness of such a title, but at the time we were merely happy to have seen the back of him.

The negotiations naturally took a considerable time, and it was the spring of 1352 before Joanna was at last able to set foot in Naples as undisputed queen. By that time she had given birth to a daughter, named Catherine after her deceased mother-in-law – we could but pray that her character would not be similar to that of the Valois shewolf – while I had been delivered of a bonny, bouncing boy, whom we named William after my unfortunate father, again hoping that he would have a more happy life than his namesake.

Our own lives now at last seemed to have assumed a permanently successful aspect, for by the end of 1351 the Black Death appeared to have spent its force, and people were able to lose some of the fear which for four years had haunted their every action.

It has been claimed that upwards of seventy-five million people died during those four years, but I take leave to doubt whether there are that many people in the whole world. In these happy circumstances, however, and with the Hungarian threat now finally disposed of, preparations at last went forward to celebrate the coronation of the King and the Queen, for which purpose the Pope sent a Legate to perform the ceremony.

This took place on 25 May 1352, the day of Pentecost, and was quite the most magnificent fête in the history of Naples, or perhaps of anywhere else.

By a happy thought, Joanna pronounced a general amnesty, which applied to everyone, no matter which cause they had supported in the wars, and this naturally completely restored her popularity with her people, who thronged the streets as she and Louis rode side by side beneath a canopy of cloth-of-gold, followed by the assembled nobles of the realm.

Alas, it seemed that my noble lady was never destined for that happiness which is, even if fitfully, the lot of us inferior mortals. There we were, following the coronation, all in procession, dressed in our finest, surrounded by laughing and cheering people, when, as we passed through the Porta Pettruchia, some ladies threw several garlands of flowers from a high window on to the handsome knight who had this day become their legal King. These garlands broke open as they drifted downwards, and the result was that Louis was half smothered by the various blooms, which entered his visor and had him coughing and choking.

His discomfort communicated itself to his horse, which promptly reared with such violence that the rein snapped. The result of this was that our new King was unseated. Louis was as brilliant a horseman as he was everything else, and, realising that he no longer controlled his mount, leapt to the ground with all the agility of an athlete, landing quite unhurt ... but the crown which had just been placed upon his brow fell from its lofty perch, and shattered into three pieces.

The event was witnessed with a wail of dismay, followed by a total silence. There was no one present who did not take the event as a very ill omen. But Louis was first to recover, and laughingly kicked the pieces of broken metal at his groom.

'It is not the crown that matters, my people,' he

shouted. 'It is the head that wears it.' And he tapped himself on the forehead as his steed was recaptured and brought forward, the rein now secured.

Yet were the people right in their forecast of disaster, for when we regained the Castel Nuovo, it was to find the Princess Catherine in the last extremities, and that evening she died.

The Princess had been unwell for some time, with a high temperature and a hacking cough, yet her condition had not been such as to excite alarm. But the fever suddenly took hold of her, and ran its course within a few hours.

Joanna was inconsolable; she readily recognised the tragedy as but another symptom of that misfortune which seemed to pursue her entire life. Louis shouldered his grief with typical manliness. He refused to allow the planned coronation ceremonies to be interrupted, and the full three days of jousting and tournaments continued. In these the King played the fullest part, and emerged the victor ludorum, as had been expected. I suspect it was only those opponents who had to face his steely eyes as they charged in the lists could truly measure his grief.

It was now, also, that he instituted the order of the Knights of the Knot, and all in all, he was hailed by the Neapolitans as the most worthy of kings.

To watch her husband's feats of arms, the young Queen – she was still only twenty-six years old – sat on a high dais, dressed all in black, as were her ladies. But if she smiled and clapped her hands at his triumphs, the pleasure did not extend to her eyes, and certainly not to her heart. For Louis, although it took him some time to realise it, had ended his marriage in anything more than name.

I do not think Joanna was angry with him for attempting to overcome the death of their daughter by action. Rather I always felt that she was envious of his spirit and mental strength. But his embraces no longer sent her into transports of joy, as every time he took her in his arms she thought of that cold, still little body which had been the fruit of their connection.

And yet, she was Joanna, the tempestuous and passionate and, dare I say it, the lascivious girl I had known and loved for so long. Her loins burned, and did so with increasing compulsion as she grew older. But these were yet early days, and I suspect that in the first instance she was merely concerned with perhaps regaining the careless pleasures of her girlhood, when she had loved irresponsibly, uncaring of the future.

As her closest, indeed, her only confidante – for she and her sister never truly regained any intimacy, and all the other companions of her youth were dead – I was naturally involved in all her thoughts, and all her desires, or, in the beginning, her lack of them, for I was well aware with what ardour King Louis approached her bed, and with what disappointment he left it again within an hour.

I had but a single remedy for this, and with my invariable devotion to the well-being of my mistress – which was naturally extended to include the well-being of her husband – I would willingly have sacrificed myself, but it appeared that he wished his wife's body, not that of her handmaiden, however beautiful.

Soon his visits all but ceased, although I then discovered, to my annoyance and indeed my humiliation, that he had indeed found some solace ... with one of the other ladies at Court!

Perchance I wept for us both. Certainly I wept with the Queen for the month following her babe's death, while assuring her that there would be many others to bring a smile to her face – without quite determining how this was to be accomplished if she was not prepared to grant her husband an entry into her womb. To my attempted encouragement she returned an inconsolable grief, for some time. Nor did she find the slightest pleasure in her son, who, as she well knew he was the result of her alliance with Bertrand of Artois, did nothing more than return memories of the crime for which she was sure, Papal indulgence notwithstanding, she was now being punished. Thus she took to sitting stony-faced in her private chamber, which overlooked the Mole and the harbour and the sparkling Mediterranean, her needlework lying idle on her lap.

I naturally tried to amuse her as best I could, and so introduced into her presence a band of minstrels, who strummed their lutes and sang their romantic ballads. I thought they were excellent, as well as comely, young men, but for a while Joanna showed little interest in them. Until I realised that her gaze was fixed somewhat fiercely on the youngest of the trio, a youth of a very tender age, who did most of the singing in a high, clear voice which quite belied the size of his codpiece. This circumstance no doubt also interested the Queen, who at the end of the recital gave a gentle clap of applause, which had the minstrels bowing in appreciation, and then, when I would have ushered them through the door, said, 'Stay awhile, young man. I would speak with you.'

The young man looked at his companions in some alarm. They shrugged their shoulders and sidled from the chamber, leaving me standing by the door in considerable apprehension. Which increased when my mistress said, 'You may close the door, Richilde.'

I obeyed, and returned into the room, where the young man was standing before the Queen, looking most uncertain.

'You have a delightful voice,' Joanna remarked. 'Where did you learn to sing?'

'From my mother, Your Grace.'

'And now you are a man, with a trace of beard on your chin,' Joanna observed. 'Yet your voice is as high and sweet as that of a castrati.'

'You flatter me, Your Grace.'

Joanna smiled at him. 'Because you are, indeed, whole?'

He blushed. 'Your Grace ...'

'Pour the young man a glass of wine, Richilde,' Joanna commanded. 'And you and I will have one also.'

I obeyed, and Joanna sipped.

'Are you wed?' she asked.

'I am too young for matrimony, Your Grace.'

'Too young,' Joanna repeated, and sighed, and when Joanna sighed, walls were wont to tremble. 'What is your age?'

'Fourteen years, Your Grace.'

'Fourteen! I was younger far than you, sweet singer, when I was despatched to the marriage bed.' Or a bed, certainly. 'I would swear that had my husband been one such as you I would have led a happier life.'

So plain an invitation had to penetrate even the skull of a thickhead, as this fellow appeared to be. He looked anxiously in my direction, as if seeking confirmation.

'I think I hear Prince Charles calling, Your Grace,' I lied with immediate tact. 'Shall I see what he is about?'

'Assist me to bed, first,' the Queen commanded.

The minstrel and I goggled at each other; this was too plain.

'And then leave this handsome youth to sing me to sleep,' Joanna continued. 'And, Richilde, there is a bag in my chest. Fetch it hither.'

I must confess this last concerned me more than anything else. Was my beautiful, imperious mistress reduced to purchasing her desires? Indeed she was not; the minstrel's codpiece was by now on the point of bursting, and indeed split a seam as between us we disrobed the Queen and placed her between the sheets. But Joanna was in one of those moods of self-abasement which were wont to overtake her, and when, an hour later, I returned, to find them both naked and tousled, she must plunge her hand into the bag and present the dazed youth with a golden florin.

'You will sing for me again,' she told him.

At that moment he would have died for her.

I cannot help but feel that part of Joanna's problem at this time was sheer frustration. Here was the most active of brains, as well as bodies, and she simply lacked the wherewithal to satisfy her constant craving for occupation, both mental and physical. She had the instincts of a mother, but Charles Martel was already revealing the dull mentality which suggested that after all he might be the son of Andrew of Hungary. Thus, in the absence of any others – and in her reluctance to conceive and risk further heartbreak – she lavished much affection on my own two children, who possessed the ebullient personalities of their parents.

She had the instincts of a lover, but the man she had loved above all others now filled her with revulsion.

She had the instincts of a queen, but found that the nobles of Naples were the most difficult of all people to rule – and I do not forget those turbulent barons of my own England, who have equally been described as unrulable. Nor was it possible to indulge in any vast scheme for improving the city, whether by building it up or pulling it down, for Naples was now suffering, in common with all Europe, from a shortage of that commodity which is even more essential than gold: people. The ravages of the Black Death had so reduced the population that finding labour for the most trifling purpose was next to impossible, and only to be obtained at exorbitant prices.

Not that there was much money, either. The costs of the war, and now the heavy burden of the indemnity to Louis of Hungary, had quite emptied the Queen's coffers.

Perhaps Joanna might have established herself the more firmly on the throne had she been willing to be as ruthless as some of her ancestors, but neither she nor her husband had the characters of tyrants. Louis, indeed, was concerned simply with the one aspect of life he could do best, the fairly taking of it, and having, I have no doubt at all, discovered that his wife was preferring other arms to his own, spent his entire time either in jousts or in fighting in any war in which he could obtain a command, whether the fortunes of Naples were involved or not.

My own fortunes took a singular turn at this juncture, with the appearance at the court of Naples of Nicola di Lorenzo.

This man, who preferred to call himself Cola di Rienzi, was of the meanest origins, his father having been a tavern keeper in Rome, for all that he put it about he was actually the illegitimate son of the erstwhile Holy Roman Emperor, Henry VII. Be that as it may, Cola had, as it were, rubbed shoulders with ourselves from an early date, for in 1343, at the age of thirty, he had been despatched from Rome to Avignon to plead the cause of reform in the tortured Holy City, for too long now the prey of rival factions of nobles. Cola, of such humble birth, represented the popular or people's party, who wished only to have their Pope restored to them to rule in peace and justice.

The pontiff to whom he appealed, of course, had been that old and lascivious friend of Joanna and myself, Clement VI, at that time but recently elected to the Papal throne. Clement would naturally have much enjoyed being able to return to Rome in power and triumph, and he had thus encouraged Rienzi to the extent of appointing him notary of the Roman civic treasury, a position still within the authority of the Papacy, and, thus armed, our hero had returned to his native city to do nothing less than accomplish a revolution which would restore Rome to its ancient glory.

His plans appeared to prosper, and on 20 May 1347, while Joanna and I were in the deepest toils as a result of Andrew's death, Rienzi had summoned a parliament to meet on the Capitoline Hill, at which he announced a series of edicts against the nobles who had for so long misruled the city. Acclaimed by the mob, he took for himself the title of tribune, with dictatorial powers.

The nobles could not withstand the popular fury, and it appeared as if Rienzi had triumphed. But like so many base-born men who have greatness suddenly thrust upon them – and not a few of noble birth, either – he now proceeded to extend his vision far beyond that of the Pope. His reforms of the taxation, the judiciary, and the politics of Rome were hailed as indicating the dawn of a new age, nor could his determination to make Rome the capital of a 'sacred Italy', whose mission would be to spread peace and justice throughout the world, be criticised. His act in sending silver wands to all the principal cities and rulers of the peninsula, without Papal authority, was, however, frowned upon, the more so when no fewer than twenty-five cities accepted his invitation to join his sacred confederation.

Naples, convulsed as it was with civil strife at the time, was not one of them.

Rienzi now went even further, and had the temerity to summon the rival claimants to the throne of the Holy Roman Empire, Louis IV of Bavaria, a member of the Wittelsbach family, and Charles IV of Luxemburg, to appear before him, that he might determine their suitability.

This was too much for Clement, who knew that Louis was his enemy. A legate was promptly despatched to bring the proud tribune to heel. This worthy Cola chose to ignore, while supporting the claims of Louis, and preparations were undertaken for the Bavarian's coronation, in Rome.

This anti-Papal movement might have succeeded had Louis lived, but unfortunately for Cola he died in this same year, leaving the Imperial throne to his rival; while Clement, as we had ourselves observed at first hand, was not the sort of man to be slighted. His agents worked amongst both people and nobles, especially the great families of Orsini and Colonna, and as a result a counter-revolution began to gather pace, to such an extent that Cola was forced to flee to the mountains of the Abruzzi, and remain there in hiding.

This should have been the end of his story, but with remarkable pertinacity, two years later, at a time when our own fortunes were in the balance and the Black Death was raging with unparalleled ferocity, he left his hermitage and made his way to Prague, to the court of Charles IV himself, whom he determined to influence with mystical prophecies. Charles did what any sensible ruler would have done: he placed him under arrest and despatched him to Avignon, where Clement, if unable to have him burned as a heretic as many wished – Cola's religious views were entirely orthodox – none the less clapped him into prison.

Here again he might have remained, and entirely disappeared from history, had not Clement died, in December 1352. This was an event which caused everyone some concern, as changes in the personality of the Pope nearly always herald changes in the policy of the Papacy. If it would be stretching a point to regard Clement as a friend of ours, we could at least remember that he was a man capable of succumbing to Joanna's charms.

Not to mention my own.

The new man we had met, only briefly, during our sojourn in Avignon. We took comfort from the fact that he was also a Frenchman, Etienne Aubert. But, unlike Clement, he had begun his adult life as a civil lawyer, and only later had taken holy orders. A protégé of Clement's, to be sure, he had soon been appointed Cardinal Bishop of Ostia, which of course is the port for Rome. From here he had also imbibed ambitions as to the restoration of the Papacy to the Holy City, and on being elected Pope – as Innocent VI – began to consider how these ambitions might be realised.

In Cola di Rienzi he conceived himself to have a ready

and potent weapon. Cola was therefore released from prison, given the title of senator, and told to prepare the Romans for the return of their Pontiff.

This task was of course not easy of accomplishment. As I have mentioned earlier, the misdeeds, and mishaps, of Boniface and his successors had raised many doubts in men's minds as to the true role and power of the Papacy. These doubts had not been assuaged by the catastrophe of the Black Death, against which priest had been as powerless as professor. The Colonnas now held sway in Rome, and were wont to defy those popes who, as they said, had separated themselves from the seat of their spiritual and temporal power. Rienzi was therefore conscious that his return to Rome would be attended by some danger, and needed to be assisted by some temporal force. With this in mind, and supported by the Papal authority, he appeared in Naples in the early summer of 1354.

Joanna was pleased to receive the revolutionary, not because she was any supporter of people against prince, but because on the one hand it was necessary for her to remain on good terms with Clement's successor, and, on the other, she had not forgotten that nearly all Italy north of Naples, and the nobles of Rome more than any, had acclaimed Louis of Hungary as he had marched south to war upon her.

In addition to all this, Cola was a fine, handsome man, now some forty-one years old, which I have lately come to conclude is near to the prime of life – I remark this with deliberation, as I am now some years older than this and have not yet, I feel, achieved my own prime. Certainly his long, straight nose, his firm lips, and his jutting chin, but imperfectly concealed beneath a short beard, all combined to suggest a character of great strength of purpose ... and not necessarily confined to politics.

Remarkably, however, Cola revealed less interest in the Queen than in her handmaiden. It is not for me to suggest that this was not the first time such an unusual distinction had been made. One thinks of Charles of Durazzo ... but Charles, eventually, and most others previously, had felt the aura of majesty added to the very real beauty of my mistress, and had refused to look further, even beyond her shoulder. It will be recalled that even Pope Clement had felt the Queen necessarily to be his first objective, however much he had clearly enjoyed the prolongation of his labours at my expense. Cola, however, was a man of the people, who regarded queens as well as princes as unnecessary excrescences on the face of mankind. He chose by beauty alone – of character as well as body – and forgot the aura.

Or perhaps, being an Italian, he had never previously known anyone with yellow hair.

Joanna was immediately sensible of the situation, and without further ado agreed to supply the senator with an armed Neapolitan escort with which to assert his papal authority in Rome. The escort would be commanded by General Alberto Cogni.

I was delighted for my dear husband, if concerned that he would again be riding into danger. I was even more concerned when Joanna took me into her boudoir and kissed me tenderly upon the lips.

'It is my intention that you should accompany Alberto,' she said.

'To Rome?'

'It is a famous city.'

I could not deny that. 'But this Rienzi, he strips me naked with his eyes.'

'Perchance he will wish to do so with his hands, my dearest Richilde. I can but beg you to lie back, and enjoy it, and think of me.'

I scratched my golden head. 'You wish me to do this, Joanna?'

'I wish you to help Rienzi to succeed in his mission. That way we will not only secure an ally upon our northern flank, we will make a friend of this new Pope. Both are eminently desirable aims. Rienzi will certainly seek to rise. A senator, according to my knowledge of Roman history, may well become an emperor.'

I could hardly argue with that prognostication, either. I understood, of course, that Joanna, much as she loved me, was at this moment anxious to remove me somewhat from her intimate service, as I had left her in no doubt that I disapproved of her dallying with base-born minstrels and the like. To this extent I would have liked to remain, as saving my dear mistress from herself I have always regarded as my principal duty on earth. But to be my own mistress for a season was a powerful attraction, and if I refused to consider the possibility of being unfaithful to my beloved Alberto, I reflected that there could be no faithlessness in carrying out the instructions of Joanna herself; what had to be done must be considered a job of work.

Perhaps with some foreboding of the future, however, I left my two children in Naples, in the care of the same governess who was attending to Charles Martel. There I felt they would be safe, and I had Joanna's permission to return to Naples in the autumn and visit them, and if then I felt secure in my new situation, to take them with me to Rome.

Neither of us suspected that I would be back in Naples far sooner than the autumn, or that I was about to encounter total catastrophe.

We set off for the march north, a group of some fifty persons, for in addition to Alberto and his score of soldiers, Cola himself had as many attendants, and Joanna had insisted upon providing me with a small household of my own, composed of servants of both sexes.

This was the first occasion on which I experimented with the new saddle which had recently been invented, especially for women. Hitherto, with much indecent flurrying of skirts and, indeed, display of leg, we hapless females had been forced to ride astride, and I may say that a long day in the saddle, with one's skirts arranged to either side, and nothing between the most tender and susceptible parts of one's body and the bony back of a horse but hard leather and folded blanket, was an experience not to be relished, even if, on occasion, it could lead to some very peculiar sensations. But this new saddle was comfort itself. It was all arranged on one side, so that only one foot was in the stirrup, the knee of the other being hooked over a projection somewhat higher up and further forward. This meant that one actually sat on one's skirt and shift rather than bare flesh, and equally that mounting and dismounting were absolutely decorous performances. The side-saddle, as it was called, had the disadvantage of leaving one less in control of one's steed, but for ordinary purposes it was admirable.

It also presented the rider to the best effect, and I may say that in my crimson cotehardie, lined with white silk, my sideless surcoat, in pale blue, and secured with the buttons which were becoming all the rage to the exclusion of ties, my crimson mantle, also lined with white silk, and my golden cylindrical cauls which exactly matched the sheen of my hair as they hung to either side of my ears, I presented a most elegant picture. Certainly Cola thought so, and spent much time riding at my side, as we approached the fabled seven hills of Rome.

I will be frank and confess that I was disappointed at my first glimpse of the Eternal City. In fact, I was appalled. Long years of civil unrest and Papal neglect had left the one-time mistress of the world in a sad ruin. The aqueducts, which as far back as the Caesars had carried a constant supply of fresh water to all the myriad baths of the teeming populace, lay holed and empty; the streets had weeds thrusting up through the ancient paving stones; the great buildings of antiquity lay abandoned, gaping caverns inhabited by bats and rats, and the ruins of the forum were lost in a jungle of tangled thickets which even spread over the Capitoline Hill.

'Of course it is a sad sight,' Cola admitted. 'It requires a leader of great vision to restore the city to its eternal glory.'

'Are you not a leader of vision, monsignore?' I inquired, as flattery, both as to his character and by exalting his rank, had to be part of my weaponry.

He stroked his beard with pleasure. 'Indeed I am, fair lady, but to rebuild Rome I first need the power.'

'Which you are hopefully about to achieve,' I pointed out.

'And a great deal of money,' he added thoughtfully.

'Which is ready to hand, once you have the power,' I suggested.

Which gave him something to think about.

But not immediately. I have mentioned our apprehensions once the seven hills came into view. These were now proven baseless. Rienzi's entrance into Rome was only surpassed, in my experience at that time, by Joanna's entry into Avignon ... and I understood that famous occasion to have been part of the machinations of the ambitious Clement. Here it was difficult to doubt the honesty of the Romans' emotion, as they cheered and wept and surrounded our cavalcade with huzzahs of joy. I do not think I am being immodest in suggesting that my own presence, and appearance, helped to stimulate the enthusiasm, but certain it is that we were escorted by this cheering multitude to the palazzo which had been prepared for the senator.

Alas, bitter experience has led me to conclude that orchestrated crowds, such as those at Avignon, however insincere, are preferable to spontaneous demonstrations, where adulation can so easily turn into hatred.

The possibility of such an eventuality was lost to us, however, as we were carried forward on such a wave of excitement, and shown our new home. Here there were quarters for Alberto and myself, a large but shady central courtyard away from the noise, and the stench, of the Roman streets, and a good deal of comfort which belied the crumbling exterior walls.

'So far, so good,' Alberto said, folding me in his arms for a brief moment. Truth to tell, his misadventures, and mine, and his advancing age – for he was several years my elder – had begun to turn him into something of a pessimist.

He went about his duties of mounting the appropriate guards on the various doors of the palazzo, while I had my attendants go about their duties of cleaning our apartments, securing some sweet-smelling flowers for the empty vases, and in general making the place into a home. There remained a great deal to be done, as there was a complete absence of drapes or even rushes upon the floor, and I could tell at a glance that even in southern Italy this house was going to be cold as the grave in January. But it was June, and we had six months to put it right, as I supposed.

And meanwhile, there was my appointed mission. That night, Alberto and I dined with Cola and several of the Roman notables who had come to welcome him home. The wine flowed freely and the talk also, this being mostly about politics. It appeared that the Colonna and their ilk had been ruling the city with a heavy hand, which was at least partly responsible for the enthusiasm with which Cola had been welcomed.

It also appeared that the nobles had debated opposing his entry, or placing him immediately under arrest once he was within the city walls, but had determined to adopt a more amenable stance, both because he came armed with Papal authority, and because of the attitude of the Roman mob, a force to be feared ever since the days of the Gracchi. That the erstwhile rulers of the city were but biding their time and awaiting their opportunity seemed obvious, but as Cola said, 'Forewarned is forearmed, and as long as the people are with me I am immune from the machinations of the nobility.'

I could not altogether agree with him, as there are such things as poisons and daggers in the night which have little to do with popularity, but as I was the only woman present I thought it best to hold my tongue. When the meal was over, however, and I chanced to find myself seated beside the senator, I murmured that were I he I would never sleep alone.

He pressed my hand. 'I have come to the same conclusion, dear Richilde,' he said, also speaking very quietly. 'And who could be a better guardian of my bed than yourself?'

I was taken aback by the directness of his approach, but could not of course take umbrage as I was under the orders of my mistress. I contented myself with uttering various inanities about flattery, which fooled him not a whit.

'What of your husband?' he asked, perceiving Alberto's eye upon us.

'That will be my charge,' I told him, taking control of the proceedings, as it was always in my nature to do.

'Then shall we say, midnight?' the lecherous fellow suggested.

Alberto was not happy with the situation, but when I explained that what I was required to do was commanded by the Queen, he could object no longer, and when I further intimated that several hours in the arms of Cola – who I assured him attracted me not in the least, which was perfectly true at that moment – would only whet my appetite for his own embrace, he became quite enthusiastic.

In making this promise I was being optimistic, or perhaps pessimistic – it is all a point of view. At five minutes to midnight I wrapped myself in an undressing robe and duly made my way to the senator's apartment. There was, I was happy to see, a guard on the door, but this fellow readily admitted me, and a moment later I stood beside the bed, in which Cola sat, reading by the light of his candle, and wearing nothing but a nightcap.

I was aware of being faintly repelled. I was still only twenty-nine years old, and if the circumstances of my life had caused it to be rather a full one, I had not yet been mounted by a man of more than forty years of age. I entirely discount my set-to with Pope Clement, in the first place because it took place on a chair rather than in a bed, in the second because as he was behind me I never had the opportunity to consider him as a man rather than a thrusting object, in the third because I was not actually entered, and in the fourth because it was clearly a punishment.

I was therefore most conscious of Cola's age and without his clothes his fine stature seemed somewhat to shrink, and I became aware that he possessed a larger stomach than I had expected, while his masculine appendage hardly suggested rampant ardour. I reflected that perhaps he did, after all, just require someone to share his bed for safety, without having to risk the scandal of being considered a man of irregular tastes, and felt somewhat chagrined, for although of course I did not like what I had been commanded to do, it has always been my nature to apply myself to each task with the maximum of endeavour, and I was more than ready for the coming sacrifice.

I could not have been more mistaken as to his intentions, or his capabilities. He put down his book and removed his nightcap, the better to peer at me. As it was a warm night I had removed my dressing-gown and laid it across a chair before going to stand by the bed.

'Richilde,' he said. 'You are an incredibly beautiful woman.'

And keeping me standing there he began to trace the outline of my body, with his forefinger, a touch so light, and yet so stimulating, I felt my knees turn to water.

I made myself stand still as his finger explored through valley and upland, wooded vale and deep, damp ravine, not forgetting twin mountain peak and rounded dune, on each of which he spent some time. Then I must kneel beside the bed while he thrust his fingers into my hair with as much relish as if it had indeed been made of gold, letting it trail through his fingers and seeming to kiss each strand. I had never before been appropriated in so complete while at the same time so gentle a fashion, and by the time he had finished his journey I would have coupled with the devil without a second thought.

But he was not yet done. Standing by the bed my knees had been the lower part of his explorations. Now he made me lie down while he discovered the beauty of my feet, kissing each toe in turn, before recommencing his fingertip travels, first on my back and then on my front. Long before he was finished this second journey I was experiencing the most delicious of feminine sensations, and by that time his lance was couched and ready, quite dispelling my earlier doubts.

He now knelt between my legs, gathered my buttocks in his arms, and, in that position, revealing a strength of muscle I had not suspected him to possess, plunged into me with a gentle force which again had me dizzily whirling through an orgasmic space. And this he maintained for several seconds before coming himself.

It was the best fuck of my life. To that moment.

I slept little that night, as the senator had a great deal on his mind: me! He was insatiable, and I reflected that if all men, as they grew older, became more sexually inclined, and more sexually knowledgeable, then we hapless women were in for a busy, albeit delightful, future.

When I staggered back to my own apartment in the early dawn, to find Alberto eagerly awaiting me, I had great difficulty in demonstrating an appropriate amount of enthusiasm, until he actually got to work. Comparisons are odious, and I will not make them. Alberto was my husband, and the handsomest of men. Suffice to say that when he left me I fell into a deep and dreamless sleep, awaking with a start about the hour of noon, and considering only how long it would be before I again took the corridor to Cola's bedchamber.

I thus had every reason to anticipate a long, hot, erotic summer lying ahead of me. Hot and erotic it certainly was. Long, unfortunately, it was not. Nor, despite my midnight revels, was it a happy one.

I well understand that a woman's place is by the stove or in the bed or at the crib, and that she is not required to partake or even be interested in the great affairs with which men amuse themselves. But queens are excepted from these restrictions, and I had spent my life as the servant of a queen. I could no more disinterest myself in politics and financial matters than I could cease breathing. Equally was it necessary for me to go abroad, almost every day, if only as far as the market, and thus I was able to observe the changing moods of the Roman people at first hand.

Because change they did, and with a startling rapidity. The mob which had welcomed Cola with shouts of joy and strewn flowers in his path had apparently presumed that his mere return would end all of their ills, his mere presence raise them once again to imperial power. That to regain the glorious days of the past might require money, which they alone could provide, laws, to which they alone must submit, and above all, a great deal of hard work, to which they alone had to subscribe, had not entered their minds. Thus from the moment Cola seized the reins of power and began his work, his popularity declined.

Undoubtedly the affections of the Roman people for their senator were also being undermined by the agents of those nobles who hated and feared him, but unfortunately this gathering hostility to his rule was far more apparent to me, going amongst them as I did, than to him, locked away in his council chambers and being told only what he wanted to hear. When I endeavoured to warn him, my apprehensions were dismissed with the reassurance that it was when people did *not* grumble that they needed to be feared.

I could not agree with this. I was too aware that what was happening concerned not only the man I had grown to adore, but my dear husband, whose appointed duty it was to guard the senator's life, as well of course as myself, as being always in his company – and known to be so by the mob. And yet there was nothing I could do about it. I felt as one tied to the back of a runaway horse, who can see a precipice approaching, but cannot escape her fate.

And so it proved. It was an unusually hot summer, thus there were more than the usual outbreaks of illness and disease, varying from the sweating sickness to bowels which turned to water, and minor irritants became major complaints. When Cola decided that the trouble was caused by the stench which pervaded the city, and determined that the drains and sewers should be cleaned, the men appointed to do the work objected. They harangued their friends, as usual urged on by the enemies of the state, and soon there was every indication of a riot.

'You are needed, senator,' came the word, and Cola, who feared nothing, immediately set forth to reduce the mob to discipline. With him went Alberto.

I saw them leave the palazzo with a heavy heart, but even I was unprepared for what followed, as the noise, which I could dimly hear in the distance, now swelled into a crescendo and soon lost any semblance to a human sound, and the next thing I saw was Cola himself running across the courtyard towards me, his face blanched and his hands trembling.

'They are mad!' he cried. 'Mad! They seek to destroy me.'

'Where is my husband?' I asked him.

'Richilde, you must hide me. Disguise me as your servant. We must escape this place.'

'Where is my husband?' I asked again, shouting myself,

and seizing his shoulder to shake him.

'Dead, no doubt! He would face the mob, sword in hand. They overwhelmed him. Richilde, for the love of God, help me!'

What a contrast, between the proud senator of only an hour before and this gibbering wreck! And what an even greater contrast between this gibbering wreck and my own dear, heroic husband, whose only thought had been to face the mob, sword in hand ... and in defence of this cur.

Yet I was conscious of the dangers of my own position, and as escape seemed to hold out the only hope of survival, escape with a man was preferable to escape by myself. Besides, I had loved this man, even if I knew I could never do so again.

'Come then,' I told him and, gathering my skirts, ran before him into my bedchamber, and there draped him in one of my own gowns, with a cowled cloak to wear on top, the folds of which, held across his face, would hopefully disguise his features and beard.

Alas for our hopes. As we returned down the stairs – the servants had all fled – we saw a mass of people approaching the palazzo, armed with swords and pikes. One of these pikes was held aloft, and on it was the head of my dear Alberto.

Was ever a woman faced with a more dreadful sight than that of a husband torn to pieces virtually before her eyes? For that is apparently what had happened. Meanwhile our own situation was serious. The mob were intent upon sacking the senator's house, and we were in it.

'Over the back wall,' I shouted, and ran for it. Cola was so terrified he hesitated before following me, and this caused his undoing. The mob caught hold of his skirts and stretched him on the floor. I do believe that at that moment they were interested only in rape, but lust for sexual satisfaction quickly changed to lust for blood when they discovered that they had obtained the naked body of the man who at that moment they hated more than any other.

Now it was my turn to hesitate, as I listened to the dreadful growl of men who have descended to the level of animals, the horrifying shrieks of Cola as he lost that appendage which he had been wont to plunge into me with such delight, the brutal laughter of his tormentors. However, within another few seconds he was dead.

It was time to think of myself, but my chance had gone. I turned back to the wall, but was seized while in the undignified position of attempting to climb over it, and brought back to face this parcel of ravenous human wolves. I presumed my last hour had come, but could not even make myself heard above the hubbub sufficiently to beg the time to pray.

However, manhandle me as they did, my assailants were yet in the main men, who found themselves reluctant to destroy so much beauty.

'She is but a harlot after all,' one of their leaders declared.

And so for execution was substituted rape, which I may say, having had sufficient acquaintance with both, is a far preferable fate, regardless of what certain ecclesiastical ladies may avow. All I actually lost was my breath, momentarily, and all I gained were some trifling bruises on various tender parts of my anatomy.

Unfortunately, sated men often revert to being beasts, and when all who wished had had their fill of me, or rather the reverse, voices were raised as to what punishment might be suitable. It occurred to me that I had already been punished, but I was too exhausted to beg, although I did consider it somewhat hard for me to suffer both of what are claimed to be a woman's most miserable fates in a single afternoon.

However, here again my unusual beauty no doubt saved me. They contented with stretching me on my belly on the floor and holding me there while the letter P for prostitute was branded upon my right buttock, following which I was dragged at the tail of a cart, naked and now bruised and bleeding, and surrounded by a baying mob of women and children, to the city gates, through which I was thrown, with a warning that if I was found in sight of Rome come tomorrow's daybreak, I would be hanged like a dog.

This experience convinced me that neither the people nor the city of Rome were worth saving.

CHAPTER 7

To find oneself naked and alone outside the gates of a city is a most undesirable experience.

I was, however, sensible that my situation could have been worse, and would indeed be worse did I not place some distance between myself and the Romans, and so, barefooted, naked and bleeding, I staggered into the wooded hill country I could see a few miles away.

And there began to doubt if I had not earlier been mistaken, and would have done better to return and be torn limb from limb; I would at least be warm while being manhandled. For it was now October, and as the sun disappeared into the west it became decidedly chilly, while I had had nothing to eat for several hours, and then only a light repast, as it was my usual custom to sit down to a large meal with Cola and Alberto in the middle of the day.

When I thought that neither of those two splendid men would ever sit down to a meal again I burst into tears, and cried even harder when I realised that I could soon be joining them in that unhappy state.

Then I came upon a remarkable deliverance ... well, in a manner of speaking.

Staggering through the gathering darkness, moving because I had no reason to stop save to collapse and die from hunger and exhaustion and cold, I suddenly beheld the glow of a camp fire. Towards this my feet directed themselves as if drawn by an invisible string. Imagine my consternation when I emerged from the trees into the midst of a large group of people, of both sexes and all ages, every one of whom was as naked as I, and as bloodstained as well.

These welcomed me with acclamation, under the impression that I was one of their own.

The horrors of the Black Death only a few years previously had caused people from all walks of life critically to reappraise their situations, their sense of values, their very existence. To many, it had seemed that the death-dealing plague was a visitation from Heaven, and might indeed be the precursor of the End of the World, however far we might be from a millennium.

Out of this soul-searching there had arisen several unusual religious orders, regarding whom the Church had not yet decided on an attitude. One of these was the sect of the Flagellants, who held that if Judgment Day was at hand, their best assurance of a place beside God was to abandon all their worldly possessions, even down to their clothes, and to spend their days begging and chastising themselves for all their sins, real, imagined, or anticipated.

It was into an encampment of this order that I had stumbled, the marks on my own back seeming to indicate that I was one of them, lost from some other band of itinerants. This presumption, being starving for a portion of their meagre rations, I did nothing to counter.

Indeed, I was happy to join them, at least on a temporary basis, for it seemed to me that here was food and companionship, if not exactly shelter, and, more important, these people were heading south for the winter – they had left it a little late to be sure – and were thus making in the general direction of Naples. Which was where I desired to be, just as rapidly as possible.

I therefore embarked upon one of the most remarkable adventures of my life. And from time to time was forced to wonder if I had indeed made a correct choice.

The concept of some fifty souls, as I have mentioned of

both sexes and all ages, not excluding children, walking along the road, more often than not in teeming rain, every one as naked as the day he or she had been born, and solemnly applying a cat-of-nine-tails to the back of the person in front – those at the very front took turns at beginning again at the back in order to have their share of inflicting as well as receiving punishment – may sound ludicrous. Indeed it was. But the very absurdity of our progress was also our salvation. Whenever we marched through a village, the entire population turned out to watch us, and once we had applied our scourges to driving away the dogs who invariably beset us, would willingly supply us with food and drink in return for the spectacle we afforded.

This was gratifying and life-sustaining. Nevertheless, having one's back constantly torn by the lash grew burdensome, even if we were very careful never to hit one another at all hard.

Even more difficult were our personal relationships. It is not possible for human beings to exist at all in close companionship, much less naked, without feeling the urgings of the flesh, except perhaps in the case of one or two saints, whose claims to total chastity I have always found difficult to accept.

But for me, sexual relations have always had to exist on a luxurious scale. That is to say, they should be accompanied by filling meals and heating drinks, and be conducted in a warm bed and between fragrant sheets, and, above all, with a partner of one's own choice. To be sure, I have on occasion been forced to adapt these views – one remembers Charles – but these exceptions have only reinforced my determination to obey my more general instincts wherever possible.

Now I found myself, by a good margin the most attractive female in our band, the object of lust from every quarter. It seems that flagellation can arouse the senses. Indeed I have heard of men unable to get it up without the application of the whip. Nor did fasting and cold seem to have much of a deleterious effect upon the men, and women, who chanced to settle for the night close to where I was huddled in a shivering mass.

I use the word chanced figuratively; there was often a queue.

Here was a difficult situation. I was the newcomer who, easily accepted, could just as easily be rejected again. Without these people I knew I had no hope of ever reaching Naples. And I was usually half paralysed with cold which could only be relieved by bodily contact.

I was therefore constrained to accept my fate on more than one occasion, but the hundred miles which separates Rome from Naples seemed more like a thousand before the walls of my favourite city came into view.

That night I crept away from the Flagellants' encampment, and made my way to the gate. The good sergeant of the guard was undecided whether I was a gift from the gods or from the devil when he first beheld me, but I soon convinced him of my identity, and an hour later, wrapped in his cloak, I was inside the Castel Nuovo.

Late as the hour was, Joanna rose from her slumber to greet me. News of the massacre in Rome had of course reached Naples long before, and she had supposed me destroyed by the mob as had been Cola and Alberto. Now she had her maids fetch warm water and herself washed my back as I soaked, and told her of my adventures.

'You poor darling,' she said, assisting me from the bath and, wet as I was, folding me into her arms. 'I was so afraid for you.'

And then, being Joanna, she must needs question me most closely, first of all on Cola's talents as a lover, and secondly on what it felt like to be raped by several men.

It was over an hour before I could escape to visit my own darlings, and be greeted by them with rapture.

Joanna was genuinely happy that I had survived, and to

have me back. But while I am certain that she regarded me as her one true friend in all the world, in my absence she had grown more determined that my somewhat severe moral outlook should not be allowed to interfere with her pleasures.

For during the few months of my absence the Queen had abated those pleasures not a whit. Rather had she increased in ardour, and now had a stable of half a dozen lusty lads who came to her bedchamber as she required. Louis of Tarento was hardly seen in Naples at all.

I was of course sensible that her delight at my safe return was tempered with a certain reluctance to accept me in my old role, but I was utterly surprised at the course she took to solve the problem.

'I am determined that your services to myself, and to Naples, should be adequately rewarded,' she announced a week after my reappearance. 'Not to mention those to Rienzi,' she added archly. 'I am therefore giving you your freedom, my dearest Richilde, and intend to find you a husband, not only to replace Alberto, but to provide you with a mate worthy of your beauty and abilities.'

I was overwhelmed. But at the same time dismayed.

'I am not worthy of such kindness, Your Grace. But how else shall I live, save as your handmaiden? And in any event, who would wish to marry a penniless ex-slave?'

'Why, no one, to be sure,' Joanna agreed. 'But I can think of a dozen men who would grovel at the feet of the Duchess of Eberli.'

I stared at her with my mouth open.

'That late Duke has recently died without issue,' Joanna explained. 'And indeed without heirs. The duchy has therefore reverted to the crown. Eberli, as you may know, my dearest Richilde, consists of some twenty square miles of the most fertile land, filled with farms and vineyards, situated in the most beautiful valley in the foothills of the Apennines, and produces an income of ten thousand ducats a year. Do you not suppose that will be attractive enough, quite apart from your own charms?'

Again I was overwhelmed, and the more so when I was taken to my new home, and saw the castle, a quarter of the size of the Castel Nuovo, certainly, but a home of my very own for the first time in my life, and rode over the indeed fertile valley which was now in my possession.

And went over the rent roll with my bailiff, a very solemn fellow named Ricardo, who did not even comment on the closeness of our names but grumbled that the returns were not sufficient.

They seemed enormous to me.

Lucia and William joined me in adoring their new situation.

But there remained the question of a husband, Joanna being apparently determined to implement this also as rapidly as possible. She was quite right in assuming that a large number of men would find their way to the door of the Dowager Duchess of Eberli, as I was officially known, and some of them were quite attractive. But I was not in a position to choose for myself.

I was, however, somewhat taken aback when Joanna, having summoned me to Naples, announced that she had found the very man.

'Fernando di Grandi,' she said. 'Could there be a better choice?'

I was astounded.

'Your Grace,' I protested, 'I am thirty years of age.'

'A year older than myself,' Joanna acknowledged. 'And we are both in the very prime of our beauty and our faculties.'

This was not a point I was prepared to argue. But ...

'Signor di Grandi is seventeen.'

'Sixteen,' Joanna corrected me.

'How can I marry a man young enough to be my son?'

'You will find it very stimulating, I have no doubt at all. And it will be good for me as well. Think of this, Richilde. Fernando's father, Roberto di Grandi, is the richest man in my kingdom. If all I hear is true, he may be even richer than myself. I shall insist on a proper marriage settlement, you may be sure. Non-returnable,' she added. 'Half will belong to you, and half to me. And then, Fernando ... you will admit that he is handsome?'

I could not argue that. Fernando already had a moustache, a melancholy expression, flashing eyes, and an outsize codpiece.

'We shall be great friends, you and I and your husband,' Joanna said.

I instantly knew what she intended, but did not protest the idea. I feared I was going to need all the help I could find.

As it proved.

I was introduced to my future in-laws and husband the following week.

This is not to say I did not already know them. Naples society is limited, and I had of course encountered the di Grandis on many an occasion. But never in the guise of prospective relatives. Indeed, the decision was already taken, and had certainly been communicated to them by the Queen.

Signora di Grandi was superciliousness itself; her son was marrying an ex-slave, but in exchange would become a duke – although the title was reserved for my husband, not of right in itself, just as my property and income were mine, and not his.

Signor di Grandi could not wait to get his hands on his future daughter-in-law, although decorum required that he touch only my hands, at least at this stage of our relationship ... but these he kissed most passionately. Truth to tell, he was a handsome fellow, and of an age, forty-five, far more to my taste than his son.

Who seized possession of me on the instant. His kisses began and seeped up my arm, while I giggled girlishly, unable to think of anything else to do. Before I knew what was happening he had traversed my shoulder and had his lips at the tops of my breasts, his chin attempting to nudge its way past my *décolletage*. I found it necessary to give him a buffet, while reflecting that I was in for an even more busy time than I had feared.

I therefore approached my wedding in a state of mixed emotions, of anticipation and apprehension. Nor was I the least disappointed.

The occasion itself was of some importance, celebrated in the great hall of my castle, with appropriate troupes of minstrels in attendance, and a great deal of wine, food and gaiety. This was most enjoyable, even if Ricardo regarded the whole thing with a lugubrious expression, almost visibly adding up what it would cost the rent roll. I on the other hand kept remembering the seventy thousand ducats Joanna had required from Signor di Grandi as a marriage settlement. She was going to keep half, of course, but I still reckoned I was ahead, at least in financial terms.

The Queen herself attended the ceremony, and was my matron of honour, leaving no one in any doubt as to my new status. She it was who finally tucked me into bed, kissed me most tenderly, and whispered, 'I wish to hear all about it.'

Well, she might have done so that night, had she not undoubtedly, like all the rest of the guests, retired in a fuddled state. I had no time for such innocent pastimes. My husband was introduced into my bed by the usual crowd, Joanna amongst them, my nightgown was raised above my chest, and he was placed between my legs, whereupon the riotous throng told us to be at it, promising to return in the morning to make sure all was well – there would of course be no certain evidence of consummation so that they would have to take our joint words.

As if there could be any doubt about it. I will confess that I had consumed as much wine as anyone, if only to put myself in the proper mood for coping with a sixteen-year-old.

Who lost no time. He was in me before the door had properly closed, and the marriage was sealed not more than fifteen seconds later.

I then considered I could relax, as it were, with a good night's sleep in front of me. Never had I been more wrong. He had merely been using up an excess which must have been accumulating since he had first been informed I was to be his bride. Now it was simply a matter of re-creating an erection.

This took five minutes in the first instance, while he played with my breasts and between my legs. Then it was again a hump and a thump.

But he was still far from finished. The next half an hour was taken up with kissing and cuddling, while, having most definitely had his way with me, he commenced to tell me how much he adored me. This was gratifying, of course, but then my ribs took another battering.

Now, surely, I thought, we must be finished, and ventured to wish the youth goodnight.

'Good night?' he cried. 'Why, it is indeed. And it has not yet begun.'

At that I lost my head, and tried to escape. But he was at the door before me, and as, although I am a tall and strong woman, he was an even taller and stronger man, I was carried kicking and screaming back to the bed.

'You are entering into the spirit of it,' he assured me, and proceeded to ram me again.

I soon ceased to protest, and reflected that to be assailed by one man seven times in one night is probably more acceptable than seven different men one after the other, as had happened to me in Rome. Besides, this man was my husband.

But that was a disturbing thought.

Next morning, none of the guests could have the slightest doubt, simply by looking at my face, that we were man and wife, before man as well as before God.

242

Joanna was delighted.

'How I envy you,' she said. 'Oh, how I envy you.'

I was tempted to tell her that she could have the loan of my husband there and then, but decided against it.

'I shall expect you in Naples,' she told me, 'as soon as you have finished honeymooning. With your husband, naturally.'

'I shall be there,' I promised most fervently.

The guests therefore departed, and I was alone with my Fernando. Except for the servants, of course.

I must be fair to my husband, and say that he was a good-humoured and, in many ways, charming fellow. To little William he was a friend, to Lucia, who was now in her ninth year, an elder brother.

This concerned me somewhat, for Fernando's weakness was that he could resist nothing feminine, regardless of age, disposition, or shape. When I was unavailable, even temporarily, he was at the serving maids, and when I menstruated, he moved out altogether, sharing his bed with one of them.

Naturally I did not object to these peccadilloes. I knew all men indulged in them ... and I was glad of the rest.

Because I was his principal joy. Again, I must confess that in many ways this was most gratifying: who does not like to be adored, and Fernando, so he claimed – and who was I to dispute the matter? – had worshipped me from afar even from before the age of puberty.

But it was an exhausting business.

I am bound to say that he far exceeded any other man I have ever met in the continuation of his passion. Now it is well known that the principal curse of womankind is man's impatience, and inability to contain his lubricity. That is why we value so much a man who has learned restraint, and timing, and the ability to use his hands as well as his member.

Fernando certainly knew the usage of hands, but to his own gratification rather than mine, specifically. On the

243

other hand, it is impossible to be ravished several times in a night, at least by a loving rather than a brutal man, without responding. Thus it would be an entire falsehood for me to pretend that I abhorred his visits to my couch – far from it.

I could not help but consider the future, however. At this rate I conceived that I would be a worn-out rag by the age of thirty-five.

The miracle was that I did not become pregnant.

I therefore waited for a reasonable time, two months, and then seized the very first opportunity to suggest a visit to Naples.

Fernando agreed without hesitation, and so we betook ourselves to that den of iniquity.

Joanna was delighted to receive us, the more so when I confided to her some of the secrets of the marriage bed. Within twenty-four hours we were dining tête-à-tête with the Queen and one of her favourites, an artist named Giotto. He was a youth like Fernando, considerably younger than either Joanna or myself, and, withal, shy and withdrawn; his grandfather had, as will be remembered, been a truly famous painter, but Joanna's young friend came from the wrong side of the blanket – and indeed only used the name in the hopes of attracting commissions – and withal entirely lacked his grandfather's talent.

At least with the brush. Apparently he suited Joanna well enough. On the other hand he was utterly overwhelmed by my yellow hair and white skin, not to mention various curves and valleys, and so he was a great relief after my husband, and while Joanna and Fernando, following our meal, retired to her bedchamber for a private conversation, from which she emerged as tousled and exhausted as ever I had done, Master Giotto and I dallied on the settee, to the extent that I finally had to guide him where he so obviously wished to go.

244

*

Master Giotto's hesitancy was a pleasant relief from Fernando's insatiable thrusts. But there was another ordeal awaiting me, the impatient anxiety of my new father-in-law.

Obviously such a man is of great importance to a hapless young bride, and even to one rapidly approaching middle-age. I felt myself called upon to regard Roberto di Grandi as a surrogate for the father I had so unfortunately lost many years before, laughed merrily at his appalling quips, and giggled girlishly when he carelessly threw his arm round my shoulders, or let his hand rest upon my knee.

Fernando and I were housed in the Castel Nuovo, of course, but we were expected to call fairly regularly at the Grandi palazzo, when Count Roberto would entertain us, or more especially, me, by showing me his library, which was very fine, and his collection of codpieces, which was unrivalled in all Italy, he informed me.

Certainly I had never seen such variety, of both size and material; it follows that the shape of a codpiece is, the shape of a codpiece.

'Are they all yours, Father?' I asked, innocently.

He laughed. 'Why, no, my dear Duchess. These are the fruits of conquest. On the field of battle, of course. How more may a man admit defeat than by surrendering his codpiece?'

A point of view I had not previously considered, but of which I had to admit the validity.

'But you have never had to surrender yours,' I murmured.

Another laugh. 'Only to fair and gallant ladies. There a man may so surrender without the slightest risk to his honour. Indeed, not to do so is the dishonourable course. Would you claim such a trophy, my dear Richilde?'

I cast an anxious glance at the door, but this the crafty fellow had shut, and indeed locked, upon our entry.

'It is yours for the taking, Richilde,' he leered. 'You will not pretend a lady of your experience does not understand the intricacies of masculine attire.'

'It is the intricacies of the masculine mind that bewilder me, Father,' I told him. 'I cannot believe that what you intend can have the sanction of the Holy Church.'

'In which case we will attend confession together,' he suggested.

'I am your daughter, to all intents and purposes.'

'I but wish to sample some of the joy you bestow upon my son. My so fortunate son,' the scoundrel mumbled, unlacing my bodice.

Well, what would you? I have always been in favour of domestic bliss above all other forms of happiness, possibly because I have known so little of it myself. Here I had married into a happy if somewhat lubricious family, and I was now being requested to make the head of that family happier yet. I felt it would have been churlish of me to refuse, and besides, since Cola, although I could never think of that despicable coward without contempt, I had developed a distinct preference for mature men as opposed to youths ... if only because they needed to stop and rest from time to time.

In this I was mistaken, at least as regards Roberto di Grandi, who was in every way his son's father. But by the time I found this out, it was too late.

We spent a pleasant week in Naples, at the end of which Joanna asked me certain pertinent questions. When I assured her that I was not at all pregnant, she informed me that she had a mission for me.

Joanna, for all her undoubted laxity of morals and the burning desires of her loins, remained always a highly intelligent and competent ruler. It was as if she could at will divide herself into two people, one the swirling temptress of the bedroom, the other the cool, calculating mistress of her realm and her people. I must confess it was this side of her that I admired most, and it was now revealed to me.

Naples was beleaguered, not at this moment in a physical sense, but financially. The treasury was all but empty, and money was most desperately needed, if only to keep the army in being.

Joanna was therefore anxious to raise funds, in great quantities, and had hit upon the obvious solution: to sell the Duchy of Provence. As she pointed out quite correctly, she had only ever been to that fair land once in her life, and then as a fugitive, and hopefully she would never return there again. Provence was of absolutely no use to the defence of Naples, the two people had nothing in common, and the requirements of the rulers of the two states, although they might exist within the same body, were as different as chalk and cheese.

Hence her reasoning, which was entirely sensible.

A sale of land, however, to be viable, requires two important factors to be present. The first is the legal right to dispose of the land, and the second is a purchaser.

As to the second, Joanna saw no difficulties; the kings of France had long cherished the duchy, and she understood from her various agents that the new king of the country, John, was a man of great breadth of mind and generosity of spirit.

The first requirement was less easily resolved, for it will be remembered that on his deathbed, Good King Robert had made the proviso that for no reason whatsoever was Provence ever to be separated from his family. When one is faced with a situation like this, there is only one authority to whom appeal can be made with any hope of success: the Pope in Rome.

Or rather, in Avignon.

Now a glance at the map of Europe will convince anyone that Naples, Avignon and Paris are virtually in a straight line from south-east to north-west – well, it is the slightest of doglegs. It therefore seemed to Joanna that an emissary on his, or her, way to negotiate the sale of the duchy to the King of France would lose no journeying time by stopping off at Avignon and first of all negotiating with the Pope.

'Her, Your Grace?' I inquired somewhat anxiously.

'Can there possibly be a better ambassador for the Court of Naples than the Duchess of Eberli? My dear Richilde, you are known and revered in Provence, and I have first-hand knowledge of how you are capable of influencing even a pope. As for King John, you cannot fail to succeed with him. By the way, I should inform you that he is reputed to be blind, and therefore you will have to allow him to touch you, rather than merely admire you from a distance.'

This, as it turned out, was a total piece of misinformation. The blind king with whom Joanna was confusing John of France was John of Luxembourg. However, as they both suffered virtually the same fates, the one who could not see vainly charging the English bowmen at Crécy, and the one who could see making the same mistake at Poitiers, this hardly seems important.

I have to confess I was attracted by the prospect of carrying out this embassy, mistakenly as it turned out in the short run.

Joanna immediately corrected my misapprehension.

'Fernando will of course accompany you,' she said.

This put a different complexion upon the matter. The concept of being fucked three times a night as well as travelling half across Europe was not a compelling one.

'Oh, Your Grace,' I said. 'I am now approaching middle age' – I was, after all, in my thirty-first year – 'as well as being a mother and having a considerable estate to manage ... would it not be best to send my husband alone? An ambassador surely needs to be a man.'

'Richilde,' Joanna said sternly. 'This embassy is peculiarly a woman's work. Fernando will accompany you and protect you, and will in addition warm your bed at night.

You are a duchess, and my closest confidante. That means you owe a duty to Naples as well as to your sovereign lady. Do not fail me in this. While you are away, both your children and your estate shall be my own special charge.'

Well, there was nothing more to be said. And so I embarked upon an adventure which made all of my previous experiences seem like nothing:

I must begin by confessing that I enjoyed travelling as an ambassadress enormously. Not even Fernando's pressing company could truly spoil the magnificence of my apparel and my retainers, the solicitude with which I was treated at every stage of the journey.

After traversing the Tyrrhenian Sea without mishap, we came safely to Marseilles, and thence made that never-to-be-forgotten journey to Avignon. Fernando, of course, had not travelled as extensively as I, and it was a considerable pleasure to be his mentor. Not that he was interested in the sights and sounds that surrounded us, save when a pretty maid hove into view.

But in Avignon, it was necessary for me to present myself before the Pope.

As may be imagined, I approached this meeting with some trepidation, remembering my set-to with Clement. But Innocent was an entirely different man. He it was who, as Cardinal Bishop of Ostia, had dreamed of a Roman restoration, and encouraged Cola upon his disastrous course.

He knew nothing of my part in that business, and I had determined not to enlighten him. Innocent was as far removed from the Clement of my acquaintance as it was possible to be. Of the strictest morals, he had gone some way to reforming the Curia, forbidding the multiplication of benefices, and insisting that the bishops return to tend to their dioceses rather than enjoy the fleshpots of Avignon.

These fleshpots too he turned his back upon. But he was not entirely without the vices of mankind.

'To sell Provence,' he muttered, stroking his chin. 'When it has been deeded for all time ... it is a weighty undertaking, madame. If I consider the matter at all, it is in the certain knowledge that Provence is French, in every possible way, and thus I may be assisting the course of history. Yet to set aside a man's Will ...'

I was by now fully cognisant of the requirements of diplomacy, without, perhaps, possessing the necessary temperament myself to conduct negotiations in a proper manner. Therefore, without further ado, I asked, 'What is your price, Your Holiness?'

Innocent was taken aback at this. But then he smiled. 'You are a singularly direct young woman,' he remarked. 'Well, then, be it so. Thirty per cent of the purchase price.'

'Thirty?'

'Take it or leave it,' the holy scoundrel said.

I took it. Joanna had given me carte blanche to negotiate the best terms and the best price I could.

The Pope's agreement obtained, I was naturally in a hurry to be on my way to Paris. But this, His Holiness now informed me, would be a waste of time.

At this moment it is necessary to make one of my small digressions into history, in order that my reader may understand the situation into which I was now being forced to plunge.

This was nothing less than a war between my own country of England, and France, which had now been going on for close on twenty years, and looked set to continue for a great deal longer. Indeed, as I write, it continues.

The cause was this: our King Edward's mother was a Frenchwoman, Isabella, the youngest daughter of King Philip IV, known, erroneously, as the Fair, on whom I have previously touched in this narrative.

I would prefer not to go too deeply into this lady's character; suffice to say that she quite outshone her cousin, our dear lady Catherine of Valois, Empress of Constantinople, in the extent of her vices and her passions. No doubt it was her misfortune to be married to a king, Edward II of England, who preferred playing with the male member himself rather than leaving it to the pleasure of the ladies. But even in our grim world the revenge the Frenchwoman took can be considered extreme. Not for nothing has she been called the She-Wolf of France.

Having become entirely fed-up with her husband's penis-pulling proclivities, when his fingers should, she considered, have been busy elsewhere, she procured herself a lover, a rough fellow named Mortimer, one of the Marcher lords, that is, a noble entrusted with vast lands and powers on condition he held the border between England and Wales, and then deposed her husband, and assumed the regency for her eldest son, our Great Edward, who was at the time merely a small boy.

Having done this she proceeded to dispose of her husband by the utterly reprehensible means of having red-hot irons thrust up his fundament. Some historians have chosen to point out that this meant his body could be exposed with no visible evidence of violence, providing he lay on his back. Others may suppose that Queen Isabella felt this was the method of demise most suitable to one who had indulged the pastime often enough, if not so warmly. Be that as it may, King Edward II was most savagely done to death, and Isabella and her paramour reigned supreme, until our hero, at the age of sixteen, seized the power, hanged Mortimer – a merciful fate in the circumstances – locked up his mother for the rest of her life, proclaimed himself King, and, looking around for fresh fields to conquer, discovered himself also to be King of France. At least in the eyes of certain jurists.

The facts of the matter are as follows: on his death in

1314, Philip the Fair was duly succeeded by his eldest son, Louis X. This unhappy prince, known as Le Hutin, or The Stubborn, was already King of Navarre, in the right of his mother, Joan of Navarre. On his father's death, he handed the throne of the smaller country to his brother Philip, in order to sit on the throne of Clovis.

He was then married to Margaret of Burgundy, by whom he had had a daughter, Jeanne, who became Queen of Navarre and founded a royal house of her own. Now that he was King, however, he was overtaken by a sad twist of fate which can clearly befall the most orthodox of princes as well as those who stray by the wayside: his wife was found guilty of adultery. In a queen, unless she possess the beauty and spirit of our own Joanna – and even then, as we have seen, this can be a risky business – or the ruthless determination of an Isabella, such a course of action can be disastrous, and Margaret was duly strangled in prison.

Louis promptly married Clemence of Hungary who did the proper thing and begat a son and heir, named John. However, Louis died before the babe was born.

Who then was to be King of France?

Louis' brother Philip now hurried from Navarre to Paris, and had himself proclaimed regent of the as yet unborn King. We may all guess what happened next. The hapless John, the first of that name in France, was born, and somehow or other contrived to die five days later. These tragedies do happen, but I am afraid they happen more often than not where an uncle is waiting to step into the infant's shoes.

Whatever the private feelings of those around the throne, Philip was the man of the moment, and claimed the crown. There remained, however, a small problem: Jeanne, the daughter of the adulteress Margaret, still a small girl, but most unquestionably the last surviving member of her father's house.

Philip of course had no intention of submitting to his

youthful niece, but even he must have felt that two childish deaths coming one on top of the other might have caused comment, so he sought a legal means of putting her aside. He set his lawyers to work, and, by hunting through history, they came up with a very ancient law of the Salic Franks, the ancestors of the present-day French, which stated that no female could succeed to the leadership of the horde.

This may have been very necessary in the fifth or sixth centuries of our Christian era, when a King was required to be the strongest person in the society, in every way. It entirely lacked force in our own fourteenth century. Nevertheless, the law was solemnly promulgated, as regards France, and Jeanne, as I have mentioned, was given Navarre as a sop.

But now Philip's own heirs became victims of their father's legal chicanery. His son Philip died young, and when he himself died in 1322, he left only two daughters, Jeanne and Margaret. Now it was the turn of the third brother, Charles, to claim the throne, to the exclusion of his nieces.

This he did by invoking this very Salic Law.

How Fate must have been smiling at this in-fighting. For Charles himself could begat only a daughter.

It was this prince who aided and abetted his sister Isabella in her murderous machinations, and gained for a brief period an ascendancy over England, with which France had been at war, on and off, for some time. But when he died in 1328, all was confusion again.

The three dispossessed princesses remained in their infancy, nor was Charles's daughter Blanche of an age to rule. In any event, as Charles had not seized the throne by force, but had claimed it legally, as he saw it, Blanche could not possibly become queen before her cousins.

Now, in England, our Edward was a boy of sixteen, already grown to manhood, and, looking back on his reign, one can have no doubt that he would have made as

253

splendid a king of France as he has of England. But this would have involved such a revolution in thought and memory by the French as to appear unacceptable. Yet a king had to be found. So the French turned to the Valois. That is, the family of Charles of Valois, younger son of Philip III, who had actually married Margaret of Anjou, Joanna's great-aunt. This Charles, of course, was brother of the Empress of Constantinople.

Charles was long dead, but his son was a man of thirty-five, and seemed in every way suited to rule his country. He was crowned as Philip VI.

Now, when this happened, in 1328, our Edward was engrossed in domestic matters, namely, removing his mother's paramour Mortimer, and incarcerating Isabella herself. It is unlikely that he gave the French situation a thought. However, as Isabella was Philip's first cousin, relations with his neighbour were strained from the beginning.

The actual reasons which led Edward to claim the French throne are various. He objected to accepting Philip as suzerain of his vast French possessions; he was encouraged in his ambitions by the Flemings, who hated and feared the French; and, to be honest, he possessed the instincts of a soldier far more than those of a statesman, and wished only to indulge in deathless deeds of derring-do.

More than any of these, he was of an extravagant nature, and had inherited an extravagant situation from his unfortunate father. In a word, he was bankrupt, and felt that a successful war might help to fill the royal coffers.

Once in this frame of mind, he was easily convinced that he was the rightful heir to the French throne. As he was, by a process of logical deduction. The truly rightful ruler of France was undoubtedly Jeanne, Queen of Navarre. But she showed no interest. Well, then, Jeanne, daughter of Philip V, should be Queen. She was too young. Well, then, Margaret, her younger sister. But she, obviously, was even younger. Well, then, Blanche, daughter of the third brother. But she was also too young. Thus, having eliminated all of these young ladies, we arrive at the son of the daughter of Philip IV, to wit, Edward of England. He was certainly not too young, and he had already proved himself a man of decision.

Unhappily, those who claim thrones, once they are in possession of them, are usually unwilling to give them up, however strong the legal arguments against them. Philip promptly produced a legal argument of his own, of which no one had previously heard, or imagined possible: this said that not only, by the Salic law, could no woman inherit the throne, but that no son of a woman could inherit the throne. As this is rubbish, every man having to be the son of some woman or other, he meant that no son of a possible woman claimant could exercise such a right, and calculated that as Edward was the son of a princess and not a prince, he was forever excluded.

The absurdity of this argument, if carried to a logical conclusion, will be apparent. Practised in England, for example, it would have meant that there would have been no Plantagenet dynasty, as Henry II was the son of Matilda, the daughter of Henry I, who claimed the throne on her father's death. There are numerous other examples. Certainly it was not an argument Edward III was disposed to take seriously.

And so to war.

The trouble with wars, at least in my experience, is that, except where a very large country determines to demolish a very small one, and accomplishes it quickly enough, they are seldom productive of decisive results. And even in the case of a profound mismatch, events do not always turn out to the invaders' advantage. Consider the contest between the huge empire of Hungary and our own small Naples.

In Edward's case, here was a very small country indeed, England, attempting to conquer a very large one, France. It was doomed to failure, this despite the fact that the French had time and again proved themselves incapable of meeting the English in the field.

When I left Avignon in the late summer of 1356 to find King John, the contest had been going on since the naval Battle of Sluys in 1337, when I, as a girl of twelve, had only recently been introduced into Joanna's household. I was now a mother of thirty-one, and still the contest raged. Edward had won a succession of victories, including the famous one at Crécy when a superior French army was absolutely routed, and yet was no closer to becoming King of France, and even further from consolidating his finances. Indeed, in 1344 he had been forced to repudiate his debts to the great banking houses of Florence, an event which caused a political upheaval in that money-mad republic.

Soon after this, both sides being utterly exhausted, a truce was agreed, and while this was in operation, Philip VI died, to be succeeded by his son, John, the second of that name if we count the unfortunate five-day reign of the infant.

This John was the king to whom I had been despatched by Joanna.

It has pleased the fancy of certain historians to describe the new King of France as John the Good. I assume they are thinking of his courtly manners, especially regarding the ladies, of which I was soon to have experience. For the rest, he was feckless, vicious, and unfaithful, as well as lacking determination, and in many ways he reminds me of all I have read of the one king of that name who sat upon the English throne.

Perhaps John is an unlucky name for kings.

Be that as it may, our John the Good had inherited a bankrupt and devastated country, but also a truce, which the English were honouring. Common sense and plain logic should have convinced him that his first priority had to be a maintenance of the peace for at least as long as was required to restore his battered country. But within a year he had an English hostage executed.

Naturally the English returned to war. John hastily sought a new truce, which was again broken, and truce followed truce for the next five years. Meanwhile John was also quarrelling, signing truces, and breaking them again, with Charles II of Navarre, known as the Bad. The soubriquet can hardly have been awarded as a comparison with his French rival.

The final upshot of all this was that, shortly before I departed on my embassy, the English had yet again decided to go to war against this trucebreaker, and this very summer Edward Prince of Wales, eldest son of the King, and known as the Black Prince from his habit of wearing sable armour, had set out from the English province of Gascony in south-western France, on an invasion, in fact a raid, into the rich country around Tours.

It was known in Avignon that he had actually started from Bergerac on 4 August, while I was still at sea. His exact whereabouts when I landed were unknown, but reports indicated that he was in fact making for Tours. His army, as I understand, consisted of some four thousand heavy cavalry, four thousand light cavalry, three thousand of the justly feared English archers, and another thousand light infantry.

To combat the invaders, the Pope had been informed that a very large French army had been raised, under the command of John himself, and had been ordered to concentrate on Blois. Assuming that it would be the French intention to stand on the defensive, the Pope suggested that if I made my way as directly as possible to Blois, I should undoubtedly fall in with the King. He also indicated that by far the wisest course, in his opinion, would be to remain in Avignon until the matter was settled.

But I was in a hurry to have the embassy done, and be able to return to my children. Equally was I encouraged by my husband, who had heard a great deal about the battles between the French and the English, and being a tyro in these affairs, was eager to witness one of these sanguinary encounters at first hand.

So off we set.

We took only a small entourage, realising that haste was essential as at any moment the two armies might fight a battle which could conceivably yet again change the map of France, and the ambitions of the French King.

It is some three hundred miles from Avignon to Blois, as the crow flies, and it is possible to take a line almost as straight, thanks to the various valleys which bisect the Massif Central. Leaving Avignon on 8 September, and riding sometimes as many as forty miles a day, we travelled by way of Vans, Langogne, Langeac, Clermont Ferrand and Montlucon, before bearing more westerly for La Chatre.

It was a journey not unattended by danger, as the continuous wars of the past generation had left the country unpoliced and the prey of what were known as 'free companies', bands of lawless men, many of them professional soldiers who had grown tired of fighting for a meagre pay – more often than not in arrears – and somebody else's profit, and had struck out on their own. To these men, robbery and rape followed by murder had become a way of life.

We escaped capture, both by keeping very alert and by being prepared to ride like the wind when it became necessary. Fernando of course huffed and puffed and declared that he had not come to France to run away, but I persuaded him that even his valour – of which I possessed absolutely no certain knowledge – could not succeed against such odds, and asked him if he wished to see his wife shamefully mistreated.

Apparently he did not.

From La Chatre, on the morning of 15 September, we turned north again, making for Chateauroux, which would have left us within two marches of Blois. And there we were at last taken.

But, fortunately, by no brigands. We rode straight into the midst of a patrol of French gendarmes, as they call their élite cavalry.

For it turned out that the very day we had left Avignon, King John, on receiving information that the English had learned of his presence and were withdrawing, had taken his army across the Loire and was now marching as fast as he could for Poitiers, which lay on the best road to the south, and along which he was certain the Black Prince would be found. Despite all that had happened before, he was determined to bring the insolent young man to battle and avenge all of those past defeats.

It was to the King that the gendarmes took our small party, as prisoners.

The French host was not all that far away. We might have been able to travel at over twenty miles a day, but for a large army (and the French numbered hardly less than thirty thousand men, with an almost equal number of camp followers, dogs, chickens, children and cattle), five miles progress in every twenty-four hours is worth acclaiming.

As Joanna had always taken steps to absent herself from Naples whenever the Hungarians had marched on her, this was the first time I had ever beheld such a sight, and I was astounded.

We came upon them when they were having their afternoon meal, the only real meal of the day. Their programme was apparently to start moving before dawn – and just to start moving took some considerable time –

and continue moving until noon, when the procedure for stopping was put into motion.

This took even more time than starting, as apparently it is quicker to pull down a tent than to put one up. Thus it was usually five in the afternoon before the campfires could be got going and the weary soldiers sit down with their women for a meal.

The King and his nobles, of course, had no part of this tedious business. They were mounted, rose when they were well-rested, rode ahead of the army or indulged in the chase as the fancy took them, picnicked by some babbling brook, and when they returned to the new encampment, their tents were already pitched, and their dinners awaited them.

They were indulging in this last pastime when Fernando and I were brought before them.

We had not been illtreated in any way by the gendarmes, who had recognised us to be persons of quality, but I still considered it necessary to protest most vigorously at the arrest of the Neapolitan ambassador. An apology was immediately forthcoming, less because I was the Neapolitan ambassador, than because, as I have mentioned, King John had an eye for the ladies, and he could never possibly have beheld anyone quite as tall and beautiful as myself. Immediately I was seated next to him, given a chicken leg to gnaw and a goblet of good Loire wine to drink, and told that I was most welcome.

The King was in fact quite a handsome man, even if he had shifty eyes, and I will confess that I began to consider whether, if he proved reluctant to purchase Provence, some of the wiles I had practised on poor dear Cola might not be equally efficacious here.

In fact, John was extremely interested in my proposition.

'Provence,' he remarked. 'It would neatly round out my domains. 'Tis the price I lack. But no matter ...' he smiled at me. 'Within the next few days I shall have encountered the English, and after I have defeated them, I shall have all the money I require. Why, I estimate that the ransom of the Black Prince alone will be three hundred thousand gold crowns.'

'Your confidence does you credit, sire,' I murmured.

'Confidence? Why, of course I am confident, madame. But this is because my victory is a mere matter of mathematics. I shall take thirty thousand men on to the field. The Prince has but a third of that number.'

I could not resist remarking, 'I have always understood that the odds against the English were approximately in that order at Crécy.'

'Crécy,' he said contemptuously. 'The dogs took my father by surprise with their tactics. Do you suppose, madame, that I propose to be surprised again? I can tell you now exactly what the Prince will do when he discovers that we are so hot upon his heels he cannot escape. He will seek a defensive position, one with his wings secured by bog or wood or village, and there he will place his men-at-arms behind his archers, and await our assault.'

I supposed I had caught his drift.

'Whereupon you will immediately continue your march, to get to the south of him, sire, thereby turning his flank. A splendid concept.'

The King frowned at me.

'That is not at all how a king of France fights a battle, madame,' he said, somewhat coldly. 'Am I a coward? Where I see my enemy waiting, there will I be found, sword in hand.'

Had I not been a duchess, I would have scratched my head.

'But if you practise again the tactics of Crécy, sire ...'

'One does not expect a woman to understand the science of warfare,' he remarked, regaining his affability, and allowing his hand to droop beneath the table to squeeze my thigh, an intimacy I was in no position to resent –

besides, it is not every day that one's thigh is pinched by a king.

'We have prepared, you see, one or two surprises for the English,' he went on. 'The principal lesson we learned from Crécy was that the mounted knight is vulnerable to the flying arrow. Now, obviously, the solution is very simple. I intend to dismount my knights, and have them charge on foot.'

This time, duchess or not, I did drive my hand into my hair, but the King merely assumed I was assailed by a nit.

'This will entirely confuse the English,' he told me. 'Nor will an armoured knight on foot present half so large or vulnerable a target as a horse, which cannot be completely encased.'

'But ...' my imagination strove to contend with a vision of five thousand armoured knights trudging forward on foot, supposing they could move at all. 'Will not your advance be awfully slow, Your Grace?'

'Ha ha!' He gave my thigh another squeeze. 'Awful is the word, madame. Oh, indeed, it will be awful to those forced to watch it approaching them.'

I did not argue further. I was aware that I was about to witness a catastrophe, supposing the battle was ever fought, for up to that moment the French had discerned absolutely no sign of the English, who, by King John's calculations, could only be a mile or two in front of them. But invisible.

Good King John had made some other calculations as well, of the kind that appear to overcome all men when about to fight a battle. Let us make merry, for tomorrow we may die. Only merry is an euphemism for a fourletter word of great importance to the continuance of the human race – supposing an adequate partner may be found.

He had one to hand.

I had early recognised that this was the way his thoughts were drifting, and when, after our meal, he explained that he would like to enter into the question of the proposed sale of Provence in some detail, and complete privacy, I felt obliged to agree.

Fernando of course objected, but then, he objected to everything which did not involve him and me in a bed. I explained to him that what I proposed to do was part and parcel of diplomacy, and that I had been entrusted with a sacred mission by our Queen which I was determined to carry out.

I then joined the King, anticipating a somewhat restful night, compared with the one I would have suffered had I remained with my husband.

My prognostication would have been entirely accurate but for the absurdity of men at war. The King and I chatted for a while – Provence was never mentioned – and shared a glass of wine, then he began to undress with great rapidity. I followed his example, and we fell into each other's arms, His Royal Highness being kind enough to make some very flattering remarks about various parts of my body, when we were interrupted by a great to-do, a blowing of trumpets and beating of drums, a clash of arms and a shouting of men.

My companion must needs throw me to one side, don his shirt, and rush outside in that indecent condition, leaving me uncertain as to whether or not I had actually been entered by a king!

What had happened was, as I have mentioned, a fairly typical example of the absurdities of war, at least as conducted in the fourteenth century of our era.

The French army might have been travelling slowly enough, but the English, laden with plunder and prisoners, were travelling more slowly yet. As it apparently had occurred to neither commander to send out scouts to discover just where the enemy was, the French had actually outmarched their enemies without being aware of it, and were already past Poitiers. The English, for their part, were hurrying by that same city, making a forced night march ... and in the darkness their advance guard had blundered into the back of the French!

Instantly all was, as I have indicated, confusion, and it seemed likely that the battle everyone awaited would be fought there and then. But no sensible general is going to engage in a mêlée in the darkness. The Black Prince hastily called off his men, and the French did not pursue. But that a battle would be fought on the morrow was plain; the French were now definitely across the English line of retreat.

With this on his mind, King John lost interest in amatory debate, as he began to prepare himself. I hurried back to the sumptuous tent given to Fernando and myself, and found my husband also arming himself with the assistance of his esquire.

'What are you doing?' I demanded.

'I am going to fight in the battle,' he told me. 'I have been promised a place at the King's right hand.'

I could not believe my ears.

'Husband, this is a fight between Frenchmen and Englishmen. You are a Neapolitan.'

'It is a battle, in which I am going to take part,' he insisted. 'How am I to gain military renown except by feats of arms.'

'And you would rather gain military renown than remain here in safety with me.'

'I shall return to you with the laurel leaf of victory upon my brow,' he said. 'You may depend upon it.'

I did not argue further. I had already experienced the pangs of widowhood, in mourning for a far better man.

Yet I must confess that the martial ardour with which I was surrounded penetrated even my reserve, and as the darkness began to fade, I dressed myself, and went out to see what was happening. My maids would have accompanied me, but I bade them stay in the tent. I did not wish to be encumbered by having to look after them.

In fact nothing at all happened that day, 18 September 1356, as it takes a great deal of time to prepare an army for battle. During the morning, while the French forces were slowly forming up, envoys arrived from the English camp, suggesting that the French stand aside and let the Prince return to his domains without interference.

These fellows were of course dismissed, and it is obvious that their mission was merely to occupy the French while the Prince found himself a suitable defensive position from which to fight the battle. This he located in a gently sloping vineyard where he could anchor his right flank on a marshy valley, quite impassable to a man in armour, and where, on a front of no more than a thousand yards, his left flank rested against rising ground. In front of his position there was a bristling hedge, and the approach was intersected by various sunken lanes, which greatly strengthened his situation.

In this very strong posture waited the twelve thousand Englishmen.

King John's army was approximately three times as numerous, and these he organised into three huge battles, or divisions, commanded respectively by the Dauphin, the Duke of Orleans, and the King himself. These masses were to be hurled, one after the other, at the English position.

That night, when all was ready, there was a great deal of toasting and singing in the French camp. There was not a man present who doubted the certainty of their victory, and I am bound to admit that their confidence was irresistible. I drank my toasts with the best of them, permitted the King to fondle me both fore and aft, sank into a drunken stupor, and was awakened with the rest of them by the sound of movement from the English camp.

'The scoundrels are trying to escape,' the King shouted, as the unmistakable splashing of water indicated that men were crossing the stream in the rear of the English position. 'To arms! To arms!'

It turned out later that the Black Prince had been

sending his baggage train, which of course contained all of his plunder, across the stream. Whether or not he hoped to follow with his army before the French were awake I cannot say, because now the French army moved forward, and he was left with no option but to give battle.

Equally he might have been deceiving us into supposing he was withdrawing in order to bring us on in disorder. If this was his intention, his plan worked magnificently. Two bodies of mounted knights, supported by the mercenary crossbowmen, galloped forward to nip the English movement in the bud, just as it began to grow light. They charged, needless to say, straight into an arrow storm, and were shot to pieces. For some time they persisted in their efforts, while I, again mounting my horse and riding to one side of the French array to see what was going on, gazed in wonder at the futile courage being displayed. Some of the hapless knights even reached the hedge and the English line, but there they were cut down.

The crossbowmen hardly got to fire a bolt.

The survivors of this first assault wearily returned to us; by far the greater number were riderless horses. But King John was not the least downhearted, and commanded the Dauphin to advance in turn.

Here was the key to the battle, in the French eyes. The Dauphin's men-at-arms were dismounted, and, after some time had been consumed in ordering their ranks, they commenced their assault.

It was as if time had determined to stand still. The awful array of armoured knights, their steel plates clanking most dolefully against each other, proceeded with the utmost slowness up the hill. It was quite uncanny, for although the French began with some bold shouts, these were very rapidly silenced; no man can march up a hill in an armoured suit and also keep up shouting – he needs all the breath he can muster. Several indeed could not mount the hill at all, and after a few steps fell to their knees and then on to their faces, quite unable to move.

The English watched this ponderous advance in total, and it may well be supposed, disbelieving silence. For several hundred years the difference between the lord and the villein had been a matter of charging, armour-clad, steed and rider. Now here was the steedless rider, still wearing full armour, clanking slowly towards his doom.

I am being derisory. It must be confessed that the French knights, however misguided their strategy, stuck to their task with the grimmest of determination. Soon the arrows began to whirr, but in a sense a man on foot does present less of a target than one mounted, and he is the more able to use his shield to ward off missiles. The result was that a large proportion of the first battle actually reached the English line. By then of course there was no semblance of a charge, and yet the knights hewed their way onwards, refusing to give way, and causing some consternation in the enemy. From my vantage point it seemed to me that the Black Prince was sending all his reserves into the line, with the exception of perhaps five hundred knights who formed his own guard. Thus the English army was almost totally committed, and the French as yet possessed two unengaged battles. Now was the time for King John to reveal his military genius, command his remaining knights to mount, and send them against the English flanks. The day would most certainly have been his.

Sadly, King John possessed no military genius whatsoever. Certainly he ordered the second battle to advance to the support of the first, but still on foot. This second battle was commanded, as I have indicated, by the Duke of Orleans, the King's brother. The King, if no soldier, was at least a man of courage. The Duke did not even possess that commodity. No sooner had he got within range of the English archers, who continued to assail the French from their flanking positions, than he and all his people turned and fled.

This mishap affected those of the Dauphin's men who

were still assailing the English ranks, and they too withdrew in disorder, leaving the English gasping but, for the moment, victorious. Yet had their casualties been grievous, and they were certainly very tired. And the third, and largest, French battle remained to be overcome.

Thus King John was still sanguine of victory. As far as he was concerned, the contest was going according to plan. Now he launched his main force against the exhausted enemy, still on foot, but confident of being able to overcome their dwindled opponents.

With the King's battle there marched my dear Fernando, waving his sword with the best of them.

Sadly, this was the last time I ever beheld my husband alive. For, unlike the French generals, the Black Prince *was* a military genius. He had taken in the situation at a glance, knew that if he allowed the massive last French battle, which alone outnumbered his entire force, to come to grips on their own terms, his victory could not be counted certain. More, he was aware that his archers had expended almost all their shafts. A lesser man might have quailed at such a situation. Prince Edward's reaction was instantaneous: he launched his entire force down the slope at the advancing French, even the archers drawing their knives to join in the fight.

The French were of course taken aback by this unexpected manoeuvre, and before they could gather their wits the English were upon them. Yet did they rally, and for a little while fought so well the outcome remained in the balance.

However, the Black Prince had not trusted in the unexpected alone. He was also aware that the introduction of an extra force into a battle, however small that force may be, can often prove decisive, and so had sent his only remaining fresh troops, the five hundred mounted knights of his personal guard, round behind the position previously held by the archers. These men took some time to reach a suitable place from which to charge, but when they did so, at full gallop into the rear of the French force, the result was horrifying. The French broke and fled in every direction, save for the armoured knights, who, on foot, could not run, and merely fell down, to be captured or slain as it took the English fancy.

I gazed in consternation at this destruction of such a magnificent array, and then realised it was time to look to myself. For the English, and especially the archers, realising that the battle was won, were now beginning to seek the French camp and whatever good things they knew were to be found there.

Amongst which they could number myself. Indeed, I had already been sighted, and if at a distance it was no doubt impossible to discern my beauty, the sight of my skirts was sufficient to have several men running towards me.

I turned my horse to ride off, and would have escaped my immediate assailants without difficulty, had not another group, unseen by me, made their way behind me. These now appeared before my startled steed, who promptly reared on his hindlegs. Here is where the so modest side-saddle becomes a curse. I lost my one stirrup, and then the reins, and slid off the beast's rump to land on my own, with a jar which left me quite winded.

My position was indecorous, sitting as I was in the mud with my legs spread, but this was the least of my troubles, for a moment later I was surrounded by eager manhood, and might have supposed myself back in Rome in the hands of the mob. In a trice it was all naked thighs and waving members, while I was held down by my shoulders, reflecting sadly that at least in Rome I had lain on dry ground, whereas here my yellow hair was rapidly turning black with mud. This diminution of my beauty did not seem to concern my assailants, who were interested solely in what lay between my now exposed thighs, save for one rascal, only a boy, who was busily tearing open my bodice to reach my breasts.

My life has, alas, forced me to become accustomed to such mistreatment, from which I have learned certain attitudes to be adopted when in extremis. One is not to attempt to fight rampant manhood unless one is sure of the victory; outnumbered as I was by some twenty to one such a prospect was unlikely. The second is that where one decides against fighting, it is best to scream, as loudly as possible. If there is no succour close to hand, this pleases one's assailant, and if there is succour, why, all things are possible. I therefore screamed, and if I say so myself, I possess a loud voice when I care to exert it. The Black Prince himself told me later that the entire army was given pause as it was assumed some gorgon had come amongst them, shrieking her vengeance.

Certainly I interested a knight who chanced to be nearby, and he came over to see what was happening.

'Sire!' I cried, using my native tongue for the first time in some twenty years. 'Save my virtue, I beg of you.'

I was of course stretching a point, as even had I been a virgin at the beginning of the battle that state was now history. But when in extremis one must use whatever comes to mind.

'English, by God!' quoth the knight, and began beating the man lying on my belly with the flat of his sword. This quite reduced the fellow's ardour, and as he subsided he was seized and thrown aside. His fellows stood around, panting; only two or three had actually accomplished their purpose.

'An English lady!' my saviour remarked. 'Could you not see this, you rascals?'

The men glowered, but some touched their forelocks, and one fellow attempted to restore my skirts to their proper position.

'I shall have you hanged,' quoth my saviour, assisting me to my feet. 'But, my dear lady, how came you to be in this situation? Are you truly English?'

He was judging my status on the basis of my clothes,

270

which were very fine, and I had no intention of disabusing him. Rather the reverse.

'Indeed I am English, sir,' I said. 'But I also happen to be the Duchess of Eberli, Ambassadress from the Court of Naples to the King of France, and ...' I gave my recent intimates the most severe of glares, 'set upon by these human wolves.'

'Duchess,' the knight repeated. 'Ambassador!' His eyes rolled with the thought of the ransom that might be had for so exalted a personage. 'His Royal Highness must know of this. You will accompany me, if you will, Your Grace.'

And so I was led off to meet the heir to the throne of England.

CHAPTER 8

I was, of course, very aware of my situation, as we picked our way through the tumbled dead, all in the process of being stripped to their skins by the voracious victors, seeking any bauble of the least value. I was, to all intents and purposes, a hapless woman who in her present condition lacked even beauty, who knew not what had happened to her husband ... and even less how this Black Prince, of whom I had heard so many tales – some of them entirely suited to his soubriquet – might regard me, especially when I appeared in so unfavourable a light.

'Is the Prince far, my lord?' I ventured.

'No, no. He is close at hand,' my captor replied.

'Then do you suppose it might be possible for me to have a bath, and perhaps change my clothing, before being presented to him? My tent is not far either, in the French encampment.'

'A bath?' He was clearly amazed. As he gazed at me, I realised that he had not the faintest idea of what lay beneath the several layers of mud, which even matted my hair.

'I assure you that it would greatly improve my appearance,' I told him.

'A bath,' he repeated, and I sadly recalled my own girlhood in England, when once a week the entire family shared the same tub, in order of age. As I was the youngest, my immersion was always in a brown sea covered with

272

a scum in which there were to be found numerous tiny insects struggling for existence.

What a contrast to Naples, where I had bathed in clean water every day of my life!

But now I was apparently back amongst the barbarians.

'You will see the Prince before anything,' my captor told me. And a few minutes later, there he was.

Edward of Woodstock was at this time but twenty-six years old; that is, he was five years younger than myself. In recent years it has become customary to traduce his reputation, as is the fate of all great men as they die and are unable to defend themselves, and it is possible that his later rule over Aquitaine together with his adventures in Spain revealed a character who had human weaknesses and even more a man borne down by his constant activity and beginning to suffer the debilities of ill health. Fortunately the future is hidden from us, and all I beheld at this first meeting was a tall and handsome knight, young and strong and vigorous, enjoying the fruits of his immense victory.

He sat at table, drinking wine and eating roasted chicken, still in full armour save for his helmet and gauntlets ... and by his side sat none other than King John himself, also wearing armour – his somewhat mud-stained to suggest he had taken a tumble – and also eating and drinking with great gusto, as if he had had nothing to do with the disaster into which he had led his people; behind the two princes there waited several more French noblemen, together with their English captors.

'How now, Dickon,' the Prince cried as we approached, my skirts trailing through the mud. 'What rapscallion is this?'

'A lady who claims to be of importance, sire,' the knight said.

'By Our Lady,' King John remarked. 'It is the Duchess of Eberli.'

'Why, my lord, that is exactly who she has claimed to

273

be,' Dickon confessed, apparently surprised.

'The Duchess of Eberli!' Edward said, rising, and thus requiring the King to do likewise. 'Madam, you will have to explain to me where your duchy lies.'

I allowed him a brief curtsey. 'It is in the Kingdom of Naples, sire,' I said, speaking English.

'But ...' he was clearly more confused than ever.

'I happen to be English born, sire,' I explained.

'And riding with a French army?'

I told him of my mission, reverting to French, and receiving supporting nods from the King.

'The Lady Ambassador and I were discussing affairs of state when your army approached,' he told the Prince.

'Ah,' Edward commented. 'Well, madam, I can only apologise for the tumble you appear to have taken, and offer you a place at my table.'

'Which I shall gratefully accept, sire,' I said. 'When I have been allowed to wash myself clean of this mud and change my clothing. My maids and goods are in the French camp ... if they have not already been ravished. I would also like to discover what has happened to my husband.'

The Prince looked at the King.

Who shrugged. 'The good fellow would fight with us. I have not seen him since we were overrun.'

'I will attend to both your husband and your maids personally,' the Prince promised. 'But you wish a bath. Dickon, take her to our women and have her seen to.'

As I was escorted away, I overheard the King remark, 'She is a most devilishly beautiful woman, Cousin.'

This sounded hopeful for my prospects, but I was considerably dashed, half an hour later, as I sat soaking in an erstwhile wine barrel, sawn in half and filled with water by the Prince's camp-followers, passing the time of day with these good ladies who were delighted to be ministering to a duchess and eagerly took turns to wash my hair and scrub my back while keeping the curious soldiery away with a stream of shoos and threats, to have the Prince himself appear before me.

I had been so absorbed by my conversation, and by learning about the conditions experienced by these women, that I had not heard Edward's approach. And indeed this was an aspect of life of which I knew nothing. There was not a woman amongst them who did not claim she had been forced, in the first instance at least, dragged from her bed and raped and thus left with no option but to trail behind the army in search of a husband. Most of them had had several of these appendages, it being the custom to seek a replacement as soon as the position became vacant, which obviously happened regularly enough with an army in the field. Several of my new friends were mothers.

And every one of them, regardless of her antecedents, had adopted a fierce loyalty to the Prince and his army. This was not for any political reason. The camp had become their lives, their sole support. To return to their homes was considered socially impossible, and to be left the victims of a conquering enemy could involve them in a great deal of unpleasantness, as the French camp-followers were at that moment discovering.

Thus it was that they quite failed to make any effort to prevent their beloved young general from approaching me, and the first thing I knew was that he was peering into my tub, the water of which, despite my muddy immersion, was not sufficiently opaque for modesty.

However, I was no blushing virgin, and my thoughts regarding my situation were already ranging over a wide field of subjects and possibilities. I thus used this opportunity to cry out in alarm, rising to my feet in my agitation. I realised my error immediately, of course, as a modest woman should, but my hands were quite inadequate to cover the entire area between my thighs and my nose, and it was some seconds before I regained sufficient control of my senses to sink back to my knees, confident that my hair, which was soaking and plastered in golden threads to my shoulders and breasts, would complete a very attractive picture.

Certainly Edward appeared to find me so, and it was some seconds before he could speak, while my attendants clustered at a respectful distance, where they could not interfere but would certainly overhear whatever passed between us.

As the Prince remained speechless, I felt I should lead, as it were.

'Sire,' I protested. 'You take me at a great disadvantage.'

'On the contrary,' he replied. 'I discover you at your most beautiful, madam. I only wish I had better tidings.'

'My tent has been looted!'

'Your belongings are safe, as are your women. They approach now, with your clothes. I spoke of your husband.'

'Ah.' I realised I might have been too hasty in my priorities.

'He is dead, madam. I regret this, but these rascally archers of mine are too often careless of rank.'

'Alas, poor Fernando,' I said.

'You take the news very well, madam.'

'Would you have me cry, sire? It was an arranged marriage, and he was a tiresome fellow.'

The Prince digested this, frowning.

'Does his death affect your standing?'

'Not in the least,' I assured him. 'I was Duchess of Eberli long before he appeared on the scene.'

'Hm. Well, madam, your ladies are here. And I have my duties to attend to. But I would be greatly honoured if you would sup with me.'

'It shall be my pleasure, sire.'

'I shall expect you at sunset.' He began to turn away, and then checked. 'Will you attend your husband's burial, madam?'

'As soon as I am dressed, sire,' I promised him.

This I did, although with some misgivings. Where several thousand men have been laid low, unless they be of royal birth it is really impossible to give any one of them a decent interment. My Fernando was merely one naked body lying amidst a score, waiting to be dumped into a deep pit. As he had been wearing full armour when he fell, his visor had clearly been raised and he had received a dagger thrust in the face, through one eye, in fact, which quite ruined his looks. There was no other mark on his body, which indicated that he had fallen from sheer fatigue as he had struggled up the hill, and had been despatched while lying helpless upon the ground. Perchance I was cold, but I could not shed a tear. He had been inflicted on me, and he had gone to his death in careless and quite unnecessary confidence, when he could have remained in safety by my side.

My thoughts were turning already to what lay ahead. On the one hand, there was the Prince's evident interest, and on the other, the unfortunate fact that I was his prisoner, and that I had to assume my mission a failure.

This was immediately brought home to me, as I sat at table between the King and the Prince. It was a splendid, if barbaric, occasion. Here we were, seated before long trestles laden with good things, from meat to wine, on a glorious September evening, with scarce a cloud in the sky and little breeze to cause us any discomfort, wearing our best clothes and our best manners ... and yet in the middle of a recent battlefield.

The English soldiery certainly were faring as well as their betters. The French soldiery were either dead or fled; those of their knights captured were dining with ourselves. But there were yet wounded and dying men from time to time crying out for succour, and horses screaming in torment to remind us of the horrors of only a few hours before.

While over all there hung the stench of death.

But my companions were disposed to be merry, although they were, for all their friendship, and indeed relationship – the Prince was actually the King's cousin – in vastly different situations.

'I should very much like to continue our interrupted discussion, madame,' said King John. 'Although I fear that I can no longer be considered as a possible purchaser of Provence, at least for a year or two. How much do you intend to ask as my ransom, Edward?'

'It is a matter I have not yet fully considered, sire,' Edward replied. 'However, shall we say three million gold crowns?'

I nearly swallowed a chicken bone.

But the King seemed offended.

'Is that all you think I am worth?' he demanded.

'Of course not,' Edward protested. 'I think it is all your kingdom can afford to pay.'

'Hm,' John remarked. 'That is a good point. The French have never been very apt at paying their taxes. Still, you understand, my dear lady, that for a while I shall be a little short.'

'I do understand, sire,' I said. 'And I shall convey such sad news to Her Grace, much as it will distress me to do so.'

'When, of course, you are allowed to return to Naples,' the scurvy fellow pointed out.

I turned to look at the Prince.

'Why, do you know,' he remarked, tossing a bone over his shoulder to one of the waiting mastiffs, 'I had not considered that point. But I suppose, technically, you are a prisoner of war, madam.'

'I am a neutral, sire,' I said, somewhat sharply. The sums of money that were being bandied about were far above anything my poor duchy could possibly raise, or indeed the entire Kingdom of Naples, supposing Joanna did not decide to write me off. 'My being on this field is entirely an accident.'

'Ah,' Edward said. 'But your husband fought with the French.'

'Against my wishes, sire. He was a foolish boy.'

'Indeed he appears so. But I shall have to consider ... in any event, you will agree that in your present circumstances, you have more to discuss with me, than with my cousin here.'

I would have no one suppose that I am promiscuous, or even mercenary. However, my life has taught me to look facts in the face and accept them where I cannot change them. I had been sent to France to sell Provence to the King of that country. To accomplish that end for my beloved Queen I had been prepared to go to great lengths. However, as the King had himself just told me, the transaction was now off, and therefore he, poor fellow, was of absolutely no use to either me or Joanna. On the other hand, I was entirely at the mercy of the most dashing and handsome prince I have ever encountered – he even outshone Louis of Tarento – and I was aware that he was unmarried, whereas King John certainly had a wife.

Not of course that I aspired to become the Princess of Wales. Well, perhaps I did, but I knew the odds were against me – although when Edward did eventually marry, a few years later, it was to a widowed lady like myself, and with a lesser portion. But that is fate. My immediate concern was to avoid adultery, which I have always abhorred. To my knowledge, up to that moment I had only committed this heinous crime twice in my life, and that had been entirely without my agreement, as my set-to with Charles of Durazzo could only be considered rape, while with dear Cola it had been duty. As I was now again a widow, I therefore entirely agreed with the Prince's point of view, and, to the King's obvious chagrin, retired to the victor's tent on the conclusion of our meal.

Whereupon I enjoyed a very singular experience. The Prince was undoubtedly the greatest warrior of his age – his father now being somewhat elderly – but he was an

279

absolute tyro at the art of love. Or indeed when it came to women at all. He was in such a complete contrast to the only other man I had bedded who was younger than myself, Fernando, that I found myself very nearly as nervous as he, and for a few minutes we fumbled uncertainly like a pair of fourteen year olds discovering love for the first time. Then my natural spirit asserted itself, and I was able to guide him, and greatly enjoy doing so.

The next few weeks were most pleasurable, as the army wended its way back to Bordeaux, the seat of the Prince's government in Aquitaine. The news of our victory had spread, and we were greeted by cheering crowds in each town through which we passed, while our people of course were in the highest spirits.

I was in the best spirits of all, as I nightly shared the couch of this handsome and gentle man, in every sense of the word, ate at his table, and thus enjoyed the best that was to be had, and felt like a queen as I rode at his side.

As the subject of my ransom had not again been raised I felt that he had forgotten it, and thus received a rude shock when we reached our destination.

'There is a fleet leaving in a week for England,' he told me. 'King John will be on it, as well as the remainder of our captives. You will accompany them, Richilde.'

'To England?' I was aghast.

'It is your home, is it not?'

'It was once my home, sire. But that was a long time ago. I now have my duchy to think of, and my children ...'

'You never told me you had children?'

'Well, I do. My daughter is now eleven years old, and my son seven.'

He frowned at me, and I remembered that I had never actually told him my age, either, which he had undoubtedly supposed was approximately his own.

'You must have married very young,' he commented.

'Ah ... no, sire. I am somewhat older than I appear.'

'I see. But it is no matter.'

'Of course it is not. Sire, I seek of you only a ship to carry-me back to Naples, and my Queen.'

'That is a matter for my father, the King,' he said. 'In any event, he would never forgive me if I sent you back to Italy without having given him the opportunity to meet you. My father,' he added, 'has an eye for the ladies.'

This was undoubtedly the understatement of the century.

However, there seemed nothing for it. Although I tried.

'And do these happy past weeks mean nothing to you, sire?' I asked, looking as beseeching as I could.

'Why, they mean a great deal, Richilde,' he said. 'I will always treasure them.'

'I would willingly remain in Bordeaux,' I suggested.

'What of your children?'

'I could send for them.'

'And your queen?'

'I would be your prisoner, sire.'

He smiled. 'You flatter me, and tempt me at the same time. But I do not think the stars have it in mind for you and I to embark upon a permanent relationship.'

I could do no more, save request that I should not sail in the same ship as King John. This request was granted.

Where had I gone wrong?

A thousand possibilities crowded my mind. Had the Prince somehow learned of my base origins? That was hardly possible, although one of my maids might have known that I was once a slave. Had I been too forward in the art of love? This was certainly possible, although Edward had seemed pleased enough with what I was doing at the time.

Or could it be simply that having enjoyed me for a month, and having learned all I had to teach him, he now desired to practise with a new partner? Knowing something of the family from which he came, I suspect this last to be the most likely. Yet I set sail in a sorely puzzled and uncertain frame of mind, because for all my luxurious surroundings and apparent wealth, my future seemed as uncertain as ever before in my life.

Ah, men! How my mind would drift back to my dear Alberto. Would I ever find another like him?

One of the odd aspects of life is that often when we do discover what we are looking for we do not at all recognize it. I possessed the most senior rank of the captives on board the ship in which I had embarked; there were some knights and a couple of counts, but no dukes amongst my fellow passengers. These fellows of course all looked forward to a pleasant voyage in the company of such a beautiful lady, and before we had even made the passage down the Gironde to the sea – which took two days so hard does the current run when the tide is rising – I had received a variety of advances. Refusing these was difficult, because the ship contained but a single cabin into which we were all crammed, some fourteen of us if my maids are included. Nor was there to be found any safety in numbers, as the men all had the same objective in mind and were therefore not disposed to hamper one another, while my maids were a frivolous lot and too busy considering whether they might not have a part to play in the looming orgy.

I therefore escaped to the deck on the first night, and found there our captain, staring moodily at the land, which lay to either side, as we were anchored to await the turn of the tide.

'Good sir,' I said. 'May I ask where you sleep?'

He glanced at me in some surprise. He was an ugly fellow, not very old – perhaps only a year or so my senior – but with a cast in his left eye and a somewhat pronounced chin, which indeed matched his nose to make him resemble the man in the moon. But he had attractive eyes, despite their discrepancy. Not that I was the least interested in the eyes of a sea captain, save in that they might guide us safely to our destination.

'Why, madam,' he said. 'With my cabin so over-crowded, I sleep on deck.'

'Would it distress you if I was to join you?'

Now he turned round to look at me directly.

'I find the cabin very stuffy,' I explained.

'You are welcome to sleep wherever you wish, madam,' he said.

'And will you protect me during the night?'

'I, madam?'

'There is no one else,' I explained.

And at that moment two of my would-be seducers appeared on deck.

'Duchess!' they called. 'Duchess! You could have relieved the army by now.'

'Vulgar fellows,' I remarked. 'You see what I mean, Captain.'

'You mean you do not wish to dally with these gentlemen?' He seemed surprised.

'Under no circumstances.'

My vehemence seemed to surprise him even more, but he advanced to the break of the poop as the Frenchmen were ascending the ladder.

'How now, gentlemen,' he demanded.

'We seek the Duchess,' they explained.

'The Duchess has a mygrame, and will rest on deck,' the Captain declared.

He was bigger than they, and he was the Captain.

'Will you rest with her?' sneered one of them.

'As it is my ship, sirs, I will rest where I choose.'

'By God, sir, if I had my sword . . .'

'Unfortunately, sir, you do not,' the Captain pointed out. 'But I have mine. Now, will you not retire?'

They did so.

'That was admirable,' I said. 'For the first time in many a long day I feel perfectly safe. May I ask your name, kind sir?'

'It is Christopher, madam.'

'Nothing but that?'

'Well, some do call me Christopher of the Bay, as this is a passage I make regularly.'

'Then Christopher of the Bay, I am entirely in your debt, and I wish you to know that at the first opportunity I will discharge my obligation.'

'To have served you is reward enough,' the gallant fellow said.

The remainder of the voyage was a pleasant one for me. True I was forced to spend it all on deck, and as it was now late October the nights were cold. But Christopher gallantly wrapped me in his cloak as well as mine. True there were some rain showers, but again I was well protected. And best of all, the poop was prohibited to the rest of the passengers, so I was in complete peace.

Christopher himself was a perfect gentleman, and did not once seek to take advantage of my position. Instead he taught me things about the sea and navigation I never knew. By the time we found our way up the Channel and into Southampton, I could even tell one star from another.

We were, of course, only a part of a very large fleet, carrying such of the Black Prince's booty as he wished to present to his father, and all of his principal captives, back to England. Thus when we disembarked at Southampton for a while the dockside sounded more French than English. But here again Christopher proved his worth.

'Her Grace is for the King himself,' he said, appropriating the necessary palfreys and sending me and my maids off with an escort, in front of the main party, who were quarrelling amongst themselves as to who should ride what. King John saw me go and shouted after me, but I merely bade my escort to ride faster.

I could, of course, have wished that dear Christopher could have chosen his words more carefully. At least they meant that I was entirely protected from any lust the soldiers may have felt for a hapless duchess riding in their midst, however they might choose to dally with my maids. They also, however, suggested that I was destined for the King's bed. Normally this would have excited rather than alarmed me, but I was concerned at the moral situation which might arise, as I had for a month been the mistress of the King's son. I was not, however, given a great deal of time to reflect, because upon arrival in London, some ten days after leaving Southampton – we were now into November, the weather had broken, and when it was not thick fog it was pouring with rain, with the result that the roads were quagmires – I was indeed taken straight to His Majesty.

How time flies. This Edward III had come to the throne two years after I was born. I have related some of the unhappy features of his early years, and mentioned the more glorious events of his manhood. In this year of 1356 he was still only forty-four, and remained in the fullest flush of that manhood. I beheld a large, powerful, full-bearded man with an uproarious laugh and a generally happy countenance. And why not, as he was the most successful monarch of his time?

He sat at table when I first saw him – as had his son – and was surrounded by extremely pretty women. Of his wife, a good and virtuous lady I had been told, there was no sign.

My escorts had brought with them letters, and the King glanced at these, while I stood before him, dripping wet and thoroughly uncomfortable ... and not a little apprehensive, for here surely was the ultimate arbiter of my fate.

A fast ship had been sent ahead of the main fleet, of course, bearing the glad tidings of the enormous victory gained by the Black Prince, and the King knew roughly whom to expect. But of course words can never adequately convey beauty, and the Duchess of Eberli suddenly became more than a name on paper to the delighted monarch.

'My dear, delightful damsel,' the King said. 'You will catch your death of cold, standing there. Come warm yourself before the fire.'

And he himself leapt over the table to escort me to the blazing hearth, his arm round my shoulder, his hand already drooping in front to discover what it could.

I knew then that my moral qualms would have to be subdued. Still, I do not think there can be many women who have slept with both the King of England and his son.

I spent more than a year in England, and it was, frankly, a tedious time.

My fears as to being faced with a huge ransom were speedily assuaged. Not only did King Edward acknowledge my legal position, but he was the very soul of gallantry, went around with a piece of ribbon tied to his thigh which was apparently the highest order in the land – created by himself – and swore that he would never ask ransom of a woman. This did not, unfortunately, mean that I was immediately allowed to return to Naples. Our lusty monarch was delighted with his new toy, and when, seeking to reduce his ardour, I confessed that he was but following in the footsteps – if that be the apt word – of his son, he merely laughed longer and more loudly than usual.

'I'll wager I fill you more than the boy!' he roared.

Actually, he did.

But I soon concluded he was my only friend in the entire kingdom, if perhaps we exclude the good sea captain, Christopher of the Bay. However, I did not expect ever to see him again as long as I lived. For the rest, I was an object of jealousy on the part of the other ladies who sought to attain my usually supine position beneath the King, and of intrigue on the part of those nobles who wished me to use that position to further their own ends. As I understood nothing of what these ends were, I was totally confused and merely aroused their ire in turn.

Queen Philippa, who, as I have said, had largely retired into private life, was politeness itself on the odd occasion on which we met, and I gained the feeling that she regarded me, or anyone who could consume the King's unfailing ardour, as a great relief to herself. The good lady had already mothered several sons for her husband, and no doubt felt that she had done her duty by her adopted country. That I did not follow her example I am bound to put down to my mistreatment at the hands of the Roman mob. My inability to conceive is the only thing I ever thanked them for.

Meanwhile, Joanna wrote letters demanding and beseeching my return. She had been alarmed to hear of the disaster overtaking King John – who was now very much a fixture at the English court, sighing every time he saw me, as there was little prospect of *his* ransom ever being paid – and her early letters were filled with relief at my survival. But impatience soon crept in, with reminders that my children were growing up without a mother. This fact I was well aware of, and was often close to despair.

Joanna was also concerned that the proposed sale of Provence had fallen through, and was anxious to have me back to try my wiles on some other prospective purchaser, I having related to her how close I had come to success with King John.

All of these matters I put to King Edward, but he was not disposed to take much account of a far-off Queen whom he had never met. Oh, if only they had! What a match that would have been.

King Edward, truth to say, was not disposed to take much account of anything save his own pleasures. He no longer even went to war, having accumulated sufficient glory for eternal military fame in the first half of his life, and having such a warlike son and heir to attend to such matters for him. It was therefore necessary for me to be patient, and wait until he had had enough of me. This, as I

287

have related, took some considerable time, and it was not until after I had lived in England for eighteen months that he told me I could return home.

I was overjoyed. It was now very nearly two years since I had last seen my dear children, or my dear Queen, and now at last I was free to go.

A passage was immediately arranged for me, back to Bordeaux, where I could look for a joyful reunion with the Black Prince, and then a promenade across the south of France to Marseilles, before finding a ship for home. I did not anticipate the journey taking more than two months at the outside, and was delighted to discover, when I reached Southampton with my ladies – English ladies these, my Neapolitans having all become married to Englishmen – that my captain was to be none other than Christopher of the Bay.

He seemed equally pleased to see me again, and was clearly flattered when I told him that I now counted myself in the safest of hands. At the moment, I was speaking idiomatically, of course.

Alas, it is strange how often one makes plans which seem to be based on the solidest of calculations, only to find them destroyed by the playfulness of fate. We duly cast off and made our way down the Solent, with a fair wind. But no sooner were we through the Needles Channel than the wind backed to the north west. As our course was in the first instance only just south of west, and the cog would sail not closer than fifty points to the wind – see what a nautical person I had become through my brave captain's teaching? – this caprice meant we could not go exactly where we wished. Christopher was not dismayed by this. 'If we must stand south,' he said, 'we will do so. The wind will have changed again by morning.'

In this prognostication he was to a certain extent correct; the wind backed again, to the west, and at the same time increased to a full gale, thus making any progress towards the Bay of Biscay downright impossible. Dawn found us in sight of land, to be sure, but faced with lowering skies and breaking seas, which had my ladies screaming and alarmed even me.

Indeed Christopher himself looked concerned. The land ahead of us was one of a group of rocks which some geographers have generously described as islands, giving them the name of Channel Islands, as they are actually in the English Channel. They are also apparently English, although much closer to France, and I could see no reason for not seeking shelter amongst them until the storm should abate.

Christopher decided otherwise. These islands, he told me, were composed of granite, and had outcroppings of this singularly hard rock in every direction, often just beneath the surface. They were also beset by fearsome tides, which might surge as hard as ten miles an hour, far faster than any known ship could sail. He thus, reluctantly, chose to run off before the wind, and seek shelter in France.

This certainly seemed safe enough from a political point of view, the disaster of Poitiers having determined the French nobility to conclude yet another truce with the fearsome English. In any event, as the good fellow pointed out, I was travelling on a Neapolitan passport.

Getting to France, otherwise than simply running full tilt into it, was a different matter. With the wind astern, the cog shot past the port of Cherbourg and round the Point de Barfleur into the Bay of the Seine, while my maids wailed their terror. In the course of this careering journey the foremast went by the board, the pumps had to be manned, and even I faced the prospect that my last hour might have come.

However, I clung to Christopher, and he to the tiller, and so we arrived at a place called, fittingly enough, Harbour, or Havre in French. Here we hurtled alongside the quay to the discomfort of several ships which were already there, sheltering from the storm, and after some discussion, conducted in both French and English, and most involving payment for damage caused by our intemperate entry, we were allotted a safe berth.

'I owe you my life, my dear Christopher,' I told my hero. 'As before I owed you my ... well ...' I could not think of a word, neither honour nor chastity seeming to fit the bill.

As he had not actually served me at all, in a literal sense, and as I was in any event feeling somewhat distraught and not a little over-excited by our adventures of the past few days, I fell into a swoon, from which he had necessarily to rescue me and restore me to life, and as it was a chilly spring day this was best done beneath the covers in the good fellow's bunk, while, my clothing being somewhat tight, he found it necessary to release certain bows to make me more comfortable.

I have never been more comfortable in my life, although when, next morning, I considered my situation, I thought it rather demeaning to leap straight from a King to a shipmaster.

Which but goes to show how little we truly understand about fate.

There was another aspect of life which I was forced to consider when I awoke, tousled and happy, listening to the wind howling through the rigging and knowing it could no longer harm me: how I was going to return to Naples.

Quite apart from the storm, which gave every promise of raging for another month or more, there was the matter of the foremast, which would need replacing before my Christopher could contemplate beating into the Bay. I would cheerfully have spent the time with him in Le Havre, having been most impressed by his gentleness and his knowledge and his general amatory powers, but he thought otherwise. He was a man of the firmest decisions, even if they were not always the right decisions.

290

Besides, dare I say it, he was even more concerned than I at what had happened, considering himself guilty of *lèse-majesté*, as quite apart from my being a duchess, the position I had filled at the courts of both the King and his son was well known. He therefore, unbeknownst to me, made inquiries amongst the local gentry, and without warning arrived on board with a certain Sieur de Malplaison, who it seemed would be entirely willing to assist so great a lady as the Duchess of Eberli on her way.

Christopher, of course, apart from being an excellent sea captain and a most entertaining lover, was a total innocent, who believed that any gentleman, even of the lowest rank, was necessarily a soul of honour. I took one look at the Sieur and realised that in all probability I was but exchanging one bed for another, and, truth to tell, after Christopher's arms I was in no hurry to sample another's.

In thus gloomily surveying my immediate future I was wrong, but this was no fault of the Sieur de Malplaison.

For the time being, I recognised that there was nothing for it, and allowed myself, my maids, and my boxes, to be removed to the shore, whence we were escorted inland, to the château owned by the Malplaison family ... after I had bidden Christopher a fond farewell, assuming I would never see him again.

The journey took some time, over rough roads, and was a dispiriting one. The Sieur did his best to make it pleasant. He was a handsome fellow, a few years younger than myself, and was most definitely pleased with his capture, as he supposed. Equally was he pleased with the clink of my moneybags, for dear Edward had left me well provided with coin to defray the expenses of my journey. It was my surroundings which filled me with gloom. Normandy had been fought over so many times in the past few centuries that it resembled a vast wasteland. It had recently been reconquered by the French, but few expected this state of affairs to last very long. Thus everything was in a state of neglect. I have already mentioned the roads. Additionally we passed apple orchards and walnut groves which were mere withered trees, and farms where not an animal save a starving dog was to be seen.

Worst of all were the people, ravenous scarecrows who crowded beside our cavalcade crying out for bread. So many were there at times I feared we would be assaulted, but the Sieur had taken the precaution of travelling with a score of men-at-arms, and these effectively discouraged any show of force.

Yet was my concern evident, and the Sieur, whose name was Ranald, was quick to take advantage of the situation.

'Indeed, travel at the moment, except in a powerful group such as ourselves, is highly unsafe. You will do best to remain at the château until I can arrange for a suitable escort.'

I sighed, and suggested it would really be best for me to return to Le Havre, where at least I knew I would be safe, if my journey by land was going to be equally delayed. Naturally he would not hear of it, and so we duly arrived at the château.

I was pleasantly surprised. The house nestled in the midst of a considerable garden, much of which was given over to vegetables and orchards; there was no lack of husbandry here. Surrounding these pleasant grounds there was a twelve-foot-high wall, castellated, behind which armed sentries patrolled, effectively to prevent any of the starving peasants from attempting to enter unless they truly wished to die.

Within the wall there was another garden, this entirely given over to flowers and fountains, and then a warm, cosy dwelling, with fires blazing in the principal rooms, and a great many servants waiting upon one's every wish.

Best of all, in one of these rooms, there was Madame de Malplaison, with her three children. I have never been so relieved in my life, for madame was clearly no woman to be trifled with. She was, I estimated – correctly – some

292

years older than her husband, and was thus about my own age. Their three daughters were respectively six, five and four: the Sieur had married young. Madame, whose name was Louise, for we soon became the best of friends, was a good-looking, buxom woman, by no means beautiful but given the appearance of beauty by her lustrous dark hair and glowing eyes. These eyes saw a great deal more than she admitted, and clearly one of the things they had seen over the six years of her marriage was that her husband was unable to keep his hands off anything in a skirt: she even appeared vaguely surprised that I had reached the château without being upended in a ditch.

This having been ascertained, she welcomed the prospect of a duchess staying beneath her roof, and treated me with kindness itself. But it soon became apparent that her husband had laid his plans with some care. In a week it would be Easter, and it was apparently Madame de Malplaison's wont to spend this most Christian holiday with her parents in Paris, together with her children. The Sieur did not accompany her on these occasions, as he and his mother-in-law were not friends.

For this holiday, therefore, he was wont to remain alone at the château.

'Do not fret, my dear,' he said over dinner. 'I shall be more than occupied with arranging for the duchess's safe passage through France.'

His wife looked at him, and then at me. I have no doubt that she knew what he got up to during her absences, and was prepared to condone such extra-marital activity, once a year, where it concerned serving maids and village wenches. But not when it involved an extremely beautiful widowed duchess.

'I will not fret, my pet,' she now retorted, 'because I have decided to stay here for Easter this year.'

'Stay here?' Ranald demanded. 'You have never done that before.'

'We have never had a guest at this time of year before.'

'But what will your mother say?' the poor fellow cried, seeing himself entirely robbed of his pleasure.

'Mama will be very angry,' Louise agreed. 'But I am sure you will manage to put up with it, monsieur.'

I could have kissed her, as I really had had no idea how I was going to cope with Ranald's advances. That her wifely jealousy, which so protected me from her husband, was to involve her in the most dreadful of fates, I had no concept at that moment.

Neither did they.

The week was spent pleasantly enough. I sat with Louise and sewed, while gossiping. I had much more to tell her than she me, for she was agog to learn that I had actually been present at Poitiers, and that I was acquainted with King John as well as King Edward. The sweet woman would utter not a word of condemnation against her King, but it was plain from what she told me that the effort of raising his enormous ransom was proving an immense burden to everyone in France, and was at least partly responsible for the chaos and misery of the country. The rest of the responsibility could of course also be laid at John's door, for having allowed himself to be captured in the first place: the Dauphin was incompetent and unsure of his authority, and no effort was being made either to assuage the peasants' destitution, or to put an end to the sporadic outbursts of violence which were taking place, by the use of force.

It did not apparently occur to my new friends that they were in any danger from these rebellions, which together have become known as the *Jacquerie*, and as they were not concerned neither was I. Easter Day duly arrived, and we attended chapel within the château, together with all the family and much of the staff. But the service was hardly over when one Montfort, captain of the guard, came up to Ranald and requested his presence on the wall.

The poor fellow was clearly upset, and so Louise and I

went along with Ranald to see what was alarming him. During the service we had been vaguely aware of a great deal of noise coming from the road leading to the village. On arrival on the wall we were even more alarmed than the captain to discover a large crowd of people, several hundred strong, and consisting of women and children as well as men, not to mention dogs, approaching us.

'What are they shouting?' Ranald inquired.

'They are shouting, "Food. And death to the Sieur,"' Montfort said.

'My God, what are we going to do?' Louise asked.

'There is naught to be afraid of,' Ranald insisted. 'When they come close enough, Montfort, you will shoot them down with arrows. I do not wish my garden disrupted.'

'Yes, monsieur,' the captain said. 'However, with respect—'

'Yes, man, what ails you?'

'Well, monsieur, that looks like the entire village out there.'

'Are you afraid of a few hundred starving peasants? Have we not fifty men-at-arms at our disposal?'

'Indeed we do, monsieur. But, on their days off, my men are wont to go into that village ... well, monsieur, you know how it is, and there is nowhere else.'

'You mean their whores may be in that crowd?'

'In a manner of speaking, monsieur.'

'Well, they will just have to shoot them with the rest. I am paying them, and I expect them to defend me.'

'Yes, monsieur,' Montfort said, but I could see he was doubtful, and indeed I felt that Ranald was treating the crisis in an entirely too cavalier manner. Alas, both Montfort and I were proved right.

Ranald deeming that it was unsafe for us ladies on the wall, we were returned to the house and told to entertain the children until the villagers had been dispersed. That done, Ranald donned his armour, but did not return to the wall himself; it appeared that he only intended to take part in the coming fracas as a last resort.

This arrived much more quickly than any of us had anticipated. There was a great to-do and a lot of shouting from outside, and within five minutes Montfort arrived at the door of the parlour, looking distinctly shaken.

'The men will not fight against their friends,' he announced.

'My God! What are we to do?' again cried Louise, gathering her children to her, while I remembered Rome.

'Why, I shall ... I shall ...' Ranald looked at Montfort. 'What do you recommend, Captain?'

'That you say your prayers, monsieur,' the scoundrel replied, and with that drew his dagger and presented it to the Sieur's throat. 'You are my prisoner.'

'What? What?' Ranald shouted.

'It is you they are after,' Montfort pointed out. 'If I give you to them they will spare my life.'

Ranald was struck dumb by this act of treachery, and Louise appeard to swoon, while her children screamed. I looked around for some weapon with which to defend my host by striking the cowardly captain on the head, but could find none, and before I could think of an alternative course of action the mob were crowding down the hallway towards us, shouting, to my amazement and relief, 'England and the Black Prince! England and the Black Prince!'

'We are saved,' I cried happily, not realising that the revolting peasants were merely playing both ends against the middle, as it were; as this was a château owned by a supporter of King John and Paris, they pretended they were acting on behalf of King Edward and London – had the château been owned by an English supporter, they would undoubtedly have been shouting 'France and the Dauphin!'

They were a horrifying looking lot, men and women, far less salubrious than those who had mauled me in Rome. But this time I was confident, and with reason. As they burst into our midst like snarling wolves I stepped forward and raised my hand.

That brought them to a halt, but possibly because they had never previously beheld such beauty.

'I heard your shouts,' I told them, 'and am greatly relieved. My name is the Duchess of Eberli, and I have but this week come from the court of the Black Prince' – I decided against confounding them with pedantic details – 'on my way to Italy.' Again, I reflected these varlets would hardly know geography and thus work out that I was apparently travelling in the wrong direction. 'The Sieur de Malplaison,' I continued, 'is very kindly acting as my host until transport can be arranged for me across France. I should be very much obliged if you good people would now leave before you commit a crime.'

Presumably breaking into a château was a crime in itself, but I trusted that this could be overlooked if they now behaved themselves.

My speech certainly had the effect of cooling their ardour, but only briefly. Then one of the louts spoke up. 'How do we know you are English?' he demanded. 'I speak English. Say something.'

'Why, my dear fellow,' I responded, 'is not the weather fine today? But not, I fear, tomorrow.'

He nodded, and looked at his fellows. 'She is English,' he said.

'But these are French,' said one beetle-browed rascal. 'And this Sieur de Malplaison lives on the fat of the land while we starve. What do you say, shall we make him enjoy his own cooking, today?'

They gave a roar of approval, and before I could intervene again Ranald had been torn from Montfort's arms and hustled down the corridor, shrieking his terror.

I feared for his life, and even more for the virtue of his wife, as she too was seized. I endeavoured to protest, but was thrust aside as the clothes were torn from her body, and I was forced to witness happening to her what had

297

happened to me in Rome. Obviously in these cases it is better to be a spectator than a victim – I had worked this out for myself twelve years before when I had witnessed the torture and execution of the conspirators against Andrew of Hungary – but yet my heart went out to the poor matron, who should have been in safety with her parents, as she was stripped naked and assaulted by several men in succession, her twisting body red with humiliation and injury.

Even more was I concerned for her children, as the little girls were also most shamefully raped.

My feelings were, moreover, concerned with my own possible fate. Even if I had been accepted as an English-woman, I was now surrounded by inflamed humanity, and thrust against a wall as I was I was subjected to many a pinch and squeeze.

But the worst horror of the day was yet to come, as people now came along the corridor summoning us to see the fun. Off we went, myself in the midst of the throng as there was no way I could escape it, and Louise and her beleaguered daughters dragged behind.

At this point I may say that to this moment in my life I had always regarded the Roman mob as the lowest form of human existence. I now realised I was wrong, and forced to the understanding that *any* mob is the lowest form of human existence, its exact place on this ghastly scale being accidental and a result of circumstances.

In Rome, the mob had been whipped up by their betters, who only wanted to get rid of dear Cola. Everything else was incidental. In Normandy the mob was whipped up by hunger and a deep-seated sense of injustice. The representative of that plenty they could not share, and that justice which always found them out, was the Sieur de Malplaison, and he was now in their hands, as they were now in his house.

Thus the unfortunate man was sacrificed to their hunger and his plenty. There was a roaring fire in the grate, above which hung a spit on which was impaled a suckling pig which we had been going to enjoy for our Easter dinner. This half-cooked animal was now removed and thrown aside, and in its place was spitted the Sieur de Malplaison.

I have witnessed many a dismal sight in my life but none to compare with the poor young man being stripped as naked as his wife and then impaled upon a sharp rod of iron. I have heard of such means of execution being performed in Eastern lands – and as I have mentioned a similar fate had recently been inflicted upon one of our own kings – but had never expected to see such a thing done myself. The screams of the struggling Sieur as he was held on his face across the kitchen table while the sharp point was inserted in his fundament must surely have awakened the dead, save for the ribald racket being maintained by those tormenting him, who while he was still living were busily castrating him and scattering pepper and salt and herbs upon his quivering body. Fortunately he was clearly dead by the time the spit, carefully guided, emerged from his throat. The spit was then placed upon the fire, and rotated by eager hands.

Louise had by now not unnaturally fainted again, while her children were screaming their heads off. I felt like doing the same, but refrained as I did not wish to draw attention to myself for fear some similarly horrible fate might befall me. Call me a coward if you wish, but in cases like this survival is what matters.

And still Louise's ordeal was not completed. She was revived by the simple method of having a bucket of water emptied over her head, whereupon she was sat at the bloodstained table, naked as she was, and offered a piece of meat – and this meat had been sliced from her husband's as yet undercooked thighs.

This was too much for me, and I swooned in turn, to awake some moments later in the fresh air of the garden. I drew deep breaths and looked up at the clear blue of the heavens, and wondered how, in such a beautiful world, men could be so vile.

But my ordeal was just beginning. My rescuer was none other than the foul Montfort, who was now grinning at me most lasciviously.

'We had best be away,' he said. 'Those louts may be sated for the moment, but they will think of you soon enough.'

I sat up and looked around me; the wretch had even procured a horse. 'My maids—'

'Must fend for themselves. They will not be killed, as they are clearly not French. And what is a little rape to a lively young woman?'

'I will not desert my maids,' I said stoutly. 'Or Madame de Malplaison,' I added.

'Madame is undoubtedly dead,' he said. 'Look.'

I looked at the château, and watched smoke issuing from the roof, while from within there came the most unholy racket.

'My God,' I said. 'The children?'

'I saw one of them spitted myself.'

'Can those be human beings?'

'We are all beasts,' he remarked, revealing himself to be a philosopher. But one with primitive methods of disputation. When I again protested that I must find my maids, he settled the argument very quickly by hitting me on the chin with his fist.

When I regained consciousness I was lying face down across the shoulders of his horse while he proceeded on his way. This is a most uncomfortable way to travel, for not only is all one's weight carried on one's stomach, which is not helped by having those bony shoulders eating into one, but in my case Montfort was spending his time playing with my behind.

I could not stop my head jerking as I awoke, and this seemed to please him.

'Back with us, eh?' he laughed. 'Well, then, let us resume where we left off. I trust you have learned some sense by now, good duchess? I will confess that I am aflame with desire for you.'

Saying which he dismounted and dragged me from the horse as if I had been a sack of coal.

I had early formed an intense dislike for this man, and his treachery to the Sieur de Malplaison had heightened my feelings. His mistreatment of me was the last straw. I therefore made no effort to resist him, but merely looked around me as he stretched me on the ground and proceeded to lift my skirts. I had already selected my weapon, a large stone, and as he was fully preoccupied with what he was uncovering, secured this by the simple means of stretching out my hand.

The lout was still wearing a mail surcoat, and a pot helmet. I was therefore forced to dissemble. Having folded my skirts about my waist, he now came up my body to unfasten my bodice, clearly intending to have a sexual feast, and totally oblivious as to what my outstretched arms might be doing.

I smiled at him. 'With your hat on, good sir?' I asked.

He laughed at my spirit, and threw away his pot, whereupon I swung my right arm and hit him as hard as I could upon the side of the head. He went over without a sound, sprawled on the grass with blood dribbling down his cheek, while I sat up and rearranged myself.

I am a woman who abhors violence in any form, but there are limits.

Montfort was not apparently dead, and I had no desire to have a murder on my hands. I therefore removed his sword, which I thrust through my own girdle, and his dagger, likewise, mounted the horse, and rode off, leaving him lying there.

I also relieved him of a bag of coin which was hanging from his belt, as of course all of my own travelling wealth was lost in the burning château. I even toyed with the idea of returning there myself, whatever the risk, to look for my maids. But I reflected that the risk was indeed great, and that these maids were English rather than Neapolitan, so that if they had survived they would probably do very well. They might even manage to regain Le Havre and dear Christopher of the Bay.

Here again I was tempted, but the thought of encountering another of those mobs was too terrifying, and so I decided to ride south-east, in which direction I felt sure lay the duchy of Provence and safety.

This was undoubtedly naïve of me. The whole of northern France was up in arms in this confounded *Jacquerie*, and it is extremely unlikely I would have got very far, had I not, that very afternoon, received a stroke of good fortune. Well, it was about time.

I was proceeding along a country lane, watching the spires of a church in the distance, very hungry and thirsty, and debating whether I could risk entering the village and seeking food and wine without immediately being stretched on my back, when I perceived, issuing from the village, a body of friars, mounted, and looking very well content with themselves.

Their white habits indicated to me that they were of the brotherhood known as Franciscans, founded by a very odd fellow named Francis of Assisi, who about a hundred years ago had abandoned a prosperous inheritance to live amidst the birds and the bees in utter destitution, hoping to teach the world that the simple life is the best. As is the case with such eccentrics, he attracted a large following of men of similar itinerant tastes, and I am sure that they accomplished a great deal of good, although obviously they were wasting their time in attempting to preach virtue to either the Malplaisons of this world or the ravenous beasts who had torn him apart.

However, I had encountered these good fellows in

Avignon, and also in Naples – they had not done a great deal to change the habits of the inhabitants there either – and although I approached them with some trepidation, as my experiences have made me wary even of men of the cloth where a shapely leg or a thrusting bosom is concerned, I was overjoyed to discern that the leader of this group was none other than Brother Jules, an old acquaintance of mine.

Now Jules was one of those men – they are quite numerous – to whom a pouting tit or a strokeable calf was totally meaningless; his pleasures were found within his own order, or perhaps with the young men who from time to time sought him out, no doubt for religious instruction. I therefore knew that my virtue was entirely safe in his company.

Better yet, I also knew him to belong to what was called the Community. The Franciscans had, at an early stage, divided into two camps, as it were, one demanding that the utmost simplicity be maintained, and all possessions rejected, as taught by their founder: these were called the Spirituals. The other group contended that to live in abject poverty was self-defeating, and sought some of the better things in life, so long as all possessions were held communally. Thus the Community.

Jules was a man who held that the better things in life were more important than most.

I therefore hurried up to him, reminded him of the last time we had met, in Avignon two years before, threw my arms round his neck, and kissed him most heartily.

His companions applauded, perhaps wondering if he was undergoing a spiritual rebirth, or at least a physical one. Alas, not even my splendour could alter Jules' persuasions, but he remained the kind-hearted, good-natured, overweight and distinctly gluttonous fellow I remembered, and within seconds I was chewing on a chicken thigh and gulping French wine from a flagon.

Meanwhile I told the friars of my recent adventures.

They were acquainted with the *Jacquerie*, and had indeed been sent by the Pope north to attempt to alleviate some of the horrors which were daily being reported. Now they had given up their mission as impossible, and were on their way back to Avignon.

Nothing could have suited me better. The friars numbered twenty, and although men of the cloth, each carried concealed beneath his habit a good long blade. This fact, together with their known determination to defend themselves, added of course to their sanctity as men of God, protected them, and me, from assault even by the bands of wild beasts disguised as men and women who were ranging the countryside. I was given a white habit to wear, the hood and cloak of which entirely concealed my feminine glories, and rode all the way in perfect safety. So becoming an abbess did I make indeed that Jules strongly recommended I abandon my life of service to the Queen and enter a nunnery. He assured me that most of the nuns were of his persuasion, in reverse, if you follow me without my having to go into indecencies, and that I should have a thoroughly good time of it with none of the dangers attached to my present mode of existence.

I will not deny that I was tempted. My adventures of the past two years had left me quite exhausted, emotionally and physically. But then I thought of my two dear children and my beloved Joanna, and summoned up the courage to go on.

And so, after an absence of more than two years, I finally regained sunny Naples.

My welcome, for all the failure of my mission, was rapturous. Joanna folded me into her arms and kissed me again and again.

'I had never expected to see you again,' she said. 'Now you must tell me all of your adventures. Everything that happened to you.'

This took some time, and I was anxious to regain Eberli

and my children, and Ricardo, to learn what had been happening to my duchy in my absence. But Joanna assured me that all was well, and I was required to linger in Naples for more than a week, while she listened wide-eyed to my encounters with royalty, and with horror to my description of the *Jacquerie.*

I did not bore her by mentioning Christopher of the Bay.

For my part, I discovered that very little had changed, save that we had all grown two years older, but even that was of no obvious importance in the case of the Queen, who at thirty-one was more beautiful, and, dare I say it, lascivious, than ever. The parade of young men to her apartments had changed even less. That is to say, their ages had not changed, even if the men themselves had. If they ceased to attend Her Grace during the week I was with her, this was simply because she loved me more than them.

From which it will be gathered that King Louis was still off attending whichever war happened to be going on at the moment.

There were certain aspects of life which had, however, inalterably changed. Charles Martel was dead.

This sad news the Queen herself told me, in the most matter-of-fact terms. It had happened the previous year, and thus she had had ample time to get over her grief, but the fact was that she had never borne the love for the boy that one expects from a mother. Partly this was because Joanna was ever a queen and a woman rather than a mother, but equally because, whether Charles's father had been Andrew of Hungary or Bertrand of Artois, they were both men she had grown to dislike more and more as any memory of their finer points faded, and she had insensibly found all their faults present in her son.

'Then who is your heir?' I asked in dismay.

'Why, my sister,' she said, adding, 'for the time being.'

This indicated that this was a situation she was considering changing, and indeed the sisters had grown even further apart during my absence. If they had adventured together, Joanna could not forget that Marie had willingly accepted her marriage to Charles of Durazzo. While Marie, with the perversity of someone at a disadvantage, blamed Joanna for Charles's disagreeable death.

There was also a question of protocol causing friction. For Robert de Baux was still alive, kept in a dungeon in the palazzo of Durazzo. This was an odd thing for the Princess to do, save for her own amusement, for she had a far darker side to her character than Joanna, and indeed many were the rumours circulating in Naples as to the fiendish tortures she inflicted upon her poor husband when in the mood.

Whatever her amusements, however, this course of action meant that she remained legally married. This might have been a ruse, to prevent anyone seeking her hand, and indeed, later events lead me to suppose this was so, but she persisted in calling herself Duchess of Durazzo, and living, as I have mentioned, in great state, in her palazzo, with her children, her son, whom she had named Charles after his father, clearly being brought up to regard his aunt as a representative of the devil, from the lowering glances he directed at the Queen whenever they happened to meet.

All of these family differences only encouraged me to escape to my own beautiful castle, and this I at last managed to do. Words cannot describe the greeting I received from my dearest Lucia and William, from my dogs and my horses, and even, to my surprise, from Ricardo, who had kept both the duchy and the books in good order, and insisted upon showing me every return.

Thus happiness.

There were problems from time to time, of course. In the first place, Joanna immediately began to consider possible husbands for me, and was amazed when I told her

I would prefer to remain a widow for a while longer.

'A woman must be married,' she insisted.

'Well, Your Grace,' I replied, somewhat boldly. 'If I could find a husband who never came near me but spent all his time out of the country ...'

She sighed. 'Yes. I regret it bitterly. But what is done is done. Yet I must have a man, from time to time. As must you.'

'No doubt I shall feel that way soon enough, Your Grace,' I said. 'But I have had too many men these past two years, and I am of a mind to live in peace and enjoy my children. The moment these pleasures begin to pall, I shall inform you.'

'You are right,' she said enthusiastically. 'Because soon it will be time to marry Lucia.'

Joanna could think of no greater pleasure in life than a wedding, and the joys that would follow for the happy couple.

'Your Grace,' I protested. 'Lucia is only thirteen.'

'Well,' she said, 'I was eight when I was married.'

'Yes, but not to cohabit.'

She shrugged. 'I was but thirteen when I yielded my maidenhead to that rascal Roberto.' She sighed, clearly thinking back to those carefree, and amazingly innocent, days of her youth. 'As were you,' she added.

'I was fourteen,' I corrected her somewhat primly.

'Next year,' she announced, 'we shall seek a husband for your beautiful daughter.'

In her description of Lucia the Queen was absolutely right. At thirteen Lucia, if I say so myself, was very nearly as lovely as her mother, but of a different variety. She had her father's dark hair, but not black as it was alleviated by my own, and my blue eyes, an amazing combination which fascinated everyone. Even more important, she had a figure every bit as voluptuous as mine had been at that age, and thus giving every promise of perhaps matching me as she grew older.

307

Unlike my unfortunate circumstances, however, at this age Lucia was entirely innocent.

I managed to persuade Joanna to postpone her wedding plans for another year, and it was not until the spring of 1360 that we got seriously to work. All manner of handsome young men were paraded before us, Joanna eyeing their codpieces and I their expressions and manners, as well as those of their parents; I am sure several of them found their way to the Queen's bed. But none to Lucia's.

'You are remarkably difficult to please,' Joanna complained when some weeks of this interesting pastime had been completed.

'She is my only daughter, Your Grace,' I said.

At this point it was necessary to return to Eberli to deal with my affairs, so the next group of suitors was postponed for a month, leaving Joanna in a very sulky mood.

It was a great relief to lie in my own bed, high in the main tower of Eberli Castle, and look out across the rolling countryside, knowing it all belonged to me. It was the pleasantest in the early morning, just after sunrise, when the birds would be twittering outside my window and I would hear the sounds of life awakening in the courtyard below, the lowing of the cattle as they were milked before being taken to pasture, the neighing of the horses as they were exercised, the wailing of one of the scullerymaids as she was whipped – Ricardo always began his day by whipping one of them, whether any misdemeanour had been committed or not – and the barking of the dogs as they were loosed.

Here I was joined by Lucia, warm and tousled from her own bed. This was a pastime in which we had indulged since she had been a babe. Indeed, William had used to join us for our morning romp, but since he had attained the age of puberty I had decided it were best to forbid him the company of two naked females less he become precocious.

My own darling however was a treat to hold in my arms.

'When will you return to Naples, Mama?' she asked.

I sighed. 'I shall have to go back in another month. This business of finding a husband is tiresome.'

'Do I need a husband, Mama?'

'Her Grace feels that you do. And she is right. A woman should be married, at least once, both to taste the joys of the marriage bed and to procreate, as is God's will.'

Lucia was silent for some seconds, then she said, 'Must my husband come from Naples?'

'Well, no, that is not essential. But it is certainly more convenient. I mean, he must be a fellow countryman of yours.'

'But is his rank important? You were once a slave, were you not, who married a mere soldier.'

'Well,' I said, somewhat regretting the frankness with which I had dealt with my children. 'I was fortunate to enjoy the favour of the Queen, and so was able to rise.'

'Do I not enjoy the favour of the Queen, Mama?'

'She loves you like her own,' I assured her.

'Then I too can expect to rise,' Lucia remarked. 'No matter how low I begin.'

'Yes, but you are already the daughter of a duchess ...' I began to frown, and look down at the beautiful, innocent face beside me. It occurred to me that my darling daughter was trying to tell me something.

She threw off the covers and rose to her knees, her splendid hair clouding about her shoulders and breasts.

'I love him,' she declared.

I sat up as well.

'Love whom?'

'His name is Pietro, and he is handsome, and sweet, and—'

'What is the name of his father?' I inquired, attempting to keep from shouting.

'Why, I suppose it is Pietro as well. Pietro the milkman.'

'The *what*?' I shouted. 'You have fallen in love with a milkman's son?'

'He is the sweetest boy, Mama.'

'And I suppose you have let him practise on your tits,' I bawled, leaping out of the bed and striding to the window. 'Ricardo!' I shouted. 'Ricardo! Fetch yourself up here with your cane. I have a subject for you.'

'Mama!' Lucia protested. 'Pietro and I are man and wife.'

Slowly I turned towards her, feeling as if I had just eaten a toadstool by mistake for a mushroom, unable to believe that such a catastrophe could have overtaken me.

'He has your maidenhead?'

'Yes, Mama.'

'A milkman's son?' I sank into a chair. 'My God! I will have him hanged.'

'You will do no such thing.' Lucia got out of bed and stood before me. 'Firstly because if you do I will kill myself. And secondly because he is the father of your grandchild.'

'The ...' I gaped at her, and then at her belly, which remained flat enough.

'I have missed my second month,' the wretched girl declared proudly. 'That is why I have told you.'

There came a banging on the door. Ricardo was there, no doubt armed with his cane and from the sound of it accompanied by half the castle.

'Shall I let him in, Mama?' Lucia asked.

'Oh ... go away, Ricardo!' I bawled. 'Go away.'

The noise slowly faded.

'Will you not bless me, Mama?' Lucia asked. 'And Pietro?'

The daughter of a duchess, married to the son of a milkman! Lucia of course kept reminding me that she was actually the daughter of a slave, which nearly made me send for Ricardo again. But there it was. The child was in love, which was actually more important to me than the disgusting condition into which she had got herself. I had

310

Pietro brought to see me, and then his mother and father, who turned out to be honest, hardworking people with not a vice visible between them.

Telling Joanna was not something I looked forward to, but I should have known better. For the Queen, whatever her sins in the eyes of moral manhood, was above all a romantic. Having loved and lost herself, she genuinely sought some spark with all the men she took to her bed – and never found it. Now she was overjoyed to hear of Lucia's dilemma.

'How delicious,' she said. 'They must have had it the first time under a bush, with the cows close by. Do you not find that romantic, Richilde?'

'Not in the least, Your Grace,' I assured her. 'Nestling amidst cowpats has never been my idea of pleasure.'

'You are effete,' Joanna laughed. 'You like scented silk sheets and a pommaded body. You must bring this young man to meet me.'

'Your Grace,' I said pointedly. 'He is going to be my son-in-law.'

'Well, of course,' she agreed.

In fact the Queen behaved with absolute decorum, although I could tell she was impressed with the size of Pietro's codpiece, I having had him properly dressed for the visit to Naples. In fact the youth was growing on me as well, not in a sexual sense – since my experiences in France I had quite turned my back upon the carnal – but as a human being, and it was with a few quiet tears of joy that I witnessed the ceremony, which even Joanna had to agree should be conducted in the relative privacy of Eberli Castle rather than the cathedral in Naples.

Of course Pietro could not remain a milkman. I appointed him Ricardo's deputy as my steward, and he settled down to learn to read and write so that he might one day be able to fulfil his duties. I also had him taught horsemanship and fencing, and felt that perhaps we might

311

even turn him into a gentleman, given sufficient time.

I thus spent a very happy couple of years, enjoying my children, and, soon enough, my grandchild, a beautiful girl who was named Lucia after her mother. I even gave some thought to a wife for William, but he was still very young and seemed to have no great interest in the opposite sex. As I recalled very clearly the dangers of precocity from my own youth, I did not press the matter.

Thus life proceeded at a very even tenor for the three years which followed my return from England and France, and I believe for Joanna as well, until we were all brought up short by the news of King Louis's death.

CHAPTER 9

This lamentable but foreseeable event took place on 5 June 1362. What was really remarkable, and must have proved a sad irritation to the great warrior, was that he did not even succumb in battle, but perished of a fever.

His body was brought to Naples, and interred in the Cathedral, the Queen and all her nobility attending in solemn state, dressed in black, with veils to hide our faces and the evidences of grief. Or lack of it, as the case might be.

In my case, I must confess, I wept copiously when I remembered the handsome young knight who had so dominated our girlish lives.

But this was a major event. Not in the sense that it directly affected the Kingdom. Joanna had always been its Queen, and she remained its Queen. But here Europe was suddenly presented with the spectacle of possibly its most beautiful woman, a title unchallenged even as the Queen entered her thirty-sixth year – save perhaps by those intimates who had considered her in conjunction with the Duchess of Eberli – who was also a woman of extreme wealth and ability as well as intelligence – albeit a slightly murky past – who was now a widow.

As may be imagined, every young gallant with but a drop of royal blood in his veins fitted himself out and embarked for Naples. For a season our society hummed with active young men, and some who were not so young, seeking Her Grace's hand in marriage.

From France there came Louis of Anjou, younger brother of the Dauphin. From Castile there came Enrique of Trastamara, bastard son of Alfonso XI: aged twenty-nine he was younger than the Queen, not that this was a deterrent to Joanna. From Portugal came Prince John, the illegitimate son of Pedro I and his beautiful mistress, Inez de Castro. From Austria came Leopold of Hapsburg. From Moravia came John Henry of Luxemburg. From Germany came Albert of Bavaria. From Scandinavia there came Henry of Mecklenberg. From Constantinople there came Michael Paleologus.

And from Aragon there came Jaime of that country.

This last name may not be familiar. Yet he was the same prince who as a seventeen-year-old youth had drawn his sword so vigorously in support of the Queen when she had been on trial before the Pope fifteen years earlier. In the intervening years he had undergone many vicissitudes in the intrigue that surrounded the Aragonese court, and had even been imprisoned for several years in conditions of extreme discomfort, as a result of which he now looked more ethereally handsome than ever.

His appearance led to a flutter amongst the Neapolitan ladies, and nowhere more so than in the royal house itself. However, in the beginning, he was no more than one amongst many, as Joanna, enjoying the sensation of being courted so handsomely, was in no immediate hurry again to tie the bonds of matrimony. Thus it was that Princess Marie considered how she could benefit from present events.

Marie, of course, suffered from a handicap when it came to selecting a new husband: she already had one. But she was not a woman to be deterred by trifles, and soon the word got out that the unhappy Robert de Baux had died in his dungeon. Close behind came the rumour that the Princess had herself visited the cell in which she had kept the unhappy lad for so long, accompanied by her servants, and watched as her husband's head was severed from his body, insulting him the while. Both head and body were certainly found floating in the harbour – separately.

Then, without wasting precious time in mourning, the Princess almost literally threw herself into the arms of Prince Jaime.

Sadly, she was rejected. It may be that the rumours had reached his ears as well, and he reflected that if both the sisters were reputed to be husband-murderers, Joanna had at least expiated her crime where Marie had not. More importantly, he had come to Naples to marry the Queen, not her heir-presumptive.

More importantly yet, Joanna herself now began to smile at him. Again it may be – she did not confide in me on this occasion – that once her sister appeared as a rival she was spurred to action. Or she may just have remembered the youth's long years of devotion and determined that she could not do better. Whatever the truth of the matter, the announcement was made that the Queen of Naples had chosen Prince Jaime of Aragon as her third husband.

It was in every way a love match, as passionate as had been the early days with Joanna and Louis. Alas, it was also the gravest error Joanna was ever to make.

For Marie took her rejection so hard that she lost her will to live, and shortly after contracted a chill and died, a sad waste of a life which had been so full of promise.

Joanna undoubtedly mourned her sister, but she was still indulging in a long and passionate honeymoon with her Spanish lover, and I observed that her true sentiment was one of relief. However, the event left the question of the Queen's heir in the air, as it were. Marie had been accepted as such throughout the Kingdom. Joanna made no effort to name another heir, immediately – no doubt she was anticipating an early pregnancy – so the various nobles of the blood made their own assumptions, which were, that if the Queen failed to produce a child by Jaime of Aragon, the Crown of Naples would pass, by default, to Marie's son, and in the event of his death without issue, to his sister, Margaret. Now this chain of events is exactly what happened. Jaime of Aragon proved unable to impregnate the Queen, no matter how hard he tried – no doubt the exertions of his youth had weakened his seed – and Marie's son Charles did indeed die without issue. This left Margaret of Durazzo as the heiress to the throne.

Unfortunately, the chain of events did not end there. It may be recalled that Charles of Durazzo, Joanna's bitterest enemy, had had a brother named Louis, an unfortunate lad who had been carried off to Hungary by Louis of that country. This Louis of Durazzo had since returned, fully grown, and fully converted into a Hungarian as well, filled with hatred for our Queen. He even attempted a rebellion against her, and had been defeated by Louis of Tarento himself, and imprisoned in a dungeon, where he had died.

In his youth, however, he had married a lady, for want of a better word, named Margaret of Corigliano, and by her had produced a son, named Charles after his uncle and great-grandfather. This Charles had now attained the age of eighteen, and nothing seemed more fitting than that he should wed the orphaned Princess Margaret.

Joanna was delighted at this match between first cousins, and, sweetly innocent of other people's vicious dreams as she was, upon realising that she was never again going to become a mother, agreed that Charles should be her heir, with Margaret as his consort.

Thus was the stage set for bloody tragedy – for both of these young people considered that Joanna was responsible for the death of their fathers – but at this time, with the Queen only thirty-seven years old and still in the very prime of her health and beauty, the future seemed to contain no pitfalls that could not be overcome by time.

*

I played little part in these political manoeuvres. Indeed, after acting as the Queen's Matron of Honour at her wedding, I endeavoured to abandon Naples altogether for a season. Joanna was fully occupied with her handsome young Spaniard, and I could therefore spend most of my time at Eberli, and enjoy the frisking of my grandchildren.

There was also the matter of William's wife to be considered, however, and so, after an idyllic twelve-month in the country, I left Pietro and Lucia in charge, and with my son returned to Naples, where I took a house and began to throw lavish parties, it being thoroughly understood that I was looking for a bride. Now there were many people in Naples, of the old nobility, who still chose to regard me as an upstart ex-slave. But there were even more who preferred to look facts in the face and recognise me as one of the wealthiest women in Italy, and the favourite of the Queen besides. As William was my only son, this larger group were happy to attend my entertainments, with their unmarried daughters decked out in all the finery they could afford.

This was amusing, but unfortunately William showed little interest in any of the beauties paraded before him, and I began to wonder if he had not copied his sister and fallen in love with some scullery maid. When pressed upon this point, however, he stoutly denied any such liaison, and I began to realise that I might have something of a problem – especially when my son announced that he wished to enter the Church.

A daughter married to a cowherd, a son wearing a cassock – it occurred to me that the Duchy of Eberli was cursed; as it had been given to me because it had fallen vacant owing to the lack of male heirs, so it seemed likely that it would fall vacant again upon my death, unless Lucia produced something more worthwhile than daughters. This I enjoined her to do as rapidly as possible, or she might end her days in poverty.

*

I was less distracted by these events, however, than would otherwise have been the case, because it was at this time that I was indeed distracted by a most singular, and happy circumstance.

I was in the process of packing up the house in Naples, William having been introduced into a suitable chapter for a barren if hopefully not altogether joyless future, when my chamberlain, Raimondo, attended me to deliver a message.

He did this reluctantly, because he was afraid it would involve me in various legal matters. And when I read what was written I immediately did become so involved.

'As we once had some slight acquaintance, milady,' the words said, in English, 'I risk your displeasure by sending you this plea for assistance. My ship has been arrested for smuggling and piracy, and I am lodged in the city gaol. I understand I am to be broken on the wheel, which I feel is an unworthy fate, as well as a most painful and humiliating one. If therefore you hold any fond memory of any assistance I may once have been able to render to your ladyship, and feel that you could help me in any way, I should be eternally grateful.

'Your obedient servant,

'Christopher of the Bay.'

I had not even suspected the dear fellow could write! But sea captains can do anything!

'The rascal assured me you would not be angry, milady,' Raimondo said.

'Angry?' I could have kissed him. Christopher, I thought. Here in Naples! And summoning me to his side!

I was at the prison in fifteen minutes, and, despite the opposition of the warders, had Christopher and his people free in another fifteen.

He looked only slightly older, and of his pleasure in seeing me there could be no doubt.

'Now am I your servant for life, milady,' he promised. 'Let us make haste, lads, and shake the dust of this place from our boots.'

'Wait just a moment,' I said. 'Why are you in such a hurry?'

'Well, milady, it seems to me to be essential to get out of Naples before those fellows change their minds.'

'There is no chance of that,' I assured him. 'My name carries a great deal of weight in this country. I cannot permit you to re-enter my life and then disappear on the instant. You will come out to Eberli and spend a season with me, and we will remember our adventures.'

The good fellow seemed doubtful, but he had no choice, as he and his people had in effect been released into my custody. I went with them back to the ship, which lay alongside the Mole, dismissed the armed guards who had been placed upon it, recalled for a few moments my adventures on board her, and then carried Christopher off.

He had been the very last man ever to have his way with me, and that was now some two years in the past. In that time I had been chaste as a nun, entirely from lack of interest in any of the men who had passed through my life. But the sight of my old friend and compatriot had aroused the most powerful feelings in my breast.

The journey from Naples to Eberli, unless undertaken in great urgency, requires an overnight stop. I was actually tempted to return to my Naples house for my first night with Christopher, but decided against it lest Joanna get to hear of it and summon me to her presence – she was confoundedly curious where matters of the heart, or of the body, were concerned. Thus we took to the road, it began to rain, and we arrived dripping wet at the village where I usually broke my journey.

The patrone was pleased to see me, however, and asked no questions when I required us both to be shown to the same chamber, where a good fire soon dried out our clothes, which we had prudently removed lest we catch cold. That done we could regard each other, while I recalled what a splendid figure of a man he was, and he no

319

doubt did the same for me. I was now thirty-nine years old, but as my eating and drinking habits were abstemious, and I spent a good deal of my time either on horseback or on foot inspecting my property – mostly to remind myself that all of this wealth actually was mine – I had put on hardly any weight, and such as I had seemed to have gone to my breasts and backside, my most important attributes in any event, looked at from a masculine point of view.

Having looked, we sought again the splendour of that day in Le Havre, and were not disappointed. Of all the men I have ever known carnally, Christopher was the nearest to my own true station in life, and therefore I found it possible to be more myself with him than with anyone else. In addition, he was my countryman. He was also most delightfully libidinous, and once he had again got over the mental handicap of realising he was actually holding a duchess naked in his arms, was more than willing to share in everything I desired. He mounted me, I mounted him, we rolled together from one side of the bed to the other, bathed in sweat and semen, while the floor creaked and the landlord no doubt supposed his inn was falling apart about his ears. I doubt we slept, save for a few minutes before dawn, and when we awoke, we coupled again.

I was utterly delighted. I had found the one man I had ever whole-heartedly desired to spend the rest of my days with, at least since the death of poor Alberto, and he and I had somewhat cooled our ardour before that sad event.

Next day, as the facilities at the inn were primitive, we hurried on to Eberli, and there plunged into steaming tubs, side by side. Lucia was amazed, as I had not told her all the details of my recent adventures, but when Christopher was dressed – I found that he was much of a size with poor dear Fernando, and looked very well in his clothes – she and Pietro were delighted to make his acquaintance.

We thus spent an idyllic week, in which we honey-mooned just as vigorously as had the Queen with her Jaime, while betweentimes I showed Christopher my estates. He was much impressed, and so I was encouraged to put forward a suggestion that would clearly never have occurred to him, because of the apparent difference in our stations.

'Dear Christopher,' I said one night at dinner, when he was beginning to intimate that it was time he returned to his ship and his crew. 'Have you not been happy here?'

'Happier than ever before in my life, milady,' as he persisted in calling me, even in bed.

'Then why do you not remain?' I asked.

'Milady?' He looked truly startled.

'As my husband,' I told him, and as this suggestion left him dumbfounded, I hurried on. 'As you know, I am a widow of some years standing, and I need a husband, a man I can trust, and who will love me as I will love him. Are you not that man, Christopher?'

'Well, milady ...'

'And do not fear for your ship. I will purchase it, then give it back to the crew to sail away to England, leaving you free of all encumbrances. Now, does that not sound a pleasing prospect?'

'It is the most pleasing prospect I have ever heard, milady, were it possible.'

'I assure you there is nothing to prevent it,' I told him.

'Save my wife and children, milady.'

I put down my knife, the better to look at him.

'You have a wife and children?'

'Alas, milady, that is the truth of the matter.'

Almost I stabbed him there and then. But I determined to be my usual calm self.

'You did not tell me of this.'

'There has not seemed an occasion, before now, milady.'

'Indeed? Do you love your wife?'

'Well, milady, how may a man not love his wife? But we

have been married for twenty years ...' I could see he was embarrassed.

'Then do you love your children?'

'How may a man not love his children, milady, even if they are utter scoundrels?'

'As is their father,' I remarked.

'I know my crime,' he agreed. 'I can but say that I fell in love with you the first time I saw you.'

'Did you, Christopher?' I cried.

'That is the absolute truth. Of course I understood that you were as far above me as the moon. That day in Le Havre was the very happiest of my life. Until this past week.'

'My darling Christopher,' I said, and our conversation degenerated into a series of grunts for the next ten minutes, from which we emerged, tousled, exhausted, and happy.

But not content.

'What am I to do, milady?' the good fellow asked.

I have never been one to break up a family. Heaven knows I have seen it done, often enough. 'You must go back to your wife, of course,' I told him. 'But Christopher ...' I rested my hand on his arm. 'Should you ever be in these waters again, I beg of you to put in to Naples, and inform me of your presence.'

He departed the next day, after a last tumultuous night, and, not for the first time in my life, I was left to consider the might-have-beens of life.

In this regard, it is of some solace not to be able to foresee the future.

Joanna, it seemed, was bound to marry unhappily. Or maybe it is that men are not designed by nature to be consorts, even of the most beautiful woman of her time.

The Queen had taken Jaime of Aragon as her husband in the spring of 1363, with her usual careless rapture. That

Jaime had had an unfortunate life she knew, but she had not delved deeply into the background either of himself, his family, or the Iberian Peninsula, which was his home.

This bleak appendage of Europe, which to many more resembles an offshoot of North Africa, from which it is indeed separated only by the narrow Straits of Gibraltar, had been overrun by the Saracens in the eighth and ninth centuries of our Christian era, save only for the far north-western corner. It was from this corner that the survivors of the Romano-Visigoths who had formed the population of the peninsula before the arrival of the Muslims, began the long fight back, which continues as I write and has been called the *Reconquista.*

Inspired by the Holy Church and a fierce pride, the Spaniards have managed to win a number of famous victories over the heathens, and although the worshippers of the Prophet retain their hold on the southern half of Iberia, the northern portion is now entirely Christian, and has been divided into a number of small but militarily vigorous kingdoms, of which the two strongest are Castile and Aragon.

To Castile, occupying the centre of Christian Spain, has fallen the task of shouldering the main fight against the universal enemy. Aragon, occupying the north-eastern coast of the peninsula, has had less contact with the Muslims, and has equally traditionally turned its gaze more towards the Mediterranean Sea in its search for expansion. It may be recalled that it was the House of Aragon which had been summoned by the Papacy to dispossess the Angevins from Sicily, which they have held ever since.

As was natural, however, the royal families of Castile and Aragon, with a common heritage and no doubt a common future, had on numerous occasions intermarried, and although Jaime himself was the son of an Aragonese father, Alfonso IV, and an Aragonese mother, Teresa d'Entenza, following the death of his mother, he had accumulated a Castilian stepmother, when Alfonso had married the Princess Leonor.

Alfonso had died in 1336, when Jaime was but seven years old, and the throne of Aragon had passed to his elder son, Pedro IV, Jaime being left with the title and appanage of Count of Urgel. Some ten or so years later he had appeared at Avignon in honour of the Queen of Naples. But immediately after that he had joined with the nobles of Aragon in resisting his brother's desire to increase the royal power. This Aragonese equivalent of our own barons' attempt to curb the excesses of King John had, unlike what had happened in England, been totally unsuccessful; the baronial forces had been routed at Epila in 1348, and it was as a result of this that Jaime had found himself incarcerated for the next dozen years. Finally released by a contemptuous sibling, he had sought his fortunes elsewhere than Spain, but he remained very much a Spaniard, with his heart firmly set in his windswept homeland.

Equally, he would not have been a Spaniard had he not dreamed of avenging himself upon a hated brother.

Meanwhile, across the border in Castile, family squabbles were equally disruptive of peace and prosperity. Alfonso XI of Castile was one of the greatest warriors in the history of Spain, and his victory over the Muslims at the Rio Salado on 30 October 1340 has seemed to put a check upon Muslim expansion for the past generation. However, on his death ten years later, he was succeeded by his son Pedro, who has justly come to be called the Cruel.

Alfonso also had an illegitimate son, named Enrique, or as we would have it, Henry, and this youth, born in 1333 and thus eight years younger than myself, for instance, had been forced to put up with the importunities and outrages of his half-brother, until, in 1356, he had fled to the court of France. There he soon found a sympathetic hearing, as the French royal house – however distracted by the disaster of Poitiers and the subsequent captivity of

Good King John – was disturbed to learn of the mistreatment meted out by Pedro to his French wife, Blanche of Bourbon. Thus it was that in 1363, Henry, known as of Trastamara, formally laid claim to the Castilian throne, with French support.

And, it was now learned in Naples, with the support of Pedro IV of Aragon, who had no love for his cousin and namesake.

This situation promised to stir the whole of Spain with war, especially when it was learned that the English, in the person no less of the Black Prince himself, proposed to support Pedro of Castile. Given Pedro's known reputation, this might seem a remarkable decision on the part of the foremost hero of his time, but in fact two of Pedro's daughters, Constance and Isabella, were married respectively to John of Gaunt and Edmund of York, the Black Prince's younger brothers, and therefore the throne of Castile, however vile its occupant, was very closely connected to that of England.

The stage was thus set for a formidable conflict, and it was one in which Jaime of Aragon was determined to play his part, for he had realised that should Henry of Trastamara and his ally of Aragon be defeated, as seemed entirely likely in view of the ability and reputation of their great antagonist, the crown of Aragon might well be left lying about, and who was more worthy of picking it up than himself?

In addition, only a year or two previously, this Henry of Trastamara had been at the Court of Naples, seeking the hand of the Queen in marriage. That he had lost, and Jaime had won, might have appeared a cause for the victor to regard the vanquished with contempt; on the contrary, Jaime had conceived a dislike, not to say an enmity, for the Castilian equal to his hatred for his own half-brother. To fight against them both suddenly became the most important business of Jaime's life.

Joanna was devastated. She had fallen very heavily for

her young husband, and was alike concerned at the thought of his marching off to war and of his separation from her bed, with all of Spain's dewy-eyed señoritas at his beck and call.

She could not of course contemplate leaving Naples herself to be at his side, so she chose the next best thing.

Thus was I equally devastated.

'May I remind Your Grace,' I said, 'that I am in my fortieth year, a grandmother, and that my last embassy on your behalf was a total failure.'

'Circumstances were against you,' Joanna said. 'But you sowed your ground well. Now I am returning you to the Black Prince, who we know has a great affinity for you, not as a prisoner of war, but as my representative. He will welcome you with open arms.'

I sighed: what she prognosticated was only too likely to be true, and I had no desire to be in the open arms of anyone save Christopher. But when Joanna had an idea in her mind it was nearly impossible to dissuade her.

'And Prince Jaime?'

It was Joanna's turn to sigh. 'You will look after him like a mother. And a sister. And, if need be, as I would myself.'

'Your Grace, you put a great responsibility upon me.' And a lot more besides, I thought. 'We do not even know if the Prince likes me.'

We had not come into a great deal of contact.

'Oh, but we do,' Joanna said. 'He thinks you are the second most beautiful woman he has ever beheld. He regards you with heavy sighs, whenever he sees you. He will be overjoyed to have you at his side.'

Presuming I was able to remain there, and not wind up beneath him.

'Are you sure you know what you do, Your Grace? You are commanding me to commit adultery, and with your husband.'

Joanna held my hands. 'I do what I must. Dearest

Richilde, you are the only person in this entire world I can trust. I love Jaime deeply, but he is a young and vigorous man. Who can tell how he will be seduced when he is away from my bed. But you, I know, will act only as your duty calls you, and you will never seek to betray me in any way. I have nowhere else to turn.'

I was complimented, and desolated at the same time, that such a woman should be so devastatingly lonely that she would resort to the body of her best friend to retain her hold upon her husband. But I made no more demur, even though my heart bled at the thought of leaving my castle and my lands, my daughter and my grandchildren, to go adventuring again.

And so Jaime and I, with a suitable entourage, set sail for Spain. Joanna herself came down to the Mole to bid us farewell, gave her husband a final kiss and a hug, and then did the same to me.

'Mind your charge,' she told me.

As if I had any choice in the matter.

The safest, if not the quickest way, to reach Toledo, was by ship to Marseilles, across the south of France, and through northern Spain. This entailed a journey of some two months, and was attended by the normal amount of discomfort. But I was an experienced traveller, and refused to be dismayed by wind or rain, contumacious official or broken bridge.

My experience also sufficed to calm the Prince, who became very agitated at every delay.

Ah, experience! It is the greatest boon that mankind possesses, provided only that it does not affect the spirit, that is, that a series of misfortunes does not so weigh down the soul that one is incapable of taking immediate advantage of any glimpse of good fortune which may occur. This happens far too often, and some men and women become totally dispirited, while others, from a lengthy excess of good fortune, become totally arrogant, whereas if I have discovered anything from life it is that good fortune and ill are but two sides of the same coin, and if one spins a coin often enough, all will balance out in the end.

This was a lesson Prince Jaime had not yet learned.

His problems began that very afternoon, when, after being warped out of the harbour, the wind dropped, and with it, our means of propulsion. In the Mediterranean, as may be known, there are no tides, and the currents are very slow-moving once one is removed from the vicinity of the Straits of Gibraltar. In the Tyrrhenian Sea they are virtually non-existent. Therefore we remained drifting about, within sight of Naples and all of the islands, for some twenty-four hours.

Jaime was less concerned with the fact that we were still under Joanna's eye, as it were, than that we were not scudding away towards our destination, and, he was certain, his own apogee. He became increasingly irritated as the afternoon wore on, and when our captain ventured to suggest that calms were a normal hazard of sea-faring, and that at the least we were in no danger of drifting on to any rocks, he became positively abusive, causing the poor captain to flee the poop deck in alarm, and the Prince's lords and my ladies to regard each other with concern.

The Prince now called for a bottle, and this was readily provided. Being an optimist by nature, I was of the opinion that by the time he had consumed the wine he would be ready for his couch. I was, however, wrong. Having consumed his bottle, he called for another, and at the same time began to eye my ladies with what can only be described as a meaningful expression.

I realised that a crisis was at hand, far sooner than I had expected, especially as the Prince's gaze seemed fixed upon a girl called Margaretta, who was at once the youngest of my attendants – she was only sixteen – and the prettiest, with flowing auburn hair, very rare in a Neapolitan, and withal a pair of breasts which might have done justice to a mother ten years her elder ... or, indeed, myself at her age. I had always put down her extraordinary mammary development to her habits of communing with herself – for want of a better term – over considerable periods of time, when her heavy exhalations could well have driven the ship along in the absence of any other wind, but was none the less very fond of the girl, who was quick and eager and obedient, and had no wish to see her become the mistress of an errant prince.

Besides, there were Joanna's instructions to be considered, and I feared that were the Prince ever to wrap his hands around Margaretta's magnificent mounds, he might never care to sample his wife again, Joanna's true beauty lying in her hair, her eyes, her legs and thighs, and above all her glowing personality – she had never, as I may have mentioned, truly been designed by nature for motherhood.

I therefore felt called upon to intervene, whatever the personal sacrifice that would be entailed, when the Prince, waving his second bottle, and thereby scattering wine from one end of the cabin to the next, expressed a desire to be left alone with Margaretta. I clapped my hands, ushered all my giggling girls on to the deck, and myself closed and locked the cabin door, with me still on the inside.

The Prince had been drinking deeply while this manoeuvre had been taking place, and only now lowered his bottle to regard the object of his lust, to discover that instead of Margaretta he had accumulated a woman who ... well, of course I was not old enough to be his mother, but from the point of view of his befuddled state, I may well have appeared so. On the other hand, I was prepared to put myself out to avert a crisis, and, if I say so myself, when Richilde, Duchess of Eberli, puts herself out, the result is beyond doubt.

Here we both made various discoveries about the other. On his part, the Prince uncovered – again literally – a woman of even greater attractiveness than his wife, and even more well-endowed than Margaretta, astounded as he was to believe this. For my part, alas, I found someone who, although vigorous enough, was really still a callow youth. As a woman who has been humped by a large number of men several of whom were extremely talented in this minor art, my heart bled for my dearest Joanna, if this was the highest standard she had been able to achieve during her grass and then real widowhood. To have lived, and perchance to die, without having known a Cola di Rienzi, a Black Prince, a King Edward, or a Christopher of the Bay, seemed a sad waste of a female life.

Needless to say, having once sampled what I had to offer, Prince Jaime must have recourse to me every day throughout the voyage, and managed to fall head over heels in love with me before we reached Toledo, but as I did not reciprocate his love in the slightest, however often I was required to accommodate his passion, I had no fears for the integrity of my mistress's marriage.

I kept him satisfied however, while at the same time, in my few leisure moments, having to cope with the disappointed tears of Margaretta. Such is the disgraceful state of morals at modern courts, and Naples ranked very high – or is it very low? – in this respect, that the silly girl had already yielded her maidenhead to a loutish fellow who had promised her the earth, or at least a wedding band for her finger, before eloping with her older sister. It was this sad mischance that had first caused me, softhearted as I am, to take her into my employ – upon payment of a suitable, what shall we call it, by her distraught but very rich father, whose only other course had seemed to be to lock her up in a convent for the rest of her days.

While in the employ of the Duchess of Eberli, all things might be possible.

Alas, I am not able to perform miracles, and while I personally found Margaretta a most charming girl and pleasant companion, the story of her mishap had gone the rounds of Naples society, and there was no young man who seemed willing to beat a path to her welcoming door. Spending the rest of her days a spinster in my employ was obviously still an improvement upon a cloister, but yet the girl felt her position keenly, and had here been presented with the chance of becoming a Prince's mistress, which in many instances can be even more rewarding than matrimony.

Now that dream too had been dashed, and by the very woman she loved and admired more than any other. I could only explain the situation to her, assure her that I was but doing my duty and that there was absolutely no pleasure in it for me, and then fold her to my bosom, no easy task.

My sole aim was to see the back of the campaign as quickly as possible, and thus return the Prince to his wife and myself to my home and family. Alas for hope. I had perhaps been misled by my earlier incursion into the European scene. Entirely by chance I had entered France in the autumn of 1356, and caught up with King John and his inept army just as it was about to fight a battle. Had I been a student of history, I would have understood my good fortune.

The fact is that England and France, at the time of the Battle of Poitiers, had been at war for nineteen years, and had in that time undertaken just three pitched battles, one of these being at sea. Thus it was in Spain. Henry of Trastamara was raising a great army, with French financing, and Aragonese support ... but it took him some years to take the field with the slightest hope of success.

Not that he ever had any in the first place.

I must pause here, lest my reader become confused, to explain how France, which when last mentioned in this chronicle had been breaking its back to raise the ransom for Good King John, was now able to put money into such an uncertain project as that of Henry of Trastamara's. The answer is a short one: Good King John had died.

He had lived a life of haphazard chivalry to the end. As France had been tardy in raising his ransom, a deal had been struck whereby one of his sons went to England to stand as hostage in his stead, while John returned to his native country to encourage his people to pay up. As may have been expected in these circumstances, he was not exactly welcomed with open arms, while as soon as he was safely back in France, his son, blessed as he was with different moral values to those of his father, had made his escape from the Tower of London and thence across the Channel and home.

Good King John was naturally shocked by this breach of the code of knighthood, and promptly returned to England to surrender himself. His people, let us admit it frankly, were more than happy to see him go. So were his sons. Thus the remainder of his life was spent in an honorable and friendly and lascivious captivity amidst the flesh-pots of London.

The whole incident, however, had further soured relations between England and France, the English regarding the French as having behaved like utter poltroons, and the French not caring how they had behaved so long as they could get their own back on the hated English. Thus, although the *Jacquerie* still raged, and heaven alone knows how many hapless noblemen were spitted over their own fires and their choicest portions offered to their besmitten wives and daughters, John's son, now King Charles V, was content to divert some of his scanty funds to secure the discomfort of the Black Prince.

Unfortunately for the French, money has never been an adequate substitute for military genius, but, as I have mentioned, actually bringing Henry and his adherents to battle took some time, and during this necessary build-up Jaime and myself and our party reached Toledo without undue mishap.

Where I was again introduced to my old lover. And

received something of a shock.

I had of course been aware that several years before Edward had married, a lady of noble but not royal lineage, named Joan of Woodstock, who was actually a widow. Now I had been a widow when the Prince and I had first met, and if I could not claim a noble lineage, I had at least been a duchess. The fact that he had packed me off to grace his father's bed as if I had been some common whore, had upset me at the time, but I had reflected that he had obviously had his eye upon some princess or other. When it had turned out that his eye had all the time been on this beastly widow – I have never actually laid eyes on the lady but I cannot believe she, or anyone, was as well endowed as myself – I had regarded the whole episode as a definite insult, but at the time, 1361, I had been fully engaged in Eberli and inclined to send England, and its scurvy ruling house, to the devil.

However, four years had now passed since the Prince's nuptials, and I had been informed that his wife was remaining in Bordeaux while her husband campaigned. I therefore looked forward to a happy reunion between two old friends, a reunion which would very likely exclude Prince Jaime from my bed for the duration of our visit, although I remained conscious of my responsibilities, and aware that it was my duty to protect him from any dangerous deviation from his wife.

My plans, however, were entirely set at naught by Prince Edward himself.

In the first place, I rapidly discovered that he was madly in love with his wife and was not prepared to dally with anyone, even someone as well accoutred, if I may coin a phrase, and of as guaranteed satisfactory company as myself. In the second place, and far more disturbing from a political and military point of view than even a personal one, the Prince was no longer the vigorous young man I remembered from even a scant eight years before. He suffered from a recurrent fever, which every so often laid him low with a virulent ague and had him shaking from head to foot, and also from a certain tempering of the spirit. The gallant knight was still in evidence when he was well and sober, but when afflicted by his illness and attempting to alleviate the symptoms with wine he could be as vicious as any man I have ever known. I have no doubt at all that it was this recurrent sickness, which indeed has recently brought him to his grave far earlier than was necessary – and may well prove a sad misfortune for England – that was responsible for his permitting the dreadful sack of Limoges a few years later.

But I am anticipating. While Prince Jaime was welcomed with open arms by Pedro and Edward, I was regarded with some misgivings by the latter, no doubt well aware that our names had been linked before his marriage, and concerned that news of my arrival in Toledo would seep back to his wife in Bordeaux.

The Prince thus took steps to present me in as attractive a light as possible to Pedro. I will remind you that this fellow's soubriquet was the Cruel. It was my misfortune to attract him in a very positive fashion, aided of course by the Black Prince's undoubted confidences.

Before I knew what was happening I was closeted with the Castilian king, and a very interesting experience it was too, holding as I do that it is necessary, whatever our hopes of the after life, to undergo every possible experience upon this earth, just to make sure, when the priest arrives to grant the last sacrament, that one may say, I have lived!

To be sure there are aspects of living which are best forgotten, and some of my own experiences I have here recalled with some trepidation and no great pleasure. Submitting to Pedro the Cruel must be numbered amongst these, and when I learned that he would bed no female without having first beaten her buttocks raw, I all but stormed from his chamber in a huff, while understanding entirely the reluctance of his wife, Blanche of Bourbon, to share his couch. I did not actually take this step, partly because there were armed guards upon the door who turned me back, and partly because I reflected that Joanna had required me to make myself agreeable to anyone who might further the cause of Jaime – my dearly beloved Queen, however sorry she was to be separated from her husband, was not above considering what an *empire* could be created by a union of Aragon and Naples.

Thus I suffered the importunities of this unhappy prince, which were of a considerably more lubricious and disgraceful nature than I had even suspected from the rumours I had heard; indeed, I rapidly became entirely sympathetic to his unhappy consort, who had absolutely abandoned his bed.

This I was not in a position to do, and however much I was taken aback by his determination to share his couch with both me and Margaretta, he having looked keenly and closely at her *décolletage* as she had bowed before him when we had first arrived in Toledo, my first reflection was one of relief, in that a man shared is a man halved, so to speak, while my conscience as regards Margaretta was salved by the consideration that she was desperate to have *someone*, and here was not just a prince, but a king!

As usual, I was being optimistic. Pedro's idea of amusement in the bedchamber was to set his two companions against each other. Well ... I had of course shared many a pleasant tumble with Joanna, both in our girlhood and during moments of extreme crisis in our later years, but catering to the whims of this depraved monster was something else again. I will not, for decency's sake, enter into any great details, but merely recount that we were, amongst other things, required to whip each other to his satisfaction. Nor did we, or rather I, obtain any relief when, having by his voyeuristic pleasures aroused himself into a fine frenzied state he plunged into Margaretta, to her decided pleasure, I may say. For having left the girl gasping and exhausted, and bruised and battered to boot, he still retained enough strength to attend to me!

My sojourn in Toledo was not a restful one, especially as I had to share the King with an ever more unhappy Jaime, who was perfectly aware of what was going on, but as he relied upon Pedro, in the aftermath of his anticipated victory, to grant him the crown of Aragon, could do nothing about it. But for the adventure that was soon to befall me, I would have counted this whole episode a most remarkable one, but in fact it paled into insignificance when compared with what was to follow.

For all my labours, and my consequent exhaustion, I enjoyed Toledo, which is a most beautiful city, wrapped as it is in the arms of the Tagus River. This volume of water, which rises in the mountains of Spain, and debouches into the Atlantic Ocean some hundreds of miles to the west, thus granting the County of Portugal considerable mercantile privileges – a town, known as Lisbon, which is a corruption of the Moorish word Luzbona, meaning 'good water', has arisen at the river's exit and has rapidly become one of the most prosperous cities in the Peninsula – performs a U-bend around Toledo, thus providing an almost unassailable moat to the south and east.

This leaves only the north-west to be defended by conventional walls, which should not be beyond the powers of any competent military commander. Yet Alfonso XI had taken the city from the indolent Moors within the last century, and now it revealed every evidence of being a most Christian city, accentuated by the restitution of the Cathedral, in which lay the bones of the Visigothic kings who had ruled Spain some eight hundred years before.

I found Toledo a delightful place, and would have over-indulged in the local delicacy, an almond paste called mazapan, but for a fear of getting fat.

However, Jaime and I were there for the purpose of fighting a battle and beating Henry of Trastamara, and this event finally took place at Navarete, or as some would have it, Najera. This village is situated well to the north of Toledo, and is in fact only a few miles south of the River Ebro.

The circumstances of this battle, probably Edward's greatest victory, need explaining. The Black Prince's main armament was of course in Bordeaux, and to support Pedro he needed to bring his people through the Pyrenees. Having visited Toledo, he had concluded, I am sure correctly, that the city was certainly defensible, and thus returned to his base of operations to mobilise his forces. This left Pedro in command in the south, and this turned out to be a grave mistake. For no sooner had the Black Prince departed than Henry of Trastamara and Pedro of Aragon marched upon their foe.

This was the moment we had been waiting for, as our Jaime had no doubt at all that he and Pedro could defeat these rebels, as he termed them, even without the aid of the Prince. Unfortunately Pedro, who was as cowardly as he was cruel, thought otherwise, and before the two forces could come to grips, had fled the city for the north.

Naturally we had to accompany him, and a wild business it was, with Henry of Trastamara and Pedro of Aragon in hot pursuit, until, as we neared the Ebro, all of our manoeuvres were brought to a halt by the news that the Black Prince was through the Pyrenees and debouching on to the Spanish plateau.

This had been no easy business, for the passes are few, and easily blocked by determined men, and Henry's Aragonese had been stiffened against Pedro's rule not only by a large contingent of Castilian rebels, but also by a renowned French soldier named Bertrand du Guesclin, with a body of Frenchmen at his back.

None the less, Edward, having convinced his opponents

that he was going to use the Pass of Roncesvalles, famous in history and legend as the place of the last stand of Charlemagne's hero Roland against the Basques more than five hundred years earlier, outmanoeuvred the allied force and marched rapidly south, fording the Ebro before they knew what he was about, and uniting his English with Pedro's Spaniards.

Then we turned about to face the foe.

We were, as was customary with Edward's battles, distinctly outnumbered. Henry's army consisted of some two thousand French heavy cavalry, more than five thousand Castilian heavy cavalry, four thousand light cavalry, six thousand crossbowmen, and a good twenty thousand infantry – a grand total of more than thirty-seven thousand men.

The Prince commanded just over half that number, of which some ten thousand were cavalry, and perhaps five thousand archers, the rest being infantry.

For the rest, it was simply a repetition of Poitiers. Du Guesclin has in recent years earned himself a formidable reputation, as a leader of irregular forces operating against isolated English-held towns and fortresses, and is regarded as a hero by his compatriots. At this stage of his career, however, he could think of no better tactical plan than the one followed by Good King John eleven years earlier, dismounted his cavalry, and led them against the English position.

The French at least knew what to expect, and reckoned that if they could once reach the English ranks, as they had done so briefly at Poitiers, they could win the day. And most gallantly they came on through the arrow storm. But there were simply not enough of them, and the Spanish knights, associated with them in this advance, soon found the sting of the arrows too severe to be borne, and fled the field.

The mercenary infantry and crossbowmen followed almost immediately, whereupon the French knights, now

338

totally surrounded and about to be annihilated, did the only sensible thing and surrendered.

The Black Prince had gained yet another astonishing victory. At a cost of hardly a hundred dead and a few more wounded, he could count seven thousand of the enemy slain and at least a similar number wounded.

Pedro the Cruel had conquered, albeit at second hand, as it were, and appeared secure upon the throne of Castile. However, fate has a way of tripping villains up. Edward duly accompanied us back to Toledo, with great pomp and ceremony, and for a while we gave ourselves to feasting and debauchery. Once or twice I even found myself in the arms of the Prince. But this was the beginning of Pedro's downfall.

Edward, as I have related, had no more truly amorous thoughts towards me, his mind being filled with an anxiety to regain the comfort of his wife. But he could not help but be sensible to me, and all that we had shared, and he was shocked when he discovered how ill used I was by his ill-tempered brother-in-law. To this evidence of domestic failings he could add his own personal experience of Pedro's shortcomings both as a ruler and a warrior; he did not forget that the Castilian King had taken no part in the battle which had secured his crown, but had lurked at the rear of the field until victory was certain.

The result of all this was that the Prince's stay in Toledo was much shorter than we had expected, and he soon marched off again, with his men, for Bordeaux.

This naturally changed the situation entirely, although I cannot help but feel that it was naïve in the extreme for Pedro to suppose so busy a man as the Black Prince would spend the rest of his days propping up the Castilian crown. In any event, no sooner had the news of the Prince's departure spread, than Henry of Trastamara, so thoroughly beaten only a few months before, again took the field. He had lost the support of du Guesclin and his

339

Frenchmen, who were as disgusted with their Spanish allies as Edward had been with his, but Pedro of Aragon again rode at his side, anxious to be avenged upon his Castilian cousin ... and his brother.

My own view of the situation was that Jaime and I should have taken our leave with the Black Prince and returned post haste to Naples, from which we had now been absent for more than two years. How I longed to see my darling Lucia and her darling babies again. But Jaime was reluctant; the escape of his brother from the field of Navarete, unharmed, had left him totally frustrated in his ambitions. While Pedro was downright determined not to let me go. So there was I, a matron of forty-three, being kept a prisoner like any eighteen-year-old girl, purely for the purposes of gracing the King's bed, and must once again await the outcome of a clash of arms.

On this occasion I was not present, when, after the invariable lengthy manoeuvrings, the two armies finally met close to the village of Madrid, some fifty miles north of Toledo, approximately two years after Pedro's triumph at Navarete – I had a touch of fever and was unable to campaign. Jaime of course went, certain that at last he would be able to seize the Aragonese crown. I thus remained in Toledo with my faithful Margaretta and the rest of my ladies, awaiting word from the north. When it came it was most disturbing. A bloodstained aide-de-camp galloped into the city shouting that all was lost. When questioned, he told us that the army of Pedro and Jaime had been utterly routed, that Henry had caught up with his half-brother and cut his throat with his own knife, and that the Count of Trastamara was now marching upon us with all his panoply, declaring himself King of Castile and vowing vengeance upon all who had in any way supported Pedro.

This alarmed me, as there was no one in Toledo who could have any doubt that I had shared the late King's bed ... and a man who can cut the throat of his own brother could hardly be considered in a better light.

'What news of the King of Naples?' I inquired.

'He escaped the field, and is retiring to the west. He has commanded me to ask you to rendezvous with him at Lisbon, where you will both take ship for Italy.'

Just like that! Meet me in Lisbon! As if half of the Iberian Peninsula, some very forbidding mountains, an army of bandits, and, worst of all, several armies of Moors, did not lie between me and that destination. Still, as the alternative seemed to be to surrender myself to the vengeance of Henry of Trastamara, I summoned my ladies, and announced that we were departing immediately.

They were not content with my decision. Better to face the enemy we know than risk the Moors, was their consensus. Margaretta, of course, was faithful to the end; we had shared so much over the preceding two years she could not envisage life without me. But I could persuade but one other girl, Joaquina, and two grooms to accompany me. Yet I was not dismayed. I had no hope of arranging a proper escort, and in that case the smaller my party the more chance of evading capture. I did manage to secure eight horses, and equipped with the bag of gold coin which never left my girdle, rode to the west.

Which brings me to the adventure I mentioned earlier. For of course my plan was a forlorn one. Our way was beset with too many difficulties, and a few days after leaving Toledo, while endeavouring to evade a band of unpleasant-looking Spaniards who seemed to be keeping pace with us to the north, we turned too far to the south, and must inadvertently have wandered across the border into Moorish Spain. Before we had the time to appreciate our error, or even to wonder why our would-be robbers had abandoned their pursuit of us, we were surrounded by villainous-looking fellows who were clearly not Christian.

My memory immediately went back to that day, when the ship on which I had been travelling with my family had been beset by very similar rascals, and as there was no chance that the most cursory examination of my genitalia could persuade anyone I was a virgin, I equally remembered the unhappy fate of my mother and sister, and clasped Margaretta to my bosom, understanding that we were in the same boat, so to speak. As no doubt was Joaquina, for although she was hardly more than a third of my age, such are the scandalous morals of modern courts there was little chance of her either being in that desirable state.

My fears seemed about to be realised, when we were torn apart and stripped. Our grooms were suffering the same fate, for the Moors are a remarkably broad-minded people, and will enjoy beauty whether it will be male or female, with the same intensity.

However, the preliminaries of rape having been completed, there came a pause. Partly this was because in removing my girdle the Moors had discovered my bag of gold coin, which was sufficiently weighty to convince them that they had hold of a lady of quality – they were too ignorant of fashion to discern that from the clothes they had just torn from my shoulders. But equally was it because they had never previously beheld such colouring or such beauty.

Their captain now put two and two together. 'You are the woman known as the Duchess of Eberli?' he demanded, in rather poor Spanish.

'I am not known as anything,' I retorted. 'I *am* the Duchess of Eberli.'

'You will be a prize for my master,' he told me, and commanded me to be covered up again, so thoroughly, indeed, in one of their voluminous cloaks, that I became quite invisible while within this disguise a white mask was tied across my nose and behind my ears, entirely to conceal the lower half of my face.

I cannot pretend to have been comfortable, but at least I was alive, and had not yet been raped. I cannot say the same for my unhappy company, who all around me were being stretched upon the ground and submerged beneath a horde of excited Moors. Oddly, they seemed to find more to interest them in my grooms than my women, and indeed such was their ardour to be at the young men that I for a moment felt as safe as I had been in the company of Brother Jules and his friends.

But soon enough they turned their attention to Joaquina and Margaretta, giving them a most thorough examination which would have robbed them of their hymens even had they still possessed such treasures.

I felt called upon to interfere to the best of my ability, and removed the mask from my face, as I found it quite impossible to speak without inhaling a considerable quantity of linen cloth.

'They are my daughters,' I declared. 'And must accompany me wherever I go.'

My principal captor peered into my face, and then into the faces of the two girls.

'You are lying,' he remarked. 'They do not look the least like you.'

'They look like my husband,' I insisted.

Another series of stares, while Joaquina and Margaretta, sitting up, and shivering from tit to toe, as was easy to discern in their unhappy state, held hands and prayed.

'You have had two husbands,' the Moorish captain decided.

'Doesn't everyone?' I inquired. 'I am a duchess.'

This confused the poor fellow, and he surrendered to my wishes. Margaretta and Joaquina were each wrapped up as was I, and then we were placed in three huge baskets, or panniers, secured to the backs of mules, for all the world as if we were some outsize prize hens, and marched off to the south.

But I had at least saved their lives, for the time being. Alas for my poor grooms, I never saw either of them again, but I very much fear they were mutilated and then murdered once their captors tired of them, for this is the Moorish way.

I was thus given to very sombre reflections as I juddered along on the back of this beastly mule. My situation was uncomfortable, to say the least, and my immediate survival seemed to promise only that my two maids and I should be subjected to some unfortunate fate when we arrived at our destination.

At the very best, I was a captive, and my hopes of joining Jaime and thus returning in safety to Naples and my loved ones were ended.

We journeyed for two days, and I have seldom had a less pleasant time, as although I was allowed from my basket to sleep, I was then pegged to the ground by ropes round my ankles and attached to the wrists of my guards, while these pesky fellows even insisted on accompanying me to the performance of my necessaries, showing not the least compunction as I was forced to reveal myself – after all they had seen my treasures before – but shouting at me in a variety of languages if I took the veil from my face.

Truly a strange people.

Margaretta and Joaquina suffered equally, nor were we given much opportunity for discussing our situation and sharing our fears. It was, however, remarkable how our approach to our somewhat murky future differed: I was concerned only with escaping our captors and regaining sunny Naples, even if I had no idea how this was to be accomplished; Joaquina, who was a Castilian, was concerned only with the indignity of having been stripped and manhandled by creatures she considered as lower than the beasts in the field, and infidels to boot, and considered suicide, again without the slightest concept of how this might be achieved; Margaretta, in her continually excited state, was totally occupied with the idea that she was going to be forced to belong to one of these hairy and distinctly sensuous beasts, a prospect she found entrancing.

And she had every idea of how it would be done.

Thus, on the third day of our journey, we arrived at the hill fortress of Antequera, where this particular band of Moors' amir held his capital. We made our way up the steeply sloping streets of the town and thus reached the castle, which was a place of some strength. Here, surrounded by curious soldiers, we were escorted into a dwelling of some size and considerable luxury, and presented to the Amir, Ali ben-Yusuf ben-Hadad ben-Nasi, to name but his immediate forebears.

He was a short, fat man, who barely came up to my shoulders, but possessed bristling moustaches, which seemed to bristle even more as our captain explained who I was. In fact he became quite excited, and before I knew what was happening all three of us were taken into an inner, smaller room, where there were some very odd-looking men, if this is the right description.

This was my first encounter with eunuchs, and my initial reaction was revulsion. But I am bound to say that they handled us a good deal more gently, and with less purpose, as it were, than our recent captors. In a trice we were naked and being subjected to an inspection by the Amir, who examined me as if he were looking for some invisible birthmark. I endeavoured to explain that I was not at my best, being sorely in need of a bath to say the least, but this did not deter him – possibly, as I spoke no Moorish, he was unaware of what I was telling him.

His examination completed, he turned his attention to the two girls, but this was altogether a more perfunctory affair, then all three of us were whisked away by the eunuchs, into what was indeed a bathing chamber, but one larger and more luxuriously appointed than any I had previously known. Here we were bathed, but not before undergoing a variety of quite unChristian ordeals, at least in my opinion.

In the first place, we were not permitted to do anything for ourselves, the eunuchs insisting on this pleasure

345

themselves . . . and as one who has not only taken the leading role in bathing the Queen of Naples but has also enjoyed being bathed by my own maids, I can assure you that it *is* a pleasure. In the second, having chosen to deal with me first, they gathered my hair on the top of my head with a ribbon, then proceeded to coat my entire body with a glutinous mixture made from sugar and lime and heaven knows what else, which had been brought to the boil. It was only just finished boiling when it was applied to me, and I allowed myself a shriek, assuming that this was a novel means of execution. I had of course heard of people being boiled in oil; to be boiled in toffee seemed only marginally more attractive.

However, this was not their intention. Instead I was made to lie on a raised marble slab, whereupon a silken cord was drawn over my flesh, cutting into the toffee which coated me, until I had been entirely cleaned of the mess. Whereupon I discovered that I had been entirely cleansed of hair as well: from the neck down there was not a single whisker to be discovered. Anywhere! I will not go into details about this operation, which was an extremely lengthy business. Suffice it to say that there are certain parts of the body in which to be invaded by a layer of hot toffee is itself inducive of very peculiar – but not entirely unpleasant – sensations. To have those same parts then invaded by anxious fingers and sliding thread leaves one feeling ready for bed, and not alone. But no doubt this was their intention.

While I was undergoing this remarkable series of sensations, our privacy was invaded by a perfect horde of women, from the very young to the rather old, who I gathered were Ali ben-Yusuf etcetera's wives and concubines, agog to see the new beauty their master had accumulated. They were all taken aback by the fact that I was obviously no blushing virgin, nor even a girl. Nor, I suppose, even a young woman. Yet equally were they taken aback by the glorious spectacle presented to them.

They remained with me, chattering excitedly, while I was now doused in a succession of tubs of water, some hot and some cold, to induce another series of sensations. My hair was washed separately, with great care by the head eunuch, and then very thoroughly towelled dry.

Behind me came Margaretta and then Joaquina, each being forced to undergo the same treatment, which left them both far more scandalised, and, I fear to say, aroused than myself, as they lacked my experience in the erotic arts.

My various inundations having been completed, the eunuchs who were attending me painted around my eyes with kohl, another of their fiendish preparations, which leaves the eyelids very dark, and manicured all twenty of my nails with henna, and rubbed my body vigorously with a sweet-smelling unguent. These attentions prevented me from properly seeing what was happening to my maids, about which I will confess I was curious, as there is a great deal of difference between undergoing an experience oneself, and watching someone else in exactly similar circumstances.

I must confess that, handicapped as I was, I suspect I learned more about the female anatomy in that bathing chamber than during my entire previous life, and even more so, when in a plucked state similar to my own, the two girls were brought to sit beside me and be decorated.

However, we were now fed a mouth-watering preparation composed of I know not what, while all the while being surrounded and fingered by these eager damsels, not one of whom was in the least decently clad as they wore voluminous pantaloons, made of sheer silk, and little bolero jackets which scarcely obscured their nipples; their feet were bare but they also wore a small jewelled cap, in a matching colour to their clothes. They were of every shape and size and age, as I have intimated, and I was interested to discover that some of them were Spaniards and undoubtedly of Christian heritage, although it did not seem to me that one could possibly remain Christian for very long in such surroundings.

Add to these charmers the attentive eunuchs, and the operation, which lasted for several hours, was quite the most lascivious experience of my life. Unfortunately, I had had an exhausting few days, and although when it appeared they were finished with me I was even more ready for bed, by this time it was solely to sleep.

Such was not to be my fortune, however. I was now taken to the chamber of ben-Yusuf, the girls being left behind, presumably for a later occasion.

This was a relief, for, as I had supposed would be the case, I was subjected to the Amir's lusts, and these occasions are best experienced in private, even if Margaretta and I had been forced to share them with Pedro the Cruel. Ben-Yusuf's advances consisted firstly in another minute examination of my now exposed charms, although he seemed less interested in those parts of my body which might properly be ascribed as belonging to Venus than in my hair, on my head, of course, as there was not a trace anywhere else. This he proceeded to separate strand by strand, and even to suck some of it, which made a nonsense of the elaborate coiffeur which had been prepared. However, as his attentions were thus attracted, I was permitted to have a little rest, and actually dozed off, to be awakened with a start some ten minutes later by a sharp slap on the shoulder.

Sitting up, I discovered that my new master had undressed himself, and was possessed of considerable manly attributes, which he was obviously eager to plunge into me. I did my best to accommodate him, as when one is in an inferior position it is best to yield. Actually, I suspect I could have strangled him with my bare hands, as I was both bigger and stronger than he, but I reflected that this might cause me to be executed in turn, somewhat less speedily, by his guards, and so I submitted, and had my first experience of Muslim lovemaking.

For this I was required to kneel on the floor on my hands and knees. Now it may be remembered that I had experienced such an unChristian assault before, from Charles of Durazzo while mounted on his infamous ladder. However, this I had felt to be a spur of the moment event. Ben-Yusuf's campaign was obviously one he had carried out on many occasions, and was of singular interest, for he seemed able to penetrate me far deeper than any man had ever before, and I will confess that for all my resolution not to surrender my essential self to such a heathen rogue, it happened without my being able to prevent it, whereupon I collapsed with him on top of me, still working away.

While he was doing this I again fell asleep, to be again awakened by the scurvy fellow battering at my buttocks. He had now completed his orgasmic cycle, but do you think I was thus permitted to have a little much-needed nap? Not a bit of it. He was still filled with sexual ardour, and I was required to manipulate him back to erection, which did not take very long, whereupon I discovered that he wished me to sit on his lap, facing him, with my legs curled round him. In this new position, no less disapproved by the Church, he found it even easier to enter me, and to reach even further, as all of my weight was descending upon him. While this was going on he fondled my breasts and for all my uncertainty as to whether or not I was now damned I have to confess I also wondered how I had managed to live for more than forty years without earlier discovering such delightful sensations.

At the end of this second tumble we were both spent in every possible sense. But as I lay beside him the wretched fellow raised himself on his elbow, and remarked, in Spanish of all tongues, 'Truly is your reputation well earned, my dear Duchess. I would love to keep you here for myself. But I fear it would disturb the peace of my harem, and besides, there is one who will appreciate you even more. You will go to al-Mumin.'

*

I was distinctly put out, in the first place that he had not earlier revealed his knowledge of Spanish and enabled us to converse in a reasonable manner instead of me being thrown around like a sack of grain, in the second place that I should have apparently established a reputation for lubricity which had even penetrated this remote spot, and in the third that I should now be handed on like a worn-out glove, or perhaps, more appropriately, a specially tasty plate of sweets. 'Have you tried this Eberli bonbon? Oh, it is very fine, I do assure you.'

However, I was in the unhappy position of not being able to do anything about my situation, and thus the very next day found myself again mounted in a pannier, and bound across the Andalusian plain for the Kingdom of Granada.

CHAPTER 10

My journey on this occasion was not a long one, as Granada lay at a distance of not much more than a hundred miles practically due east of Antequera, nor was it particularly uncomfortable, for the plain across which my escort and I made our way was flat and featureless, while, although I suppose I was still very much a prisoner, I was a prisoner of importance, a gift to the King, no less. I was attended by four ladies, and generally treated with a good deal of respect.

I was also accompanied, to my great relief, by Margaretta, for if ben-Yusuf had been at one with his officers in not believing the girl was actually my daughter, he accepted that she was my principal maid.

Poor Joaquina, alas, he retained for himself. If this appears surprising, as she was the least beautiful or accomplished of the three of us, she yet possessed a powerful attraction for the amir: she was Castilian, and he enjoyed bedding a female belonging to his hated enemies far more than he sought beauty or sexual prowess. Our parting was not obviously tearful, for the simple reason that we had no idea we were to be parted, and, indeed, I never saw her again. I like to think that she became a mother, and grew old and fat and eventually resigned to her fate in ben-Yusuf's harem, supposing, as happened quite regularly in that society, he was not murdered soon after we left and he and his wives stuffed down a well.

Such is life in the Muslim world.

We could therefore count ourselves fortunate. The plain across which we were travelling was, however, also dry and dusty, and we were required not only to travel in these dreadful panniers, the movement of which was the closest approximation of a ship in a rough sea than anything else on dry land, but also to keep ourselves constantly wrapped in our haiks or cloaks, as well as always to wear our face masks or yashmaks, which were highly uncomfortable in such a confined space. In vain did I insist we were perfectly capable of riding, and astride if need be; such an art was apparently not only considered indecent by the Saracens, but impossible for a woman.

I was therefore right glad to see the towers of Granada rising in front of us, after a very long week.

I have touched on the history of Spain. The *Reconquista* had now been going on, and gathering pace, for over a century, with the result that the Moors had gradually been driven from their amirates, until, at this time, the Kingdom of Granada was the last viable Saracen state in the peninsula. All others, such as that of Antequera which I had just left, were no more than outposts of the Granadan State, which, from its seaports of Malaga and Almeria, dominated the south-east corner of Spain.

Granada itself nestles in the foothills of the Sierra Nevada Mountains, a formidable range, whose greatest asset, however, is the constant flow of sweet water that descends from its snow-clad peaks. It is said that the first Moors to arrive on the site, coming as they did from the arid wastes of North Africa, were entranced by this ever-ready supply of so precious a commodity. Certain it is that Granada is a place of flowing streams and bubbling conduits.

It is also the site of the most beautiful building in Europe, and I speak as one who has travelled a good deal.

This edifice is known as the Alhambra, and was some four hundred years in the building. It had just been completed when I first beheld it.

Alhambra means the red fort, or palace, as the case may be. It was in fact both a fort and a palace. The fort, which dominates the plain below, had been the first to be built, and was a place of lofty towers and grim battlements. The palace had been built on behind it over the centuries, and it was into this that I was escorted to be presented to the Amir, Abd al-Mumin.

I was immediately alive to the beauty of the place, not only the red stone exteriors, but the intricate interior carvings, in which motifs praising the Muslim God, Allah, were repeated time and again to excellent effect.

These exterior apartments however paled into insignificance when I was taken into the inner courts, one in particular surrounding a fountain which was supported by several stone lions, from whose mouths water constantly issued. On the gallery above this court were the trellis walls of the harem, the device enabling the inmates to look down on the scene below without themselves being seen, while beyond a huge arched doorway lay the reception hall of the amir himself.

Here there were a great number of men, all turbanned and bearded and armed to the teeth, clad in flowing robes; I would not have known which was to be my master save for the fact that al-Mumin was the only one to be seated.

He was a young fellow, which interested me, with a good figure and full beard. He appeared a great improvement upon my last captor. For his part, while he was interested in the appearance of an embassy from his inferior, he had of course no idea what he was receiving, as I remained totally bundled up. However, he soon changed his mood when I was taken into a chamber adjoining the harem, and there disrobed for him by his eunuchs.

As I had still not managed to pick up any Arabic – well, when had I been granted the time? – I had no idea what he was saying, but from the gleam of his eyes and the manner in which he fingered my appurtenances, fore and aft as it were, I could tell that he was greatly pleased. Thus I was again removed to the bathing chamber, and made ready for him.

It would be tedious to relate my experiences at the hands and lips of al-Mumin. Suffice to say that he was a Saracen, and therefore inclined to look at sexual matters in a reverse manner to good Christians; that he was little more than half my age and virtually insatiable; and that he was my master in a fashion that no man ever was before, or, I am happy to say, since.

The first, I am bound to confess, I thoroughly enjoyed, so much so that I began to doubt whether the true position of man and woman in amatory discourse, as ordained by the Holy Church, *is* the true position at all, as dictated by nature. A man can *do* so much more on his hands and knees, provided the woman is also thus situated, of course. He can reach further with his member, and he can use his hands to much better effect, while, let us be honest, the back is more able to bear the weight of a humping fellow than the stomach.

The second was exhausting. I had had some of this with dear Fernando, and had not supposed the experience would be repeated. And now I was more than ten years older than when Fernando was being a nuisance.

But there was nothing I could do about it, because of the third. Al-Mumin was very conscious of his prerogatives, and he was one of the bloodthirstiest men I ever met. He delighted in winding bowstrings around people's necks himself, or in cutting off their hands, or, when really aroused, indulging in a rather unpleasant form of execution known as impalement, when the victim is stretched on the floor and a wooden stake is driven up his, or her, fundament, by strokes of a mallet until often enough it emerges from the breast. Obviously I have never actually experienced such a punishment, or I would not be relating this tale, but I can say without hesitation, from the shrieks

354

of those whom I was from time to time forced to watch undergoing such torment, that it has to be the most agonising form of death ever devised by man, especially when the executioner is slow about his strokes.

A man given to such amusements was clearly not to be crossed, in anything, and I was forced to submit to his requirements and wait for better times. However, even al-Mumin could not fornicate every moment of the day, and I was therefore allowed some time to myself. Initially, much of this I spent fast asleep, recovering from past excesses and hopefully regaining my strength for future. But I was awake often enough to consider a good deal of what was going on about me.

Al-Mumin had about fifty concubines in addition to the four wives allowed him by Muslim law, and all of us occupied the harem, from which we were summoned, as required by our lord. Betweentimes there was very little to do save look down through our trellis-work wall at the men in the Court of the Lions below us – speculating on their sexual capabilities – and gossip. Unless of course, as I have mentioned, there was something interesting going on, such as an impalement, when we were allowed out as a group, suitably veiled and cloaked, to enjoy the spectacle.

For the rest our principal pastime lay in bathing. In the interior court of the palace there was a large pool, again guarded by stone lions, and by a horde of eunuchs as well, where we ladies were allowed to disport ourselves to our hearts' content.

This was far and away the best time of each day for me, for although I may refer to this inner sanctum as an interior court of the palace, it would be entirely wrong to suppose that we were surrounded by high walls. To the south lay the bulk of the palace, to be sure, and to the west the walls of the fortress, from the battlements of which we were carefully secluded by a thick stand of trees. But the Alhambra is built upon the slopes of a hill, and to the north and east there was nothing to obstruct our view, the defensive walls being some fifty feet below our patio.

Due north, we looked down on the city itself, a teeming multitude of people, few of whom seemed aware that they were the cynosure of fifty pairs of beautiful eyes. To the east we looked at another high hill, at a distance of perhaps two miles. Here the further defences of the city had been erected, a formidable wall, constantly guarded, even if the frontiers of the amirate were a considerable distance away.

Remarkably, I was the only inmate of the harem who spent her time looking at that distant wall, and wondering if I would ever find myself on the far side of it. The others, even Margaretta, were thoroughly reconciled to their lives and spent their time either playing with each other, aimless games, or in gossip.

It may be wondered how Margaretta and I managed to take part in any gossip, ignorant as we were of the language, but a good dozen of al-Mumin's women were Spanish, captured in battle or on raids north of his border, and with these I at least was able to converse quite freely, and was even in demand, as I could inform them about events in the towns whence they had been so cruelly plucked, and even, in one or two cases, bring them up to date on the affairs of their families.

But they, I soon discovered, were of an intellectual capacity no greater than those of the Saracen or African women who shared our captivity.

My first true experience of harem life was, in fact, at once revealing of my sex and disturbing. There we were, some fifty females incarcerated together: I was actually the eldest at over forty; the youngest was no more than fourteen. Now here I have at once to correct a mistaken impression held by many, who suppose that an omnipotent and sexually active young man would stock his nuptial chambers entirely with women to whom he was profoundly attracted. This was not the case. Al-Mumin, all-powerful as he was, was yet bound by custom, than which there are no stronger bonds.

His wives were the daughters of amirs or noblemen with whom he wished to sustain a close alliance. This is part of the business of kingship, and takes no account of beauty or desirability. They at least had the privilege of adorning their master's bed at least once a month, as it was necessary for him to seek legitimate heirs.

What then of the concubines? But these were no less dictated by custom, in most cases. Every year a selection of the most attractive nubile virgins were presented at court, in order that the Amir might make a choice of new blood, as it were, for his bed. Of those presented he generally chose four. But in these cases also the choice was too often dictated by the necessity to keep some powerful commander in close allegiance. For it would be a grave mistake to assume that being taken into the Amir's harem involved a derogatory step. Quite the contrary. At the very least, the girl was assured of board and lodging, at the very highest level, for the rest of her life, safe from all the perils of the world, her only risk that of being caught in the act of adultery, in which case followed execution by the most unpleasant means that occurred to the Amir, providing only that the guilty lady was not exposed to the public gaze – the current fashion when I was in Granada was to confine the errant in a sack with four cats and four rats, and suspend her from the battlements until all movement within the sack ceased. However, I am bound to say that with regard at least to the Amir's harem, chance would be a fine thing; during my sojourn in Granada only one of his wives was executed, and none of the rest of us ever found out how she gained access to any man other than our lord.

So here we have fifty ardent females dependent upon the erectile prowess of but a single male. I have indicated that al-Mumin indeed possessed exceptional powers. But as he was wont to bestow them on one or two favourites, there was simply not enough to go round. The concubines were therefore divided into three classes, as, I am given to understand, obtains in most harems. All of them, myself included, were known as *guizde*, the selected ones. This marked us out even if, and there were some, we remained virgins, having never actually gained our master's bed. The higher rank, those who had had such an honour, were known as *iqbals*. But being an *iqbal* did not necessarily confer any rights to possessing what we all sought. Higher than they were the *odaliks*, those who had been summoned by our master more than once. As al-Mumin was a man of very definite tastes, there were only four *odaliks* in the harem. Of these I was the most popular, with my master.

Obviously, therefore, I was the most unpopular, with my fellow ladies. What particularly seemed to irritate them was that I was old enough to be the mother of most of them. That I should have preserved so much of my beauty, and be apparently so very desirable, smacked of witchcraft.

However, as it was obvious that I was an innocent party, as it were, whose attendance on al-Mumin was entirely dictated by his lust and not mine, my companions in distress gradually came to accept me, and wished to welcome me to their bosoms.

Unfortunately, this is by no means a figure of speech. Fifty ladies, exposed to every aspect of eroticism, and with but the scantiest means of alleviating their desires, must necessarily turn in one of three directions. I have heard it said that men in prison suffer the same problem, but they, of course, have only two possible outlets, unless they happen to be in solitary confinement, when they are reduced still further.

The ladies of the harem, however, possessed three, because of the constant presence of a large number of eunuchs, all highly trained in the requirements of the female sex. Now there is a question which may well be asked: if lonely ladies, possessing eunuchs, have three options open to them, and unhappy gentlemen, lacking eunuchs – or even with them – possess only two, what do eunuchs, lacking everything, possess? Here again I must dispel a popular fancy ... that these unhappy creatures feel nothing. I can assure you that this is not the case. In addition, this business of castration requires investigation, not something I would ever have dreamed of doing in normal circumstances ... but my circumstances at this time were clearly far from normal.

Castration can take one of two forms, in my experience. The first, and more common, is where root and branch are swept away. But there is a second, where only the testicles are removed, leaving the member intact, and as liable to be aroused as that of any whole man. More important yet, as this form of eunuch cannot ejaculate or climax in any form, once stimulated he remains ready for battle for an indefinite period, as long as his heart is sound. To my consternation, I discovered that there were three young fellows of this class attached to the harem – but I later learned that it is a cruel master who entirely deprives his women of creature comfort.

As may be imagined these impotent stallions were in great demand, and I have seen them mounted when they were in the last stages of exhaustion. But there were yet only three. The remainder of the ladies had necessarily to make do with fingers and lips, either their own, those of their fellows, or those of the remaining eunuchs.

Imagine! I cannot claim, entirely through force of circumstances, to have led a sheltered life, and from time to time in these pages I have felt called upon to criticise the lubricity of my own dear Queen, but never in all my days had I been a witness to such unbridled sexuality as continued, day and night, in the harem of al-Mumin. When, during my scanty moments of leisure, I was not being caressed most seductively, I was being eyed speculatively by the eunuchs, or being offered dildos of the most suggestive sizes and shapes, mostly that of the member of some heathen god or other.

Of course I largely resisted these blandishments: I

simply lacked the energy or the desire to cope at once with al-Mumin and a host of lesser attractions, but still it was a sorry situation for one of Naples' premier duchesses to find herself in, and I determined to find myself out again as rapidly as possible.

Sadly, Margaretta, given less opportunities to grace her master's bed, entirely succumbed to these regrettable pastimes, nor had I the heart to admonish her.

Dedicated as I was to escaping from this life of humiliating servitude, which was also downright boring, the question remained, how was this to be done? There could be no doubt that were I to essay and fail, the fate al-Mumin would command for me would be a great deal worse than that fate-worse-than-death which I had already experienced on several occasions. And any venture was fraught with the peril of discovery, for one could never tell when the girl or the eunuch in whom one confided, and even, perhaps, to whom one permitted the occasional liberty in search of at least an emotional slave, would not perform a volte-face because of some imagined slight, and betray one to our master. It was necessary to keep my own council, and watch and wait, to no great purpose. I had all but despaired, when, after I had been immured for something over a year, the situation changed suddenly and dramatically. In short, there was a palace revolution in Granada.

These events, I have been informed, are common enough in Muslim countries, where the fear of incurring the wrath of God by assassinating one of His anointed is not as severe as in Christendom. They are, however, difficult matters in which to be caught up.

It was my misfortune – but as it turned out, my fortune – to be actually sharing al-Mumin's divan in the middle of the night when the conspirators burst in. I happened to be facing the door, and awake, when it opened, and I had now seen enough of life to understand that when a man enters his master's bedchamber unsummoned and unannounced and with a drawn sword in his hand he means to use that weapon. Even more does this apply to several men. I therefore immediately disengaged myself from al-Mumin's sleeping embrace, and tumbled over the edge of the divan to lie on the floor, from where I listened with pounding heart to the grunts and cries from above me.

The matter was concluded in seconds, whereupon the assassins remembered me, and I was dragged to my feet, to gaze at al-Mumin's head being tossed on to the floor.

'Slit her throat,' said one of the conspirators. 'Every creature of al-Mumin must die.'

'Agreed,' said another, licking his lips most lasciviously. 'But first, we will play with her a little. I have heard much of this golden-haired woman.'

'Do you play with her if you choose, Akbar,' said a third man. 'We have the rest of the harem to despatch. But remember to bring us her head.'

Whereupon they hurried off, carrying al-Mumin's head by the hair, and leaving me at the mercy of this fellow Akbar. Or was he at my mercy? For while the murderers had spoken Arabic, I had during my year picked up sufficient of the tongue to understand every word.

Forewarned is forearmed, they say, and I had no intention of tamely submitting to having my throat cut. My experiences with the cowardly Montfort, captain of the Sieur de Malplaison's guard, had made me realise that a man when in the throes of passion is at his most vulnerable. Akbar was a man. Thus I allowed him to remove his clothing, while giving a perfect imitation of a virgin shivering with fright at the sight of her first nude male, even helped him to drag poor al-Mumin's headless body from the bed and dump it on the floor, lay upon the bloodstained sheets and spread myself most invitingly, and when he grasped my buttocks to turn me over, said, as seductively as I could manage, 'But, master, if you have heard so much of me, will you not sample what I truly have to offer?'

This gave him pause for thought, both because I had spoken Arabic and because it was apparent that I was not as afraid of him as I had earlier appeared. Indeed, for a moment I feared that I had given the game away. But lust always outweighs caution, and he flung himself upon me. Whereupon I wrapped both arms and legs round him, and commenced to roll. We were much of the same height, but I was the stronger – he was a weedy fellow – and in a trice we had left the divan and descended heavily on to the carpet, Akbar underneath. His head hit the floor and for a moment he was dazed. While he was in this position I sat on his chest, seized his hair in one hand and his beard in the other, and raised and lowered his head to and from the floor with as much violence as I could muster.

Thus constrained, he lost all interest in what was happening. But I could see that this was merely a temporary state, and I was thus forced to take a regrettable decision. However strange it may seem, in view of the circumstances in which I have so often found myself, the reader of these pages will know that I had never to that moment taken a human life, at least knowingly – what might have happened to Captain Montfort after I had laid him out was between him and his god, if he possessed one, which I doubt. But now I did not see I had any choice, if I was to have the least hope of escaping with my life. I therefore picked up the unhappy fellow's scimitar, and with a single stroke left him as headless as al-Mumin.

The ease with which this was done quite surprised me, and left me breathless for some moments. Perchance I even shed a tear for the poor fellow. But now was no time for womanly weakness. I therefore dressed myself in his discarded clothes, thankful that we were so much of a size, and for the Saracen habit of wearing flowing robes which amply concealed my own ampleness. My hair I bound very tightly behind my head, and as the haik descended over my brow not a trace of gold was to be seen.

My complexion remained a problem, of course, but there was nothing for it, and so, bloodstained sword in hand, haik held tight and half across my face – and having taken the precaution of securing to my girdle the bag of gold which al-Mumin kept in his sleeping chamber and from which he was wont to reward those of his bed partners who had been especially pleasing to him – I strode from the chamber like the veriest Muslim warrior.

Circumstances were in my favour. The Alhambra was a bedlam of shouting men, shrieking women, and wailing eunuchs. Death and destruction was on every side, and was the occupation of everyone, whether giving or receiving. In addition, except where torches flared or precious drapes had caught fire, it was utterly dark. No one sought to interfere with me as I went about my apparent business, which in the first instance involved a return to the harem in the hopes of finding Margaretta.

This, however, was no simple task, for the harem itself had been invaded by the conspirators, and the women, not unnaturally, saving those who had immediately been seized for rape, had taken the opportunity to get out. I do not think many of them had any idea of making their escapes, as the harem was all the life they knew, and survival outside of it was an improbable achievement. Pretending as I was to be a man, I was indeed accosted by more than one of the women, for I presented the picture of a tall and young and strong fellow, just what an abandoned *guizde* might regard as a gift from the gods. Now, I knew these women, and they knew me, so I dared not speak with them, but thrust them aside roughly as I continued my quest.

I actually found Margaretta, still in the harem, being mounted by an anxious fellow who was totally oblivious to his surroundings until I tapped him on the shoulder with my sword. Then he raised both head and body, which

363

made it the easier for me to despatch him, as I had no wish to run him through while in situ, as it were, and thereby run the risk of injuring Margaretta.

Margaretta stared at him, and then at me, in consternation, but made no sound, obviously reflecting that at times like these rapid changes of scenery had to be accepted. The silly girl only screamed when I released my haik to reveal myself.

'My God, Your Grace!' she shrieked. 'What have you done?'

'Probably saved your life,' I replied. 'Now haste. We are leaving this place.'

She was by now sitting up, and in response to my words drew up her knees and gathered the remnants of her clothes about her, protectively. 'Leaving? To go where?'

'I will decide that when we are safe,' I told her.

'It is safest to remain,' she suggested.

'To become the plaything of whoever triumphs in this affair? Are you a man or a mouse?'

'I am a woman,' she retorted, truthfully enough.

I was tempted to lay her out and remove her by force. But I doubted that I possessed the strength to carry someone like Margaretta very far – she had put on weight during our sojourn in the harem. Equally, if she wished to stay, she would only be a hindrance to me. At the same time I could not just turn my back on her, as she might very well start screaming the moment I attempted to leave, and give my identity away.

Circumstances often force us to act in an abnormal way. As with Montfort, I now realised that my actions must be forceful and unhesitating if I was going to survive. With the hilt of my scimitar I struck poor Margaretta a brisk blow across the head which stretched her senseless on the floor, and hurried from the room.

A few minutes later, finding myself in the courtyard, I simply mounted the nearest horse and rode off.

*

364

I was not of course yet safe. Imagine, a lone woman riding through a Muslim country, and dressed as a man. This is regarded with disfavour by most peoples. In our Christian countries women so attempting to disguise themselves are usually burned as witches. I had no idea what might be the Muslim way of dealing with such a situation, but I could not suppose it would be any less painful.

On the other hand, I was not without resource. The entire country, as news spread of what had happened in Granada, descended into chaos, and I possessed the bag of gold I had taken from al-Mumin's chamber, while my height and bloodstained scimitar convinced most people, at least from a distance, that I was no one to meddle with – and I was careful to let no one come very close and thus discern my sex, except when I was forced to buy food. But on these occasions the vendor was usually more interested in my gold coins than in my person.

For the rest, I slept under the stars, thanking them that Spain, at least in the summer, is such a warm country, and made my way up hill and down dale, heading steadily east.

My journey took some time, as it is about three hundred miles from Granada to the coast, in the east; it is closer in the south, but I had learned during my stay in the city that the south was the most thickly populated area, and I felt this would be a mistake. Thus for most of my time I proceeded alone, and found it most enjoyable; it was, in fact, the first time in my life I had ever been left entirely to myself.

My routine was invariable. I rose early, bathed if there was a stream nearby – and I usually sought to find one before stopping for the night – dressed myself, and began my day's march, leading my faithful horse. I seldom rode him, as I was concerned that he be at all times less weary than myself, just in case we should need to make a hasty getaway ... as happened on more than one occasion.

Proceeding by easy stages, and keeping an eye on everything that I passed, I usually came upon a hillside hamlet at some stage during the day, whereupon I held my haik across my face, slapped the sword on my hip, and purchased food. As I lived mostly off fruit and vegetables – I had no means of cooking any meat – it was often possible to buy several days' supplies at one stop, and thus cut myself adrift from risk of recognition as a woman for that period. Come midday, I found a lonely spot and siestad like any other of the natives, before resuming my journey in the early evening, and stopping when darkness fell.

Of course it was not all as simple as I have made it sound. Apart from bands of hill robbers, there was more than one occasion when I was beset in the villages, and had to leap into the saddle and cut my way out. But as I was always ready to do this, no one ever brought me down; before I saw the sea I had become quite an adept with the scimitar.

Of course I lacked a great deal. A change of clothing for one thing, and my diet was a simple one, while I bathed in cold water and drank nothing else. Yet I was happy, or I would have been happy, but for a remarkable development: throughout the six weeks I spent on my journey, I did not menstruate once. Could I possibly be pregnant again, after all of these years? Then al-Mumin truly had possessed a potent lance, poor thing. But really the thought of being confined and constrained for the year or so it takes to bring a child into this world and adequately feed the babe was most disturbing, especially at a moment in my life when I needed all my strength and vigour.

As it turned out, and to anticipate somewhat, I was not pregnant, but had reached that age in life when pregnancy ceases to be a practical possibility. I have been told by others that this is a sad occasion, often accompanied by fits of the most profound melancholia, and seriously affecting one's womanly habits, abilities, desires and enjoyments.

Well, possibly this is so for some, even many. It was never so for me. Perchance I was just too busy at the time it happened to feel anything more than relief. And as time went by, I was merely aware that a great burden had been lifted from my shoulders. Or possibly lower down my body.

My business was to get back to Naples just as rapidly as possible. And this I found quite easy to do. I rode into a seaport known as Alicante, which it seemed traded with all the Mediterranean, Muslim or Christian. Here I soon discovered a ship flying the Neapolitan flag, boarded it, requested a private interview with its captain, and revealed myself.

He had been a somewhat truculent fellow before, but when he found himself face to face with the Duchess of Eberli, he was perfectly flabbergasted. He told me that I had been supposed dead this past year, and that the Queen had worn mourning for three months.

'Then she will be the more overjoyed to see me,' I said. 'So let us make haste, signor. Haste.'

And so, home. To be folded in Joanna's arms, as she made me tell her time and again of my adventures, and I could see that her brilliant imagination was placing herself in the harem in my place, and considering all the amazing experiences I had had as if they had happened to her.

Naturally, she also wished news of her husband. But much as she had once loved her Aragonese prince, his lengthy absence had caused a diminution in her regard for him. For the silly fellow had not after all returned to his beautiful bride, but had been persuaded by the Portuguese with whom he had taken refuge to continue the fight, and indeed he never did come back to Naples; four years later he fell in battle against Henry of Trastamara and his half-brother.

I am anticipating. Even on my return, which took place

367

in the autumn of 1371, Joanna had abandoned any hopes of having her husband return to her bed, and was, as was her wont, satisfying her undiminished desires with a succession of lovers. For a while after my return, indeed, she shared her bed with me as she had me recount my adventure time and again. There we were, two ladies who would never see forty again, as ardently loving of each other as when we had been young girls, despite the river of blood that had flowed between and beneath us during the thirty-five years of our acquaintance.

But much as I loved my Queen, my heart was naturally more attracted to my castle and estates, my children and grandchildren. I early found an opportunity to visit the monastery where William had incarcerated himself, and discovered him well and prospering, very much the favourite of his prior, although equally very much the monk, who insisted upon having me kneel beside him and pray for my deliverance from the catastrophic spiritual effects of my incarceration in a harem – as he supposed would necessarily be the case.

I humoured the boy, but had a much more interesting session with his prior, who was just as interested as Joanna in the domestic arrangements of the Saracens, and sighed heavily when I described these, especially where they pertained to young boys or still partially equipped eunuchs. This interest naturally made me pause for thought regarding what the future might have in store for William – or perhaps had already delivered – but I reflected that it takes all sorts to make the world, and that my son had chosen his vocation for himself.

More satisfying was my return to Eberli, and the welcome of dearest Lucia and her husband, and growing family, for she now had three children, and the youngest was a boy, named Louis, in whom I saw the hope of my house.

It is a great boon, not to be able to foresee the future.

*

My existence therefore resumed its even tenor, or it would have done, had not Joanna determined that I should marry again.

This I was entirely reluctant to do. As I approached my fiftieth year, I did not suppose I would ever again either adventure, or be in danger of my life, and so saw no reason why I should allow that life to be disrupted by some over-anxious male. If I thought of men at all, in the abstract, it was of Christopher of the Bay, but as I had heard nothing of him for several years I had to presume him either dead, or forgetful. If I chose to think of men in the concrete, there was Guido, Ricardo's son, who was twenty years old, very virile, satisfyingly handsome, and my willing slave. But as I am not by nature promiscuous – not, at least, in the sense that, like Joanna, my emotions are in a continual state of arousal – his visits to my bed were irregular and often at considerable intervals, as I found the management of my estates, the sequences of nature, the life cycles of my animals, and my crops, to give me as much pleasure as any man.

But Joanna was adamant, and she was my Queen. More to the point, she had already found the man.

His name was Danilo Focchi, and apart from the somewhat sinister connotation of the surname – which of course only applied if I considered it in an English sense – he was in fact someone I might have chosen for myself, had I been in the mood. He was tall, broad without being stout, and of a clearly athletic build. He was younger than myself, but not disturbingly so, as had been poor dear Fernando; Danilo was forty-six. He also possessed the most splendid manners, dressed well, and sat a horse as well as any man in the kingdom.

What he did not possess, unfortunately, was any fortune whatsoever. It was a sad tale. His father's property, a considerable one, had been overrun by the Hungarians during the wars of the late forties, and utterly devastated. Danilo, then just coming to manhood, was left an orphan, and a destitute one. To a young man of spirit, there was only one way in which to recoup his finances and so he took up the profession of arms, serving as squire to our late, great King Louis of Tarento. Indeed, I remembered him from this period, although I had seen little enough of him, and taken even less interest in his affairs, bound up as I had been in my own problems.

As King Louis's faithful follower, Danilo had done a great deal of fighting in various parts of Europe, and earned himself a considerable reputation as a warrior. It was not until after his patron's untimely death that his thoughts had returned in the direction of earning a fortune for himself.

This he did with remarkable celerity, selling his sword, and his brains, to various warring princes, mainly in the north of Italy, and emerging as a famous and wealthy condottiere. Then, reaching the age of forty-five, he had determined to put matters of the sword behind him, and retire to his native city, there to live out the remainder of his life in peace and prosperity.

But as we all know, man supposes, and God disposes, especially where the man has been careless, or, in the case of Danilo, over-cautious. Well aware that he had made a host of enemies amongst those he had fought and conquered, and that these villains might well be waiting to avenge themselves once he had divested himself of his mercenary followers, he determined that the safest way to regain Naples was by ship. But his vessel was overwhelmed by a storm, and went to the bottom, taking all of his accumulated treasures with it. Danilo reached the shore utterly destitute.

In this sorry state he had eventually regained Naples, and attained an audience with the Queen, who remembered him well as a faithful follower of her late husband, and no doubt in other ways as well, for Danilo had ever been a handsome fellow. However, he was well on the wrong side of forty, and Joanna's penchant had increasingly gone in the other direction as regards men. Thus she determined that his long and arduous service should be rewarded by giving him a rich wife.

Nor did she consider that she was in the least inconveniencing me. Quite the contrary, as she held that the only inconvenience a woman could suffer was to be without the always immediate support of a man, and she was unaware of my relations with Guido, as I feared to lose the boy.

I understood of course that there was nothing for it, but on our wedding night, after the affair had been consummated and the madding crowd had departed, I determined to stabilise the situation.

'That was a most delightful thrust, my pet,' I told my husband.

'And for me. You are quite the most beautiful fifty-year-old I have ever encountered, my dearest duchess.'

It occurred to me that he might have phrased his compliment differently, but I did not wish to quarrel upon my wedding night.

'You say the sweetest things, my darling,' I riposted. 'However, you have placed your finger on the nub of the matter ... well, you have already done that, but I am now speaking metaphorically. And yet realistically. I *am* fifty years old, as you have just reminded me—'

'And have the figure and the vigour of a twenty year old,' he interrupted, thus proving that he was intelligent enough to learn.

'The vigour, at the least, is in short supply,' I pointed out. 'And apt to be rapidly exhausted. I must therefore, sadly, have your agreement to certain rules and restrictions.'

'Yes?' he asked, commencing to look a trifle anxious.

'It is simply that I have become rather set in my ways over the many years I have walked this earth,' I told him. 'And I fear to presume so far as to require you to conform

371

entirely to my habits. I therefore consider that it would be best for us to have separate apartments at Eberli. When I desire your presence, and it shall be at least twice a week, I do assure you' – I felt it necessary to throw this in lest he become too discouraged – 'I shall summon you, but at other times we shall follow our own paths. I shall continue to manage and supervise my estate, and you will do … why, I do not know what you prefer to do with your time, monsignore. But be sure that I will encourage it.'

I was anticipating something of a crisis, and bracing myself to be firm, but to my surprise he agreed wholeheartedly that when people had reached our ages – I could have wished he would not keep harping on this lamentable aspect of the situation – such an arrangement was not only desirable, but necessary, and equally that he had no wish to intrude upon my prerogatives as mistress of Eberli.

I was greatly relieved at his understanding, and was very anxious to make him understand as well that I knew all about masculine failings – which, when one is young, one considers as strengths and even virtues. I therefore said, 'And of course I understand that should your virility be such that twice a week is insufficient for your needs, you have my permission to seek the alleviation of your distress elsewhere.' I knew that men will do this anyway, and it is a useful asset in times of domestic strife to have this matter settled in advance.

Again, he seemed entirely gratified.

'However,' I added, 'I have no wish to be in any way aware of anyone sharing your bed save myself. I make this plain, monsignore. Should adultery ever be flaunted in my face, the woman will immediately be expelled from Eberli, with all the ignominy I can muster.'

'I do assure you that contingency will never arise,' he promised me.

And so I assumed the burden of my third marriage with every promise of domestic bliss. I did not of course love

Danilo, any more than he loved me. It was an arranged marriage, for our mutual convenience; my money for his protection. As I did not consider that I needed his protection, while there could be no doubt that he desperately needed my money, I naturally felt myself to be the senior partner, quite apart from the question of age, and in this respect set out to enjoy myself.

For I regarded my accommodating view of his private affairs to extend equally to myself, and continued, from time to time, to entertain Guido in my boudoir while we discussed matters of mutual interest.

As for Danilo, I assumed that he similarly occupied himself when not required to occupy me. Life assumed a very civilised tenor. Twice a week I let him know that I was eager for his embrace; four nights I enjoyed an uninterrupted slumber, and on the seventh Guido brought me up to date on affairs below stairs.

This is not to say that my husband did not spend a great deal of time in my company. He was intensely interested in the management of the estate, and would accompany me on most of my tours of inspection. Indeed, he hinted from time to time that if I would like to dismiss Ricardo, he would be happy to take over the entire control of my affairs. This, however, I declined to do; I trusted Ricardo far more than I did Danilo.

No doubt he was aware of this, but he remained always the soul of charm, paying me gentle compliments, and going out of his way to please me, while in the evenings he would strum his lute and sing in a deep, clear voice, or else we would play at chess, at which game he was expert.

Often enough we entertained Lucia and her Pietro, and to my delight Danilo was as courteous to them as to myself, and liked nothing better than a romp with his step-grandchildren.

Equally, when William obtained leave of absence from his monastery to visit his mother, Danilo went out of his way to be charming to the boy. More, he seemed determined to act the father, and he had never actually shown such a wish as regards Lucia. It did my heart good to see William and Danilo together, and they spent a great deal of time tête-à-tête, or else riding to hounds, or discussing this or that. Danilo indeed even invited William to visit him in his private apartments, a privilege he had never extended to myself!

But I was happy to see my son happy, and when the time came for him to depart, we all of us wept.

No doubt I should have left well enough alone, but I am after all a woman, and curiosity is one of my besetting sins. As time went by, I became increasingly intrigued by my inability to discover any evidence that Danilo was taking advantage of the carte blanche I had granted him to pursue whatever took his fancy when he was not engaged with me. I had expected to be able to observe various of my female employees casting me sidelong glances, or even whispering or giggling behind my back, activities on which I was determined to stamp with the utmost severity: Ricardo was always present with his whip.

But not a trace of adultery could I discover, save in my own bed, and this began to trouble my conscience. I could not of course openly investigate the matter, and it therefore rested for some time, while I felt ever more concerned about it, until William returned for a visit once again. Naturally I greeted him with open arms, and indeed I was thoroughly proud of the way he had turned out, for although a priest he was at once tall and powerfully built, had an open cast of countenance, and a great deal of confidence in his demeanour. In short he was a man of whom any mother could be proud.

To my concern, however, he seemed less eager to greet me, his flesh and blood, than Danilo, who was merely his stepfather, and within minutes of their first embracing the two men were closeted in Danilo's apartments.

I should like no one to suppose that I am a fool, and

hope to have revealed enough in these pages to dispose of any such misapprehensions. My principal fault, as I see it, is an overwillingness to discover good in all about me, often at considerable cost to myself.

Equally, I believe I am the most broadminded of women. Well, circumstances have forced this upon me.

But a mother's feelings for her son are of a very special variety, perhaps even more special than the relationship between mother and daughter. It may be that in the male offspring we women seek to discover all the virtues that might have been lacking in the lad's father, especially when that father has long gone to his grave. Equally, perhaps, do we fear to discover the weaknesses we remember so well, and which may have been passed on to the son.

But the fact was, I could remember no weaknesses possessed by my dear Alberto, save a slight tendency to pessimism, and this was in no way reflected in William's sunny character. On the other hand, my late husband had been a most libidinous fellow, well, we only have to consider the liberties he took with a queen's maid, which, while productive of many happy hours, eventually brought him to his sorry end. I have never been one to criticise sexual prowess, even when carried to extremes, and it may be recalled that my principal fear when acquainted with William's decision to enter the priesthood was that he would be deprived of those moments of ultimate bliss.

I was now forced to accept that he had in no way been deprived of such moments, only undertaken them in somewhat different circumstances than I personally would have recommended.

Now it may well be that a woman who had spent most of her life as the *intimate* confidante of the Queen of Naples, not to mention more than a year in the harem of al-Mumin, should have considered her position in the light of that Biblical exhortation that only he who is without sin should cast the first stone. Outraged motherhood knows no such limitations.

I therefore took my way along to Danilo's apartments, by no means sure how I intended to handle the situation, and in fact retaining a faint hope that there might be no situation to handle.

Alas for optimism. I decided against knocking, threw open the door, bent such a stare upon the servant who was within and undoubtedly had orders to keep all visitors out that he congealed and became unable to move or utter a sound – his ultimate employment of course rested upon me rather than Danilo – and thus gained the bedchamber, where I discovered the two objects of my quest naked upon the bed, and disporting themselves in a perfectly indecent manner.

For several moments there was total silence, as we contemplated each other. But in fact my anxiety having been allayed, as it were, by the fact of the situation, I found it difficult to maintain the necessary level of outraged anger. Which is not to say that I did not remain deeply angry, and indeed insulted, or that I was not very concerned at the misfortune which had overtaken my son.

'Well, monsignore,' I remarked.

Danilo was on his knees on the bed, a ridiculous sight. 'You required me to provide my own entertainments, madame,' he protested.

'But not with my son,' I pointed out, coldly.

'I assure you, Mama, that there was no harm in it,' William said.

'I will speak with you later,' I told him. 'Get yourself dressed and go to my apartments.'

William looked at Danilo, almost as if he would have resisted, but Danilo gave a quick nod. The boy got out of the bed, dragged on his clothes, and hurried from the room.

'Were I to report this matter to the Queen, and she to the Archbishop,' I told my husband, 'you could find yourself at the stake.'

'William would be beside me,' he retorted. 'Would you

376

really carry matters that far? As the boy said, there is no harm in it.'

That seemed true enough. And yet my sense of outrage was returning, when I reflected the number of occasions this man had had his way with me, while no doubt thinking all the while of some handsome yardboy.

'It is none the less unnatural, and universally condemned,' I insisted.

'Are you going to pretend that you have never had an unnatural desire, and indeed, gratified it?' he inquired.

Well, obviously that was not a question I cared to answer; I was indeed rapidly coming to realise that my position was indefensible.

Not that I intended to surrender. 'In all the circumstances,' I said, 'I may be prepared to let the matter rest. However, there are two rules which I am now making, to take effect as of this moment. The first is that you shall never enter my apartments again. The second is that William never enters your apartments again. Is this understood?'

'But ... if I am not allowed to come to you, my dearest Richilde, we no longer have a marriage.'

'For the sake of appearances you may remain at Eberli,' I said. 'But the rules stand. If you would prefer to leave and seek your fortune elsewhere, that must be entirely your decision.'

'I shall appeal to Her Grace the Queen.'

'You may appeal to whomever you wish. I do assure you that Her Grace will listen to me far more than she is likely to listen to you.'

With that I left him. I had no fears of anything he might attempt. Danilo might have been a lion in battle, but he lacked that moral courage which is necessary to take a stance and see it through to the bitter end regardless of rumour and contumely, and the risk of failure.

Equally I was not concerned about my domestic

arrangements. Guido had always been a far more enthusiastic lover than Danilo – I now understood why – and in
fact yielding my privacy only once a week instead of three
times suited me much better. In addition, Guido, as
befitted his station, was entirely servile and obedient to my
whims, where Danilo was inclined to give himself the airs
and pretended powers of the husband.

As for what he did in the privacy of his own bedchamber
I preferred not to think.

Dealing with William was a more difficult matter, but I,
wisely, I think, determined not to approach the subject on
the basis of sin, but simply on the utter impossibility of
having my son as the lover of my husband; to all intents
and purposes this was incest. William quite understood
this point of view, and was utterly contrite.

The secret was thus confined to us three, and no doubt
Danilo's valet, and there it remained, for if, as I suppose
was inevitable, William felt constrained to confess to his
Superior, we all know the secrets of the Confessional are
sacred.

As to what other secrets William might share with his
Superior, these I dreaded to consider.

Danilo and I therefore carried out our merry farce for
some years. Whenever we were called upon to attend a
function in Naples we travelled as man and wife, and even
shared a bedchamber, although I always most pointedly
arranged a bolster between our naked bodies, nor would I
ever allow my heart to soften even to his most pitiful
entreaties.

Having settled my domestic affairs to my own satisfaction, not even the romantic and carnal concerns of the
Queen seemed likely to upset the even tenor of my
declining years. Prince Jaime died, as I have recounted, in
1375. Joanna was then forty-nine, and like myself, had
passed the supposed climacteric. But again like me, she
was finding life as enjoyable as ever, and no sooner was the

news of her widowhood confirmed, than she again let it be known that she was available.

As with a dozen years before, suitors flocked to her door. But this time she was more discerning, and in addition to health, some pretensions to looks, and pronounced sexuality, she made it a prerequisite of marriage that her husband should spend the rest of his life in Naples.

This of course ruled out most of the princes, who had ambitions of their own, as well as duties to fulfil, and eventually Joanna settled for a minor Count, who called himself Otto of Brunswick. From which it will be gathered that he was a German. He was in fact a scion of a family known as Habsburg, who owned a duchy in Austria, and were causing some amusement in the Holy Roman Empire by repeated suggestions that they might aspire to the Imperial throne themselves. It is of course well known that the position of Holy Roman Emperor, however exalted it may sound, is really a matter of which candidate has the most money to spend, and is least likely to offend the sovereign princes over whom he will be titular head. In this respect the Habsburgs had admirable qualifications, to which they had added another: as a family they were numerous, and their plan of campaign appeared to be to marry off these sons and daughters – particularly the daughters – to whomsoever might possibly eventually support their cause.

Now Naples was of course not a part of the Empire, but it was a thriving and reasonably powerful kingdom, and no doubt the Habsburgs felt that a marriage alliance with the most famous woman in Europe could do nothing but enhance their chances. In this they were utterly wrong, as Joanna's glorious star was about to set, but I do believe the marriage would have proceeded anyway, for it was a genuine love match. I have said this before about Joanna's liaisons, and no doubt all of them were, in the beginning, only to founder upon male ambition. Otto, although some years younger than Joanna, sought to do nothing more

379

than serve her, in every possible way, and be at her side no matter what the future might bring. He thus embarked upon a most difficult course.

For the time being, however, all seemed well. Joanna appeared blissfully happy with her fourth husband, her kingdom prospered, and so did the Duchess of Eberli, preparing to decline gracefully into old age. Not that I felt a whit older than on my twentieth birthday, far from it, even if I had sundry aches and pains and my attempts to teach Guido the various Saracen positions for making love – several of which are more suited to a contortionist than a passionate pair – had to be abandoned because I simply was no longer supple enough.

Of course there always lay that shadow of the death of Andrew of Hungary across both Joanna and myself – we were the only two survivors of that sad period of our lives – but even that seemed buried forever when Joanna at last accomplished something she had been striving for since her accession: she had a Neapolitan elected as Pope. Alas, this manoeuvre, which might have seemed to secure her kingdom for the rest of her life, was to be the cause of her undoing.

To explain this, it is necessary for me to delve back into the recent history of the Papacy. I have already recounted in these pages how following the upheavals at the beginning of the century only French candidates were to be found for the Holy See, and these had opted to remove themselves to the security of Avignon and the protection of the French monarchy rather than expose themselves to the uncertain humour of the Roman mob.

This sensible precaution was of course not regarded with much favour by the Romans themselves, or by the non-French cardinals, who conceived, correctly, that the Roman Church had now become a French Church. However, as long as those in power in Avignon were men of spirit and determination, such as Joanna's and my old friend Clement VI, there was not much that could be done about the situation.

Clement had died in 1352, as it may be recalled, and his successor had been another Frenchman, Etienne Aubert, who had taken the title of Innocent VI. Again, as it may be remembered, it was Innocent who first contemplated returning the Papacy to Rome, and to this end despatched dear Cola upon his futile and fatal mission. The exploits of the Roman mob in tearing Cola and Alberto to pieces quite abated Innocent's desire to live amongst them, and the matter was then dropped, Innocent devoting the rest of his life to reforming the Papal Court in Avignon – which greatly needed attention – and in vainly attempting to reunite the Roman and Byzantine communions.

Innocent's successor, in 1362, was yet another Frenchman, Guillaume de Grimoard, who took the title of Urban V, and who actually carried his predecessors' plans to fruition, returning the Papal Court to Rome on 15 October 1367, while I was campaigning in Spain. This might have been expected to end the affair, as well as the Babylonian Captivity. Not a bit of it. The Romans proved, as ever, ungovernable, and after some three years Urban packed his bags and returned to France. The Romans were upset about this, and even publicly begged him to stay, while they invoked the support of a famous mystic, Saint Bridget of Sweden, to warn him of calamity – unfortunately she did not specify for whom – were he again to abandon Christianity's centre.

Nothing would sway the Pontiff, however, and off he went. As far as calamities went, his was immediate: he died that same year.

Urban was succeeded by none other than the nephew of Clement VI, who had made him a cardinal at the disgustingly early age of nineteen, and had clearly been grooming him even then for the ultimate power. This youth, who bore the same name, Pierre-Roger de Beaufort, as his uncle, was now a virile man of forty-one, and took power

381

as Gregory XI, this despite the fact that he had never been ordained as a priest. To such a sorry state had religious affairs been reduced.

Unwisely, Gregory also began considering a removal to Rome. This attitude was of course not entirely inherited. There were many reasons attracting the Pope back to St Peter's, not least the continuing struggle between England and France which was devastating the latter country and even from time to time lapped at the environs of Avignon itself. Concomitant with this was of course the extreme weakness of the French kings. The Popes had first taken up residence in France when sure of the protection of the formidable Philip the Fair – provided they understood their subservience to that monarch. Now they were still regarded as being at the behest of the monarchy when that monarchy no longer had the power to protect them.

In addition, there was a large body of non-French – mainly Italian – cardinals whose votes had to be gained, at great expense, every time there was an election, and who kept hankering to return to their native land.

There may even have been some genuine feelings concerning the fact that Rome was the Eternal City; Avignon had no such claims to immortality.

Whatever the true reason impelling him to so disastrous a step, Gregory XI returned to Rome on 13 January 1377. The event was hailed with acclamation all over Italy, and we in Naples were not backwards in coming forwards with our congratulations. Obviously, having sold Avignon, Joanna had nothing further to gain from having the Pope as her tenant, but in any event she was on the best of terms with Gregory, who remembered her in all the glory of her youth and beauty as an appellant at his uncle's court nearly thirty years before, and having such an admirer in close proximity seemed to promise a period of tranquillity which would see us both into our graves. After all, Joanna was now fifty-one, I was fifty-two ... and Gregory was a mere boy of forty-eight.

However, after only just over a year in Rome, Gregory died, on the night of 26/27 March, 1378.

Now, who am I to question the sudden death of a young, strong, active man, and suggest that it may not have been merely the result of too hearty a dinner, as was suggested at the time? I can only put forward what is an established fact, that, like Clement, Gregory had found a year in the company of the Romans more than sufficient, and had announced his determination to return to Avignon. Clearly the Romans did not wish him to go, and no doubt someone was there to give utterance to the aphorism, better a dead Pope than a French Pope.

The event, none the less, took everyone by surprise. Except perhaps those who had been privy to the plot, and these certainly included a majority of the Italian cardinals, who were now determined to end the succession of French popes which had obtained for the better part of the century. Almost at the same moment that news of Gregory's sad end reached us, we also received a delegation of cardinals, proposing to the Queen that she agree to allow the Archbishop of Bari, Bartolomeo Prignano, to be put forward as the Frenchman's successor.

I happened to be on a visit to Naples when these events transpired, and was actually with Joanna when the proposal was made to her.

'Prignano?' she inquired. 'Prignano?' And then turned to me. 'Prignano!' she cried. 'Could anything be better?' She smiled at the Roman envoy. 'We will send for the Archbishop immediately.'

Signor Prignano had been born in Naples itself, in 1318, that is to say he was eight years older than Joanna, which meant he had known her, at least by reputation, all of his life. However, no doubt fortunately, as we then thought, as he had lacked any influential uncles or cousins, his progress in holy orders was slow, and it was not until he was well into middle-age that he had reached the higher echelons of the Church. When Joanna had been fighting for her survival against Louis of Hungary and earned the disapproval, it had seemed, of all Christendom, he had been nothing more than a parish priest, and whether or not he had joined in that disapproval had been quite irrelevant. When more than ten years later, he had finally become a bishop, Joanna had already been confirmed in her crown and her prerogatives – and, officially, in her innocence – by the Pope, whom all bishops had to accept as knowing what he was about.

At this time Prignano had first met the Queen. I doubt very much whether Joanna ever thought much of him, or thought of him at all, but he was a Neapolitan, and she was pleased to see one of her own subjects rising so high. During the preceding ten years, it may be recalled, I had been preoccupied much of the time, or it might have occurred to me to tell the Queen the story of one of our own English kings, Henry II, who had been very pleased at the slow but steady elevation of an Englishman, and a friend of his, by name Becket, to an archbishopric, whereupon he had discovered that archbishops can be the most difficult of men. Henry in fact found it necessary to have this Becket despatched by some faithful knights, a precaution which Joanna had not had the foresight to take. She remained indeed convinced that all of our troubles were at an end, and that Prignano was the most loyal and pliable of her subjects. It was difficult to argue this point, as I knew absolutely nothing about the arch-bishop, while of course King Otto knew even less, having been resident in the kingdom for only a few years. Thus neither of us made any attempt to dissuade the Queen from her course. And to be frank, there was no cause for alarm during the first few weeks after Prignano, having been summoned before Joanna, was informed of the honour which was about to be his.

He was becomingly bashful and self-effacing. 'Oh, Your

Grace,' he protested. 'I am but a humble priest, totally unfitted for such high office.'

'Nonsense,' Joanna declared. 'Your record, both for administration and devotion, is second to none. And did not Pope Gregory make you one of his chancellors, for just those qualities?'

'Well, this is true, of course,' the scurvy fellow confessed. 'But I none the less would beg leave to decline the honour of succeeding him, Your Grace.'

'Nonsense,' Joanna repeated. 'Christendom needs an Italian pope. More, it needs a Neapolitan pope. And you are the man, my dear archbishop.'

Thus blindly do we rush upon self-destruction.

Prignano allowed himself to be persuaded, duly travelled to Rome with an escort of Neapolitan cavalry, and was there greeted with acclamation by the populace. His election was a mere formality; white smoke was issuing from the chimney of the Vatican almost before they had got the fire properly lit, as even the French cardinals realised that, if it was time to humour the Italians, they could hardly do better than this humble little man who seemed afraid to say boo to a goose.

The election took place on 8 April 1378, Prignano assuming the name of Urban VI. That done, we all settled back, anticipating a peaceful time, and received the shock of our lives when, in his first sermon as pope, Urban delivered a stinging criticism of the lives of the rich. In this general castigation he included his benefactress, and even made several scurrilous allusions to her unhappy past.

'The wretch!' Joanna exclaimed when a transcript of the sermon was brought to her. 'The ungrateful wretch. What can we do about him, Richilde?'

'Alas, Your Grace, as we have elected him Pope, I do not think we can do anything about him. He is an old man. Let us be patient.'

I was ever an optimist. Having attacked the Queen,

Urban now proceeded to attack the other cardinals, criticising their lifestyles – cardinals all paid lip service to clerical celibacy and at the same time kept a string of mistresses – their luxurious standard of living, their venality ... particularly regarding the amassment of wealth by the sale of indulgences, which guaranteed that one's loved ones, having died, would spend as little time as possible in Purgatory before being taken up to heaven and a seat on the right hand of God.

Sadly, none of these dear departed ever returned to tell the rest of us how rapidly this elevation had taken place, or even more sadly, to tell us whether or not they had really wished to be elevated to what can only be described as a somewhat austere existence, however eternal.

The cardinals, and particularly the French cardinals, resented these attacks. They also resented having to attend Rome, which they disliked on account of the climate, which was hot and malarial, the people, who were hot and unpredictable, and above all, the food, which was not hot, and to French palates, inedible. They therefore took themselves back to the fleshpots and organised brothels of Avignon, and, once there, realised the extent of the mistake they had made in yielding to the Italian demands for a native pope.

From this realisation it was but a short step to another understanding, that they had only yielded to Italian pressure through fear of the Roman mob. This in turn indicated that Urban's election had been irregular, and therefore invalid.

The French were too cunning to attempt to defend their position from Avignon, but returned to Italy, although not to Rome, as they declared that their lives would be in danger in the Holy City. Instead they established themselves at Fondi, and invited all the cardinals to join them in order to choose a new, and legal, pope. Predictably the Italians stayed away, and the French therefore elected their own candidate, Robert of Geneva.

Many libellous things have been written about Robert of Geneva, and it is therefore worth recalling that he had as many qualifications for the papacy as anyone else, and a good deal more than most. He had served as bishop both of Therouanne and Cambrai, and had been made a cardinal by Gregory XI. He was thus an experienced man of the Church. But he was even better qualified than that, for as Papal Legate to northern Italy, he had commanded the Papal army that had ended the Florentine revolt, in the course of which campaign he had destroyed the town of Cesena and massacred four thousand of its inhabitants.

Clearly therefore, Robert was no man to be trifled with, even if it could be doubted if such a formidable soldier would really make a good pope. Most unfortunate of all, however, he was a cousin of the French King. This, alas, made him equally a cousin of the Queen of Naples.

For the time being, we in the Castel Nuovo or out at Eberli viewed these stirring events with mixed but unemotional feelings. Clearly our enthusiasm for Prignano's election had been misplaced. However, we regarded the prospect of there being two popes – as Urban showed no inclination to step down – as being an entirely religious problem, and one which might indeed turn out to our advantage. Certainly we had no intention of becoming involved.

As if involvement in the affairs of the Church can ever be avoided.

Having been elected, Robert, taking the title of Clement VII, determined to settle the question of who was rightful pope by the first means which came to the mind of a soldier – force of arms. In this regard he was apparently well situated. The Papal army which had followed him to the conquest of Florence and the destruction of Cesena was still mobilised. But, knowing the difficulties of taking Rome itself, which has bedevilled commanders throughout history, from Alaric and Hannibal to more recent generals, he undertook what appeared to be a brilliant tactical stroke, and had a company of French men-at-arms enter the city unannounced, whereupon they seized the famous castle of St Angelo, which had been built more than a thousand years ago as a tomb for the Emperor Hadrian, and pronounced Pope Urban deposed.

Such an announcement was premature. The Pope was still at large, and retained the loyalty of the Roman mob. Clement, hurrying behind his forlorn hope with the Papal army, found the gates shut and himself faced with an entire people. At this juncture, the gallant garrison of St Angelo surrendered rather than risk their lives.

The men-at-arms were indeed allowed to leave, and join Robert's forces, but now it became apparent that the entire country was in support of Urban, and that maintaining himself without an ally was going to be difficult. But he knew where one was to be found, and directed his march on Naples.

Joanna was here in a difficult position. If she had supported Prignano's elevation, she now knew this to be a mistake. Additionally, she was French herself, and on the whole had received nothing but co-operation from the various French popes who had held office throughout her life – she could expect none from Urban, judging by his sermons. Even more important, Robert appealed for her assistance in the name of cousin.

Thus she welcomed Clement VII with open arms, and announced her determination to install him in the Vatican, by force if need be.

The result of this was that Christendom very rapidly divided into two camps, as it now possessed two popes. France, naturally, Scotland, Castile, Aragon, Burgundy, as well as, of course, Naples, supported Clement. Northern Italy, Portugal, England, the Scandinavian countries and the eastern states such as Poland and Hungary, backed Urban. Germany, which included Austria, varied from one side to the other. It will not escape even the most casual reader that this division of opinion, although possibly sincere, occurred entirely along the lines of current political rivalry. Thus it was natural that whichever side England supported, Scotland would choose the other. The same went for Spain and Portugal, while Florence and her neighbours had every reason to dislike Clement for his excesses when invading them. The Germans of course had a long history of disagreement with the Papacy and were merely seeking a Pope who would support *their* point of view.

However, all of these countries could take their stances and air their opinions at their leisure, sure of a great deal of time elapsing, and indeed, perhaps a resolution of the entire business, before they would have to draw a sword in defence of their positions. We in Naples were not so fortunate. No sooner had Clement taken up residence amongst us than Urban began issuing *denunciamentos* from the Vatican, beginning with anathema and gradually working himself up to excommunication of the anti-pope and all who supported him.

These Papal missiles, which are, after all, only words, are actually no stronger than the determination of the people who receive them, and no doubt in France Urban's thunderings were regarded with amusement. In Italy they were a different matter. Additionally, whether those of superior intelligence believe in them or not, they can certainly be used by the unscrupulous to twist the minds of the unwashed masses, particularly where there are axes to grind.

In Joanna's case there were many of these. Top of the list was that dreadful youth – only he was now a grown man – Charles of Durazzo, who for all Joanna's generosity in making him her heir, could remember only the death of his uncle, the imprisonment of his father ... and the fact that he *was* heir, and were the Queen to be removed by Papal decree, the Kingdom would be his. While his appalling wife had been brought up to believe that Joanna was the cause of all the misery her branch of the family had ever endured: she even blamed the Queen for her mother's death.

Before, therefore, we had properly understood what was happening, Charles and his wife had fled Naples, joined the Papal army, and declared Joanna deposed.

Joanna, with her usual insouciance, dismissed this as a mere gesture. 'My people will support me,' she declared. 'They adore me.'

Clement, however, felt that mere adoration might not be sufficient, and promptly abandoned Naples and took ship for Avignon, where he was surrounded by friends. Imagine, after all the tribulations he had brought upon us! God knows – at least I hope and pray that He does – that I am a devout Christian, but I am bound to say that not one of the several popes I have encountered in my lifetime have encouraged me to believe that He guides the choices made by the cardinals, or even approves of them.

It may be supposed that with the cause of the argument removed, our relationship with the Vatican would have immediately improved. Unfortunately, matters had gone too far. Charles of Durazzo's property in Naples had naturally been confiscated in view of his rebellion, nor could he have any doubt as to his fate were he to return there and surrender himself. Equally Urban had to be certain that he had earned the undying enmity of the Queen, and if in these pages I have endeavoured to present the true side of Joanna's character, wayward, certainly, amoral, certainly, but yet at bottom kind and generous, those who considered themselves her enemies could only remember that past enemies of my sweet lady had usually found themselves dead.

Despite the departure of Clement, therefore, Urban continued to hurl anathema at the Queen, and to declare that every Christian knight had a duty to his religion – and his Pope – to bring down this foul murderess, this sorceress, this child of Beelzebub, this cancer in the side of the church, etc, etc. Thus encouraged, Charles of Durazzo found little difficulty in raising an army, and we found ourselves once again embroiled in civil war.

Shades of 1346. The trouble was, it was now 1381. This had certain advantages. Joanna had lost the fearfulness of youth, and, far from considering flight, which was available to her as cousin Clement could hardly have refused her asylum in Avignon, determined to fight for her throne and her prerogatives. In this resolution she was fully supported by her most faithful servant. Actually, I have very little choice. My name was associated with the Queen's in the general condemnation, some idiotic cardinal going so far as to wonder if I were not actually a reincarnation of Beelzebub in female form, and I could not doubt that whatever fate overtook Joanna would also be meted out to me, whereas for me to desert her would have left me friendless in a hostile continent. As soon as the rebel army therefore began to spread across the countryside of Naples, I abandoned Eberli and fled to the city, to place my men-at-arms and my wealth at the disposition of my Queen. Lucia and Pietro and their children naturally accompanied me, as did Ricardo and Guido.

Best of all, Danilo also indicated his willingness to fight, for, whatever his faults, he was just about the most experienced soldier in the kingdom.

Joanna welcomed us all with open arms. But fifty-five is a sad age to have to abandon one's home and possessions, and begin to fight for one's life.

Joanna naturally counted heavily upon the support of her people and the warlike abilities of her husband. Nor was she disappointed. Otto was like a man possessed, patrolling the battlements, marshalling his forces, confronting the vast army commanded by Charles with the utmost determination, and always ably supported by my brave Danilo. But here again we were undone by age, the age of the city, and its inhabitants.

the age of the city, and its inhabitants.

It may be recalled that the Neapolitans had ever shown a reluctance to fight for their Angevin rulers. Indeed the alacrity with which they had opened their gates time and again to the armies of Louis of Hungary was downright indecent. And then they had been a hardy and warlike people, whose principal entertainment upon a Saturday afternoon was breaking a few heads. Now a generation of peace and prosperity, while generally recognised to have resulted from their Queen's wise and beneficent rule, had totally sapped their warlike spirit, and we were hard put to find sufficient men to man the walls.

Yet fight we did, with great determination, sustaining a siege of several months. It would be tedious to recount the various assaults, the hiss of the flying stones hurled by the trebuchets of our enemies, and of the arrows delivered by their crossbowmen, the shouts of attackers and defenders, the clash of steel upon steel, the screams of the wounded and the groans of the dying. These soon became commonplace.

Our so-called Christian antagonists even produced a fearsome-looking tube which, filled with an explosive device, hurled a stone ball in our general direction. I say this advisedly, because I do not believe any of these 'cannonballs' as they are described, ever actually hit any part of Naples.

Yet we could hardly doubt that we were in a losing position. Although the harbour remained open, such was the power of the Papal interdict that the shipping using it was severely limited, and this in turn limited the quantities of necessary supplies which could be brought in to us. People began to grow hungry, even as almost every family in the city mourned a dead or maimed brother or father or son. The two factors combined to induce a weariness with the resistance.

Joanna of course refused to countenance that there could be any weakening of the will to win. She was as active as her husband, tending the wounded, mourning the dead, even appearing on the walls in full view of the enemy as she encouraged her soldiers. This was truly perhaps her finest hour. Sadly, it was unavailing. Unbeknown to us, certain poltroons were in communication with the enemy, seeking the preservation of their lands and titles should the monarchy change hands, and this being confirmed, they opened the city gates in the dead of one night.

Even the sentries on the Castel Nuovo had been suborned, and Joanna and I, sleeping in each other's arms as we had as girls, were suddenly awakened to find the royal apartments occupied by enemy soldiers, and Charles of Durazzo standing above our bed.

CHAPTER 11

For queens more than for ordinary people, awakening to find strange men at one's bedside is a startling experience. The immediate reaction, to summon one's guards and have the intruders despatched, is rapidly overtaken by the realisation that the guards themselves must have been suborned or despatched, or the men could not be there at all.

And when one of the men is your principal enemy ... Joanna clutched the covers to her throat. 'What means this?' she demanded, her voice high but steady, even if she must have known she was in the most dire straits of her entire life.

I certainly knew it, and had no desire to sit up at all, but only to lose myself in the bedclothes and hope to be overlooked.

'It means, dear aunt, that your life of crime has come to an end,' Charles told her. 'Your city has fallen, and you are under arrest.'

I felt Joanna shudder against me. 'By whose authority?' she demanded.

'I have the papal interdict.'

'Which papal interdict? That of Rome is worthless.'

'I consider it to be entirely legal,' the scoundrel said. 'Get out of that bed.'

Joanna tightened her grip on the sheet. 'You expect me to leave this bed before you? Before your people? You are outrageous.'

'My dear aunt,' the wretched fellow said. 'Rumour has it you have appeared naked before at least a thousand men. Should half a dozen more disturb you?'

Joanna gave him a look which should have caused him to drop dead on the spot, and then threw back the covers and stood up. The Queen was now fifty-six years old, and yet she gave them all pause, not least her nephew. But he recovered himself. 'And that evil creature who haunts your shadow.'

What a description, when I remembered what this lout's own uncle had done to me. However, there was nothing for it, and I stood beside Joanna, entailing another somewhat longer pause in the proceedings.

Charles was now definitely overcome, and it was left to the priest who stood at his shoulder to remark, 'Truly are these creatures of the devil, my lord, able to turn men's heads. Let us away with them.'

I clutched Joanna's arm, assuming our last moment had come, but it turned out that, having been commanded to dress ourselves, we were merely being removed clandestinely from Naples, lest the populace riot in our favour. But it had been that very populace which had betrayed us in the first place.

None the less, discovering as we did that we were not immediately to be murdered, we commenced to worry about our loved ones.

'My husband?' Joanna demanded.

'Is my prisoner,' Charles told her.

'I wish to see him.'

'Your wishes no longer have any power of fulfilment,' he said. 'Besides, the fellow is wounded. He is not a pretty sight.'

'That is all the more reason for me to go to him,' she cried.

'And I have said you will not.'

She stamped her foot, but there was no redress.

'Am I allowed to inquire after *my* husband?' I asked.

This time his smile was positively evil. 'He is also my prisoner, Duchess.'

'What of my daughter? And her children?'

'Your daughter. Yes, of course. She is being attended to
... by my men.'

I endeavoured to strike him, but was prevented, and
indeed for the next few minutes suffered severely as these
members of his escort were given the right to amuse themselves at my expense.

I am bound to say they were a sorry lot, and hardly fit
to kiss the hem of a woman who had shared the couch of
al-Mumin, much less fallen into the hands of a Roman
mob. That I was buffeted, and on occasion lost my breath,
was the worst I really suffered.

Joanna was naturally concerned. 'Can you not stop
this?' she demanded of her nephew.

He bowed. 'They will stop when they are spent. Be
thankful that I do not extend their privileges to include
yourself, dear aunt.'

Joanna could therefore do nothing to help me, but in
fact my discomfort was a short one, in that sense, for
Charles was also well aware that there remained within
Naples a considerable body of men, and women, who still
supported the Queen, even if they might have had to agree
to the general surrender, and that his possession of the city
would be put in jeopardy should Joanna be rescued. We
were, therefore, that night taken from the Castel Nuovo,
heavily cloaked and veiled, and conducted to the castle of
Muro, an old Durazzo stronghold, some miles from the city.

Here we were incarcerated, together, and were able to
cling to each other, contemplate the future – which
seemed distinctly unprofitable – and regret the past.

'Had I only sons,' Joanna moaned. 'To support me and
avenge me.'

I reflected that I did have a son, and he had proved of
small support to *me*. In this condemnation I was, as it
turned out, premature, but I none the less felt distinctly
bereft.

I also had a daughter, who so far as I could gather had

been forced to suffer the lot of every conquered woman. Well, I had suffered such a fate myself more than once without more than temporary discomfort, and I could only trust that Lucia possessed my strength of mind and determination to survive.

Joanna soon recovered her spirits, and became certain that her Otto would escape his captors and lead an avenging army to rescue her. This seemed to me a remote contingency, and I was more able to share her second conviction, that Clement's faction would overthrow Urban's, and our rehabilitation would result. This too was of course wishful thinking. Having got a pope of their own once again in Rome, the Italian cardinals were not going to relinquish their prerogatives.

However, as it later turned out, Joanna had become a kind of hot potato. Charles had been declared King of Naples by Pope Urban when the Queen had been interdicted. But Urban, being a simple fellow and incapable of seeing a problem through to its bitter end, had in this instance looked no further ahead than the hopeful military defeat of Joanna and her replacement by a monarch who would support his papacy. What one does with a deposed monarch, especially one who still commands a fair amount of support in her country, and, even more important, how one sets about anointing and crowning a king when there is living a queen who has already been anointed and crowned, were problems which only occurred to the hapless fellow after Charles's victory.

Urban's overwhelming ambition was in every way to legitimise his position. Thus he did not dare denounce all the previous Avignonese popes as being usurpers, as their election and rule had been accepted by all Christendom. In a papal sense, his enemy was Clement and no predecessor. It followed therefore that anything decreed or promulgated by a previous pope, in his capacity as vicar of God and mouthpiece of the Deity, necessarily remained valid. And a previous pope had utterly exonerated Joanna from all crimes. Nor could it be argued that since her return to Naples in 1352 the Queen had proved the best and perhaps the most enlightened monarch in Christendom. That she had supported Clement was a black mark, to be sure, but it required a simple act of abnegation by the Queen, declaring her mistake and offering to kneel before the Pope in Rome, entirely to restore her to all of her prerogatives.

Charles of Durazzo was haunted by the possibility that this course might suggest itself to Urban, to rid himself of his difficulties and in return, of course, for a promise of support for his papacy from Joanna ... and that Joanna might agree to it. Which would leave Charles out on the end of a very long limb already half sawn through.

It was therefore a matter of some urgency for him to have the affair settled, just as rapidly as possible. No doubt he appealed to Rome for a decision, and found himself relegated to waiting – we had ourselves experienced the lengths to which Papal procrastination could go.

When the Pope eventually did advise Charles, we were made aware of it immediately. We were informed that His Grace the King of Naples – 'What effrontery!' Joanna exclaimed – would be calling upon us with regard to a matter of great importance, and were required to wear our best.

A selection of our clothes having by now been brought to us – indeed to this moment our captivity had merely been a business of incarceration, for we had been treated both well and with the utmost respect – we were happy to comply with Charles's wishes, and Joanna, indeed, had seldom looked more uncompromisingly regal.

This was just as well, in view of Charles's proposal for ending the stalemate. He arrived accompanied not only by several of the great nobles of state, including the Papal Legate and a clutch of priests, but also by several scribes, from one of whom he took a very official-looking document.

'Having considered the matter of Your Grace's position,

398

and your criminal activities,' Charles announced, 'the nobles of Naples have reached a decision as to your future.'

Joanna merely snorted.

'It has been decided that you will sign this document of abdication,' Charles continued. 'By which you renounce all claim upon the throne of Naples, all the prerogatives you once enjoyed, and all the wealth you have amassed. In return, you will be allowed to leave this country and go wheresoever you wish to live, taking with you such of your companions as you wish...' he allowed his gaze to play over me, 'and even to be joined by your husband. To sustain Your Grace, an income worthy of your station will be paid every year by the government of Naples, it being clearly understood, however, that should you, or any of your entourage, ever again set foot within the bounds of our kingdom, he or she will be instantly punished with death, and all payments by the government of Naples to yourself will immediately cease.'

He paused, and gazed at his aunt, who was gazing back. Not unnaturally, in these circumstances, some of the upstart's arrogance diminished.

'It is a very fair offer, Aunt Joanna,' he protested. 'More fair than some of my adherents thought proper.'

I will confess that, fair or not, it was an offer I would have unhesitatingly accepted, on the basis that once we were free and out of Naples we could reconsider our position. But then, I am neither a queen nor the descendant of kings.

'Fair?' Joanna demanded. 'How can anything be fair which deprives a citizen of her birthright, a queen of her throne? But even if it were fair, it is quite unacceptable, before man and before God. I have been anointed queen of this land. Only God may take away my rights as queen.'

Charles licked his lips, somewhat anxiously. 'What are you saying, Your Grace?'

'That you may take that document, and yourself, from my sight.'

'You mean you refuse to sign it?'

'Exactly.'

'You cannot refuse,' he said in desperation. 'It is the will of the people of Naples.'

'I obey the will of God, and will preserve the prerogatives of my ancestors.'

Charles opened his mouth and then closed it again, looked for help from his aides and could find none, and fell back on first principles.

'You will find me an implacable foe, Aunt Joanna,' he declared.

Joanna snorted again.

I was now afraid that Charles might fall back on the methods so beloved of his uncle, and seek to obtain direct proof of Joanna's guilt, by means of a confession wrung by torture from an accomplice, which might even stand up in a court of law. And, of course, there was only one accomplice remaining from those far-off days.

However, in the first instance my apprehensions seemed to be groundless. The villain was undoubtedly considering ways and means, and, as it turned out, seeking advice, but there were difficulties, again as it turned out.

While he was weighing the pros and cons of maltreating me in the balance, however, he discovered that he had to hand a means of what he believed might soften my resolve never to betray my mistress – the body of my husband.

I have to confess that I was heartily relieved to discover it was Danilo I was going to see, when I gained the foul dungeon, as I was afraid that Charles had managed to lay hands upon dear Lucia, who, as I had heard nothing of her since the day Naples fell, I had to believe was either dead or had escaped, but even so it was a distressing sight, for Danilo had been divested of his clothing, and clearly been subjected to a great many indignities. Some of these, possibly, he may even have enjoyed, but he was certainly looking distinctly woebegone when I beheld him.

Again, like his uncle, Charles seemed to be assuming that the sight of my beloved husband so exposed and about to be tortured would bring about my entire mental collapse; the poor fellow was unaware of the peculiar relationship which had existed between Danilo and myself for some years.

Which is not to say I did not greet him with open arms, and pressed him to my bosom several times, to his evident gratification.

'Enough of this,' Charles said, when we had billed and cooed for several minutes. 'If you would enjoy the company of your husband much longer you must make a confession to me, here and now, of your complicity, with the late Queen, in the murder of her first husband, Andrew of Hungary.'

'I assure you that I know nothing of that business, monsignore,' I protested.

'And I assure you that you do,' the rascal countered. 'And that if you do not admit your crime, and that of the late Queen, immediately, you shall watch your husband suffer most dreadfully.'

I refused to admit the terror which was hammering on the gates of my consciousness. 'Monsignore,' I said, 'to what avail will a confession on my part contribute? Her Grace has been exonerated by His Holiness himself.'

'Because no evidence was adduced,' Charles pointed out. 'But you, Richilde, I promise, will suffer no such impediment to free speech as was inflicted upon those earlier conspirators, when put to the question. I but invite you to co-operate with me now, assure me that your answers will incriminate the Queen, who is most undoubtedly guilty, and I will assure you in turn that the question as administered to you by the court will be of only a passing painfulness, providing you do not attempt to change your testimony, and that your execution will be the swiftest and most merciful that I can devise: the garrot, which I am assured is a matter of no more than a second between life and death.'

'Your offer is most generous, monsignore,' I said. 'But I repeat, I know nothing of that event.'

'Very well, madame. You have made your choice.'

Danilo was unhappy with the situation. 'You cannot so abandon me, my love,' he protested.

I embraced him once more. 'You must have courage, my dearest heart,' I said. 'Do not be afraid of these louts.'

He did not appear to be reassured, with good reason. I was now escorted to a chair, and made to sit there, to watch my husband tortured. Danilo was secured by his wrists and ankles, each to a separate rope, and in this somewhat humiliating posture was hoisted from the floor by means of a movable beam of thick wood, his ropes being suspended from four equally movable arms extending from the beam itself.

This beam could be placed over any object in the room, according to the whim of the torturer, and for Danilo the object chosen was a wooden pyramid, which was man-handled into the centre of the room. This pyramid, as pyramids do, rose to a sharp triangular point, and it was on to this point that Danilo was lowered, several times. Able to control his posture by manipulating the various arms holding the ropes – very like a puppeteer might do – these foul fiends were able to make him suffer in a variety of ways. They began by holding his entire body parallel with the floor, face up, and then lowering him so that the apex of the pyramid ate into the small of his back. From his shrieks and frantic heavings I have no doubt this was extremely painful. Fortunately they soon tired of this and turned him over to introduce the apex into his belly. But of course there were more interesting places for them to explore with their miserable toy. My Danilo was made to sit on the wooden stake, his legs pulled part so that it was introduced most unpleasantly into his anus, his body being carefully guided to the right position by two of his eager tormentors, whom I quickly discerned were of a similar sexual leaning as himself.

All of this was horrifying to watch, as were my poor dear husband's screams dreadful to listen to, when I could hear them, for most of the time I was screaming even more loudly than he – I had, after all, had more practice – while I tried time and again to rise from my chair, but was always restrained by my guards ... but with my usual ability to observe and reason, no matter how unfortunate my situation, I early recognised that it was apparently no part of Charles's plan to destroy my husband. The slightest carelessness when he had been placed on the pyramid on his back, for example, could have broken his spine, and equally a small miscalculation with his private parts could have reduced him to a bloody and sexless wreck. None of these ultimate misfortunes happened, and as I watched him it dawned upon me that Charles was experiencing the same emotions as had plagued his uncle thirty-six years earlier when confronted with me. Although, of course, in a somewhat different manner.

I was considerably reassured by this, and it was not very long before I was proved to be correct, as suddenly the Duke seemed to tire of the sport, and the questioning, and dismissed all of his people, including the priests and the scribes, with a wave of his hand, commanding them to take me with them.

I was thus forced to leave my husband again, to heaven alone knew what fate – although I had little difficulty in surmising what it was going to be – and was conveyed back to the Queen's chamber, where, as was her wont, Joanna made me recall everything that had happened.

'Do not fret, my dearest Richilde,' she told me. 'We shall be avenged.'

Alas for her confidence. My dearly beloved Queen and life-long friend was drawing to the end of her days, all unaware of the fate hanging over her. For it appeared that Charles, despairing of obtaining any of the evidence he required, had determined on what was, after all, the simplest means of solving his problem, sure that Urban needed Neapolitan support so desperately in his struggle against Clement that he would grant absolution for any crime which contributed to that end.

Thus it was that this very night we were again rudely awakened – I only just having nodded off due to my concern as to what might be happening to Danilo – to find ourselves surrounded by several men, all of whom wore black cloaks and black hoods, and presented a most sinister appearance.

Joanna reacted as imperiously as ever. 'What means this intrusion?' she demanded. 'Are we not to be allowed a night's rest?'

'Remove the creature,' said one of the men.

Before I could defend myself I had been dragged from the bed.

'Oh, Richilde!' Joanna cried. 'How my heart bleeds for you.'

My poor darling clearly assumed I was again to be put to the question. Now she was surprised to be dragged from the bed herself and thrown on the floor. Before she could catch her breath or I could understand the horror which was unfolding before my eyes, the mattress on which we had just been lying was also pulled from the bed, and thrown on top of the Queen, entirely obscuring her naked figure. On top of this mattress four of the black-robed men now threw themselves in turn, pinning it to the floor.

The Queen's slight body made hardly an impression upon the cloying feathers. For a moment or two it moved, and then subsided, while the murderers pressed ever harder. I opened my mouth to scream, and had a gloved hand closed over my lips, while another went round my waist to hold me motionless. I could at least bite the glove, but was unable to penetrate the leather – although as I have excellent teeth the fellow did grunt – and stamp with my feet, but this had little avail, and in fact the whole ghastly tragedy was over in a matter of a few minutes.

The leader of the band of assassins waved his hand, and his men rose from the mattress. Another wave, and the mattress itself was lifted. Joanna of Naples lay there, a crumpled, dwindled heap.

The leader knelt beside her, took a knife from his girdle, and cut into that lilywhite wrist. No blood spurted.

'It is done,' he said, with some satisfaction.

'What shall we do with this one?' inquired the man holding me, endeavouring to free his glove from my teeth.

'Bring her before the council,' the leader said. 'Let us hear what she has to say.'

Thus, in a darkened bedroom, naked and defenceless, died the most exceptional women of her age. Or perhaps any age.

Her murder left me desolated, and I have been desolated ever since. Yet I have always possessed the instinct of self-preservation. Thus when I was dragged before the tribunal, as I have described at the beginning of this book, I felt certain that nothing could now harm the Queen, who was surely already standing before the greatest Judge of all, and that it was therefore time to look to myself. And, hopefully, be able to regain my child and grandchildren.

I thus told the story of the Queen's life, which was, necessarily, also the story of my life, with the utmost fidelity. It took some time, and I was exhausted by the end of it, the more so as I perceived that I had been wasting my time. There was not a spark of pity or understanding or sympathy to be seen in the faces in front of me.

'You have condemned yourself out of your own mouth,' the chairman said. 'You may persist in your claim that you knew nothing of the plot to murder Prince Andrew, yet are you an accessory after the fact, who was content to aid and abet the late Queen in all of her nefarious practices, up to the very day of her death. You are in every way as guilty as she. But worse. Your confession establishes beyond all doubt that you are a witch. Will you not now admit that all of your actions, and those of the Queen, were dictated by your foul masters, of whom Beelzebub is but the greatest? Answer.'

I understood immediately what they were after, of course. To assassinate an anointed Queen is about the most heinous possible crime, as Charles was well aware; Joanna's crime, that of despatching an *un*anointed prince who was also an unwanted husband, had haunted her throughout her life. Nor may a Queen be condemned, living, as a witch, except through due process of papal law, and everyone knew how Joanna had survived one such process many years before.

But with the Queen dead, if it could be proved that her closest companion and bosom friend was a witch, it might well be possible to have it accepted by the world that the Queen had herself been tainted with the dreaded evil, and that therefore her death had actually been an act not only of justice, but of mercy to herself.

This determination on the part of Charles and his minions obviously placed me in a most invidious position. With Otto and Lucia disappeared, Danilo a prisoner, William incarcerated in a monastery, Ricardo and Guido fled, I had not a friend in the world. Indeed, considering those who still regarded me as an upstart foreigner and a bad influence on the Queen, I possessed nothing but enemies. Nor, I knew, would there be any sparing of pain or indeed bodily destruction for me. I might still be beautiful, but I was considerably older than Charles and his minions, and if I was going to be condemned as a witch, and therefore burned at the stake, a few broken bones or torn pieces of flesh experienced beforehand would make little difference in the eyes of the law.

Yet was I determined to resist them to the last breath of my body. I have never been one to surrender meekly to misfortune.

It may be recalled that but for my unfortunate experience at the hands – if that is the correct expression – of Charles of Durazzo, I had not personally been involved in the misfortunes suffered by the conspirators to the murder of Andrew of Hungary. Indeed, from that day I had not been inside a torture chamber save as a spectator, the most recent occasion being the mishandling of my poor Danilo.

It was now necessary for me to brace myself, as it were, for the real thing, for the first, but hopefully the last, time in my life. Indeed these misfortunes are usually for the last time in one's life, and should therefore be considered the more deeply.

My inquisitors turned out to be a bevy of young priests, who took to their task with great gusto, while necessarily obeying all the rules of their hideous profession – I am speaking of them as inquisitors, of course, and not as men of God, although in my circumstances it was difficult to tell the difference.

These young men, forced by their calling to undertake an entirely unnatural life, at least in sexual matters, were like children unwrapping a prize parcel, as they in the first instance, having conveyed me to their dread dungeon, removed my clothing.

Well, I had expected nothing less, so it is not to be supposed this caused me any blushes. But what followed was singularly unpleasant, as it was now necessary for them to prove that I had indeed had contact with the Devil, failing which I could hardly be considered a witch. This relationship with the Devil is always considered to be an affectionate one, in the course of which Beelzebub or whoever one's particular demon happens to be, plants at least one kiss upon the body of his beloved. This kiss has the power of anaesthetising the point of contact, as it were, according to the learned doctors of the law; thus, should any part of the human body be found to be insensible to pain, it has obviously been in contact with the Devil's lips.

Now you may know, and I may feel, that such a supposition is absurd. Not the doctors of the Inquisition. Even to suggest that it might be in opposition to all the laws of medicine was sufficient to condemn one as a witch out of hand. The result was that my first ordeal was to be searched for the Devil's Mark.

This is normally done by pricking with a needle, whichever part of the body seems likely to be affected, or, more usually, happens to attract the interest of the Inquisitor. In the case of a hapless female who retained some pretensions to beauty this proceeding is better left to the imagination. Suffice to say that the piercing of my nipples, the pricking of my nose and ears, and between my legs, sufficed to induce shrieks loud enough to have awakened Beelzebub, had he been inclined to come to my rescue, and certainly convinced the scoundrels who were holding me down and amusing themselves that no devil could have preceded them.

Unfortunately, the rigours of my life, and most especially the various exposures to the elements of my body, which, in keeping with my hair, was unusually white, as on the occasion when I had marched with the Flagellants, or bathed in the open air with the *guizdes* of al-Mumin's harem, had caused a degree of freckling on my skin, and in places normally well concealed by my clothing even one or two moles.

I had never considered such blemishes too deeply before, save to be aware that they were blemishes. Now I discovered to my concern that they were virtually devoid of feeling, especially when the pricking needle was in such expert hands. For a thrust into my flesh would produce a scream and of course a gush of breath, so that if a second prick was made immediately, and into a far less sensitive area, I was quite incapable of responding.

This pleased them greatly. They clapped their hands, shouted to the world that they had found the Devil's Mark, and led me away to be put to the question.

Now, obviously I have seen more than one person so mistreated, and I feared the very worst, remembering the heated iron chair of Bertrand de Baux or the ladder of Charles of Durazzo. To my surprise, however, while I was made to sit upon a bar of wood, with my legs dangling down one to each side, which suggested all manner of sinister connotations, I seemed merely to be made as comfortable as possible. Although my ankles were secured to rings in the ground, rather tightly, thus pressing my buttocks into the wood, and my arms were carried behind me and secured to rings set in the wood itself, any chance that I might fall backwards and hit my head, as I would assuredly have done in normal circumstances, was prevented by a stout wooden rest, also attached to the bar, which was placed against my back and secured there by means of screws into the bar at its lower end. This left me absolutely rigid and unable to move anything save for my head, while my trunk was thrust forward in a somewhat unseemly fashion from, if I may be excused the phrase in view of my circumstances, tit to twat.

I naturally found this somewhat threatening of abuse, but once again my immediate fears were set at rest when one of the Inquisitors, smiling most kindly, held a beaker of water to my lips. Nothing was ever more welcome, and I smiled at him in return.

Meanwhile, his accomplices were seating themselves around me, pads and pencils in hand, while the first began the questioning, which is, as everyone knows, to a set formula.

'How long have you been a witch?' asked the first.

'I have never been a witch,' I replied.

This amused them, and my friend offered me another drink from the jug of water, which he had refilled. Well, I was no longer thirsty, but I did not wish to offend him, and so took another hearty swig.

'Why did you become a witch?' asked the second Inquisitor.

'I have never had any reason to become a witch,' I answered.

More smiles, and more water.

'I do assure you, sir, that I am no longer thirsty,' I explained to my friend.

'But you must drink, Your Grace,' he insisted, and poured more water down my throat.

I was now beginning to feel quite bloated.

'How did you become a witch, and what happened on that occasion?' asked the third Inquisitor.

I was becoming somewhat irritated. 'I never became a witch,' I shouted. 'So nothing happened.'

Instantly my smiling friend was at my side again, with another full beaker of water. I shook my head. 'I have had enough.'

'One can never have enough water,' the scurvy fellow pointed out.

'Well, I wish no more at this time,' I told him.

'But you must,' he replied, at the same time gesturing to his fellows. These laid down their pens and papers, and proceeded to grip my jaws and force them apart, while a third inserted a kind of spout into my mouth, and down this the fourth poured another liberal quantity of water.

I was now feeling distinctly uncomfortable.

Meanwhile, the Inquisitors had resumed their seats, and the fourth question was asked. 'Who is the one you chose to be your incubus? What was his name?'

'I cannot think,' I protested. 'Good sirs, permit me to visit a privy.'

'We are not concerned with your creature comforts, woman,' the scoundrel said. 'Give her some more water.'

'It is the water that is the trouble,' I shouted.

But to no avail, and more liquid was poured down my throat. Naturally, I endeavoured to take at least a small revenge by relieving myself there and then, but the unfortunate fact was that very little of my intake had reached the point of departure, as it were, and I was only aware of feeling as if I were about to burst; certainly my internal organs all felt as if they had been distended to twice their normal size.

There was only one way to arrest this growing agony, even if I understood that to incriminate myself and then refuse also to incriminate the Queen might be to expose myself to far greater mistreatment – but if I was forced to take any more water I felt I would go mad, and perhaps incriminate her anyway.

'Wait,' I shouted. 'I will answer your questions. But permit me to visit the privy.'

'That is very sensible of you,' said the Head Inquisitor. 'Then I will begin again. You will visit the privy when you have answered to our satisfaction. How long have you been a witch?'

Having decided to go along with this charade, and naturally being in a great hurry to get the business over and relieve myself, I was determined to dazzle them with my confession, and hastily recalled everything I had ever heard, or read, about witchcraft, which was a considerable amount. 'Ever since I can remember. I became a witch at my mother's knee.' Well, she, poor lady, was long beyond caring, I was certain.

Sensation! They wrote busily. And there was no further offer of water.

'Why did you become a witch?'

'Because my mother wished it.'

'How did you become a witch, and what happened on that first occasion?'

'My mother rubbed a certain ointment between my legs, and gave me a broomstick. I mounted on this stick, and flew away to where the Devil awaited me.'

More sensation, and hurried whispered conversations. They had never had such a confession before.

'Who is the one you chose to be your incubus? What was his name?'

'I did not choose anyone. They were presented to me by my mother.'

'They?'

'There were several of them.'

'Their names, woman, their names?'

'Why, one was named Beelzebub, as I recall. Then there was a fellow named Asmodeus. And one called Apollyon. There were also two fellows named Behemoth and Leviathan. Oh, and I have forgotten poor little Lucifer. I liked Lucifer best.'

They were now positively beside themselves with excitement; they had never encountered someone who claimed to have been seduced by all the devils in hell.

'Which one of the devils was your master?'

'Well,' I said. 'I suppose you would have to say Asmodeus. He was the biggest, in every way.'

'What was the oath you were forced to render him?'

Joanna and I had often discussed the terrible business of witchcraft, so there was a good deal to remember, but it was mainly a matter of letting my imagination run riot.

'Why,' I said. 'To do his bidding at all times. To abominate the Church and all its works. To murder babies and stick pins into good women at every opportunity. That sort of thing.'

'How did you make this oath, and what were its conditions?'

'I kissed his backside, and then his member, understanding that if I broke my oath I would be sent to Heaven for all eternity.'

They crossed themselves at such blasphemy. But were still concerned with detail.

'Which finger were you forced to raise in taking the oath.'

'The middle finger of my right hand,' I assured them.

'Where did you consummate your union with your incubus?'

'At a sabbat,' I replied without hesitation.

'What demons and which other human beings participated at the sabbat?'

'I have told you of the demons.'

'Tell us of the human beings.'

'Why, they were such as Bertrand de Baux, and his brother, and Charles of Durazzo, and Louis of Hungary ... oh, and I nearly forgot, Pope Clement VI.'

'Your Grace, you blaspheme,' they remonstrated.

'You are asking me questions, and I am replying,' I argued.

'Then tell us this, was not the late Queen also present?'

'Never.'

They muttered at each other, and then resumed.

'What food was eaten at the banquet?'

'Bats' dropping and turnips, unborn babe and new potatoes. Sautéed.'

'How was the sabbat banquet arranged?'

'We all sat on the devils' knees.'

Amazingly they were writing all of these nonsensical answers down with great concentration; they had not even stopped to inquire how we had managed to eat an unborn babe without first devouring the mother.

And still they persisted.

'What music was played, and what dances were danced?'

'Pan supplied the music with his pipes, and we all danced back to back, rubbing our arses together.'

'What did your incubus give you for your intercourse?'

'A really good ram.'

How busily their pens moved.

'What devil's mark did your incubus make upon your body?'

'Those you have found. The places he kissed me.'

'What injuries have you done in the name of the Devil?'

'It would take too long to list them all.'

'Do so.'

'Well, there was the woman Boccadocio whom I caused to miscarry, because she stepped in front of me on the street. And the boy Gilberto whose member I caused to tie itself in a knot because he would not lie with me. And ...'

I streamed off another twenty-odd imaginary instances, all of which were written down, but with growing impatience, as I had not told them what they truly wanted to know.

'You must speak of your part in the death of Prince Andrew of Hungary,' one said at last.

'I know naught of that.'

'But you were the Queen's servant, and you were present.'

'I know naught of that,' I repeated.

They sighed, and resumed.

'The injuries of which you have spoken, can you undo them?'

'Of course, if I choose. Am I not a witch?'

'What herbs or what other methods can you use to cure these injuries?'

'I rub two sticks together, and utter the magic word, abracadabra.'

'Have you also bewitched animals?'

'Of course. Are you not aware that Farmer Gregorio's cattle no longer give milk?'

'Why did you do this?'

'He allowed them to wander on to some of my pasturage at Eberli.'

'Who are your human accomplices in evil?'

'My sister Constance, my brothers Henry and Richard.'

'And the late Queen?'

'Never the late Queen. Her Grace abhorred witchcraft in all its forms.'

Once again they muttered at each other in frustration, before continuing.

'Why does the Devil give you blows in the night?'

'I expect he enjoys it.'

'What is the ointment with which you rub your broomstick made of?'

'Semen, mainly.'

'How are you able to fly through the air? What magic words do you use?'

'I use abracadabra. This is the word that releases me from my earthly form. Why, do you not realise that if I wished, I could release myself now from these bonds, and your presence, and simply disappear?'

Oh, would that had been possible. But none the less they were terrified, and huddled close together, before they could bring themselves to ask the next question.

'What tempests have you raised, and who helped you to produce them?'

'My greatest success was the big storm of 1365,' I said. 'Asmodeus was my helper. Do you not recall that the campanile of the cathedral fell down?'

I had, of course, been in Spain in 1365, but they were too agitated to remember this.

'What plagues of vermin and caterpillars have you created?'

'Whatever is crawling about your bodies at this moment, I placed there,' I assured them.

More agitation, and some surreptitious scratchings.

'What do you make these pernicious creatures out of and how do you do it?'

'I cut the members from newborn male babies, and tickle them until they come back to life.'

Their hands were trembling as they wrote it all down. But we had reached the end of the interrogation; there was only one question left.

'Has the Devil assigned a limit to the duration of your evil-doing?'

'One thousand years,' I declared.

They uttered a shriek, and fled the room.

Gaolers came in and released me, and allowed me to relieve myself of my discomfort. Then I was again clad in my penitential shift, and marched back to face the Grand Inquisitor, who had been joined by several notables, amongst whom I observed Charles of Durazzo himself.

The Grand Inquisitor had also had the time to peruse my answers. He was made of sterner stuff than his clerks.

'You are a self-confessed witch,' he pointed out.

'That is correct, monsignore.'

'Thus, have you anything further to say before this tribunal pronounces judgement upon you?'

'I demand the right to be heard in public,' I said.

'That demand is denied. You are sentenced to death. However, I am disposed to be merciful, and promise that your death will be quick and painless, if you will now complete your confession.'

I knew what he meant, but preferred to appear mystified. 'What more can I say, monsignore?'

'You can acknowledge what we all know, that the late Queen was your accomplice in all of these ghastly deeds.'

'That would be untrue, monsignore. Her Grace knew nothing of my midnight forays, nor would she have approved of them if she had.'

'Woman, do not prevaricate with me. Your immortal soul is in danger.'

Well, as to that, if I had ever believed that God indulged in or approved of the insensate cruelty practised by those who take his name in vain here on earth, I would indeed have become a worshipper of the Devil, who at least promised an amusing time.

'My soul belongs to me, monsignore,' I told him.

'You will find out differently soon enough, if you persist in defying this court,' he snarled.

'I cannot implicate the Queen,' I insisted. 'Because she is innocent.'

He half turned his head, to catch Charles's eye; the new King of Naples gave an angry, and, it seemed to me, despairing shrug.

'Very well, woman. Richilde Benoit, sometime Duchess of Eberli, as you have chosen to live your life in the shadow of the Queen, as her creature, it is our decision that you shall die, in her shadow, and as her creature. You will spend tonight in silent communion, and at dawn tomorrow morning you will be taken to the place of execution. Your flesh will be torn with red-hot pincers and you will be scourged with iron-tipped whips. Then you will be burned alive, and left in the flames until not a vestige of your being remains. Take her away.'

My knees were weak, and I had to be dragged down to my dungeon. No doubt I have ever been an optimist, but I was so certain of my own innocence, so sure that my absurd answers to the absurd questions which had been put to me would at least be understood by the Grand Inquisitor, that I had presumed my life would be safe. Of course I now realised that as the only witness, apart from the assassins themselves, to Joanna's murder, my own death was an absolute necessity.

It was none the less awful to contemplate, and I had a great deal of contemplating to do, as it was only four o'clock in the afternoon when I was sentenced, and there were thus more than twelve hours to go before my execution.

I paced the floor until I was exhausted, and then threw myself upon the pile of straw which was apparently intended to act as a bed. But I was in no mood for sleep, as I reviewed the events of my not uneventful life, and worried about my children, and felt already the burning pincers on my flesh, recalling those dreadful scenes from my youth. Yet sleep I did eventually, to be awakened with a start as my cell door opened.

I sat up, and stared at the figure behind the candle, tall and clearly masculine, shrouded, as had been my inquisitors, in a black cloak and hood. Behind him there was another priest, somewhat smaller, but similarly clad.

'Is it time already?' I whispered.

'Time,' he said, closing the door behind himself.

My heart nearly stopped beating.

'William?' I whispered. 'My God, William!'

He held his finger to his lips, and came closer, to kneel beside me. I put my arms round him, and hugged him as tight as I could.

'Oh, my darling boy,' I whispered. 'But how come you here?'

417

'I am to confess you,' he said.

'And let us make haste,' said his companion. 'It is a sad thing to have a condemned felon as a mother.'

'Why, you are absolutely right, Tomaso,' William agreed, and stood up. Before either myself or the unfortunate Tomaso understood what was happening, my son had placed the candle on the floor, raised his habit, removed from beneath it a stout stave, and struck his companion across the head; Tomaso collapsed on the floor without a sound.

I stared at William in consternation, and he smiled.

'Let us indeed make haste.' He knelt beside the stricken fellow, and rolled him to and fro as he removed the habit. 'Do you also undress, dearest Mama. I am sorry to ask you to do this, but it is necessary.'

'Oh, William,' I said, removing my gown. 'But if you aid me to escape, you will be as condemned as myself.'

'I am already committed, Mama. And is not mutual condemnation an honourable state, for a son, as regards a mother?' he inquired.

'But ... where can we go?'

'It is arranged,' he promised me.

'And Lucia?'

'That too is arranged.' Expertly he tore my gown into strips, with which he bound Tomaso's wrists and ankles, and gagged his mouth.

I could not demur longer, and pulled on the discarded habit. Indeed, it was only the fear that my children would be involved in my catastrophe that had held me back in the first place; I would far sooner have died endeavouring to escape, fighting my pursuers to the last breath in my body, than be merely tortured to death. So although I did not understand how William was going to work this miracle, I willingly obeyed his instructions, donned the black robe and raised the hood over my head, and then followed him from the cell.

At the end of the corridor several guards were gathered,

418